# Novellas & Stories

# Novellas & Stories

MELJEAN BROOK

CAROLYN CRANE

JESSICA SIMS

# CONTENTS

# The Blushing Bounder

## A Tale of the Iron Seas

BK 0.4

## MELJEAN BROOK

# Chapter One

THE NEEDLES IN MISS LOCKSTITCH'S LEFT HAND COULD HAVE sprung from Temperance's fevered nightmares. Not even *her* hand, but an embroidering machine *shaped* like a hand, the steel contraption hadn't disturbed Temperance at first glance. It had seemed more of a curiosity, and she'd been so desperate for conversation that when Miss Lockstitch had appeared at the door of their small flat, Temperance had actually *thanked* her horrid husband for arranging a companion to begin sitting with her every day.

She ought to have known. From the moment Edward Newberry had forced a kiss upon her, Temperance's life—what little remained of it—had been one dreadful episode after another: deceived by Newberry's seemingly honorable character, shunned by her family and employer, forced to marry the man who'd instigated her fall, moved across an ocean from Manhattan City to filthy London, and denied the gentle care of a sanatorium, where she might have spent her final years in privacy and comfort.

And now *she* had become the horrid one, staring rudely at another's affliction. Sitting in the chair opposite Temperance's sofa, Miss Lockstitch had laid her palm over a blue cloth stretched across a round wooden frame, and positioned the frame over her thigh. Temperance simply couldn't look away from the score of needles rhythmically jabbing through the back of the woman's steel hand, the twitching fingers that seemed to control the needles' speed and the pattern of the colored threads. At Miss Lockstitch's knee, a muffled clicking and slight up-and-down of her toes told Temperance that *another* apparatus had been grafted onto the woman's leg—which now explained the pretty bow that had been tied over the knee of her trousers. Beneath the fall of cloth she embroidered, Miss Lockstitch must have quietly exposed the machine in her leg that was working in tandem with her hand. As she worked, Miss Lockstitch spoke of her upcoming marriage to Constable Thomas, as if it were perfectly normal to carry on a conversation with her contraptions half-exposed.

Perhaps it was. Perhaps, in London, it was. Temperance hadn't yet met a person who hadn't had a tool attached to their body in some fashion, or a prosthetic limb to replace it. Miss Lockstitch lived in a boarding house full of other seamstresses, all members of the lockstitch guild—and, Temperance assumed, all fitted with similar contraptions.

"Mrs. Newberry?"

Her gaze darted up, met Miss Lockstitch's enquiring look. Beneath her curling blond fringe, the young woman's brow had furrowed with concern. Heat climbed into Temperance's face. Though the seamstress had turned her focus away from her cloth, the clicking of the machine hadn't ceased; she didn't know how long Miss Lockstitch had been watching her, waiting for a response.

Temperance scrambled for an excuse. In the first hour of her visit, Miss Lockstitch's replies had been marked by shyness and uncertainty. She'd slowly become more comfortable, speaking more quickly, asking more questions. No matter Temperance's feelings about the terrible machine, she couldn't bear the thought that her rudeness would make the young woman feel unwelcome.

And she *was* young—only eighteen, by Temperance's estimate. Perhaps that age could serve as the excuse she needed.

"Forgive me, Miss Lockstitch. I found myself wondering…I had heard that the Horde waited until the children raised in crèches were almost fully grown before altering them for labor. Yet you must have been only nine or ten years of age when the revolution drove the Horde from England. Did I misunderstand?"

"Not at all." Miss Lockstitch glanced at her hand, and in her faint smile there seemed a combination of pride and loss. "I had a blacksmith create it for me two years past."

She'd *deliberately* let someone remove her hand and attach that contraption to her body? Temperance struggled to contain her horror. "Why?"

"How was I to compete and to find employment if I did not?" A frown creased the young woman's brow, as if she were uncertain how Temperance could have missed an obvious point. "I was apprenticed to the guild shortly after the revolution, but who would hire me when my stitches were so much slower? When they were sometimes uneven? I would hardly be useful in any of the shops, and a burden upon my guild house."

The need to be useful, the fear of becoming a burden. Temperance understood both very well. "I see," she said.

"I understand why this surprises you, but it was a necessary step, and all to my benefit. My machine is more advanced than the Horde embroidering devices are—and my fingers function as all fingers do, so the apparatus is still useful when I'm not working. There are many older ladies who only have the use of one hand." Miss Lockstitch's eyes narrowed, evincing a shrewdness that Temperance hadn't seen within her before. "Without this, I could never have advanced within the guild. I could have been named seamstress, but my voice would never carry as much weight, and my purse would always be light."

She spoke so blatantly of money? Such vulgarity. But perhaps this was the way of London, too—and hadn't Temperance once done the same, confiding in Edward Newberry about her expectation of a small inheritance? Was not her openness the cause of his deception and her current situation? She could not condemn this woman for vulgarity without also condemning herself, and Temperance refused to take the blame for Edward Newberry's actions.

Still, it was uncomfortable to hear such plain speaking.

With her face coloring again, Temperance nodded and shifted her legs on the sofa, rearranging the thin cotton blanket over them, hoping the activity would also serve as a break in the conversation. She no longer wanted to pursue this topic.

The clicking paused. "Are you in need of assistance?"

"No." Temperance smiled and leaned back against her pillows again. "I was only adjusting my blanket."

Miss Lockstitch hesitated. Her teeth pressed against her bottom lip before she admitted, "I ought to have told your husband when he asked me to sit with you, but I am not...I am not entirely familiar with illness. If ever you need something, please ask it of me. I might not know to do it, otherwise."

And here was the simplest way to be rid of her, Temperance realized. She only had to say that the woman would be of little help when her consumption worsened again, and Newberry would have to find someone else. Perhaps someone without an unpleasant contraption fixed to her hand and leg.

But Miss Lockstitch herself wasn't unpleasant, and Temperance's horrid husband would probably find someone awful to visit with her, simply as punishment.

"There's not much to be done now, anyway," Temperance said. "If the coughing begins to take me again, there are compresses and poultices that can ease the strain. But we will speak of these at a later date."

Miss Lockstitch's smile was soft and grateful. "Is it very difficult, this illness?"

Difficult? It was *killing* her. She could not cross a room without feeling winded, without her heart fluttering like a weak bird— *she* could not, though her sisters had once nicknamed her Temperance the Tireless. Her hands, once so steady and strong, could not hold a sketching pencil for more than ten minutes without shaking. Her fingers had thinned to twigs, and she could not bear to look in the mirror, to see the hollows in her cheeks, her sunken eyes, her pale skin. At night, she awoke shivering in her own sweat, out of dreams where she watched herself slowly waste away to nothing.

But she only smiled faintly—*did she appear ghastly yet when she smiled?*—and said, "It is tiring, sometimes."

Relief softened the other woman's features. "I am glad to see that it is nothing like bug fever. My guild mate Jenny came down with that after a steamcoach crushed her leg, and she was like a furnace to touch, with boils all over her face, and they had to put her in ice just to keep her alive. The physician said her bugs were working so hard to heal her that they all but killed her."

Bugs. Temperance didn't know how she spoke so casually of the tiny machines living within her body, especially as they were called *bugs*. How could she not spend her day scratching at her skin, trying to get them out?

Even worse, knowing that those bugs had been used by the Horde to control everyone in England until the revolution—and after they were dead, turned them into monsters.

How could Miss Lockstitch bear it? Though Temperance supposed that never becoming sick would be one small benefit. "So you've never taken ill?"

"No." Miss Lockstitch shook her head. At her knee, the embroidery machine began clicking again. "I don't know anyone who has been, aside from yourself."

"But there are physicians?" Temperance should probably contact one, before too long—though she didn't know what a London physician could do for her. What would he know of consumption?

There was little to be done anyway. Her husband had pressed the idea upon her that she might let herself be treated with the bugs, but she could not—she *would* not—become the monstrous thing that the infected became after they were dead. She *would not* allow her body to transform into a ravenous walking corpse, like those that had devastated all of Europe.

The nightmares of becoming a zombie came as often as the nightmares in which she wasted away to nothing—and in them, she hardly looked any different.

"There are physicians," Miss Lockstitch confirmed. "Problems arise now and again when a girl in the house delivers a babe."

From Miss Lockstitch's easy tone, Temperance gathered she was speaking of problems *other* than it being an unmarried girl delivering the babe.

Yet another difference between London and Manhattan City—

perhaps the biggest difference of all. After one forced kiss, Temperance had been shackled to a lying lecher, yet no one here thought anything of an unmarried woman bearing a child.

"And then, of course, the babe will need to be infected with bugs," Miss Lockstitch continued. "It's always best for a blacksmith or physician to make the blood transfusion. In fact, the physician who infected Molly's last babe is father to the jade whore paired with your husband."

Shock slapped Temperance, made her mouth drop open. "Father to the *what*?"

Two pink spots appeared high in Miss Lockstitch's cheeks. "Perhaps that isn't kindly said. I'm speaking of the inspector, Mrs. Newberry— the woman your husband has just been assigned to assist during her investigations."

"Detective Inspector Wentworth?" Temperance hadn't realized the inspector was a woman.

This wasn't jealousy catching at her throat. Her husband was welcome to a wh…a woman like that. Perhaps it explained why he'd never pressed his attentions upon her—Temperance ought to be *thankful* he'd found someone else to force his giant body upon, even if he likely used her inheritance to pay the woman. And it wasn't the pain of disappointment, either. She couldn't possibly be more disillusioned in Newberry's character than she already was.

It was only a cough that formed this ache in her chest, a cough waiting to start up again and wrack her body apart.

"Yes, that's her name," Miss Lockstitch said. "My Thomas tells me that the superintendent considers it a personal favor that your husband agreed to assist the inspector, and that Newberry will himself advance to inspector sooner because of it."

Temperance didn't care what he did. "Will he?"

"My Thomas says so. There was a time, we considered waiting to be married until my Thomas made inspector, too, but he couldn't tolerate the thought of escorting that woman." She shook her head, as if to express her intended's stupidity. "He ought to have done it, no matter what she is. But he wouldn't, and so instead of waiting to marry an inspector, I'll be marrying a constable. I told him I won't wait for the other. Did you wait long before you married?"

How long had Temperance waited after her father declared that she had a choice between living the remainder of her life working on her back, or marrying Edward Newberry?

"Just one day," she said—and that only three weeks ago.

TEMPERANCE HAD JUST SETTLED INTO BED WHEN SHE HEARD HER husband come into the flat. Quickly, she dropped her book to her lap and snuffed her bedside lamp. If he did not see the light, perhaps he would not bother to check on her, and she would be spared his presence for almost a whole day's span.

But she had no luck. The tread of his boots approached her bedroom—and then silence, as he paused. As he always did.

Even in happier days, he'd paused. How very long ago that seemed, though it had only been two years since she'd first taken a position as governess to Baron Shiplan's two young daughters. Two years since she had first noticed the constable who'd patrolled the park where she'd daily taken her charges for exercise and fresh air. He had not been the only constable, of course—but there had been no others so tall, with shoulders so wide, and hair so red. There had been no others whose nod and rumbling "ma'am" as she passed gave her a shiver, and no others who had charmed her with a deep blush the first time she'd offered a smile and a "constable" in return.

And it had only been a year and a half since she'd been sitting on a bench, watching the Shiplan girls skate on the frozen pond. A year and a half since she'd turned to find him holding a handkerchief that she'd dropped on one of the paths—he'd paused a few feet away, as if working up the courage to take the final steps, to speak. His face had burned when she'd thanked him and taken the handkerchief, her gloved fingers brushing his.

In the year that followed, how many times had she turned on that bench to find him standing, waiting for her invitation to come closer? Not that he'd sat with her, oh no—that wouldn't have been proper. But he could stand at the other end of the bench, and they could speak softly enough not to be overheard.

She had told him *so* much. Her life seemed to start at his first pause, and she told him all of it. Every bit, beginning with how she was born the youngest daughter of the estranged youngest son of a viscount. She had laughed at herself as she'd described her seasons and her family's efforts to find her a husband—she was too tall, too plain, and too poor to secure more than pity—and yet her constable had looked at her as if she were beautiful. She had told him how pleased she'd been to find a position as agreeable as governess to the Shiplans. And when her grandfather had begun to wither away, she had confided that sometime in the future a small inheritance would be hers—very small, but enough to keep a flat of her own, if she dared defy convention and live by herself. What would it matter if she did? At twenty-four, she was all but a spinster; in another few years, she would very firmly be one. What harm would it do if she used her money in a manner that would make her most happy?

*No harm*, he'd said, and it was the first phrase he'd spoken that hadn't been accompanied by red cheeks.

Very casually, she had mentioned him in her letters to her sisters—the constable from the park who blushed so charmingly. Perhaps she mentioned him too many times; Prudence had replied with the caution that men whose blood rose so easily were usually *Men With Appetites*. Temperance couldn't believe it of her constable, however, not when he'd been so unfailingly kind and courteous. Indeed, she was certain that if he knew how the sight of his ungloved hands could make her blood run hot, if he knew that she often sat on the bench with her thighs clenched and pressed so, so tightly together, her constable would only blush—he would not give in to appetites. She had thought to respond to Prudence that perhaps men whose blood rose so easily created *Women With Appetites*—but she hadn't written that, of course. She'd only thought it.

Then six months ago, she spent three weeks in bed coughing and sweating, and with no appetite of any kind. Her constable had waited then, too, and after three more weeks had passed and she'd finally had strength enough to return to her bench, he was already there. She'd seen the clench of his hands, as if he forced himself not to reach for her. She saw how he swallowed and turned his face away when she told him that if the illness came again, if it worsened, she would not spend her inheritance on a flat, but a sanatorium surrounded by a park, so that she could live out the remainder of her spinsterhood in quiet and peace.

For a while, that hadn't appeared to be her future. She'd been a bit weak and tired, but capable of teaching and fulfilling her duties. She had hope—until she was struck by the debilitating coughing again, the night sweats, and she'd begun to shed weight like water. An advance on her inheritance was given, and arrangements were made with the sanatorium. She'd bundled her things, and she'd still been strong enough to walk with her employers and their children out the front door to the waiting steamcoach.

But Edward Newberry had been waiting, too. For a farewell look, she'd thought, and her pleasure had been so great that she'd been unable to stop her smile—the same smile that had always been her invitation when she turned to find him waiting near her bench.

She had not cared that he approached her now. How lovely was it, that she would see him a final time, that she had an opportunity to say good-bye? It was a blessing. An improper one, perhaps, but she had been short on blessings of late, and she would not turn away from this one.

Except that day, he didn't pause at all. With his eyes locked on hers, he'd advanced swiftly, cupped her face in his giant hands, and kissed her.

He kissed her though Baron Shiplan struck him across the back with his cane, shouting that he was a filthy cur. He kissed her though two footmen tried to wrestle him away from her—and though she regained her senses halfway through, and began to struggle, too. He kissed her until the Shiplan girls were pulled away from the scene by their mother; as they went the elder one said, *"That is only the man she speaks with in the park every day,"* and the focus of everyone's outrage shifted to include Temperance.

Newberry had been dragged away, Temperance sent to her father's home. In tearstained letters, her sisters confessed that they'd known how she'd encouraged the constable, and they hadn't done enough to warn her against it. The sanatorium's directors heard rumors of her wanton behavior, and suggested another location for Temperance to spend her remaining years. No one would have her, no one wanted her, and suddenly it mattered little that Edward Newberry didn't know who his father was, and his late mother had been an actress who'd entertained a string of men throughout her career, and that he was three years younger than she. Her grandfather's solicitor met with Newberry—now unemployed as well, dismissed from the police force for his unbecoming conduct—and it was agreed that he would have her inheritance if they married and moved to London.

He'd immediately agreed; Temperance had taken a day longer. When she'd seen him again, moments before they were wed, she'd asked him— still hoping that he was her friend who'd simply been swept up by an impulse—whether he'd planned all of this to happen when he'd kissed her: the marriage, the inheritance, and London?

*Yes*, he'd said, and his answer had shattered that hope.

She'd been sick on the airship journey from Manhattan City to Bath. She'd been sick on the locomotive to London, on the steamcoach from the station to their flat—and feeling sick again, listening to him pause outside the door, and remembering how deceived she'd been, how *stupid* she'd been, for smiling every time he'd paused before.

Nothing left of her heart allowed a smile now. She closed her eyes when the gentle knock sounded, followed by the creaking hinges. Light spilling in from the small parlor warmed the darkness behind her eyelids.

His voice came, low and gruff. "Forgive the disturbance—I saw your lamp through the window as I was coming in, and hoped you hadn't yet fallen asleep."

Drat. "I'm awake."

"How did Miss Lockstitch work out?"

She was vulgar and wore a disturbing contraption in place of her hand. "Very well," Temperance said, and because it was ridiculous, she opened her eyes.

His big body filled the doorway, nothing but a silhouette. He'd removed his domed hat and the shape of his shoulders seemed less stiff than usual. He must have also taken off his uniform jacket...which meant he stood at her door in his shirtsleeves. *Oh.* She closed her eyes again, trying not to remember the night when she had woken in a sweat, not only from the sickness but the sweltering summer night, and he'd heard her walking about and had come to the door of his room. He had been very solid, her husband, as if he spent many hours in a pugilist's ring rather than simply patrolling a quiet park.

"Have you thought more on the infection?"

The memory of his bare chest dissolved easily. "I have told you, I will not end up…a thing. And you *know* I will. You've heard of the zombies as well." Ravenous, mindless—consuming other humans, filled with *bugs*. It was unthinkable. Only a horrid man could think a short lifetime could be worth an eternity of *that*. "I do not understand why you pursue this. You have my money. Is that not enough?"

"It's not hardly enough. You *must* risk—" he began, but the exertion of her anger had squeezed at her lungs, caught at her throat, and the cough had ruptured up, cutting him off. Then another, and another, until her throat was raw and her muscles aching and blood spotted her handkerchief. She curled up on her side, bracing herself against each wracking cough, tears slipping into the pillow. He crossed the room during her fit, and as the coughing eased his hand made warm circles on her back. But she could not bear his touch, not when she had wanted it for so long and now it came like this.

"Leave me be," she whispered. "Let me sleep."

He paused, then, and she thought he might refuse. But he turned away, quietly closing the door behind him, and she struggled up in her bed and fixed her draught of laudanum. The bitter medicine coated her tongue, her throat, and was all that she could taste as she lay back again, listening to her husband move about the flat, retrieving his cold dinner from the stone slab in the larder. Chair legs scraped lightly against the floor in their small dining area, then there was only quiet as he settled in to eat.

The laudanum warmed her chest, weighed down her limbs. She closed her heavy eyelids, and it was so easy to imagine him sitting at their table in his shirtsleeves, at the table that was so similar to the one she'd once imagined for her own flat. A cozy combination of rooms converted from an old mews, she wouldn't have wanted anything more—except that this was in London, and she shared the flat with a deceitful man, and she was dying in it.

# Chapter Two

THE NIGHTMARE CAME, AND SHE SAW HERSELF EMACIATED AND pale and ravenous. Temperance opened her eyes to the dark, heart pounding, her linen shift twisted and clinging with sweat. As always, the laudanum weighed on her chest, pressed her into the bed, and she had a moment of terror that she wouldn't be able to get up, that she was already dead.

But her legs moved, and she swung her feet to the wooden floor. From the other room, she heard a deep coughing. Newberry, but he didn't suffer as she did. His cough was of his own making.

Desperate for air, she opened the window to the warm night, but it wouldn't be *fresh* air—not in London. The gray haze of smoke that hung over the city during the day was still visible at night, the glow of the gas streetlamps casting a dirty yellow into the dark sky. She breathed it in, though the filthy air would kill her faster and was already clawing at her husband's lungs, air that she could hear being made dirtier in the distance, on the busier streets of London, the never-ending rumble of the steamcoaches and lorries and carts belching their exhaust.

Their second-level flat overlooked the cobblestone alley between the mews and the lockstitch guild's great stone house—an aristocrat's house, perhaps, before the Horde had come and most of the nobles had fled to the New World. She looked to the end of the alley. Miss Lockstitch had told her that a park lay not far away, the Embankment alongside the River Thames. From there, she would be able to see the bridges, the colorful tents over the Temple Fair, and the crumbling tower that had once broadcasted the radio signal the Horde had used to control the bugs.

She would like that—the tower was only a curiosity, but the Embankment's gardens sounded like heaven, and the strange amusements of the Temple Fair diverting. Perhaps she and Miss Lockstitch could hire a cab this week, and if Temperance could not manage a walk through the gardens, at least she could sit.

Feeling light, lighter than she usually did after a draught of laudanum, Temperance idly glanced to the other end of the alley, and realized that she was still in her nightmare. What else could that man have sprung from?

Tall, so tall that the blond woman he faced only came up to his middle, his eyes burning orange like the bowels of a furnace. His legs were long, thin compared to the bulk of his torso, and deeply jointed, bent far over at the knees though he stood upright—almost like the front legs of a mantis, but these were his *only* legs, and she saw the glint of metal instead of green.

And *he* was rumbling, too. It was not only the distant traffic. Wisps of steam wafted from the back of his head. Was it even a man? Temperance could not tell anymore, and it looked as through her nightmare was ending, because the blond woman had turned away from the rattling man, as if they were leaving the alley. But, no—not over yet. The man's metal hand flicked out to his side, then back around, and came down over the woman's head.

The woman crumpled to the ground.

Temperance screamed. And screamed again, scrambling away from the window as the man suddenly rose up in a great hiss of steam, *bounding* toward her, springing as high as their second-level flat, his orange eyes glowing with the fires of hell. Her next scream caught in her throat, became a cough, and another. Her bedroom door crashed open,

Newberry shouting her name, and she flung herself toward him, because he was horrid but also so big that even a nightmare could not get through him. Strong arms hauled her up against a wide chest, and he demanded to know what had happened, but she could not tell him, she could only cough and point to the window.

Cradled against him, Temperance fought not to hide her face in his shoulder as he carried her over to look—but the man wasn't there. The alley was empty but for the figure still crumpled on the stones. Newberry's body stiffened slightly when he saw her, his arms holding Temperance a little tighter.

"I'll send for the inspector," he said.

NEWBERRY KNEW BETTER THAN TO MOVE A DEAD BODY BEFORE the inspector came—she had said so very firmly when they had met that morning, and she'd laid out her expectations for him. He was not to call her 'lady,' even if it chafed his bounder sensibilities to refer to an earl's daughter as anything else. She would be called 'sir,' following the precedent set by Superintendent Hale, who had come to London from Manhattan City after being denied a position on the police force because of her sex. While she conducted an investigation, he was to keep his eyes open and his mouth closed, unless she asked for his opinion; if he could prove himself with sensible replies, she would eventually allow him to offer his opinion unsolicited. And if someone spat at her, if a passerby tried to hit her, if it looked as though a mob might come after her, she would appreciate very much if he stepped in.

He hadn't needed to as of yet. And though she'd also instructed him to leave any body alone, he bent her rules to verify that the woman didn't have a pulse, and that he wasn't leaving her injured on a cobblestone street while he waited for the inspector to arrive.

No pulse. And considering that a gash in her skull exposed smashed brains, the reason for it was clear.

Newberry glanced up to the well-lit window on the mews' second-level. Temperance stood there, her fingers pressed to the glass. She'd demanded that he leave her alone, that he go perform his duties.

She still did not understand. Above all else, his duty was protecting her, keeping her safe, keeping her alive. And he would do it, no matter how she hated him. So he watched her now, and though pain stabbed through his chest when she deliberately turned away, at least he knew she was well. He would bear *anything* to know she was well.

And he would bear anything to see her get better. The shredding of his heart was the price he'd paid, the choice he'd made when he'd kissed her, when he'd offered to marry her and move her to London. But it would be worth it to see her strong again.

If only she weren't so all-fired stubborn.

The huffing engine of a steamcoach announced the inspector's arrival—a cab, Newberry noted, and she was accompanied by a young man and a boy or twelve or thirteen, one brown-haired and the other light, and both of them looking hastily dressed. Buttoned up in her inspector's jacket and trousers, the inspector appeared irritated with them, but in a familiar sort of way. Brothers, perhaps, though they shared none of the inspector's Horde features.

She left them behind to pay the driver, her gaze sweeping the length of the alley before coming to rest on the woman's body. "Constable Newberry." She gave him a nod before crouching next to the woman. "I suppose you have none of your equipment."

"No, sir. I am to be issued my equipment and a police cart tomorrow."

"All right. I've called for the body wagon. We'll ride back to the station with it." Bending over the head wound, she drew in a sharp breath. "He was either very angry, or very strong."

Strong, by Temperance's description. But the inspector hadn't asked for his opinion or a report yet. "Yes, sir."

She sat back on her heels, and her gaze lifted to the lighted window. "You have a witness?"

"Yes, sir. My—"

"First tell me what you see, constable." She gestured to the woman's body. "Pretend that you have not heard anything at all. What do you see here?"

A test, he realized. She looked up at him, her expression inscrutable, but he felt that her eyes were taking in his every thought, every emotion, looking to see whether he'd cheat and use the information he already knew. Swallowing, he studied the body.

"She's female, blonde, thirty or thirty-five years of age," he said, and felt his face heat at the obviousness of that, but the inspector only nodded, as if telling him to go on. "She was likely born in a crèche, because thirty years was before the revolution, and the apparatus on her arm suggests that they altered her, as well."

"Not always, but go on."

"It's a cutting tool. A cleaver? We might find a guild mark on her arm, and that will help us identify her."

"You know of the guilds and their marks already? How long have you been in London, constable?"

"A few weeks. But we live next to the lockstitch house." He gestured to the building. "It would be difficult not to see."

"You'd be surprised how many people see very little in this city, constable."

"Or hear very little," he said. Though Temperance had screamed in terror through an open window, no other windows were lit. No one had come out to the alley to help or to see what had happened.

"And most say very little, too. What else?"

Was there more? He studied the cobblestones around the body, noted a broken brick, the smear of blood and hair on the corner. Temperance had not mentioned a brick. In the dark, she probably hadn't seen it. "He used that to hit her with. But why? If it was a machine, the metal of his arm would be just as efficient—if not *more* efficient."

"Just as she would have used her cleaver to defend herself, yes? It would be natural, instinctive, to use a weapon in your arsenal that you are intimately familiar with. But he must not have given her the opportunity, struck her from behind."

"Yes, sir. And if he grabbed a brick close at hand, this probably wasn't planned, but something done in the heat of the moment."

"Very good, constable. You'll find that most of the murders we investigate are the same—for many of us, controlling our more extreme emotions after the Horde's tower was destroyed became a difficult exercise. Most likely, he became angry, and reacted—but of course we will try to find him and ask." She paused. "You will not irritate me if you offer your opinion now and again. Now let us go and talk to your witness."

She stood and looked to the man and the boy, who had been

standing quietly at the mouth of the alley. They were both sizing him up, Newberry realized, and he suddenly felt like a lumbering giant next to the petite inspector.

"Henry," she said. "Please watch over her until the wagon arrives."

The man nodded. "We'll be here. Shout if you have any trouble."

"I think I shall be all right with the constable here." Turning on her heel, she gestured for Newberry to follow, telling him, "Those are my brothers, Henry and Andrew. You outweigh them both together, and already nag at me less. I think this shall work out very well. Now, tell me of this witness."

"My wife, sir."

"She saw the body from your window?"

"She witnessed the murder itself, sir."

"I am fond of your wife already, constable. Was she able to describe this person?"

"Yes, sir. She said he looked like Spring-Heel Jack."

The inspector frowned, looked at him. "Who?"

DETECTIVE INSPECTOR WENTWORTH DIDN'T LOOK ANYTHING LIKE the caricatures of the Mongol officials that Temperance had seen in the newssheets. She did not have bulbous lips or slitted eyes that barely opened, and her body was not misshapen, fat-bottomed, and slope-shouldered, with a curving spine. Indeed, she was rather pretty, with smooth black hair wound into a knot at her nape, emphasizing the roundness of her face and the delicacy of her features rather than concealing them...though Temperance wasn't certain she would *ever* become used to seeing a woman in trousers, particularly snug ones. At least Miss Lockstitch's had been wide and loose, like the bottoms to a Lusitanian hunter's habit, so that when she stood it looked as though she wore a long, tailored skirt.

But trousers or no, it was good to see her, to see a face that wasn't pale. Although none were of Horde blood as the inspector was, men and women of every color walked the Manhattan City streets, and this woman's presence suddenly made London feel a little more like home.

The inspector's gaze swept the rooms once and Temperance twice.

The straight line of her mouth curved slightly when Temperance gave her the sketch.

"This is what you saw?"

"Yes." Temperance pointed to the second sketch, where the man's legs were no longer deeply bent, but almost straight. "And this is how he looked as he sprang toward my window."

"Will you show me the view?"

"Of course." Winded by the time she reached her room, Temperance had to slow and catch her breath. "It…is here."

The inspector gave her another long look before nodding. "Thank you. Constable, you didn't see this machine?"

The inspector had asked him so that she could take a rest, Temperance realized. All at once, she felt wretched. Miss Lockstitch had called this woman a jade whore, but given the difference between the caricatures and reality, given the Horde's history within this land, Temperance began to understand that the name wasn't a literal one.

"I didn't see it, sir," he said. "I came into the room after she screamed."

The inspector glanced at the bed—wide enough for two, but clearly only used by one. Temperance felt her cheeks flame, and her husband's lit like a bonfire.

*It is my illness*, Temperance wanted to say. But it wasn't. Even if she hadn't been consumptive, the horrid man wouldn't have been welcome in her bed.

"I see," the inspector said. "Do you have a window in your room, Newberry?"

"No, sir."

She looked down at the sketch in her hand. "Tell me about Spring-Heel Jack. Who is he?"

"He's no one, sir," Newberry said. "At least, not anymore."

"Dead?"

"No. He never was anyone, not exactly. The stories about him started up about fifty years ago. First, in the newssheets, reports from the people he'd attacked: a baker's daughter from Prince George Island…" He stopped. "That's the long island that lies east of Manhattan City—"

"I've seen maps of the New World, constable," the inspector said.

"Yes, sir." He flushed and cleared his throat. "And there was another attack on a vicar, which startled his horses so badly he was thrown from his cart. Those incidents both had witnesses, and everyone described the assailant the same way: with springs on his feet, the wings of a demon, and he spat blue flame."

"But this one did not have wings," Temperance put in. "And the flame of his eyes was orange."

Newberry paused for a moment, looking at her, and she remembered that they had spoken of this once, with him standing beside her bench. She had known of Spring-Heel Jack, but had not known the full truth of the story until he'd told her.

Still holding her gaze, he continued, "There were other sightings, and the description always the same. The newssheets speculated that he was a man who'd lost his legs in an accident and had them replaced with springs—which turned him into a madman, bounding up and down the island and Manhattan City. Everyone else held the opinion that he was the devil."

"Only bounders would be so terrified of prosthetics and demons," the inspector said. "And what was it truly?"

Newberry looked a trifle disappointed—and Temperance had to admit she was, too. This had been one of her favorite shiver-tales as a child, but the inspector did not look a bit impressed.

Though compared to the horrors of the Horde occupation, Temperance supposed a springing man-devil was nothing.

"Well, sir, no one knew who was behind the attacks until the incident in Cromwell Square. Spring-Heel Jack bounded in front of a countess's carriage as she was leaving a ball, and the fear gave her the vapors. She didn't recover for several weeks—and never ventured outside her home again."

"So, the lower classes were tormented and no one could stop it. But a countess fainted and the game was up."

"Yes, sir."

"And someone either pointed a finger or confessed," the inspector guessed.

Temperance met Newberry's eyes again, saw his suppressed smile and had to stifle her own. Truly, this woman could take the fun from everything.

"Yes, sir. Apparently, a group of young lords—including the countess's eldest son—had created Spring-Heel Jack on a lark. It was something of a betting club: they made wagers, daring one another to appear in the costume. Points were given based on the number of mentions the incident generated in the newssheets."

"A lark? Did they have nothing better to do with their time?" The inspector shook her head. "And now so many bounders are returning to England. Are these pranks what everyone in London has to look forward to?"

Temperance couldn't say. She only wondered, "What is a bounder?'

"It is us," Newberry said.

The inspector's mouth suddenly closed. Her lips pressed together, and embarrassment darkened her cheeks. "Yes. I'm sorry. But it has been very frustrating watching the people who fled England two hundred years ago return now—and so many of them filled with ideas of how to better us, and so eager to tell us how improper we are."

"I see," Temperance said. She understood all too well how maddening that could be—particularly when she had done nothing that was improper.

"But I was not thinking of you in this way. It has been the titled families returning for their estates and Parliament seats, most often. Also, I have heard that Constable Newberry was let go from the Manhattan City police force for improper behavior, so in my mind, I had already excluded you both from that category."

A beet could not have been redder than Newberry. "You've heard that, sir?"

"Yes. But don't worry, constable. Unless you did something truly awful, such as forcing yourself upon a woman, I shall not hold it against you—and Superintendent Hale has already assured me that your character is sound."

It took her husband a few moments to find his voice, and Temperance could hear the roughness in it, the shame. "Her mother knew mine," he said. "And Hale's husband was the reason I joined the force."

"I heard he was a good man." The inspector looked to the sketch again. "This club of bored rich boys—are there many of these sorts of clubs in Manhattan City, constable?"

"Yes, sir. Not of that sort, exactly, but there's a fair number of brotherhoods and such. Most are dedicated to remembering the glory of England—or restoring that glory."

"So they sit and talk."

"Mostly, sir."

"Then we can likely rule out a repeat of this Spring-Heel Jack incident."

"It does seem unlikely, sir."

"All right." She looked out the window as a rattling, huffing wagon pulled up to the end of the alley. "There are the body collectors. Have you anyone to stay with you, Mrs. Newberry?"

She glanced to Newberry, then to the guild building across the alley. "Perhaps we could wake Miss Lockstitch?"

"No," the inspector broke in, apparently changing her mind. "Stay here, constable. He knew he was seen; he might return. I will need you in the morning at the station, and we will go and speak with the victim's guild, discover who she is, and show this sketch around. Perhaps someone will recognize this machine. Walk with me down to the wagon, constable."

Temperance peered through the window, where two men had begun rolling the body in a cloth. They hadn't even restrained her first. "Don't they fear she'll wake up on the way?"

The inspector paused. "Who will wake up?"

"The woman who was killed. They are only rolling her into a sheet. Will that stop a zombie?"

Brows arching high, the inspector looked to Newberry, who blushed. "I confess, sir, I wondered the same thing."

The woman's gaze suddenly flattened, her mouth compressing into a tight line. "You think she'll become a zombie, constable?"

"Yes," Temperance answered for him. "Won't she? This is what we've been told. What we've *always* been told."

"And I've been told that bounders believed this, but didn't think they were *that* stupid. But they are?"

"Apparently, sir."

"By the starry sky…then listen to me now: She *won't* wake up. None of us will, unless we're infected with different bugs when they bite us. The zombie bugs are *different*." Lifting her face to the ceiling, the inspector heaved an exasperated breath, then turned for the door again. "All right.

Constable, with me. And do not speak unless I ask you to, and until you've proved yourself again."

# Chapter Three

WHEN THEY REACHED THE ALLEY, THE INSPECTOR SAID, "My family lives at Number Eight, Leicester Square, constable. Tomorrow morning, you will be there with your wife. My father will infect you both."

Dear God, he wished it could be so. "I'm sorry, sir, but I cannot. Not unless she agrees, and I won't do it unless she does."

She stopped and gave him a hard look. "Do you realize that your wife is *dying*, Newberry?"

Just hearing the words made it impossible to breathe, as if an iron fist grabbed his heart, pulped it into nothing.

The inspector must have seen. Her face softened. "She *must* be infected, constable. And you as well. The black lung kills more New Worlders in London than any other cause, and it would be easily preventable if they weren't so damned afraid of the bugs."

"I would, sir. But she's afraid. Terrified. I can't force her into it. I have already forced too much."

But he would if it came to the end, Newberry knew. If her condition continued to worsen, he'd force her to take the injection. It would be an unforgiveable trespass, but if she lived, he would never regret it.

"You've forced too much? How so, constable?"

"She'd never have come here on her own. She'd never have married me. So I compromised her."

Her eyes suddenly burned with anger. Her voice was flat and cold. "What does that mean, constable?"

"I kissed her."

The inspector didn't immediately respond, as if waiting. Then her lips pursed. "You kissed her?"

"Yes."

"And they made her marry you."

"Yes."

"Incredible." Shaking her head, she started toward the wagon again. "Bounders are simply incredible. I thought you must have shagged her, and that was stupid enough a reason, especially if she'd been forced into a bed by the man they wanted her to marry. I am glad you did not tell me that, at least. But compelled to marry for a *kiss*?"

Newberry had stopped in place, choking on his embarrassment and shock. He'd never *heard* such language from a woman—and from an earl's daughter! Good God, be merciful on her.

The inspector glanced back, frowning…then suddenly grinned. "Oh, Newberry. After you spend more time with me on the docks, you'll be saying it, too."

"I would *never*!"

"Or the act, I suppose?" Her expression suddenly changed to alarm. "By the starry sky, Newberry—do not have an apoplexy! I see that I will have to go easy on you to begin."

If she didn't, Newberry feared he would not live through it. Only through rigid control had he never let such thoughts enter his mind, and she only had to say *shag* and he was imagining Temperance, the flex of her fingers as she sketched in her book, the feel of her lips and the taste of her heated mouth. If he was always filled with lust, how could he return home? She would see it, and that would be too much. On top of everything else, it would be too much if she hated him for that, too.

"Please go very easy, sir."

"I will. Go on back home, then, constable. I'll see you at my house in the morning, regardless of whether you convince her." She sped up a bit, and when her brother Henry turned to face her, she called out, "The rumors about bounders and the zombies are true!"

Their laughter followed him back to the mews.

WHEN HER HUSBAND RETURNED, TEMPERANCE WAS NOT HIDING in her room. She sat on the sofa with her legs tucked under her blanket, her mind racing frantically.

"Is it true?" she asked the moment he came through the door. "Do you think it is true?"

He didn't immediately answer, taking the armchair opposite. His bulk filled it, twice the man of any other man she'd met, and all of it solid. She could still feel his strong arms around her, holding her close to his chest.

"I don't know," he finally said. "I'll ask to see the body tomorrow. In that way, we could be certain whether it has risen or not."

"But even without that evidence, you believe the inspector was telling the truth."

"Yes." He rubbed his big hand over his face. "Before we were here, how could we know? But there are always people who die and are not found until later. Several every night in a city this size. Why have they not risen? If it only takes one bite to spread the infection, even two or three would devastate London. Yet no one takes precautions against them. Windows are not boarded up, people walk freely at night. At the station, I was given no instructions about what to do if I came across one—yet they have told me to be wary of ratcatchers and of the eels in the river. And so it's only sensible to believe that there aren't any zombies here."

That seemed sensible to Temperance, too. She met his eyes and saw the same bemusement that she felt. All of this time, they'd believed that everyone in England became ravenous zombies after their deaths. *Everyone* she knew in Manhattan City had believed it, but knowing that their ignorance had been shared with thousands of other people did not make the embarrassment upon learning the truth any less. The inspector had not laughed at thousands of people; she had laughed at *them*.

Temperance was glad that he'd been with her to share it. Split between them, the humiliation was easier to bear.

She saw more in his eyes now, too—the speculation, the same as hers. In a low voice, he said, "If it's true, then you wouldn't become one after taking the injection."

Would it be so easy? Her heart filled with hope, with fear. "I wouldn't be able to return to Manhattan City after I was infected, though. Not without a bribe for the officials."

"A bribe as large as your inheritance?" He held her gaze. "I have saved it for you, in the event that was what you wished to do with it."

Her heart stuttered, and she pushed her hand to her chest. "You have?"

"Yes." He rose to his feet and started to his room, but paused at the end of her sofa. "But I wonder, Temperance: After everything that occurred, what would you want to go back to?"

He closed the door quietly behind him, and left her wondering exactly the same thing. What was left for her in Manhattan City? Her family had blamed *her* for Newberry's kiss and turned their backs. Her friends had quickly become distant. She wouldn't find useful employment—and she would need it if her inheritance was used up in bribes.

And there was another question to wonder about, too. Newberry had lived a full life in Manhattan City. But if he had not married her for the inheritance, then what on earth had drawn him to London?

N EWBERRY HAD LEFT BEFORE TEMPERANCE ROSE THE NEXT morning, late, after hours of being unable to sleep. Miss Lockstitch came, and their conversation was filled with the murder. Several of her guild mates had woken at the sound of Temperance's scream, and a few had seen glimpses of the machine—though, of course, no one had come out while the inspector was there and reported what they'd seen.

Temperance drew another sketch, and Miss Lockstitch pulled her embroidery from her large pelisse, but before she could fit the frame over her knee, Temperance stopped her, gasping, and left her sofa for a closer look.

It was astounding work. A delicate, intricate design of flowers and leaves, the stitches so tiny they were all but invisible. "This is *beautiful*, Miss Lockstitch. I've never seen the equal."

Smiling and pink cheeked, the young woman said, "Thank you."

"Do you create the design yourself, or only embroider it?"

"I create it."

"It's stunning." Temperance could not have said whether it was worth losing a hand over, but she wasn't blind to the pride and joy the woman was feeling now. Perhaps those feelings *were* worth some pain, some loss. She returned to her sofa. "As part of my governess duties, I used to teach two girls how to stitch small items, and I barely had the patience for it. To see this, to know it was done in one day…it is simply amazing. Your clients must be spoiled."

Miss Lockstitch flashed a grin. "I make them pay for it."

Temperance had to laugh. "As you should."

Setting the frame over her knee, and her hand over the frame, the needles began clicking away. "Mrs. Newberry, the other girls in the house and I had wondered…you were a governess. Did you also teach reading?"

"In several languages, yes."

"Do you think—when your illness passes—you might agree to teach us?"

*When her illness passed.* Not since her second decline had that been a hope. But even if she was infected, even if the bugs cured her, would she stay in this flat with Newberry?

Temperance didn't know. But she could make a promise. "If I am here, I will," she said.

Newberry returned earlier than she expected. It was only just after noon when he came into the flat, scooping his domed hat from his head. He gave a polite greeting to Miss Lockstitch, and when his gaze met Temperance's, she rose to speak with him.

"Have you discovered who she was? Have you discovered who he was?"

"We know who she was, yes—she was with the butcher's guild. We still don't know who he is, but we're looking for him."

But her husband wasn't looking for him, he was here— *Ah.* "The inspector worries that he'll come back for me."

"Not only the inspector," he said, and she couldn't speak for a moment, until she noticed that Miss Lockstitch had been gathering her things.

"Abigail," she said, "perhaps we will take that walk tomorrow."

"I look forward to it." She gave Newberry a nod as she passed. "Good day, constable."

Temperance returned to her sofa while Newberry went to the window, watching the alley until Miss Lockstitch made it back to her home. After a few moments, he hooked his hat beside the door, unbuckled his uniform jacket. "A walk?"

"A cab, in truth—at least for most of the distance. She said the Embankment is lovely, and I don't think I could manage the Temple Fair, unless they have a great many benches throughout."

"But you'd like to visit that, too?"

"Yes."

"Then we will." He extended his arm to her. "Let me help you up, and you can make yourself ready."

Her gaze fell to his hand. She tried to remind herself that he was horrid, *horrid*…but either she didn't care, or she wasn't convinced of it anymore. Slowly, she slid her fingers against his, felt his warm clasp. When he pulled her up, his head was bent, and she was looking up at him—and tall Temperance, plain Temperance, she would only have to keep going, to rise up on her toes to meet his lips.

She did not, but for a long, breathless moment she waited, recalling how his eyes had locked on hers as she was running away to her death. She recalled his strong hands against her cheeks, his firm mouth. She recalled the joy she'd felt then, her first kiss—her *only* kiss—and it had come from her constable. She recalled the wonder of it before the baron had begun to beat him, before she'd remembered herself and fought to get away.

Now, letting go of his hand, she started for her room. But she could not stop thinking: What harm would it do if she forgot herself again?

# Chapter Four

THE SPIDER RICKSHAW WAS EITHER AN ABSOLUTELY TERRIFYING contraption or an exhilarating one—or perhaps both, but after five minutes, Temperance couldn't even determine whether *terrifying* or *exhilarating* were any different. She had laughed and shrieked from almost the very beginning of their ride, hiding her face against Newberry's arm as their small cart darted between lumbering lorries, as they were nearly flattened by oncoming steamcoaches, and daring another look again as they passed men and women riding in their slower—and perhaps safer—pedal buggies.

At the front of their cart, their gray-haired driver pumped his sturdy legs against two long hydraulic levers, and beneath his feet was a flurry of spinning wheels, clanking gears, and the clickity-clack of segmented metal legs that carried them at speed.

Newberry laughed as often as she, though he didn't hide his head even once, and as the arched stone gate marking the entrance to Temple Fair appeared at the end of the Strand, he said, "I don't know why I didn't think to do this earlier."

Temperance knew why. It was because, before today, she'd never invited him to sit beside her—and now, all but squished on a small bench between his solid body and the side of the cart, she'd had more fun than she could recall since...

Ever.

*That* was horrid. And she ought to have thought of it earlier, too.

The spider rickshaw finally slowed as they came out of traffic and passed through the gate and beneath the first giant, striped tent. The scents of roasted meats filled the air, barkers calling out their goods from all sides. The stalls were widely spaced, with many more rickshaws and buggies rolling through. Temperance realized she wouldn't have to walk at all, and was glad of it—her illness would not put a damp rag over their time here today.

Newberry called to the driver over the noise of the rickshaw and the crowds. The rickshaw stopped, and Newberry hopped out, holding up his hand in a gesture for her to stay. She did, watching acrobats in colorful pajamas perform their tricks on a rope hanging between two large balloons. A boy with a stack of magazines announced the release of the latest Archimedes Fox adventure. Two women bounced past the rickshaw, wearing nothing but corsets and sheer skirts. Temperance's cheeks flushed, but she turned to watch them—as did almost everyone else, and she laughed as heads rotated with the predictability of an automaton's as the women walked along.

Within a few minutes, Newberry returned carrying three foaming mugs of bark beer—one for the driver, she realized, which made her love him all the more.

She *loved* him.

And because she did, Temperance smiled at him as he climbed back into the cart. His face reddened, and he took a long gulp while she sipped hers, suddenly and inexplicably shy and embarrassed.

The rickshaw began clicking along again, but she barely saw the amusements they passed. Should she hold his hand? Rest her fingers on his arm? Or dare more, and rest them on his leg? Should she let it fall casually between them, where his thigh was pressed against hers?

This was agony.

"Are you well? Has this been too much?"

Startled, she met his concerned gaze. "No. I'm well. But you, sir, have foam on your lip. No, let me."

She stopped his wiping fingers and swept her thumb against the corner of his mouth—and then there was only his mouth, and the tightening of her thighs, the deep hollow ache that she'd known before. Temperance knew what would fill it, that her constable could make that ache disappear, but she could not now, not yet.

Not when she couldn't even cross a room.

She let her fingers fall from his lips, and slipped her hand into his. Holding her gaze, he lifted her palm to his mouth, pressed a kiss into the center—and the ache eased, a little, and yet somehow dug ever deeper.

"Edward," she said, and rested her head against his shoulder.

He didn't let go of her hand. He held it through the blue tent's twisting maze of stalls, where she tossed a coin to the twirling, dancing men with rollers for feet, who spun so fast that she dizzied simply watching them. He held her hand through the yellow tent, where a woman with a small furnace beneath her belly roasted chestnuts. He offered to buy a bag for her, and she laughed until her head was as light as the floating lady, who somehow lived within the hydrogen-filled bubble of her balloon.

And he was still holding her hand as they passed into the orange tent, where he stiffened ever-so-slightly at her side—as if sitting up straighter, though his posture was already quite tall. Near the center of the tent, she saw the inspector in her uniform and hat, flanked by the man and boy who'd accompanied her the previous night. The inspector stopped a woman, showed her a paper—the sketch of the machine, Temperance realized.

"Are they here looking for him?" she wondered.

"They must be." He nodded. "It is the right place for such a machine, isn't it?"

Temperance supposed there was no other place for it. The inspector spotted them, and a slight smile curved her mouth, her hand lifted in acknowledgment, before stepping into the path of another man, showing him the sketch.

A thorough woman, Temperance thought. "Do you suppose— Oh, dear God!"

In horror, she watched the inspector's head snap to the side, her hand flying to her mouth. The man had *struck* her. Temperance shouted, rising from her seat. Her brothers started after her assailant, who turned and ran from them. The rickshaw jolted as Newberry bounded from the side—*Good Lord, he was quick*—straight into the path of the running man, and Newberry did not even stagger as the man barreled into him. He simply gripped the smaller man's shoulders and lifted him up, a foot above the ground, and shook him until Temperance heard the man's teeth repeatedly snap together.

*"Never again!"* he roared, and in his rage his face was as red as his hair, all of him terrifying and huge.

And yet she wasn't afraid. She wasn't afraid at all.

The inspector came up, her lip dripping blood over her chin. Newberry set the man down, grabbed him by the scruff.

"What do you want done with him, sir?"

"Just let him go." She sounded incredibly weary, and Newberry did. The man immediately began to run. "He's not worth the time, or dragging you away from your wife." The elder brother started after the man scampering away, and her voice sharpened. "Henry! Just let it go. And thank you, constable. You see now why your presence is needed during my investigations."

"I do, sir."

The inspector nodded. "All right, boys. Let's move on."

Newberry climbed into the cart again, still stiff with anger—and Temperance was shaking, too. Her hand found his, and she clenched it tight.

Such a man he was. Such a man, to immediately leap to a woman's defense.

Yet she had believed, she'd truly *let* herself believe that he had forced a kiss upon her for money? "I am so sorry, Edward," she said. "I am so sorry."

His brows drew together. "For what?"

"When we were married, you said that you'd planned the kiss, you'd planned it all. But it wasn't for the money, was it? It was so that I could come here and perhaps be healed."

"Yes." His voice was gruff.

His face blurred in front of her. Oh, why tears now? "Thank you," she said.

Big hands cupped her face, but he didn't respond. Perhaps, like her, his throat had closed and wouldn't allow even another word.

But she struggled through the pain in her chest, because she had to know— "Do you love me, Edward?"

"More than my own life."

She laughed, and threw herself into his lap, and there—in the center of the yellow tent at Temple Fair—pressed her lips to his, and kissed him until she could no longer breathe.

Which wasn't nearly long enough.

His thumbs brushed away her tears. She settled in next to him again, and though she wasn't physically closer—they'd been crushed together all this time—she *felt* closer, as if the press of their sides and their legs were not just where they touched, but where they were joined, connected.

She took his hand. "I have loved you for years. And I— Oh." Her fingers tightened on his thigh. "Edward, look."

Beyond his shoulder, walking down one of the twisting side paths through the stalls, a man was wearing a huffing machine suit. Temperance's heart began to pound, and she saw now why the legs seemed deeply jointed—they were like stilts with springs and hydraulics, with his natural feet standing on pegs at the suit's upper thighs. The boiler had been strapped to his back and rose high over his own head, yet shaped at the top like a face with eyes—glowing orange from the reflected light in the furnace.

Newberry let go of her hand, climbed out. "Go quickly, and find the inspector. I'll keep near him, and wait for her. Find the Horde woman who was just hit!" he called to the driver.

"All right," she said, but the man in the suit had already stopped, was peering down the path toward her. "Oh. Oh, he recognizes me."

"*I didn't mean to!*" came a desperate shout. "*Let me be! I didn't mean to!*"

"Go!" Newberry turned, just as the machine suit spun and the man began to run. "Go!"

She watched Newberry sprint down the twisting path after the man, and then the rickshaw lurched into motion, a rapid clickity-clack darting through the crowd, and this time Newberry wasn't there to keep her from bouncing around. She gripped the side of the cart, her heart fluttering painfully, and this was not exhilarating at all, but simply terrifying.

Just as she was about to be sick all over her feet, the rickshaw stopped. Temperance shouted out, "Inspector Wentworth! Newberry is after him!" and the woman took off at a run, brothers close behind, but Temperance was already coughing, coughing, and could not run at all.

"Follow them, please!" she managed to tell the driver, who gave her a wild grin and pumped his legs, and they had almost caught up to the inspector when she darted down a side path, and the cart tilted wildly as the spidery legs all seemed to shift about in one great heave, and Temperance was suddenly facing the same way, tasting bark beer in her mouth.

Ahead of them, she saw the springing machine, bounding, bounding, bounding beneath the roof of the striped tent. The crowd grew heavier as everyone came into the middle of the path to see, and soon even the driver's honks and shouts wouldn't move them ahead any farther.

It was not that far. Not that far. Temperance couldn't speak for coughing, but she gave the driver a heavy coin and gestured for him to wait.

He nodded, and she began to weave her way through the crowd, pain stabbing her lungs with every cough, and blood in drops on her handkerchief. The machine had stopped bounding, but people in the crowd ahead had begun pushing back, as if trying to get away. Temperance clung to a stall post, legs almost too weak to keep her upright, and she would stay here, she decided, so that she wouldn't be trampled and because Newberry could find her on his way.

Rising above the shouts came another noise, a high-pitched whistling. Oh, and she knew that sound. A boiler with its vents blocked and its pressure rising to the point of explosion. And as the crowd cleared, she saw it: the man trapped in his suit, with Newberry and the inspector frantically working to get him out. The inspector seemed to be shouting at him, and Newberry shook his head, and Temperance wanted to scream at him to *run! run!* but she couldn't even breathe. And finally, the man came away, Newberry staggering back as a buckle suddenly broke free, and then the inspector was running, and Newberry running and carrying a murderer.

The explosion knocked Temperance down, knocked almost everyone else down—and those left standing ducked to escape the flying shrapnel. Shaking the ringing from her ears, she looked up. The inspector was standing, her brothers were standing…and Newberry was not getting up.

She couldn't hear the inspector over the shouts, but as she staggered to her feet the brothers were lifting Newberry between them, carrying him at a run—too fast, and they were past her, and she could not even call out.

A hand touched her shoulder. She looked round, and the inspector frowned at her, shook her head. "Newberry's lucky. The man we pulled out wasn't."

*How lucky?*

The inspector seemed to read her face. "He'll be all right. They're taking him to my father," she said, and suddenly swept Temperance up in her arms—carrying her easily, even when she began to run.

Good Lord. The bugs did this?

Ahead, she saw the brothers flag down a steamcoach, but they didn't wait for Temperance and the inspector. With a great bellow, it started off, and the inspector tossed her into the waiting spider rickshaw and shouted a direction to the driver as she climbed in.

They scuttled off at speed. Temperance gripped the side of the cart to keep from jostling into the inspector. Her breathing had eased, a little, but she saw the inspector's gaze fall to her bloody handkerchief, saw the hardening of the other woman's eyes.

"They're taking him to my father," she said, "but with this sort of abdominal wound, he's likely to become septic after the surgery, do you understand? Without the bugs he'll probably die. He *needs* the transfusion."

Was she asking the wife's permission? Yes, yes. Temperance nodded wildly.

"Newberry told me last night that he wouldn't do it unless you did first."

*Oh.* There was no question, then. She would waffle about saving her own life. She wouldn't do the same with his.

"I will," she said.

\* \* \*

IT WAS SIMPLE FOR HER. TEMPERANCE LAY ON A SOFA, WHILE THE inspector's father with his brown beard and sharp eyes gave her an injection of his own blood through a small hollow needle. Then he gave her a sleeping draught, and when she woke in an unfamiliar room, it was the next day, and her chest did not hurt, and her legs were not weak, and she walked down a stair without needing to cling to the banister.

The boy—Andrew—met her at the bottom of the stair, and led her to the back of the house where Newberry lay upon a table, a blanket over his hips, his chest bare and his stomach covered in a bandage. He lifted his head and saw her, but the red stubble on his cheeks had darkened his skin, concealing most of his blush.

She took his hand. "Good morning, constable."

"Good morning, wife." His eyes searched her face. "How do you feel?"

"Wonderful. And you?" She looked to his bandages.

"His lordship says that I'll be completely healed by this evening. He'll let me leave after dinner."

"So all is well, husband?"

"Yes."

For her, too. Temperance rested her cheek on his shoulder and wept.

# Chapter Five

I T WAS NOT THE FIRST TIME TEMPERANCE HAD DINED AT AN EARL'S
house, but it was the most pleasant. No one cared that her husband
sat at her side, and she did a *very* good job of not staring at the
countess's strange mirrored eyes.

But though it was pleasant, she did not want to sit. For months now,
it seemed that she had always been sitting, or sleeping, or in her bed. She
wanted to walk and run all the way home, and then dance with Newberry
around the rooms of their cozy, perfect little flat.

Perhaps they noticed her impatience. After dinner, the inspector wore
an amused expression as she walked with them to the waiting steamcoach.
Newberry assisted Temperance inside the carriage, then turned to the
inspector, gave a nod.

The inspector closed the door after he climbed in, and said through
the open window, "It has been quite the day, and this is the first night
that you are both in full health since your marriage began. I won't expect
you early tomorrow morning, Newberry."

She rapped on the carriage's side. It jolted forward, and in the dark

Temperance didn't know if Newberry's face was as hot as hers, but she guessed that it likely was.

"Is she always so bold?" Temperance wondered.

He sounded as if he were choking. "I believe so."

Temperance could not be. She took his hand, and that was enough as the steamcoach traveled the short distance down Whitehall, then west to their mews.

Newberry seemed satisfied as well, though when they reached their flat and lit the lamps, it seemed his blush had not yet faded. Still he was, as he'd always been, the perfect gentleman. Her heart pounded as she readied for bed. She climbed beneath the sheets and then she waited.

And waited.

She heard his bedroom door close. *Ah.* Retrieving his things to move into here, no doubt.

Still, he was taking a very long time. She passed it by remembering how his chest had looked. How his lips had felt. Her shift grew uncomfortably hot, and she wanted to tear it away, so that she would be nude when he finally came to her.

Burning with frustration, she sat up and called, "Edward?"

He appeared at her door a moment later, hair wild, gaze darting to the window. "Yes?"

He'd been in bed, she realized. Sleeping—or trying to. Suddenly aware of her bare breasts beneath the thin shift, she pulled her sheet up to her chin.

Temperance almost lost her courage before she found it again. "I thought you might sleep with me from now on."

His blush covered his face, his neck. How far down did it go? Her gaze dropped, then stopped at the linen stretched over his hips, the tent tall enough to house a fair. Her fingers shook, and the ache started again, so needy, so deep.

"I think that you would like to come to bed, too," she said. Oh, and how *she* wanted him to.

His eyes closed. His voice was tortured. "I haven't…before."

So? "Neither have I. But I'm sure we'll manage to fit everything into the right places."

He nodded, and her heart thumped as he approached the bed. She scooted to give him room. He lay on his side, his feet at the very bottom. Gently, he stroked her cheek.

She touched his, felt the heat. "My sister once warned me that a man who blushed so easily was probably a *Man With Appetites*."

His fingers stilled, and worry crept into his eyes. "I might be. I want so much, Temperance. But I don't want to frighten you. Or hurt you."

He was the sweetest, most perfect man. She brought her face close to his.

"You cannot hurt me, Edward."

His nod was small, a bare movement of his head. Their lips were close. His ragged breath swept across her mouth before he filled the distance between them.

And, *oh so sweet*. His kiss was a slow taste, a tease against her lips before he opened his mouth on a groan and took it deeper. His hands found her waist, hauled her against his rigid body. She felt the hard press of him against her hip, and she'd never, *never* have imagined that simply knowing how he wanted her could strike sparks through her body, could make her squirm against him, until she was panting and wet—so wet!—between her thighs that she could not even look at him when he first touched her there. *Wanton*. But he didn't push her away; it only seemed to inflame him, tearing her shift up over her body, his mouth suddenly hot on her nipples and his fingers pressing inside her.

She gasped, squeezing her thighs around his hand. Edward stilled.

"Am I hurting you?"

Unable to speak, she shook her head. But now his mouth was slower as he bent his head, the suction of his lips and tongue at her breast matching the languorous movement of his hand. Tension began to roll through her, some deep, awful, wonderful tightening that seemed to cramp at her calves and push her hips into wild gyrations, leaving her crying out his name and sobbing for some release—and suddenly it was there, in great pulsing waves that shook her, shook her like the convulsions of a cough, but so luscious.

Edward's mouth found hers again, his hips settling in the cradle of her thighs. She felt him, thick and probing. She closed her eyes and stilled as a new ache formed, moving deeper, deeper, and her fingers dug into his shoulders. He groaned and his weight came over her, the ache not so painful anymore but just so *there*, it was all that she could feel.

His body shook. With her hands on the bunched muscles in his shoulders, she urged him to move. He withdrew and surged, and that easily Temperance forgot herself, forgot everything but the strength of his body, the sweetness of his mouth, the heat of his skin. The tension came again, building, and she strained to meet it, rising with him, falling, circling her legs around his hips to hold him close, arching her back as it swept through her, coming again and again with each heavy thrust. He called her name then, his body suddenly still but for the pulse of him deep within.

With a groan, he settled over her. Temperance wrapped him in her arms, felt the heaviness over her chest that was her constable, pinning her to the bed—and for the first time not making her fear that she was dead, because she'd never been so alive.

She kissed his jaw. "I love you," she said, and laughed as he rolled over, carrying her with him. "And thank you for saving my life."

"Saving you saved mine," he said gruffly.

"I'm glad," she said and smoothed her hand down his side. His blush rose, and she grinned. "I ought to warn you that I've just discovered that I'm also a *Woman With Appetites*."

He smiled. "Then it's a fine thing we're in London. No one will come when you scream."

She laughed and lowered her head. Yes. A fine thing to be in London, indeed.

# Vixen

## Jessica Sims

# Vixen

MIKO HATED IT WHEN PEOPLE SHOWED UP ON HER DOORSTEP. It was the one reason she'd moved to the country, after all. Well, one of many. Modern life involved a great many people crammed into very small spaces, and that was difficult to deal with when you were a were-fox with the constant need to shift to fox form. But even more than that, just being around men made her hormones sing. Were-foxes weren't called vixens for nothing. Out in the wild, a fox vixen was prone to, well, polygamous relationships, and that carried over to their human counterparts. Spend a few hours of time around a man? She'd start to feel the need to select a mate. But if men weren't around? No problem. No needs. No worries. No mates. Just peace and quiet, where she could relax and paint to her heart's content.

Add in the fact that the country was serene and involved very, very few door-to-door salesmen, living outside of the city in an old farmhouse was perfect for her needs.

So it was irritating to see two men on her big wrap-around porch.

Even more irritating, they'd rung the doorbell three times now and didn't appear to be going anywhere. She'd have to answer at some point because every time it rang, it broke her concentration. Sighing, Miko dumped her pencil into the Mason jar that held her artist supplies and left her studio, moving across the old farmhouse to the front door.

As she pushed through her kitchen, a particular object caught her ire—a delicate green bonsai tree on the counter, a leafy green oasis in the clutter. Another one of her mother's gifts. She hadn't realized her mother had left one the last time she came over. Seeing the bonsai just made her even more irritated, and she grabbed it and swept it into the garbage before continuing on to the front door.

That was her mother—never taking no for an answer. No matter how many times Miko told her to butt out, she'd completely ignore her daughter's wishes. Maybe it was a were-fox trait to be stubborn and independent beyond all reason. Her mother didn't even like the term 'were-fox'. She preferred 'kitsune'.

Miko preferred were-fox. Which pretty much told everything about her relationship with Yui Woodward.

Miko jerked the door open, about to snarl something unpleasant through the screen. She didn't need her roof redone, wasn't interested in selling the mineral rights to her land, and certainly didn't need to buy candy bars or Girl Scout Cookies or have her lawn mowed. As soon as she glimpsed the men on her porch, though, she stopped.

If these men were roofers, damn, maybe she *should* get her roof redone. Because…wow. Every hormone in her body went instantly on alert. Both men were gorgeous, in that odd, mismatched pair sort of way. One was enormous, with big, broad shoulders, huge muscled arms, and a close-cropped skullcap of dark hair. It should have made him frightening except for the fact that the look in his soft brown eyes was warm and mild, as was the smile curving his mouth.

His companion was slightly more compact, his frame that of a swimmer rather than a bodybuilder, and his blond hair fell in loose, tousled waves across his forehead. Where his companion had warm eyes, this one's sharp blue eyes sparkled with a dangerous, fun gleam. Miko could tell at a glance that they were polar opposites. The mild one and the wild child.

And judging from the mischievous look in the blonde's eyes as she sized them up, they knew it too.

Immediately, her fox nature began to react. When a desirable male was in the area, her natural instinct was to preen and pose to make herself more attractive. To slide her hands slowly over her body when she knew they were looking. To give a man hot, possessive looks to let him know she was interested. Two handsome men? Well. It was an immediate turn-on, and she licked her lips, her voice pitching low. "Can I help you two with something?"

"I sure hope so," said the blond, grinning at her. He hadn't missed her quick appraisal—and approval—of their appearances.

The dark haired one cleared his throat, the hint of a blush tingeing his cheeks. He pulled out his wallet and approached the screen door. "My name is Jeremiah Russell, and this is Sam Thorpe."

Miko kept the smile on her face. "And?"

"Yui Westwood sent us."

God. Not another one of her mother's matchmaking schemes. Miko raised a skeptical eyebrow and crossed her arms. "And I shouldn't tell you both to fuck off…why, exactly?"

Sam licked his thumb and raised it to the breeze, waiting a moment for it to change. As soon as it did, she knew.

They were shifters. Just like her. Here on her doorstep. Two cat shifters, if her nose was correct. Her eyes narrowed. Well. That either made things really interesting, or really annoying. Either way, she couldn't turn them away from her door. Miko opened the screen door, gesturing for them to come inside. "I should have guessed."

"Your mother said you should call if you have concerns," the darker-haired one began in a mild voice.

"Or if you're just wowed by our charm," the blond added with a grin and clapped his friend on the back. "Though this behemoth might make you a little anxious."

Again, the darker one showed signs of embarrassment, but it was a good-natured embarrassment. As if the two ribbed each other all the time and the blond just happened to get the upper hand. Sam and Jeremiah, she reminded herself, trying to memorize their names. Sam the cocky blond and Jeremiah the sweet, overgrown brunette.

She wondered if they teamed up for everything. A throb of heat flashed deep inside her body, making her pulse flutter.

Frowning at her instant response, Miko shut the door and moved toward the kitchen. Annoying visitors or not, she had to offer hospitality to fellow shifters. "Can I get you guys something to drink? I need to make a quick phone call to my mother."

"Of course," said the tall one easily.

She poured two glasses of iced tea into tumblers and reached for the phone, cradling it to her ear and turning her back to her guests. The phone's short cord kept her in the room, which she found irritating; the two feline shifters would be able to hear everything her mother said, even through the phone line. Shifters of all kinds had amazing hearing.

"*It's about time you called,*" her mother said into the phone, in Japanese.

Miko drummed her fingers on the receiver. Her mother always spoke Japanese, but mostly did it to annoy her daughter, who hated reminders of who and what she was. For once, though, it was working in her favor. She doubted either of the shifters in her house spoke Japanese. She replied in Japanese. "*Mother, why are you sending strange men over to my house?*"

"*Not strange men. Two shifters,*" Yui corrected. "*They will help you this week.*"

"*What do I need help with?*"

"*Did you find yourself a mate? Is he there to protect you?*"

"*God, Mother. Do you have a one track mind? I'm twenty-seven. Is that what this is? Matchmaking? I don't need your help with men—*"

"*You are headstrong and foolish and you—*"

"I'll call you later, Mother," Miko said loudly, in English. "When you're ready to have a real conversation."

"*Miko-chan,*" Yui warned, "*listen to your mother—*"

"Gotta go," she said, and hung up. Miko stared at the phone, and then pinched the bridge of her nose. Why had she even called her mother? Yui didn't approve of Miko's quiet lifestyle and thought she should spend her time recruiting men to service her were-fox needs if she didn't take a mate or two. Her mother—still incredibly beautiful at fifty-five—had a harem of men that she kept at her disposal, and constantly had a new boyfriend in the wings. As a child, it had been confusing. As a teenager, it had been humiliating. When she'd grown up, she'd vowed that she'd control her own were-fox nature better. No harem of men. No constant stream of new boyfriends that zipped out of her life as quickly as they zipped in. Miko preferred a quiet, celibate life.

Her mother clearly had other ideas.

Miko turned. Both of the men were still studying her, standing where she'd left them. Though one blushed at being caught staring, the other returned her frank look with a smile. She sank down in one of the two chairs, indicating that they should do the same.

At her cue, the tall one sat, awkwardly. *Jeremiah*, she reminded herself. "My mother probably told you that I need a big strong man around the house to see to all my needs. She's wrong. I don't need anyone."

Jeremiah rubbed his face, a blush moving across his cheeks. "Actually, she hired us to be your bodyguards for this week."

Miko sat up in surprise. Bodyguards? But both of them were so attractive. Surely that hadn't been just luck. "Oh."

Sam seemed to want to fill the silence with small talk. "This isn't what I expected," he said, glancing around her messy house with surprise. "You're not what I expected."

Annoyance flared in her. "Oh?" What were they expecting from a were-fox? A room full of sex toys and a guy in latex chained up in the corner? "What exactly *were* you expecting?"

Sam the blond gave her an assessing look. "We thought you wouldn't be, you know." He rubbed his nose and grinned. "Pretty. Young. What with you living out here on your own. Heck, I was expecting a bunch of cats and some knitting."

Jeremiah put his hand over his face. "Sam..."

"What?" His partner looked surprised. "I'm just telling her the truth."

Miko smothered a laugh. All right, then. They weren't here to jump in the sack with her, despite what she'd suspected. She relaxed a bit, and wondered briefly if they even knew she came from a family of fox shifters. "And what is this about, exactly? Why did my mother send you to be my bodyguards?"

Jeremiah's face grew serious, his brown eyes growing darker. "The local hunt club has a new chapter leader. An English one."

She frowned. "So what does that mean?"

Sam finished downing his iced tea, then reached across her low table to grab Jeremiah's and drink it as well. "Rumor has it that he's started a fox-hunting club."

Her breath left her lungs. "Fox hunting? That's…that's not allowed. It's illegal."

"It *is* illegal," Jeremiah said calmly, glancing over at Sam, then back to her. "But we have it on good authority that it's happening, nevertheless. Another were-fox—Hayami—was chased through the woods by several men on horseback with hunting dogs."

Miko sucked in a breath. No wonder her mother had sent them. "Hayami's my cousin. Is she all right?"

Why hadn't anyone told her? Her mother had said nothing on the phone, simply started in on her usual tirades, and Miko hadn't known to ask. Guilt surged through her. She should have known that Hayami had been attacked, but…she didn't keep up with her family. It was easier than answering nosy questions, seeing her cousins and mother with an endless string of men, the appraising looks she got from their dates, and her own involuntary response.

Her mother seldom took Miko's opinion into mind, choosing to drop by—or send people by—to remind her exactly who and what she was. Family was complicated. Family expected things. Family expected her to embrace her nature fully, and she'd spent years fighting that very thing. Still, hearing that her cousin had been hunted filled her with fear and a little bit of shame. She hadn't known.

"She's fine," Sam assured her. "But until this gets this sorted out, other shifters have been assigned to shadow the local foxes." He gave her a sideways glance and muttered. "And you are definitely a fox."

"Sam," Jeremiah warned, then gave Miko a bit of an embarrassed look. "You'll have to ignore him. He's a blowhard, but harmless."

And they expected her to smile prettily and ignore that obvious invitation? If so, they didn't know were-foxes. Even though a small voice in her head said she should ignore it, she couldn't help but turn to Sam and give him an equally assessing look. Her gaze crossed over his shoulders and down to his crotch, and focused there. "He's not bothering me. I'm a big girl. I can handle myself."

At that, both men's eyes gleamed.

* * *

IT WAS STRANGE, ADJUSTING TO HAVING TWO MEN IN THE HOUSE when before it had only been her. She wasn't sure if she liked the intrusions or not.

"Can I set my laptop up in here?"

Miko glanced back to see Jeremiah re-entering the house, a large leather satchel slung over one shoulder, a garment bag across the other. Obviously, he was ready to stay at her place a few days.

The sight irritated her. "I don't have a choice, do I?" How would she possibly concentrate with strangers crawling all over her house? She needed silence to concentrate, and just knowing they were there was already like a burr stuck in her coat.

He gave her an almost apologetic look, deep brown eyes mild. "I know you don't want us here, Ms. Westwood, but we'll be out of your house as soon as we know you're safe."

"I know you're just trying to do your job, even if it's an annoying one." Miko swept past him, opening the door to one of the guest rooms and indicating he should enter. "But please, don't call me Ms. Westwood." It did, indeed, make her think of gray-haired cat ladies.

Or her mother.

Again, the soft, gorgeous smile. "Miko, then."

The soft ripple of his voice did dangerous things to her insides, and she clamped her legs tight together to quell the ripple of desire. "That's right," she said, trying to keep her voice light. She moved out of his way as he entered the room and set his things down.

"Where are we staying?" asked Sam from behind her, and Miko turned. He lounged against a wall, that same sly, charming grin on his face. A grocery bag of clothing slung over his shoulder. No computer for him, and his sunny curls were a mess, his shirt un-tucked. She guessed that he was the type to go through life charging ahead, whereas Jeremiah was the cautious partner.

For some reason, she liked the thought of that—they were like a study in opposites. Sam with his charming, boyish grin and devil-may-care attitude. He'd be a spontaneous, inventive lover. Jeremiah would be more thoughtful, slow and seductive and devoted entirely to her body.

Not that she was thinking about things like that.

Flustered by how quickly her thoughts had turned to sex and mating,

Miko stepped aside and gestured at the room occupied by Jeremiah. "I've only got one guest room."

He tilted his head, grinning. "Got room in your bed for me?"

It was on the tip of her tongue to blurt out a 'yes', but two things stopped her. One—she didn't want any strings on a relationship right now, and having Sam in her bed for an unknown number of days could end up being awkward. And two, the thought of aggressively selecting Sam over Jeremiah with the soulful eyes felt somehow wrong.

She liked them both, and at the same time, was irritated at both for being here. Her fox instincts told her that either would be a good mate and a strong sexual match for her, and both were clearly interested. Even if she did feel like picking one, which would it be? If she picked one, would it destroy his relationship with the other? The were-fox in her was possessive; she wanted both men. And most men? Didn't want to share their bed—or their woman—with another man. Sure, it was a great storyline in pornos, but she'd quickly found out that reality was far, far different than the movies.

It was a messy situation, and Miko hated those worse than anything. Clamping her thigh muscles together tightly again, she waved a hand at the door. "You figure out which one of you gets the bed. I didn't ask you to come here, and I'm not going to hold your hand and tuck you in."

With that, she quickly moved down the hallway and out of their presence. Time to make a strategic retreat, and to regroup and relax.

"MAN, SHE'S HOT," SAM SAID, TURNING TO GRIN AT JEREMIAH. "I can't believe she's a were-fox."

"On her mother's side, according to Ms. Westwood," Jeremiah replied mildly, plugging his computer into the wall. "And because her family hired us, that means that you need to leave her alone. No harassing her because she's sexy."

"So you thought she was sexy too?" Sam said with a wicked grin.

"It doesn't matter if I did or not—the point is that we're here to do a job, not to gang up and seduce a young fox alone."

"So you're interested in her too?"

Jeremiah was quiet for a long moment. "Yeah. But we have a job to do first and foremost, so she calls the shots."

"Agreed," said Sam. "Let the best man win."

"Nobody's winning anything. She's a person." Jeremiah shook his head. Sometimes Sam could be a little too competitive, especially when it came to a gorgeous woman.

"Does that mean you're not going to make a play for her?"

Jeremiah smiled. "I didn't say that."


THERE WAS NOTHING QUITE LIKE A GOOD RUN THROUGH THE FOREST to clear her head. That was why Miko indulged herself, despite the warnings she'd been given. She was aware of the danger, all right. And she'd decided to take precautionary moves against it, too. She could scout the area, look for the scent of hunting dogs and horses, and determine what the boundaries of their hunting grounds were.

On her back porch, Miko stripped out of her nightie and let the evening air caress her skin for a bare moment before she allowed the fox to take over. The familiar rippling and bunching of her muscles shivered through her body, and she bent to her haunches as her form changed. Within moments, she was in animal form, her fox tail swishing. While her nose was keen in human form, her senses were nearly overwhelming in fox form. Scents immediately crowded in—the putrid smell of something dead in the distance—roadkill maybe—the overwhelmingly crisp scent of leaves and earth, the stink of the garbage cans on the side of the house, magnified a dozen times thanks to her sensitive fox nose, and the cat-and-human smell of her two houseguests.

Miko darted into the wilderness. She'd picked this house because it was out in the country. Thick trees and wild underbrush were her only neighbors for miles. Usually she passed through the nearby golf course that backed up to her property (there was something so very attractive about the scent of cut grass, both to her and the rabbits), but with Sam and Jeremiah's warnings rumbling through her mind, she changed paths and ducked under the nearby barbed-wire fence. Though the house was fenced, her property extended for several acres in all directions, which gave her plenty of hunting grounds, she thought, her four paws dancing down a scent trail. A squirrel tonight, maybe. She liked squirrels.

She always lost time when she did a run. Maybe it had something to do with her fox-mind, or maybe it was that she reached a kind of Zen-state when it was just her, the ground inches away, and the wildlife around her. Whatever it was, she was enjoying herself.

Until she heard the horn.

When it first pierced the night air, she thought it was a figment of her imagination. Deep, sonorous and loud…and quickly followed by the baying of hounds.

*Shit.*

Not only were Sam and Jeremiah right, but they'd misjudged where the hunters would go—tonight they were even on private property. *Her* property. In the distance, she could hear the pounding of horse hooves, and that was enough for her—Miko slunk into the underbrush, tail tucked, and began to run back to her house.

The hounds continued baying, having picked up her scent, and the adrenaline and fear began to rush through her, making it hard to concentrate on anything but her small black paws along the dirt and grasses. Home. She had to get home. They couldn't get her there. She'd be safe at home. Home.

One of the hounds bayed alarmingly close, and Miko nearly careened into a tree. She needed a hole to hide in, somewhere to burrow and be safe— So distraught, she nearly missed the gleaming eyes of the predator that lurked in the bushes. A large cat emerged and Miko skidded to a halt, backing up. Oh, hell. She'd gone from bad to worse…wait. The sinewy, golden cougar paced past her, sniffing the ground, then took off.

Not two steps behind it, a tufted lynx bounded past.

Must have been Sam and Jeremiah in their changed forms. No predator would turn down a tasty morsel of a fox, even if she was a tiny one. And the scent of them—annoying and yet intriguing—was filling her nostrils again.

She didn't overlook her good fortune in having them suddenly appear. Miko made a break for home and clambered up the porch, where her robe still lay discarded, and hastily began to change back. The moments of change were the most vulnerable. The hair on her body prickled at the thought of being caught mid-change, but she was back in human form within moments, and pulled on her robe. She was breathing hard, her hands shaking. That was…surreal. To think that someone had been hunting her—hunting her cousin Hayami as well. Her regular hunting grounds were no longer safe. It was rather upsetting to think about.

Upset or not, Miko grabbed a long handful of honeysuckle vines from off the side of the porch and began to drag them over her scent trail. The flowers would obscure her scent long enough to not draw small predators back to her home. It was a familiar ritual, one that she always took upon herself when she changed forms. She'd been surprised once by a hungry stray, but never again. She might be part fox, but she had a human brain, and she wasn't about to paint a big sign on her yard that said "Come and eat me!"

That done, Miko stared at her yard. What she needed was a drink. A nice, stiff drink. Maybe a hot toddy. She went inside, glancing back once to see if the boys had returned, then put a kettle of tea on and got out the whiskey. She needed a drink, because she'd been scared out of her wits tonight, and because her mother had been right after all. Both left a sour taste in her mouth.

The two men returned a half-hour or so later, when she was on her second toddy and feeling a nice, warm buzz in her stomach that soothed her jittery nerves. They looked rather pissed off at her too, especially Sam. He hadn't even bothered to finish dressing before storming into the house. His feet were bare and he'd barely tugged his shirt down over his chest. She caught a peek of flat, tanned stomach and a thin line of hair below his navel before it was hidden from her gaze.

Shame, that.

Jeremiah was a few steps behind him, buttoning up his shirt, jeans slung low on his hips. His mouth was a grim line of disapproval.

Amazing—the two of them in various states of undress did crazy things to her fox libido. She shifted in her seat, feeling suddenly flushed. "Welcome home."

"What the hell were you thinking," Sam burst out first, crossing her kitchen to stand over her, arms crossed over his chest in disapproval.

Miko studied him with sleepy eyes, the alcohol already affecting her system. With his wild curls and lithe, energetic body, of course he was the lynx. It fit him so well. Behind him, Jeremiah slunk against the doorframe, always hanging back, always cautious. Big. Graceful. Cougar suited him.

Sam was still standing over her, though, demanding answers. So Miko looked up at him and gave him a lazy glance. "I'm not a prisoner. This is my home. And I wanted a run, so I went for one. I kept away from the country club grounds, but it seems they are not sticking to just the grounds." When Jeremiah made a frustrated noise, she raised a hand. "I thought I was safe, but I was not. It was a stupid move, and I won't do it again." She stood slowly from the table, eyeing both of them. "If I'm naughty again, you both have permission to spank me."

With a meaningful look at them both, she poured out her drink and left the kitchen, sashaying down the hallway. She knew she shouldn't tease them—*knew* it—but the faint sound of Jeremiah's second groan was *so*worth it.

MIKO WOKE UP THE NEXT MORNING FEELING RESTLESS. SHE KNEW it was all in her head—the sensation of being crowded. She could hear her house guests talking downstairs, making themselves at home as they cooked up breakfast. *How very cozy of them*, she thought with a wry twist of her mouth. Add in the fact that she more or less wouldn't be allowed to go on a run until the fox hunters were taken care of, and her skin was practically crawling with confinement. It was a feeling she hated, so she took a quick shower to clear her mind, dressed, then locked herself in her art studio. At least there she could channel all this nervous energy and make something productive.

She emerged many hours later, stomach rumbling. The sun had gone down some time ago. The artistic fervor had died away, leaving her with nothing but an empty stomach and a strangely sated mood. Drawing really did make everything better. Rubbing the graphite smell from her nose, she wandered into the kitchen.

And paused. Both men were at her kitchen table, sprawled in repose, their legs extended under the table. Empty bottles of beer decorated the table, and a few crumpled dollars lay at the center of her table. Each man held a hand of cards, and both perked up with interest at the sight of her.

"Hi," she said, feeling a little breathless at the sight of them, so relaxed in her kitchen. She could look at both of them for hours on end, just gazing at two opposite but equally beautiful pieces of masculine flesh.

"Hungry?" Jeremiah said, getting up from his chair and offering it to her. "I can make you a sandwich."

So thoughtful. They'd bought groceries for her, too? Normally she just ordered takeout. "A sandwich would be nice," she said warily. Miko watched his ass out of the corner of her eye as he bent over the fridge, pulling out bags of lunchmeat. It was tight and firm, and his pants hugged him at just the right spots.

Damn, she really needed to get laid. Distracted, she glanced over at Sam and noticed him smiling at her. He'd seen her looking at Jeremiah, and he didn't seem to mind. Interesting. She wondered if the two had ever partnered before. The thought sent a hot flash of desire coursing through her body, and her return smile to him was wicked indeed.

"What are you boys playing?" she said, picking up Jeremiah's facedown hand. A queen was sandwiched between a king and a jack, but the rest of his hand was garbage. She ran a finger along that queen. Lucky gal—slid between two handsome guys.

Okay, now she *really* needed to get laid if a hand of playing cards were making her fantasize.

"Poker," Sam said, lifting his beer and taking a swig. "Do you play?"

She laid Jeremiah's cards back down and leaned over the table slightly, grinning at Sam as an idea struck. "Not for money."

His gaze dropped a little, watching her breasts plump as she pushed against the table. He swallowed hard. "No?"

"I've only played strip poker," she confessed.

Sam leaned across the table, giving her that roguish grin that made his blue eyes light up. "You interested in playing tonight?"

In the kitchen, she noticed that Jeremiah got very still, and she glanced over at him. His body radiated sexual tension, and the glance he tossed over at her was smoldering.

"Oh, I'm definitely in," she said.

Jeremiah recovered and placed the sandwich in front of her. So thoughtful—he'd even sliced it into two perfect triangles. Miko rewarded him with a beaming smile and took a bite. "Thank you." He glanced around her dining room. "You have any extra chairs?" Her small table only had two chairs—she'd been too cheap to buy more and she never used this table anyhow.

The lack of chairs did pose a bit of a problem, until another brilliant idea struck her. Miko stood, sandwich in hand, and gestured at the chair she'd just vacated. "Jeremiah, you can sit here. I'll just sit on your lap."

She could practically hear him swallow.

The men folded the cards back into the stack, and Sam began to shuffle with expert, casual hands. She watched his hands; she liked them—strong, with thick fingers and calluses that showed he worked with his hands. She'd have bet money that Jeremiah had lean, long fingers and softer palms. He looked like a computer jockey.

Jeremiah looked reluctant, so she slid out of the seat and patted it, indicating he should sit. His dark eyes were hot upon her as he sat down, slowly sinking into the wooden chair, gaze unmoving from her face. When he'd sat in the chair, legs slightly parted as he tried to relax, she slipped one leg over his and straddled his knee, giving a slight wiggle to remind him that she was there. As if he could forget.

"Shall we play?" Miko leaned over the table, smiling. The angle would give Jeremiah a nice view of the curve of her ass and the small of her back, and she intended for it to. Even better, the move pushed her breasts against her arms and Sam's gaze was immediately drawn there.

She was having far, far too much fun toying with the two men.

"Rules?" Sam said, his voice husky.

"We all three play," she said slowly, thinking. "Winner takes off nothing. Second place, nothing. Loser has to remove an article of clothing. Simple."

Sam dealt the cards with a faint smile on his face. Around the table he went, dealing three hands in a slow, leisurely fashion. When she had five cards in front of her, Miko picked up her hand, careful to pull it close to her chest so Jeremiah wouldn't see it. A trash hand—five different cards, all four suits and nothing that matched. Ugh. She snuck a peek over the cards at Sam, but his face was inscrutable—that slight smile still curved his mouth.

Jeremiah shifted under her legs, her only indication that he was still there and paying attention.

Miko kept two clubs and tossed the other three down. "Three cards."

Sam dealt her three. "How many for you, Jere?"

A card slid close to her elbow. "Just one."

Damn.

She said nothing as Jeremiah picked up his new card, but his knee jiggled a little again. She wasn't sure if that was a good jiggle or a bad jiggle.

"I'm taking two," Sam said, then discarded his and pulled two new ones. This time, he didn't bother hiding the smile that spread across his face. His blue-eyed gaze slid back to her. "What do you have?"

She still had nothing. A pair of threes, but that wouldn't win anything. Miko laid the cards down, face up. "I have crap. You two?"

Jeremiah leaned over her, his shoulder brushing up against her back. Prickles of awareness fluttered over her skin, and she resisted the urge to lean back against him. "I have a flush," he said in a low voice, and she could feel the warmth of his breath against her bare shoulder. With precise hands, he laid out all five cards—all hearts.

Well, that certainly beat her.

"Full house," said Sam, showing his fan of cards. Kings and deuces.

She was the big loser. Disappointment flared briefly—Miko was competitive and liked to win—but it was quickly replaced by a teasing excitement. "Guess that means I lose."

"Guess so," said Sam, grinning at her with invitation in his eyes.

She stood slowly between Jeremiah's legs, thinking. What to take off first? Her sleeveless linen wrap-blouse? That would be what they expected her to do, and she didn't get her kicks off of what was expected. Her sandals? Too lame. A watch? Earrings? Even lamer than shoes.

So Miko reached for the snap of her shorts and undid it, slowly teasing the zipper downward. A quick glance through her lashes showed that both men were riveted to the movement, and the air became heavy with tension. With careful, languid motions, she eased the fabric down over her hips and shimmied slightly, until her shorts fell to the floor, exposing her panties to both eagerly awaiting men.

"Are those..." Sam began.

"Ruffled," Jeremiah finished, sounding as if he were dying. He might have been—the black ruffles on the back of her lacy panties were probably bare inches away from him. She'd picked her lingerie deliberately today, thinking of the two men, though she hadn't anticipated the fun of strip poker.

And she was definitely having fun. Far, far too much for her own good.

Miko returned to her perch on Jeremiah's lap, straddling his knee between her thighs and giving it a slight squeeze with her inner muscles. At his groan, she couldn't resist a slight smile and a wink at Sam, who looked as if he'd cheerfully kill to trade places with his partner. "Next hand," she said, voice light and coy.

Sam dealt again, and this time Miko watched his hands, just in case her first bad round of cards had not been a fluke. To her surprise, this hand was decent. She kept a pair of jacks and a king and indicated that she wanted two cards. The guys also drew two cards each.

Her pull was excellent, though. Another king to match. "Two pair, kings and jacks."

"Beats me," Jeremiah said, leaning over her again and turning his cards over. "Nothing."

"Ditto." Sam's hand was nothing but a pair of tens.

She rubbed her hands and grinned, getting to her feet. "Let's see both of you take something off, then."

"Both?" Sam gave her a skeptical look.

"Both of you." So it was a bit of a rules-bend. It was strip poker—this stuff wasn't set in stone anyhow. "It's you two versus me, right? So if I win, I remove something. If you two lose, you both remove something. Seems fair to me."

"You could always just pick one of us," Jeremiah said reasonably. "My hand was worse than Sam's. I lost."

"Why should I have to pick between both of you?" Miko's hands went to her panty-clad hips, assuming a flirty stance that belied the quiver in her stomach. "I can handle you both."

"Both at once, eh?" Sam said, a slow, lazy smile crossing his face. "Big words."

She simply cocked her hip a little more and gave him a smile, inwardly disappointed that he didn't seem to be taking her suggestion seriously. "Oh, definitely both at once. Don't you worry about me. Just worry about taking those pants off."

On cue, both men reached for their zippers. She didn't know where to look first. Sam was in front of her, so she concentrated on him. Down his pants went, revealing an all-over body tan and vibrant blue boxers. That was a shame. She was curious to see the size of his cock, she admitted to herself. He had such a lovely, compact build with the perfect amount of muscles that she was hoping the economy didn't carry over to his dick. Speaking of…she glanced over her shoulder at Jeremiah.

No boxers there. His jeans were pooled around his ankles and dark gray boxer-briefs hugged every inch of his package. Oh, my…that was rather nice. And big. All over.

This game had just gotten very, very interesting. "So are we going to all just stand around for the next round?" She arched an eyebrow at Jeremiah.

"Why don't you sit with me, then?" Sam said, sliding back into his chair. "If you're so fired up to spend the game seated, anyhow."

A challenge. Well, she couldn't let that pass her by. Miko moved over to his side of the table and trailed her fingers along the table, waiting for him to scoot his chair out so she could perch on his leg like she had with Jeremiah.

Sam didn't pull out his chair. Instead, he patted his leg and indicated that he was ready for her to sit down. Between his lap and the table-top, there were only a few inches, just enough for her to squeeze in. His ploy was totally obvious. The question was, did she accept his dare or did she decline it?

She'd never backed down from a dare before, especially not one by a man she was considering as a potential mate. And if she was honest with herself, it had been a long time since she'd had a relationship, and both men were tweaking her interest. She was considering both of them.

So she eyed Sam's lap, put her hands on the table, and slid in. She could hear his breath suck in slightly as she settled in, her ass flush against his erection.

"Deal," she said, her voice husky.

Sam dealt again, reaching around her to do so. His hands brushed against her arms as he laid out each card.

Her next hand was decent, but Jeremiah's was better. Her loss. Miko shrugged and undid the buttons on her shirt, letting it slide off her shoulders and down her back. Now she straddled Sam in her panties and bra only. Jeremiah had said nothing the entire time, simply watching her with hot, unrelenting eyes. He didn't tease or play like Sam, but she knew he was just as interested, just as intensely fascinated with where the game was going.

She lost the next hand again. Her eyes narrowed when Jeremiah quietly revealed three aces. "Is that just luck or something more?"

He gave her a slow, sweet smile. "Are you implying that I'm cheating?"

She didn't want to offend him. Who knew how proud cougars were? Maybe they were as stiff about their honor as she was about her sexuality. "No," she said, backing off. "Just thought that maybe you wanted to see my breasts a little more than Sam here."

"I can't think that's possible," Sam interjected, and he gave his hips a little roll, bouncing her and making her gasp at the feeling of his cock pressing against her ass. Heat and want flooded her body.

Sam slid a hand up her back. "Want some help?" His fingers tugged at her bra snap.

Miko shrugged, reaching behind herself to undo the clasp with expert hands and letting it fall free as well. The air conditioning made her nipples tighten, as did Jeremiah's gaze. She felt Sam strain under her, trying to catch a glimpse. Her breasts were not large or bountiful, but they were high and tight, and her nipples were small and dark. She liked her breasts, and judging by the look on Jeremiah's face and the way he shifted in his chair, he approved as well. Her hands glided lightly over her breasts before she leaned over the table and tossed her cards away. "Next hand."

To her surprise, her next hand contained the three aces that Jeremiah had won with in the last round. She didn't question the fact that the three aces seemed to be chained together since it was currently working in her favor. Miko stood and gestured for the two men to remove an article of clothing. In front of her, Jeremiah slowly removed his shirt, pulling it off his body, and her mouth went dry at the sight. God, his chest was perfect. Six pack abs, tight, tanned, with only a trail of hair descending down his navel. "Very nice," she said. Very, very nice. His shoulders were large and defined with muscle. Not too much, just enough.

She glanced behind her at Sam's body, and was delighted to see that his was equally hard and lean. Where Jeremiah was tanned, bulging muscle, Sam was a bit more compact, leaner, every muscle in his chest finely detailed. Jeremiah might be built like a brick house, but there wasn't an inch of fat on Sam, down to the smooth plane of flesh below his navel. He had a large tribal tattoo covering an entire shoulder, a sunburst design. She decided she liked it.

"One more hand?" Sam suggested, running a hand around the waistband of his boxers, as if he were itching to get rid of them. Her nipples tightened at the sight, and she felt the curious urge to feel both men pressed against her.

Her fox hormones were going wild with two seductive men at hand. Instead of picking between them or leaning one way or another...she wanted both. Both hot, nearly naked bodies pressed against her own. Sandwiching her between them. Both mouths and four hands roaming over her needy body. A shiver rushed through her.

"One last hand," she agreed.

"Winner take all," Jeremiah said in a low voice, and that sent a bolt of heat through her. What was there to take? Other than their bodies. A visual of her pinned between them, one feeding his cock into her mouth as the other rammed her from behind—rolled through her mind like a hurricane.

The three of them stood around her small dining room table, watching with strangely tense faces as Sam slowly dealt three more hands, and Miko turned her hand over. Three aces. He'd obviously given her the winning hand this round. She laid the cards out on the table and glanced over at Sam. "So, how many rounds were *really* dealt?"

His mouth lifted at the corners and he gave a little shrug. "Were we not supposed to cheat?"

She didn't know whether to be annoyed or amused. "So how am I supposed to know if this was just an excuse to see me naked?"

"Are you going to tell me you're not even slightly interested in seeing my cock?" He gestured at Jeremiah. "Or his?"

She didn't like how Sam was trying to take control of the situation. Or rather, she liked it, but she knew that if she wanted to keep them in control, she needed to take charge once more. So she slid over to Jeremiah and cupped his straining cock. "I have a feeling that if I wanted to see this, we wouldn't have to play games. All I need to do is ask."

Jeremiah brushed his fingers along her jaw, a look of longing on his face.

"However," she said softly, "that won't be tonight. I want to be the one to call the shots. Understand? My body, my house, my rules."

With that, she left the room.

THE NEXT DAY, SHE AVOIDED THE TWO MEN. PARTLY BECAUSE SHE wanted them to understand that she had the upper hand in their relationship, and partly because she needed to get her head back in her work. She had a deadline, and she was going to miss it if she didn't pay attention and start producing some pages. So she locked herself in her studio and worked. About midday, there was a knock at the door, and she answered it, only to see a sandwich and soda had been left for her. The deliverer was nowhere in sight.

It was nice to have someone fixing her lunch. The men seemed to respect her boundaries. And she could have sworn that a short while later, she heard the vacuum running.

After she'd gotten her daily allotment of panels drawn (and then some, she'd been on an artistic tear), she emerged from her study.

Her house had been cleaned, top to bottom. Floors swept, rugs vacuumed, and her shelves gleamed as if they'd been dusted. Even the burned out lightbulbs on her track lighting had been replaced. Miko knew she was a pretty terrible housekeeper—when the urge to draw came upon her, she tended to ignore everything else, and since it was just her in the house, it didn't matter if a few lightbulbs went unchanged or an inch of dust piled up. But seeing that someone else had cleaned her house for her? That was…nice.

She could get used to having the guys around. Putter around the house, fix her leaky faucets…satisfy her needs. Ugh. Surely she wasn't thinking relationship? Or worse, *relationships*. They'd barely even gotten past the flirting.

Still, she found she couldn't shake the thought.

A head poked out of her kitchen. Sam looked over, grinning, and waved a spatula. "Hey, dinner's almost ready. How do you like your steak?"

"Rare," she replied automatically. "I'm a fox, remember?" She liked a fresh kill as much as any other were-creature.

"Oh, I remember." He winked at her and again the spatula waved. "Everything about you is tattooed into my brain."

"Only your brain?"

"For now." He grinned, the look so boyish and appealing that it was hard to resist.

She found herself smiling back. "Where's Jere?"

"Upstairs. Working."

She nodded, realizing that she didn't know what either one of them did for a living, other than working as hired muscle for other shifters. She gestured at the stairs. "I'll tell him that dinner's ready."

Sam nodded and disappeared back into the kitchen, and she could have sworn she heard whistling.

It was odd. Her kind either avoided men or embraced a promiscuous lifestyle. Her mother had done the latter—lover after lover entering and leaving the house during Miko's childhood. The fox hormones made it a lifestyle choice that few could resist.

Miko had resisted, though. After seeing her mother's relationships dissolve over and over again and her mother's liveliness turn to bitter unhappiness, Miko had resolved to have better for herself. Her father had been a nice blond country boy from Montana, and he'd been unused to her mother's were-fox ways, or her Japanese customs. They'd broken apart when Miko was very small, and she rarely ever saw him. After that, Yui went through lover after lover, discarding them like used tissue. Every break-up was filled with drama, and it taught Miko a valuable lesson: a simple, monogamous relationship wasn't right for a were-fox.

So she avoided them like the plague. Miko'd had the occasional lover, but when she grew restless, she knew the cause. One man wasn't enough to suit a were-fox's needs, and so she'd quietly break off the relationship. Her job offered her a lot of flexibility; she could live in the countryside by herself. Didn't need to be around others, male or female. She didn't need anyone, she didn't depend on anyone, and without the opposite sex around, she didn't feel the need to be promiscuous. It was lovely and freeing. It was…kind of lonely, too, if she admitted it to herself. But she usually didn't.

Miko knocked on Jeremiah's door and then entered a moment later, hoping to catch him off guard. He glanced up from the computer screen and gave her the slow, thoughtful smile that she'd learned to associate with him. "Miko," he said in greeting. "I hope you don't mind if we cleaned up a little. It's the least we could do since we're staying in your house."

She shrugged, moving over to his side and peering at his laptop screen. "I don't have much of a choice since my mother sent you to stay with me."

He looked pained at her words. "I hope we're not too much bother."

*Oh, you bother me,* she thought. *On a whole new level. That's the problem.* "What are you working on?"

He scratched the back of his head, ruffling his thick brown hair. "Just retrieving some files off a server." He gave her a quick look. "I do network security when I'm not tied up in...other things."

"And Sam?"

"Sam's a plumber."

She'd have thought they'd have matching jobs to go with everything else they did. "A plumber and a computer geek? What makes the two of you team up?"

He shrugged. "Sam was my roommate in college. He dropped out, I didn't, but we remained friends. We're still roommates. We work well together, and he's a good wing-man on the X-box."

How very...dorky. Still, at least they were normal. She could live with that. "I don't have an X-box."

His shoulders lifted in a shrug. "We weren't staying here long, remember? Just until the fox hunters go away."

"Right," she agreed, but it sounded hollow. Already she wasn't looking forward to their leaving. How sad was that? "Dinner's ready," she said, and left the room.

The steaks were terrific. For some reason, that depressed her. Better yet, it made her antsy. She needed a good shift and run through the wilderness. But she couldn't, because she was trapped here. Stuck with two handsome, sexy men that she knew were terrible for her easy, quiet life but she wanted them anyhow.

It was driving her nuts. Miko threw down her fork. "I need to get out."

Sam wiped his mouth with his napkin. "You want to go to town?"

"No, I want to go for a run."

"Absolutely not," said Jeremiah. "Not until the hunters have been stopped. And until they're caught in the act, you're not safe."

"They can't be out hunting every night," she argued.

"This is Texas," Same said. "You think hunting every day is out of the realm of possibility?"

He had a point, but she refused to give in. Her mind raced. "So the plan is to simply wait for the law to do something?"

"It's not a great plan, but those are our orders, and we're going to follow them," said Jeremiah.

"They're not my orders." Miko stood from the table and gave them both an impassive look. "It's not your life being put on hold while we wait for this thing to blow over."

"Isn't it?" Sam retorted. "We're here babysitting you to make sure you don't run off straight into a pack of rabid hunting dogs. Again."

Miko flinched.

"Sam," Jeremiah said in a placating voice.

"That's not what I meant," Sam said, wiping his mouth with his napkin and giving her a frustrated look.

"Isn't it?" The sad thing was that she understood his frustration—she didn't like sitting around and waiting any more than they did. She understood it, she really did. "No need to apologize to me, Sam Thorpe. I can't wait for you to get out of my hair either."

And with that, she turned and left the room.

"THAT WENT WELL," JEREMIAH COMMENTED AS MIKO STALKED OUT of the room.

Sam gave him an angry glare. "She's being impossible."

"She's not the only one." Jeremiah stood and began to calmly clear the dining room table, even though he was disappointed that she'd left. He always missed her when she wasn't in the room. Just her presence warmed him. "You told her we were babysitting her. Of course she's going to get offended."

Sam raked a hand through his messy hair, and frustration made his jaw clench. "That's not what I meant to say. I just...hell." He grabbed a few of the discarded forks and began to toss them onto the plates that Jeremiah held. "She gets to me. I worry about her."

Jeremiah remained silent, his thoughts caught up with the petite were-fox. He recognized the look on Sam's face—he wanted Miko for himself. And if he was a good friend, Jere would back down and let Sam have her, because Sam needed a good woman in his life. Except the thought of backing off and seeing her with Sam left him with mixed emotions. He'd be happy for his friend, but Miko...

He couldn't let her go. Even the thought of backing away left a sour taste in his mouth.

"I want her, Jere," Sam said in a quiet voice. "And I know you do too."

Jeremiah swallowed. Thoughts of Miko flashed through his head. Miko, smiling up at him over a hand of cards. Miko with a smudge of graphite on her nose, bent over her art table as she worked on a sketch. Miko, naked and arching up from her chair, her small breasts tight with longing. No, he couldn't back off. "I do. So the question is, what do we do now?"

Silence hung in the room for a long moment. Neither man had the answer. Trying to quell his own emotions, Jere left the plates in the sink and paused, bracing himself against the counter. He wasn't ready to give up on her just yet, but he was torn. Sam was his closest friend, and he wanted him to be happy.

He gripped the edge of the countertop and glanced over at the door frame, where Sam waited.

"No other option, brother. We have to let her choose," Sam said.

Jeremiah nodded. But he knew very well that her choice would tear the two of them apart.

Sam gave him a hopeful look. "Do you suppose she—"

"Nah," Jeremiah said. "Wishful thinking, there."

EVEN THOUGH THE MEN WERE CONTENT TO WAIT AROUND HER house, Miko was not. She stalked up and down on her big wrap-around porch, her mind full of rushing thoughts—of the men in her house, the hunters, and, oddly enough, her mother. She headed back into the kitchen and picked up the phone again.

"*Miko-chan?*" Yui said softly when she picked up. "*Is everything all right?*"

The worry in her mother's voice made Miko sick with guilt. She never called unless something was wrong, and immediately she felt like a jerk. It wasn't her mother's fault that Miko had issues reconciling her fox half. It wasn't her mother's fault that hunters had moved into the area. It wasn't her mother's fault that Miko hadn't known about Hayami. Her mother had tried, and Miko had interrupted her, accusing her of matchmaking. She sighed. "*Hello, Mother.*"

Yui's voice was mild, tentative. "*I worry about you, Miko-chan. Are you well?*"

"I'm fine," she said softly, in English.

"*You do not take good care of yourself, daughter.*"

"I know." Miko grimaced and leaned against the wall. "Look, Mother, I'm sorry. I know I should keep in touch more. I just get…caught up in things."

"*You want control over yourself. I understand these things,*" her mother said in a wry voice. "*When I was your age, I fought hard to be a normal human girl so I could please your father and make him happy. And in the end, I had to realize that I could not fight my nature. It is who we are, Miko. We are kitsune. It does not make us wrong. It just makes us different.*"

She sighed. Normally she would roll her eyes at her mother's teachings, but for once they had a ring of truth. She was so tired of fighting her attraction to Jeremiah and Sam. Would it be so terrible to choose one? To bring him to her bed and end this awful war with herself and her hormones? But even as she thought it, she knew that wasn't the answer.

The fox wanted *both* men, of course. And that was the part she kept getting stuck on. Even if she could pick just one…how fair would it be to try to build a relationship, only for him to discover that he wasn't enough for her after all? That she'd crave more than one man to sate her restless fox side?

That was the tricky part.

"Thank you, Mother," she said softly. "For sending them this week. They've been a big help."

Her mother gave a soft, knowing chuckle. "*I sent you more than one strong man, Miko-chan. Your kitsune would be quite happy with two men in your bed, you know."*

Oh jeez. How quickly they went from a truce to TMI. "Thanks, Mother," she said dryly. "I'll keep that in mind."

*"It would do you good to embrace your fox side, Miko-chan. Trust your mother."*

Embrace her fox side. A horn blared in the distance, so faint that human ears would never catch it. Miko stared out the window. She could embrace her fox side. Once and for all. "I will, Mother. Thank you. I'll come by tomorrow."

Yui made a pleased noise of surprise.

"Gotta go," Miko added quickly, before her mother could say anything else. "Love you."

She hung up the phone and stepped back outside onto the porch. In the distance, her heightened senses picked up the faint sound of a horn again, and her hands tightened into fists. Who was it the fox club was hunting now? Hayami again? One of the other foxes? Or was her mother next?

No matter who it was, she couldn't sit idly by and wait for something to happen. It was sweet that her two protectors were concerned for her safety, it really was. But her fox form had a human brain, and she didn't intend to end up as prey.

She could take care of this if she embraced her fox side, like her mother said. Fighting the inevitable only meant hiding from the world, and she was tired of hiding.

Putting her hands to the window screen, she peeked through the glass to the interior of the house. The men were speaking in the kitchen, neither looking in her direction. Perfect. Now was an ideal time to carry out her plan. Miko began to head back to the kitchen and then stopped. This conversation needed to be private. She slipped her cell phone out of her pocket and began to dial, walking down the porch to get away from the windows and any possibility that her conversation might drift to the wrong ears.

"Information," said the voice on the other line. "What city and state?"

"I need the police department in Little Paradise, Texas." Miko took a deep breath and lowered her voice. "I have a crime to report."

The woman on the line made a startled noise. "A crime? Are you all right?"

"I'm fine," Miko replied. "The crime hasn't happened yet."

"Oh." The operator got very quiet, and then cleared her throat. "I'll connect you through."

The line got quiet, and then a second operator picked up a few moments later, this one male. "Little Paradise police department. Can I help you?"

"Hi. I'm going to give you an address," Miko began, realizing she probably sounded a little crazy. "There's a crime in progress." She quickly rattled off the street address, and since she was outside of the city, gave them landmark specifics.

The cop paused for a moment, and she could hear him typing. "What kind of crime is it?"

Oops. She hung up on him, wincing. Hopefully that vague threat would still get them to come out. Because if not, her little plan was going downhill fast. She tucked her phone back into her jeans pocket, and then began to remove her shirt.

The plan? Set herself up as fox-bait, drag the hunters right to the cops, and then escape before anyone would even notice she was gone. Her problem would be taken care of, the local foxes would be safe from the idiot hunters, and she'd finally get the two men out of her hair and her house back to herself.

So why did it feel like such a lousy idea? Why was it so very depressing to think of waking up and having an empty house tomorrow morning?

THE SOUND OF A NEARBY HUNTING HORN CAUSED BOTH MEN TO come out of their funk. Sam cocked his head slightly, listening for the telltale thunder of horses' hooves in the distance. To his side, Jeremiah got to his feet, a grim expression crossing his face.

"Where's Miko?" he asked.

Sam put down the wrench and wiped his hand on his shirt. Thinking about how dinner had turned sour had bothered him, and when Sam was bothered, he worked with his hands. He'd spent the past hour fiddling with the leak in Miko's faucet, and had completely lost track of time.

He'd thought that Jeremiah was in the other room, placating her or trying to make her understand his—their—frustration. But maybe not. "She's not with you?"

"No. I haven't seen her since dinner."

The hounds bayed nearby, and the hunting horn sounded. The skin on the back of Sam's neck prickled. It was obvious they'd found something. On a hunch, he ran out to the porch…and stared at Miko's discarded t-shirt and the pile of her clothing. "Shit! Jere, she's run off."

Even as he stripped down and began to transform, Jeremiah was at his side, doing the same. Their goal was Miko's safety, and as the horn sounded again, off in the distance, he desperately hoped they weren't too late.

*R*UN, RUN FASTER. *D*ART UNDER BUSHES, WEAVE THROUGH THE *grasses. Wiggle down a foxhole and come out the other side.* Miko's brain rambled directions to her, as if that could make her small black paws move faster, or stop her tail from twitching in anxiety.

The hounds were nearly upon her, the hunters hot on their heels, the horn braying in her ear. Her plan had seemed better from the safety of her porch. In fox form, her thoughts became frantic, fleeting and wild, and she struggled to maintain a sense of control over her emotions, even as she ran for her life. All she had to do was get to the road, where the police would be waiting. The fox-hunters would be caught red-handed, and her life would be her own again.

Providing she didn't get caught first.

Providing she still wanted things—all things—to go back to normal.

A beagle bayed in her ear—too close. She slammed to the left, darting under a bush and veering away from her path toward the side of the highway. She had to—they were trying to corral her, shepherd her in a roundabout way toward safer ground for them, whereas she kept picking paths through bramble and under barbed wire fences and whatever she could to throw them off. It still wasn't working, though—one was so close she could smell the scent of cheap dog food on his breath.

Something snapped at her tail, and it stung, fur ripping. He'd nearly caught her by her tail! Miko gave a little yelp and darted again.

She heard a growling roar, and then the sound of a cougar-scream. Miko's already fraying nerves splintered, and it took her a moment to calm and realize that the men had come to her rescue, again. She could smell them now, a mixture of Sam, Jeremiah, and wildcat blending with the scent of the hounds and the hard, earthy smell of the dirt beneath her feet.

Behind her, the hounds scattered as the two cats appeared. One yelped, and just like that, Miko felt the heavy pressure of her followers lift off her back—they weren't so close on her tail any longer. A rifle shot rang out, the horn brayed again, and chaos reigned.

One of the cats—the lynx, moved in step behind her, and she knew what he was thinking. He'd trail her, make it seem as if he were hunting her, and the dogs would scatter because of the difference—and dangerousness—of the new hunter. The hunt would be over.

They were going to ruin her plan.

She was out here risking her neck, and they were going to destroy everything for her. Fury shot through her mind, and when Sam sprinted forward slightly, moving to her left—an obvious herding motion—she darted through his legs and cut across the underbrush.

Back toward the highway again, where she could hear the faint wail of a siren.

The hounds began to bray once more, sensing her escape, and the chase was on again—this time it was dogs, hunters, and shapeshifting felines all chasing after her tiny fox form.

If it wasn't for the fact that she'd be dead if they caught her, Miko would have laughed at the situation.

There, in the distance—the highway. Red and blue lights flashed, and she could hear the jingle of a police officer, the buzz of his radio. *Don't see anything out here*, he was saying to the radio. *Confirm address?*

She ran straight for him.

It must have been an unusual sight—a tiny fox darting out of the woods to cross the empty highway. A pack of dogs hot on her heels, then behind them, a wild cat or two, and then hunters on horseback. She wanted to stop and admire her handiwork, to see the expression on the hunters' faces as they realized they'd had the worst of luck and had landed in the lap of a law-enforcement official. But the hounds were still on her tail (literally), and so she continued to run, circling wide. She could skirt the edges of the golf course and trot her way back home, safe and sound.

"Stop there," she could hear the police officer yell at the hunters. "Put down your weapons and call off those dogs!"

Excellent. The horn rang out again, and the dogs began to fall back. Miko wanted to do a happy dance, but she kept running, because she wasn't an idiot and—

Something grabbed her by the scruff of her neck.

Panic shot over her again, and Miko writhed, feeling the bite of hot jaws over the back of her neck. A predator had her! She squirmed, paws flailing, as she was lifted off the ground.

But then a moment later, she was overwhelmed with the scent of Jeremiah and cougar, and she realized that the jaws on her throat were merely carrying her, like a kitten, and she relaxed slightly, though her instincts would not allow her to completely relax with his mouth around her vulnerable throat.

The lynx stepped in place next to them, and then shot ahead slightly, taking the path that Miko normally did, back to her house.

She was sure they were furious at her, but she didn't care. Happiness shot through her body, deflecting away all anger. The hunters would be taken care of, and she and her fox cousins would be safe. She'd done it. She'd taken care of the problem.

Maybe there was something to this fox-thing after all.

Several minutes later, they arrived back to her porch, and Jeremiah's lanky cat form slunk up the steps, then deposited Miko on her discarded clothing like he would a delicate cub. The fur on the back of her neck was damp from his mouth, and her tail stung from where the hound had bitten the fur off. Her natural instinct was to stay in animal form until the stinging went away—it wouldn't take long and she healed much faster in fox-form, but her adrenaline was still pumping after the rush through the woods and the success of her plan.

So she crouched low on the porch and began to change back to human form.

Miko was the first one to fully retain her form, and when she did, a patch of skin on her buttock throbbed, the skin raw. She put a hand to it, wincing. Perhaps she should have stayed in fox form after all.

A quick glance over showed that the two men were finished transforming, tanned skin rippling. Sam got up from a crouch, rising to his full height next to her and she got her first look at his fully naked body.

He was beautiful. His flesh was sleek and toned, not a spare muscle or hint of fat anywhere on his body. A swimmer's body, an athlete's body, with a hard chest and corded shoulders. His cock, she was happy to see, was long and beautiful—everything she'd wanted it to be.

Behind him, Jeremiah stood slowly, his naked body was a thing of beauty as well. He wore a dark frown on his face, though, and strode forward, checking her over to ensure for himself that she was healed. His hands ran over her body with worry.

"You risked your neck," Sam said in a low voice, striding toward her. "Of all the stupid, crazy things to do—"

"I knew what I was doing," Miko protested, but her words died as Sam stepped behind her and knelt, examining her wound.

"It was still incredibly foolish," Jeremiah said, sliding his hands over her arms, checking for wounds.

It was an incredible turn-on. Both men had their hands on her, bare flesh touching her own. Desire flooded through her, and a small sigh of pleasure escaped her throat. She wanted both of them. Together. Forgetting all about the rawness on her buttock or the fact that both men were currently pissed at her, she reached for Jeremiah with one hand, and Sam with the other.

"Miko," Jeremiah breathed, gazing into her eyes. "What are you trying to tell us? What do you want from us?"

Sam said nothing, but she felt his hands circle her thigh, felt the gentle press of his mouth against her buttock, nipping at the place where her skin had been abraded.

Miko shook her head. "I...I can't choose between the two of you. And I don't want to."

She trailed her hand across Jeremiah's jaw, then down to his naked chest, splaying her fingers across it. She could feel his heart beating rapidly underneath her palm, felt the warmth of his skin. Her other hand—the hand on Sam's shoulder where he crouched behind her—lifted, and she felt Sam kiss the palm. Flutters of heat moved through her.

"You want to do this?" Jeremiah whispered, then leaned in and cupped her face in his hands.

"Don't you? Both of you?" she asked, then leaned over and bit at his thumb gently.

Sam's fingers brushed down her thighs. "Then I suggest we go inside," he said in a low, husky voice. "Much as I admire your porch, I don't know if the neighbors will approve of you keeping house with two guys."

A laugh bubbled out of her throat and she wrapped her arms around Jeremiah's neck. "I don't have any neighbors."

He lifted her into the air, pulling her body close to his. She felt as light as a feather in his arms. Jeremiah was so strong, so built. She glanced backward to see if Sam was still with them, needing him there too. He had retrieved her clothing from the porch and locked the door behind them, then bounded up the stairs after Miko and Jeremiah.

Jere hesitated a moment, clearly torn between moving to the guest room or invading Miko's bedroom.

For some reason, that touched her. Even though they were going to take the next move, he didn't want to push her. She liked that about him—about both of them. So she leaned in and bit at Jeremiah's shoulder gently. "My room has the biggest bed."

"Your room it is," Sam agreed behind them, and she felt his hand run down her back in a light caress.

Jere swung the door open and the three of them entered her bedroom. Her room was an absolute mess—the only part of the house where the men had studiously avoided going, so it wasn't neat and tidy like the rest of the farmhouse. And she didn't care, either. With a fluid motion, Jere tossed her down on the big king-sized bed and she stared up, waiting.

Her gaze slid over to the nearby dresser, next to the window. Her mother's little bonsai tree sat there, no worse for the wear considering she'd tossed it out. Oddly enough, she was glad to see it. "Did one of you—"

"It looked like it needed a home," Sam said, then his hot naked body slid onto the bed next to her and she forgot all about bonsai trees.

His mouth landed on hers in a hungry kiss. His lips were on hers, coaxing and teasing with soft tugs, his tongue sliding into her mouth to suggest further delights. Slowly, he stroked at her tongue with his, tasting her. Then again, in a more rapid motion, giving her an entirely different suggestion.

Miko kissed him back, biting at his tongue with little nips when he tried to stroke into her mouth again. Warm, large hands began to caress her body, and she realized that while Sam was coaxing her mouth with his own, Jeremiah was stroking her skin with his hands. She could feel his knuckles sliding over her side, grazing the edge of a breast and trailing down to her hip, over and over again as Sam's mouth possessed her own. It was a thrilling dichotomy—stroking hands and thrusting kisses.

One large hand slid further down on her thigh, making her raise her hips in anticipation. So far, Jere's caresses had been light and undemanding. Which was lovely, but she was getting anxious for more. Her hand reached for his hair, finding his close buzz and rubbing along his scalp, enjoying the textural difference between that and Sam's soft curls.

Sam bit lightly at her lip, distracting her. A small noise of pleasure escaped her throat and she tangled her free hand in his hair, as well. So intent on the driving focus of Sam's possessive mouth, she almost missed it when Jeremiah's hand slid down the length of her thigh and stroked her sex.

The small pleasure-noises she'd been making turned into a full-throated moan.

"You are so beautiful," Jeremiah whispered against her hair, his large fingers sliding down the seam of her sex, then resting on her thigh, pushing her legs open. She gladly obeyed, arching slightly on the bed to let him know that she enjoyed his touch.

Sam's mouth pulled away from her own and began to move down her neck, kissing and nipping and biting. First her jaw-line, then down her throat, across her collarbone and working his way down to her breasts. "I've been wanting to put my mouth on you for days," he breathed on her nipple. His lips brushed it slightly, and then he paused. "...decide if you taste as good in person as you do in my mind."

"And do I?"

His tongue swiped out of his mouth, flicking across her nipple. "Better. Much, much better."

A shiver of pleasure moved through her. Jere's fingers grazed her sex again, not quite ready to take the next step. Always cautious and thinking of her, that Jeremiah.

Miko slid her hand from the back of Jere's head to his neck and pulled his mouth down toward her own. She needed to taste him. As his lips met her own, his fingers slid along the wet seam again. She angled her head slightly, gazing up into his eyes. Her hips lifted at the same time, and his finger penetrated the lips of her sex, sliding to the hot valley below, and both of them sucked in a breath.

"More?" Jeremiah leaned in, his mouth hovering close to her own.

"More," she agreed, and pulled his mouth down to her own.

Another hand slid down to the crook of her knee, and she realized Sam was pulling her other leg apart, far apart, until both her legs lay spread in a wide vee. He continued to work at her nipples, giving each one tiny, ticklish bites and nipping at them until it drove her mad. Jeremiah's mouth on her own swallowed her moans of pleasure, but she didn't think Sam minded.

Jeremiah's tongue thrust deep into her mouth, and his fingers slid down her sex again, and penetrated the slick warmth. Her muscles clenched around his finger as it slid into her passage, and he groaned at the sensation.

"How long has it been since you've been with a man, Miko?" He slid his finger out slowly, then pushed back in, stretching her, teasing the slick wetness through her passage. "You're so tight."

Sam groaned and buried his face between her breasts. "Christ, don't tell me that. I'm going to come all over her like a schoolboy if you keep that up."

The mental image made her giggle. "It's been a few years."

"Sweet Jesus, that has to be a crime." Sam's mouth trailed down her belly, lapping at her navel.

Jeremiah's finger plunged deep again, almost at the same time that Sam's tongue dove into her navel, and a bolt of desire flashed through her. "It's complicated," she said, forcing herself to try and breathe regularly. And failing. They were doing amazing things to her body, and it was making her mind cloud up. "Were-foxes…aren't…like…others." Oh god, his finger plunged in again and her words died in a low moan, her hips raising. "Foxes…are…promiscuous…We have a hard time settling with just one mate."

"How about two mates?" Sam teased, and he shifted against her, moving lower. His mouth brushed against the curls of her sex, his breath hot.

Her entire body tensed in anticipation, and she could feel her thigh muscles clench, still pulled wide by their hands.

Jeremiah pressed light kisses to her jaw before moving back to her mouth once more. His finger thrust again, so hard that her hips raised and a whimper of pure lust escaped her throat. "You don't have to answer that, Miko," he breathed against her mouth. "Just be with us. We'll figure out the rest later."

She wanted to speak up and say something then, but Jeremiah's mouth found her own again, and his finger thrust once more, distracting her. Before she could recover from that, Sam's mouth slid even lower, and his tongue dipped into her sex, searching for her clit.

When he brushed against it, she screamed. Her fingers clenched against the back of Jere's head, nails digging into his skin as her hips rose once more.

Both men chuckled, and she made a sound of disappointment as Jeremiah's fingers slid away from her sex, only to be replaced by Sam's hot, seeking tongue. His hands kept her thighs pulled wide, and Jeremiah sat up, licking her wetness from his hand with intense eyes. When he'd licked his fingers clean, he knelt over her and began to give attention to her breasts, pressing them together and trailing his tongue over her nipples and the valley between.

Sam's mouth was driving her wild as well—his tongue seemed to know the exact places to touch as he licked and sucked at her clit, teasing it with tiny, rapid circles. He flicked his tongue against it, then would slide his wet mouth down her sex until he plunged his tongue into her, mimicking Jeremiah's fingers, then moving back to her clit once more. He did all of this with smooth, unhurried motions that made her think he'd planned just this very thing—or at least thought about it—for a long time.

The thought was so erotic that her body tensed with the onset of an orgasm. As if both men sensed this, they began to work at her body even harder, trying to push her over the edge. Jeremiah bit gently on one of her nipples, his thumb flicking the other one, while Sam thrust his tongue against her clit with rapid, insistent motions. She came, ripples of pleasure shuddering through her body, the orgasm swelling over her like a tide.

Sam sat up slowly, his lips gleaming, a naughty smile on his face. He still sat placed between her legs, but his cock strained, inches away from her damp sex. As she inhaled, stretching slightly with the exultation of her amazing orgasm, he rolled his hips forward slightly, his sex sliding along her own wet one.

That was enough to get her going again. Miko sat up in bed, brushing aside their hands and pulling her legs together. She sat on her knees and put a finger to her mouth, as if contemplating what to do next, her other hand running down her stomach.

"Tease," Sam said in a low, husky voice. His hand went to his cock and he stroked it, knowing that she watched with avid eyes.

"A tease implies that you're not going to get what you want," Miko said in a light voice. "And I'm not that kind of girl."

Behind her, Jeremiah straddled her on the center of the bed, so his large thighs framed her own. She could feel the heat of his cock nudging against her buttocks, and the mental image sent new ripples of excitement through her. Knowing the image it would present in Jere's mind, she wiggled on her knees for a moment, and then leaned forward, until her face was in Sam's lap. Her lips played along the head of his cock for a moment, then she pulled away.

Ignoring his groan, she trailed a fingernail down Sam's thigh. "Why don't you lean back? And I'll…lean forward."

He obeyed her command, moving until he lay flat on his back, his head resting on her pillows. His cock jutted into the air, the length appealing to her senses. Such a long, thick cock. Both men were spectacularly endowed, she had to admit to herself. No complaints from her. She knelt forward, wanting to place that hard, thick length against her tongue, taste the salty moisture beading on the head of it. She knew the motion would place her ass into the air slightly, giving Jeremiah a nice, long look at it, and she knew she had a nice ass.

Both men groaned as she moved, and she saw Sam's fists clench in the blankets as her tongue flicked out and swiped across the head of his cock. The length of it was beautiful, and she wrapped a hand around it, squeezing to test the hardness, before leaning over and swirling her tongue against it again.

"Christ," Sam breathed.

Jeremiah's hands were on her ass, massaging and flexing the soft skin, and she rolled her hips suggestively against his hands. His mouth brushed against her skin, and she felt him bite at the flesh there, sending another jolt of excitement through her. She moaned, then slid her mouth over the head of Sam's cock.

One of Sam's fisted hands went to her hair, tangling in the long, black locks. No pressure for her to move forward, just anchoring her there and letting her know how much he liked the attention. Encouraged, she leaned forward even more, and began to take the long, hard length in, sliding it deep inside her mouth.

Jere's hands tightened on her hips and he slid a finger between her legs, teasing and fingering her sex once more, and a shudder rippled through her. "Lift your hips," he whispered, punctuating the command with a languid thrust of his finger deep inside her.

She did as he asked, spreading her legs low and wide, excitement thrilling through her. Sam's hand knotted hard in her hair as she sucked his cock deep into her throat, moving down the base of the shaft and then back up again, working him with her mouth over and over again.

Miko felt Jere shift behind her, felt his large hands on her hips again, and then felt the head of his cock nudge against her spread, wet sex. That was all the warning she received before he thrust into her in one swift motion, burying himself to the hilt.

She moaned around Sam's cock, her muscles clenching as Jere thrust into her again, hard. Sam's hand pressed the back of her head down, encouraging her to take him deeper, to work him harder.

Again, Jeremiah thrust into her, rocking her to her core. His hands pinned her hips in place, but it didn't stop her from rolling her hips with each thrusting motion. At first, he thrust slow, hard, deep. But with each thrust, he began to pick up speed slightly, until he was pounding into her from behind, the force of his actions causing his sac to thump against her clit in a thrilling way. Over and over, he thrust into her, as she worked Sam's cock with her mouth, pulling him so deep that he butted against her throat, his cock filling her mouth and hands.

"So...fucking...beautiful..." Sam said, punctuating each word with a thrust into her mouth that she gladly took. Her moans of pleasure were muffled by his cock, but still loud enough that both men could hear them. Her hips worked frantically as Jeremiah continued to thrust into her, his motions swift, sure, and controlled.

"Come for us," Jere demanded in a low voice. "You came against our mouths, now we want to see you come against our cocks."

Miko cried out and shuddered with that, the second orgasm rushing through and hitting her deep. She slid Sam's cock out of her mouth and rubbed it against her face as the orgasm came over her, crying out over and over as Jeremiah continued to thrust, the orgasm building instead of ebbing, until she climaxed all over again, her internal muscles tensing around the cock deep inside her.

With that, Jere cursed and his fingers dug into her hips, almost painfully so, as he came, cock spurting deep inside her.

Sam's hand knotted in her hair, pulling her toward him. His hand gripped his cock and he shot his milky cum on her breasts, the hot liquid sliding over her skin as he yelled his release, then pulled her against him so she fell forward on him. Jeremiah pushed forward as well, his hips still locked firmly against her backside, the three of them stacked together like a sandwich.

They panted for long, languid moments, no one daring to break the silence. Then Jeremiah pressed a kiss on Miko's shoulder as he disengaged himself and got up. Miko rolled over in the bed, laying on her back, Sam's sticky warmth still spread across her breasts—and now on his chest.

A towel landed on her face. Miko pulled it off her head and frowned, glancing over at Jeremiah, who wore a distinctly boyish look on his normally serious face. "Clean yourselves up, ladies and gentlemen."

"Such a sweet talker," she teased back. "Telling us that we're too dirty for you."

"Not too dirty for me," Sam said, and began to wipe her down with the towel.

That was sweet, she thought, though she said nothing until he was done. Jeremiah returned to the bed a few moments later and pulled her close to him, and when Sam had finished cleaning himself, he did the same. They lay sandwiched together, the two men with their arms linked around her body.

"You've done that before," Miko mused.

"Used a towel? All the time," Sam said.

She pinched his shoulder, grinning. "No, I meant what we just did. Sharing a woman. The two of you have done that before." She should have guessed as much when her mother had hinted that she'd sent over two men. It sounded like something her mother would have thought of. She knew Miko was sensitive about her kitsune side and wouldn't be happy with an endless string of mates. But two men dedicated to each other and devoted to her? That would keep her fox happy for a long, long time.

Once again, her mother was right. Irritating.

"Does it bother you if we have shared a woman?" Jere asked.

"Mmm," Miko said, tracing a finger on Sam's chest as Jere's big hand cupped her hip. "Actually, I prefer it. But I'm new to this. I've never had two men in my bed at the same time."

"That was beginner stuff," Sam said. "We're just breaking you in."

She laughed.

"Our last relationship was with a were-lynx. Female," Jere said in a low voice, his mouth pressing against her shoulder in a casual kiss. "But she couldn't…" He let his words trail off.

"She didn't like two men. It made her tired," Sam said bluntly. "She wanted a normal relationship."

"Ah," said Miko.

"You?" Jere asked. "Was this…what you wanted?"

She nodded. "I liked it. Far, far too much for my own good," she said with a laugh, snuggling down between them even more. She loved the sensation of both warm bodies pressed against her own, hands on her thighs and breasts and all over her body. It was sensory overload…and it was exactly what she needed in a relationship to keep the fox inside her happy. "And you're not the only ones with relationship troubles in the past. All my old relationships fizzled because were-foxes are generally insatiable. I wore out my old boyfriends."

"Poor, poor things," Sam said in a grave voice. "To think that a beautiful, insatiable were-fox is a problem."

"It is," she said seriously. "Our nature is to want more than one mate, and to want them often. It's just like foxes in the wild, and it doesn't translate so well to human relationships."

And that was an understatement. Which was why she felt so comfortable with the two men. Knowing that they'd shared women in the past sort of made things perfect...

Except for the fact that they were sent here for a task, and that task was done.

Miko sighed.

"What?" said Sam.

"Well," she said, trailing a finger over his chest. "We've just gotten together and the two of you are going to have to return to Fort Worth. You'll have to leave." Sure, it was only an hour away, but it wasn't the same as having them under her roof, spending all day together.

"Oh, I don't know about that," Sam said.

"It's going to take several months for us to determine that the threat is taken care of," Jeremiah said in a grave voice. "What if the hunt club returns? We'd want to make sure you're safe."

"Plus, your pipes are terrible. I think this house needs a top-to-bottom plumbing remodel," Sam added. "And I'm expensive—and slow. But I'm thorough."

"I noticed," she teased, her heart feeling light. "I could use a server overhaul too."

She felt Jere tense against her in surprise. "You have a server?"

"Nope," she said, and laughed. "But I could probably use one for my art. Put up an online gallery for my comic art."

"So that's what you do in your room all day," Sam teased. "Here I thought you were up there drawing naked pictures of women. At least, that's what I was fantasizing about."

Jere chuckled against her shoulder, his breath warm.

"It is what I'm doing," she pronounced in an overly-innocent voice. "I draw panels for a hentai manga. Lots of tentacles and naked chicks. Mostly naked chicks."

"Holy shit," Sam breathed. "You could quite possibly be the world's most perfect woman."

"Perfect for both of us," Jeremiah agreed, pulling her closer to him.

She couldn't have agreed more.

# Kitten-Tiger & The Monk

A Disillusionists Novella

## CAROLYN CRANE

# Kitten-Tiger & The Monk

SOPHIA SIDWAY, THE MOST POWERFUL MEMORY REVISIONIST IN Midcity, always got what she wanted.

And if she wanted to be rebooted—to be stopped—once and for all by the Monk, then that's what would goddamn happen.

But she had to find the Monk first.

She doubted the Monk was a real Monk, considering he was part of the disillusionist gang. They said the Monk was the most dangerous disillusionist. That was hard for her to imagine—some of those disillusionists were pretty dangerous. Each of them was unbalanced in some way: too much fear, too much anger, too much grimness—basketcases, in other words. Dangerous basketcases, considering they used their craziness as weapons, thanks to Packard.

Sophia snorted. Only Packard would find a way to turn people's neurotic tendencies into crime-fighting powers.

According to the rumors, the Monk had so much dismal darkness inside of him that the other disillusionists weren't even allowed to meet him. Apparently the Monk worked in total isolation. That's all she knew.

The dull and steely elevator doors closed. There were only two buttons on the old metal panel—one button for the bottom of the tower, one button for the top. She punched the top one and straightened her safari jacket.

She'd seen the most evil, the most twisted of villains transform into productive citizens after the disillusionists were done with them. That's what the disillusionists did—they went around attacking and rebooting lawbreakers, causing deep and profound changes.

The whole idea of disillusionment terrorized Midcity's criminal class. Who wanted to turn over a new leaf? To suddenly be a wonderful person?

Sophia did.

The elevator jerked and began to rise.

Sophia was so sick of herself. Thanks to her particular genetic mutation, she could erase the truth from people's minds and replace it with whatever she pleased. She couldn't erase further back than a day, but a day was enough. It was a kind of godlike power, really, and she abused it to its fullest possible extent. She could steal anything, from a stick of gum to the most important event in a person's life. Since she'd been working for the Mayor, half the news stories in the *Midcity Eagle* were made up by her, even though witnesses would swear they saw what they saw. Because she'd revised their memories.

Revising memories was a robbery of the most invasive kind, like stealing a part of their life, a part of who they'd become. The new memories she'd implant were cover-up lies at best. At their worst, they destroyed lives, and could set off murderous frenzies.

Sophia knew other people whose genetic mutations gave them strange powers: there were telekinetics, dream invaders, telepaths, force fields guys, and more. (Highcaps, they were called, short for high capacity brain function.) But as a memory revisionist, Sophia trumped all other highcaps. She was rock, paper and scissors. People had no idea. And, if they did, she would erase their memories and put in something different.

She couldn't even say when she'd begun to hate herself; she'd lived with low-level self-loathing for a while. Lately it had gotten a lot worse. God! She'd crawl out of her own skin if she could.

The Monk would disillusion her, make her stop. He had to.

The elevator rose by slow lurches toward the Tanglemaster's tower, some twenty stories up. *Creak.* It was corrugated metal, inside and out, designed more for freight than people. Not like anybody used it, except the Tanglemaster.

She sighed and crossed her arms. The Tanglemaster was the only one who knew where the Monk lived—mastermind Packard told her so a couple months ago. It had started as a game, her trying to get Packard to reveal secrets about the mysterious Monk. She remembered how his eyes twinkled when she'd pressed him on it.

*Why do you want to know where the Monk is?* Packard had asked.

*Because it's a secret you won't tell anybody else,* she'd replied coolly.

He'd laughed about her always getting her way, and he promised that meeting the Monk would be an unpleasant experience, though he seemed highly amused at the idea. Then again, everything amused powerful Packard.

She'd replied that being told *No* was a very unpleasant experience for her, too.

More amusement. Packard knew she was a memory revisionist—did he think she'd try to revise his memory? She'd never had the guts to try a revision on Packard. Luckily, she didn't have to, because, for whatever reason, he'd revealed that only the Tanglemaster can find the Monk. *If he feels like telling you, he'll tell you. Even I have to go through the Tanglemaster to get to the Monk,* Packard had said.

The floors went by. Seventeen. Eighteen.

Damn good thing she'd gotten this lead out of Packard early on—Packard was long gone now. He would *never* help her now.

She planned to ask the Tanglemaster outright first. *Where do I find the Monk?* If he refused to tell her, she'd erase the whole interaction from the Tanglemaster's mind and approach him again, with trickery. Then money. Then threats. *You never get a second chance to make a first strike,* her dad used to say when Sophia was a kid, holding her proudly on his lap. *Unless you've got my kitten-tiger with you.* That was Sophia—kitten-tiger. She'd been manipulating people's memories for so long, it was like breathing.

The tower elevator clanked to a halt.

Kitten-tiger Sophia stepped out into a small, dark vestibule. The door to the Tanglemaster's control room stood ahead of her. To the right, a little scratched-up window provided a view of the Tangle. Formerly known as the Sidway multi-turnpike, the Tangle was a hulking and misshapen rollercoaster-like traffic structure. Darkness had fallen now, and headlights and red brake lights swirled over it like ants.

Ugh.

This lead she'd gotten from Packard better be worth it—she avoided the Tangle at all costs, even if it meant going an hour out of her way. It was a bad sign that only the Tanglemaster knew how to find the Monk. It meant that the Monk probably lived down in the Tanglelands—three square miles of lawless wasteland down below the turnpikes, a kind of city-beneath-the-city, a mutant and misfit war zone that was worse than ever, thanks to the sleepwalking cannibals.

Her brown high-heeled boots created a hollow ring on the corrugated metal floor. Some women liked 'fuck me' footwear, but Sophia went a step beyond, with *Don't fuck with me* footwear—all the better to announce her around town. Sophia Sidway: efficient and trustworthy advisor to the powerful. A woman to be feared.

She knocked.

A voice from inside: "It's open."

She stiffened. *That voice.* Was it him? *No way.*

Louder now: "Door's open."

Heat flooded her face. It *was* him. The one man she'd never wanted to face again, back in Midcity! She could still turn and leave, but she wouldn't. Couldn't. Had to see. In a kind of trance, she turned the handle and pushed the door open.

Robert's back was to her; he seemed focused on a console of flashing lights and monitors, but she'd know that big set of shoulders anywhere. His trunk of a neck. He still kept his brown hair in a short, choppy cut, just like ten years ago. There were holes in the elbows of his big gray sweater. The thing needed patching. His jeans needed patching, too. Hiking boots all muddy.

Robert Ferguson. The man she'd loved….and then violated and betrayed. Robert was the Tanglemaster?

Sophia wondered suddenly if Packard had sent her to Robert as a perverse joke. Was it possible Packard, with his scary powers of insight, knew their history, knew how she'd betrayed Robert? She hoped not.

Even Robert didn't know. All Robert knew was that she'd abandoned him during his darkest days—coldly and inexplicably left him.

Robert didn't know that she'd *caused* those dark days. He didn't even know she was a memory revisionist. That was the nature of her power as a memory revisionist. They never remembered how truly awful she was.

*They* never remembered, but she did.

"What?" Robert barked, not looking up.

"What the hell are you doing here, Robert?"

He spun around, surprise showing on his face. And then it was gone, replaced by a squint—part anger, part bewilderment. Hardness around his eyes and his cheekbones made him look less boyish than he once did. At first glance, a person might say Robert was a plain-looking man. He had a face that was strong and sturdy and well-built as anything he'd ever created; his particular mutation gave him the power to interact with buildings, changing their shape and extending force fields over them.

Her family had always considered him to be dumb highcap muscle. Human scaffolding, the Sidway construction crew used to call him. But once you got to know Robert, you knew he was emotional and artistic, and that his face was full of feeling and nuance. You knew how his brown eyes danced when he got excited about an idea. You knew how that tiny gap between his front teeth made his rare smiles friendly. You knew the hurt in his gaze could seem bottomless. You knew he was beautiful.

She wanted to turn and leave. But also, she wanted to place her warm palms over his smooth cheeks, to put her forehead to his forehead, her breast to his breast, just like she used to. She wanted to breathe in one moment of their old love—just one. She could live on a moment like that.

"What do you want, Sophia?"

She clenched and unclenched her empty hands. "I can't believe you're here." She stepped forward. "I thought you'd left Midcity forever. After…" She motioned out the windows. The Tanglemaster tower was like an air traffic control tower, but the windows didn't look out onto the sky; they looked down onto the insane interlace of highways that made up the Tangle, the most disastrous public works project in Midcity history.

A decade ago, she'd manipulated Robert into staying around to work on it. Even with him as part of the crew, it was doomed. It had cost her father his life, brought down Sidway Construction. Her mother fled the country. Sophia had lost everybody she loved because of that turnpike. "After you, you know…"

His gaze hardened. "Well here I am."

"Right."

"And I'm busy."

Having practically grown up with him, she knew all his modes, including this one—the hard guy. It never ran deep. But that was then.

Her gut roiled. "I don't get it," she said. "You're free. Don't tell me you've been here in town working as the Tanglemaster all this time. I mean, what the hell? This is what you're doing? This? Sitting in this stupid tower working traffic controls?"

He gave her a hard look. "Word of advice. Don't go into career counseling."

Her heart nearly flipped out of her chest as he turned back to his screens and lights. Why would he say that about career counseling? For a moment, she worried he knew what she'd done. What she was.

No way.

He despised her because she'd supposedly loved him, but as soon as things got hard, she took off. That's how he would see it.

In truth, she'd violated his mind, ruined his most cherished opportunities, trashed their trust, and *then* she took off.

She'd heard mastermind Packard talk about how idealists and visionaries had grim and dark flip sides. And if they crashed down hard enough, they stayed down. Is that what happened with Robert? He'd been an artist, a visionary. She'd imagined him in a brilliant career somewhere. Why was he being the Tanglemaster? A robot could practically do this job.

He flicked a few switches.

With a sickening spread of shame, she realized that this was her fault. She'd reduced the man who'd loved her to this.

She could have tracked him down afterwards and told him the truth; maybe it would have repaired some of the damage she'd done. But she didn't have the guts to tell him. She was so weak, so selfish. Was she even capable of love?

Seeing his face, it was painfully easy to remember the strong and direct way he used to gaze at her—the intensity of his gaze back then was diamond-hard, but the commitment of it made it vulnerable, as though he put every bit of his heart into the way he looked at her. His gaze used to feel like a challenge. That sounded silly but it's what it felt like at the time, that his gaze contained a challenge to rise up to meet him, to offer him the ragged and reckless honesty that he offered to her. And she'd really tried to. For a while, she'd been a better person under that gaze. With Robert, she'd felt fully and completely seen. Fully and completely loved.

Back then she would have rather had her soul ripped out of her than lose that gaze, to have Robert look at her the way he looked at other people. Wary. Shuttered.

The way looked at her now.

She had to find the Monk. He would stop her, punish her. Make everything right somehow, though she wasn't sure how.

Robert was typing into a keyboard. Monitors flashed through views of cars lined up on dark, snowy entrance ramps. So many people, so many cars. The Tangle was like its own little city, covering two square miles, they said, and reaching dozens of stories into the sky.

What was Robert doing here? She'd imagined him somewhere glamorous, like Paris or Los Angeles.

An awful thought came to her. "Fuck," she said, slipping up next to him, butt on the edge of the table, which lined the entire length of the wall under huge windows. "Tell me you're not holding the whole thing up."

"You need to go." He flicked another switch. He still wouldn't look at her. "I can't have you in here, dude."

It stabbed her that he'd call her that. They used to call each other that as a joke. She moved sideways, coming almost between him and the console. "Tell me you're not stabilizing that motherfucker with your force fields."

She stared at him. Waiting.

No reply.

"Let it crash," she said. "It deserves to die."

"You wound me, Sophia. The Tangle is my greatest masterpiece ever."

"Fuck!" she said. "You *are* holding it up!"

* * *

H E LIFTED HIS CHIN, HEART PUMPING WILDLY, AND LOOKED AT her. Staring into her eyes had once been a compulsion, like staring into something vast—the Grand Canyon, or a star-glutted sky—and the harder you looked, the vaster and more impossibly glorious it seemed, and you had to keep looking, to somehow find a way to take it all in. A dangerous, foolish thing, staring into Sophia Sidway's big brown eyes. She'd probably revised him the last time he looked at her like this, maybe even the last hundred times. He sometimes wondered how much of his late teens were even real. "You think I'm strong enough to hold up the entire Tangle?" he asked.

"You could sure hold up part of it."

Warily, he watched her eyes. She thought he didn't know what she'd done to him. "What do you want?"

With a flicker of sadness she looked out the window. She looked the same as before, with some exceptions. Her brows seemed harder, more coiffed and perfect. So did her clothes. But that hair was the same bright red. "How unstable has it become?"

"Ten seconds to tell me what you want, or I throw you out and bolt the door." He said it in a low voice, so she would understand that he meant it. He *did* mean it...except for the hateful little part of him that still wanted her.

She crossed her arms. "I need to see the Monk."

He smiled, startled. He ought not to react at all, but he had to do something with the shock. He turned her words over in his mind: *I need to see the Monk.*

"Packard told me to ask you to take me to him," she added.

Robert struggled to keep his expression blank, wondering why Packard would reveal even that much. He squinted. "What? The Monk?"

"Yeah, the Monk. The one and only. Mister I'm-such-a-dangerous-disillusionist-nobody-gets-to-meet-or-work-with-me guy. Except you and Packard apparently. I need to see him." With a toss of her head she flicked her thick hair out of her eyes. "It's cool. You don't have to pretend they're an urban myth—I know they're not. I'm in on the whole psychological hit squad thing. Weaponizing their inner darkness and all that. Zinging criminals, rebooting them. I personally know all of the disillusionists. Well, except the Monk. But I'm practically one of the gang. I worked with them to bust the Dorks, did you know that? I was in on that."

Sophia went on to describe a stakeout of some sort; she still supplied too many details when she was up to something.

She stopped. Crossed her arms. Had she realized what she was doing? "Just tell me where the Monk is and I won't bug you anymore. I just need to go see him." This in her tough-girl tone.

"Nobody just *goes* and *sees* the Monk," he said.

"Do you think Packard would've told me to ask you if he didn't want me contacting the Monk? If he didn't want me getting this communication to the Monk?"

"You're telling me Packard has a communication for the Monk?"

"Something like that," she said.

"I'll get a message to the Monk." Why was he talking to her? He loathed her. Hated her—in a strange, energizing way.

"It can't be like that. It has to be me," she said.

"Nobody sees the Monk except his victims." Why did she want to see the Monk?

She frowned. She'd always hated to be told *No*. "What is Packard going to say when he learns you've refused?"

"I don't give a crap." He pulled away and moved to his computer.

"What are you doing?"

"Rush hour," he said, typing a note into an open document. "I'm at work here." He rested a palm on the cement desk, which was connected physically to the entire structure of the Tangle. The smooth plane between his palm and the flat desk came alive, and he felt through it, out into the concrete and rebar, the twists of road, snaking in on each other. He could feel the cars as a kind of force. He could feel the distress of the drivers. The insane pointlessness of it all. The Tangle was a part of him. Or more, he was a part of the Tangle. He was sunk so deep into it, so at home in it, he barely ever left the tower. He had a home in the Irish quarter, but he almost never slept there; he preferred to stay working on the Tangle.

Everybody hated the Tangle, talked about the Tangle, wrote angry editorials about it, but nobody had ever recognized it for what it was.

Nobody but Packard, anyway. Packard had understood it immediately, and he'd sought Robert out so that they could talk about it. Packard had even made Robert laugh about it. Packard was Robert's number one fan. His only fan.

"Why won't you tell me where the Monk is?" She placed herself directly in front of him, between him and the console. "Is this about some vow you've taken?"

Ah, yes, this was how she'd do it. Fish for the obstacle and figure out the way around it. Then she'd erase his memory of her visit, and come back at him, as if she were arriving anew. Lather, rinse, repeat.

He slid his palm over the desk. It hurt that she was here—hurt with a biting and vicious kind of pain, like sinking frozen toes into a bath of steaming hot water. And you have to pull out your feet because the pain is too sharp, yet you long to put them back in, to feel the warmth. You just want it not to hurt.

"The answer is no."

"Robert. This is an extreme situation," she said.

"Why?"

"Will you take me to him if I tell you why?"

Robert picked up a paperclip, as if he was considering her question. Then, "Nope."

Silence. She would hate that, of course.

"I think the fact that Packard sent me trumps any vow you've made to keep the whereabouts of the Monk a secret."

"I only deal with Packard."

She leaned forward and he sucked in her bright scent; another few inches and he could taste her lips, plunge into the warmth of her mouth. "Are there no circumstances in which you'd bring me to the Monk?

"None," he said, highly aware of his heart speeding up, his cock hardening. The memories of all the times they'd fucked—the tender hours on the roof, slowly, slowly worshipping each other. Or their brave and inventively dirty scenarios in ruined places, untainted by the boringness of porn—it was as though the memory of that was in his cells, his body, and it was being pulled out by her nearness. They'd been so much more than lovers—they'd been soulmates, artistic collaborators, best friends. She'd encouraged his dreams and his hopes. And then she'd demolished them.

She said, "Haven't you ever heard the saying, *Only a fool is certain and immovable?*"

"Well, I guess we know what that makes me."

Darkness passed over her face as she straightened up. "Don't. You're not."

"You still don't get to see the Monk." He began to unbend the paperclip. He could interface with the atoms of the most massive skyscrapers in Midcity, making the walls soft as quicksand or hard as rock; he could use his force fields to prop up entire buildings for repair workers, but he couldn't get a stupid paperclip to go the way he wanted.

"Robbie, you are so crazy. You know that?" She snatched the paperclip from his fingers. "Look what you've done." She held it up accusingly, leaned nearer, and looked into his eyes. This was something she used to do: lean in near, right before they kissed, while holding him off with a hand, and the space between them would feel so alive. And then they would devour each other. It struck him now as a convenient distance from which to revise his memory. "Paperclips, dude. This is not your medium."

"How do you know?"

She snorted, twirling it between two fingers, eyes on his. A memory revisionist locked into your mind through your eyes—he knew that now. She would stare at you, and eventually there would come a point of no return where you couldn't look away. Once she had you, she could go in and rub away your recent memory, the way you might rub a word off a chalkboard. She could leave a blank there, or put something new in. Would she have the audacity to put Packard in? Commanding him to take her to the Monk? No, she wouldn't. She didn't know his and Packard's relationship well enough. Sophia was a user and a liar, but she wasn't an idiot.

He took back the paperclip, bent it some more.

"You have an eyelash about to go into your eye," she said.

"I do?"

She leaned nearer. He liked feeling her face near his. He wanted it to last.

"Oh, Robbie hold still." She touched his cheek, brought his attention back to her, leaning closer still. Should he let this happen? Had he left himself enough clues?

"An eyelash hair. Let me get it out." She held up a finger. "Okay?" She waited until he met her eyes again.

"Okay." He promptly broke their gaze and set the paperclip on the desk, in front of where he usually faced.

"Come on!" She laughed and clapped a hand on his shoulder, held his chin with her thumb and her finger, smiling into his eyes. She was so beautiful. "Hold still."

He gazed at her now, soaking in her touch. He would do this. He would let her revise him, and they would play this scene over and over. He didn't need to remember the specifics; memory was overrated. Relationships were overrated. Everything was overrated. There wasn't a point to anything, wasn't that what he always told his victims? No meaning, nothing to believe in. That's what he told them as he destroyed their faith in whatever they cherished, as he destroyed their faith in things they might someday cherish. He had the power of force fields and a terrifically dark despair that Packard had taught him to weaponize, and this made him more dangerous than the other disillusionists—she'd heard right about that part. He worked in isolation, rendering his victims as empty as he was. He took their hopes, their dreams, their faith, their everything—just what Sophia had taken from him.

Hardcore criminals tended to benefit from disillusionment in the long run, often with a change of heart. They would build back new hopes and dreams and beliefs. Humans were designed to hope.

But not him. Not anymore.

And now there was this. The woman he used to love, touching his face, acting as if she cared. He would let her revise him, he would see what she was up to. Her powers didn't allow her to take more than a day, but she'd likely only take her visit. Hell, let her take what she pleased. Robert was the Monk. He cherished nothing. This one fact made him far more dangerous than she could ever be.

He looked into her eyes, allowed himself to relax into her hold. It seemed more intimate somehow than being in her arms, than fucking her, even, because she was showing him something secret and true about herself. He wanted to see more, to see this thing she did. Of course he would have seen it before, but she would have erased it from his mind, and he wanted to see it now—to see *her*. He wanted her bared to him, not physically, but metaphorically. Maybe the repulsion of seeing who she was would sink in somehow, break him of wanting her. Warmth crept up his neck as he breathed her in; his fingers itched to slide onto her thighs. What would she do? He imagined sliding his hands further, around her ass, pulling her against his rock-hard cock, kissing her, tasting her lips, her tongue, invading her right back. Yeah, that would derail her control. Sophia hated surprises, hated to be derailed, which would make such a kiss all the more exciting

Christ, who was he fooling? He wanted her, that's all. He was like a pathetic trained dog. He clenched his jaw against the want, the heat. If he touched her like that, gave in like that, he'd hate himself.

He'd let her have her coy little intrusion, and then he'd make her sorry she'd ever messed with him.

He felt when she had him. He was still generating thought, but things were soft. Things grew fuzzier. A strange calm descended over him.

A LITTLE AFTER FIVE O' CLOCK ROBERT COULD SWEAR HE BREATHED her in—not so much a perfume or whatever so much as...*her*. Unmistakable Sophia. You didn't spend your formative years obsessed with a woman only to forget the sensation of breathing her in. With her bright scent came all the heart-swelling emotions of that time—the love and the lust, the anticipation of seeing her. The bewilderment. The rage.

Was he hallucinating? He'd always thought her scent was a mixture of her hair, her soaps, and her sweat, blended together. Why now? He looked around the tower office, eyed a magazine in the little pile of mail in the corner. Was there a perfume sample in there or something?

But it was too specific, too her. The emotions that came with it felt nearly unbearable. He'd loved and dreamed so hard with her, and fell so far.

He thought of the green scarf she'd left it in his little room in the conscripted labor barracks of her family compound. He never told her he had it; he'd just kept it for himself, to touch to his cheek. Until the day he figured out what she'd done.

He spread his hands on the desk, feeling down into the Tangle, searching for grounding.

And then he saw the paperclip. A paperclip in the shape of an S, right in the place where he put to-do notes, as if the S was a note to himself. Again he looked at the clock. Was it late? Had he lost time? His computer was asleep; he'd assume he'd been daydreaming if it wasn't for the scent, the paperclip. Would she really come back after all these years and *revise* him yet again?

*No.* Not possible.

Yet...

The idea energized him with a strange fury. What could she want? Did she think he didn't know by now that she was a memory revisionist? Of course not. She saw him as a dupe. Always had.

Was the paper clip the only clue? No, there had to be more. He shuffled around the folders, feeling like a detective of his own habits. Would he have typed something? He woke up the machine and went to the last document open, and there it was, right up there on the screen.

*She wants to be taken to the Monk.*

Robert stared at the line for a long time. The Monk? Only Packard knew he was the Monk, and Packard was long gone. Or was he? Did Packard need him? No. And if he did, he wouldn't send Sophia.

Robert had met Packard over ten years ago, right after the Tangle was complete. Packard had burst into Robert's tower. "It's brilliant," Packard told him. "I can't stop looking at it. I can't believe what you've done here!" Packard got Robert to take him through it, inside and out. Packard had wanted to stop, to ask questions at every point. He wanted to know how it affected Robert to externalize his hopelessness like that, to keep all that chaos going.

Then, a couple years later, Packard had invited him to that weird Mongolian restaurant of his and asked him to work as a disillusionist. Packard wanted to teach him to zing out his immense darkness—he said Robert would be a natural. Packard usually only taught regular humans to be disillusionists, but he was making an exception with Robert being a highcap. On and on he went with the reasons, until he got to the only one that mattered: Robert would stay sane longer, which meant he'd be able to work on the Tangle for more years. *Your life's work*, Packard had called it.

Scary level of insight, that Packard.

Robert looked at the words on the screen again; words he'd typed himself. *She wants to be taken to the Monk.* Taken. At least Packard hadn't divulged that he, Robert, was the Monk. But why tell at all? There had to be something in it for Packard—that was how Packard rolled. But what? Surely he didn't think Robert would actually reveal anything to Sophia.

*She wants to be taken to the Monk.* She.

He smiled bitterly. Still only one *She* in his life.

Robert had practically grown up at the Sidway family compound, though not in the main house, like Sophia. No, he lived in the workers' housing from the time he was maybe five. It wasn't exactly a prison; it was more a dorm where the workers couldn't leave, because they were working off gambling debts or they were immigrants working off illegal passage, and the alternative was being killed. Robert stayed because it was the only home he knew, aside from vague, fuzzy memories of something before it.

He was raised by the illegal immigrants and gamblers working off Sidway debts. Some became like fathers, and it was heartbreaking when their terms would be up, and they'd leave. A few of them were charged with teaching him reading and math, but they all pitched in, and he enjoyed helping them at the construction site.

Even at the age of five, he could smooth walls and stabilize framed-up buildings so that the men could crawl around on top. Of course, Robert had special privileges the men didn't have, too. For example, he got to have his own dog—Baron, a small beagle-terrier mutt, and he got to keep Baron with him in his tiny room on cold nights. And he played outside with Sophia and her friends out on the grounds, when he wasn't at the construction sites.

The story went that Boss and Mrs. Sidway had found him on their doorstep and, instead of giving Robert up to the awful Midcity orphanage, they'd given him a home and started him in a trade. Robert felt it was a fair shake, especially as he grew older and came to understand that most highcap kids had it far worse. Most highcap kids had to hide their powers or be rejected; his powers were embraced, and he learned how to strengthen them, even use them in spectacular ways that sometime awed his crewmates; they and the Sidways were the only ones who knew what he was. And of course, he loved the work, loved to help shape Midcity's biggest and most glorious residential and commercial properties. He was glad he didn't have to go to school; it made him happy to work on buildings.

Robert's ability to stabilize structures, or to change the form and surface of metal and steel, enabled Sidway crews to slap up buildings at four times the speed of human-only crews—for a fraction of the cost.

At the age of thirteen, Robert could create a force field that would hold up a three-story office building. He could go from one site to another, setting up force field after force field, or removing the ones that were done. He could touch a stone wall and interface with its atoms and, after an hour or more of concentrated thought, he could form elaborate frescos, or strange, ultra-modern gargoyles, though anything artistic like that was forbidden.

He and Sophia grew close when they were around fourteen. He'd sneak off construction sites and she'd sneak away from school and they'd meet, two rebellious and high-spirited teens, offended that anybody would forbid their friendship.

By age sixteen, they were in love. The forbidden-ness helped stoke it, especially the fact that Sophia's dangerous and criminal father might literally kill Robert if he knew they were having sex. But the love was real enough—for Robert, anyway. Robert's love for Sophia infused everything he did—his secret art projects became bolder, brighter. He stabilized bigger buildings, and smoothed out the most pathetic sheetrock jobs. Even the way he walked across a construction site was lighter. His love for Sophia animated his life, and stoked a fire in his chest so bright, sometimes he felt like the sun was blazing inside his heart. He loved Sophia's bravery, her sense of play and her mischievous ideas. He loved her flaming hair and ivory skin, and the way her veins showed through the skin on her hands and ankles. He loved the two splotches of pink that would appear on her China doll cheeks when it was cold outside. He loved the pale red-gold of her eyelashes—so light as to be nearly translucent, like whispery blonde feathers around her eyes. And he loved her toughness. She was his protector and he was hers.

When he was seventeen or eighteen, he got the bug for finding his parents, and Sophia became his passionate ally. Even then she hated a closed door, a secret, the word *No*.

They scoured news stories, birth records. Sophia became convinced that her dad would've gotten a private investigator to hunt down Robert's origins. *He wouldn't leave anything to chance—he would want to know who you are*, she'd assured him.

One night when her parents were out at one of their endless parties with Midcity's mobster elite, Sophia and Robert broke into her father's office. They found Robert's file in with the other workers' files, but it wasn't the investigator records they expected. The file contained letters and papers full of numbers. Interest calculations, it seemed, though it never said what for. Robert rifled through. The dates went back a decade, some a bit more. Some were signed by a Nance Perkins.

Sophia had grown silent. She knew what she was seeing—Robert could tell, and he bullied it out of her.

*It means gambling*, Sophia told him. *Loans to cover.*

Robert was well aware by then that Sidway Construction was only the most visible of Boss Sidway's moneymaking operations, but what did gambling debts have to do with him? The woman was his mother? That was the implication? Did his mother have debts to Sophia's father, or somebody her father controlled?

Sophia tried to get him to forget it. Robert refused. The other letters were scrawled, hard to read. There was one paper at the end—a sum in the six figures on the left side, and the letter "R" and "13 yrs" on the right, and a line below both with signatures and dates.

Sophia paled. She was a pale girl with pale lashes, but she'd paled more.

*What? R isn't me!* Robert said. *I was only five when these were written.*

*Thirteen years of service*, she finally told him. *You're paying off her debt right now and you'll be done when you turn nineteen.*

Robert remembered sinking to the cold floor, surrounded by the papers, like a bird in a sad nest.

His mother had sold him.

He pressed his hands to the marble tiles, thinking to level the Sidway mansion, to level the world! But Sophia wrapped herself over him. *We're a family, you and me and Baron*, she reminded him. *We're in this together.*

*We'll make it right together. We'll think and be smart and be together forever.*

Robert buried his face in her shoulder. He vowed to find his mother and rescue her. Then he vowed to find his mother and rage against her. He would leave Sidway—let Boss Sidway's goons track him down and kill him. No, they might kill his mother. He would help her. She was a victim. He would to tear apart the world!

And then he'd cried.

He'd always imagined his mother had been a scared teen girl giving her baby to the richest family she could find. Wanting the best for the baby she loved.

Sophia had held him. And then she'd asked him: *Do you wish you didn't know? If you could not know, would you prefer it?* Robert remembered the question seeming odd. Too serious, somehow.

*Hell no,* he'd said.

A minor crash on clover fifteen jolted him out of his reverie. He dispatched emergency vehicles and rerouted traffic. He hated to see such a thing; contrary to what one might think, he did what he could to promote safety on the Tangle…well, short of destroying it and thereby making it off limits to drivers, which would be the ultimate safety fix.

He picked up the S paperclip, twirled it while watching the cars reflow, thinking about Sophia's offer to erase his memory of their discovery about his mother. He didn't realize back then that it was indeed an offer. He didn't know then that she was a memory revisionist. Why had she kept her highcap nature from him? She knew he was a highcap.

She convinced him to stay at the compound, and let everything seem normal. Though a Google search turned up nothing on his mother, they would track her down, she'd said, determine the situation. One of the immigrants had been killed for leaving—Boss Sidway had made sure Robert and the other workers all got a look at the body. Would Sidway hunt and kill his mother if Robert left? And he and Sophia wouldn't be able to see each other. She reminded him of the plans they'd made to travel the world, to be artists together. Of the projects they had in process.

Robert had a vision for public art that involved modifying urban landscapes, of taking the decrepit and making it strange or beautiful. Sophia was more of a two-dimensional artist—she had piles of sketchbooks full of imagined landscapes drawn in colored pencil. However, she'd often collaborate with Robert, sketching out new possibilities for installations—she'd look at a photo of an alley and decide that it needed this or that detail, or a shape here, an object there. The possibilities she saw felt so right as to almost feel inevitable. Vivified landscapes, they'd call them. Though Robert could will matter into specific shapes, it was tough-minded Sophia who'd dream up the bold and the glorious. Her entire way of being was a kind of gift to him as an artist. And as a man.

It was only later that he'd realized the talent of Sophia's that he so admired—the knack for visualizing that which seemed to belong—was precisely what made her such a powerful highcap revisionist, so good at creating false memories.

Maybe there were clues, but he'd never noticed. All he saw was his brilliant, passionate Sophia with her big intense gaze, red hair glowing in the streetlights.

They'd sneak out at night and vivify spaces by enhancing shapes, and adding new forms. It didn't matter that their work would be trashed eventually. Vivification was illegal—technically it was property damage—and also temporary, like a moth. Many of their ideas had been inspired by the great urban sculptor, Grentano, with whom they were both obsessed.

They sometimes vivified hidden alleys. Sophia would paint a mural on one side and Robert would add cool geometric shapes or strange gargoyle heads to the other. Sophia would sign her work with an "S" but Robert didn't need to sign his—whenever a force field highcap like him modified a structure, it took on his seal, like a fingerprint. Robert's was a tiny bird.

They once vivified the undersection of the old highway bridge. They climbed up the decrepit wooden structure to where the supports joined in a rough "Y."

Robert could remember Sophia clinging onto a dark wooden beam above their precarious perch, laughing, vowing to kick Robert's ass for getting her to climb up there. She hated heights.

He'd teased her; it had been her idea to place the faces so high.

*I can't help if it's where they needed to be,* she'd told him. Robert remembered the feeling of pushing his will into the wooden surfaces, the faces slowly emerging, and the feeling of loving Sophia more than ever. She was usually so fierce and bossy, but being out of control made her more relational, even in the way she spoke of the people down below. *They're all just finding their way,* she said. *Even the creeps, they're just finding their way.*

He'd stood up against her, then, and he'd kissed her. He loved his fierce and bossy Sophia all the more when he saw her heart—that's how he felt, like he was seeing her heart.

Lovers. Artistic collaborators. Robert had felt like they were unstoppable.

He blamed Sophia's parents, Boss and Mrs. Sidway, for victimizing his mother. They'd presented her, no doubt, with an impossible choice. Maybe they'd even entrapped her because they heard her child was a highcap who could manipulate force fields. He'd dreamed of destroying them once he got Sophia safely away.

Not that he completely excused his mother—he was her child, her little boy. She should've found another way. Robert's search for her went on, fruitlessly. Years later he'd dug up an old missing persons case in Iowa that seemed like her. He feared the worst.

Sitting there in his Tanglemaster tower, Robert twirled the paperclip S.

Being so utterly discarded by his mother and then, even more painfully, by Sophia, had revealed to him some essential truths about the pointlessness, hopelessness, and utter solitude of human existence.

He should thank them, really.

But now, ten years later, here he was a grown man, and the thought of Sophia visiting him sent his heart beating right out of his chest. Monstrous.

Back when they were eighteen and supposedly in love, Robert and Sophia had learned that the great sculptor Grentano was taking on an apprentice to travel the world with him. Sophia had encouraged Robert to apply.

It would be an awesome opportunity to work with the amazing Grentano, and of course Sophia would go too. It would be the start of their new life. Sophia also encouraged him to apply for group shows, scholarships to the finest academies as a back-up plan. *It's time to get out of this cow town,* she'd said.

Eventually, the flurry of rejections came. The schools didn't want him. The group shows didn't want his modern gargoyles. Worst of all, Grentano had hated his slides. Grentano suggested he stay in construction.

All this was around the time the Sidways were bidding the massive twenty-story multi-turnpike project, a billion dollar project that would be impossible without Robert. Not that he cared. But after the rejections, Sophia talked him into staying, at least for the turnpike.

*No sense in rushing out of here until there's something to rush to,* she'd said. They would save money, plan together. They had to be smart. He agreed; he would stay for a while longer and they'd think of a new plan. Naturally, the rejections saddened him, but he didn't lose faith in his vision. In fact, he was mostly frustrated to have to wait to get Sophia away from her twisted, dangerous parents.

Some time after, Robert was up by the railroad yards working on one of his modern gargoyles when a sixty-something man drove past; he stopped his car, got out, and confronted Robert, demanding to know if he was Robert Ferguson—he recognized Robert's style. When Robert told him that he was, the man wanted to know why Robert had rejected three scholarships and a Grentano apprenticeship to stay in construction. Why bother applying in the first place?

Robert was dumbfounded.

The man, an art professor, insisted he'd personally spoken with Robert on the phone, that Robert had accepted the scholarship and had promised to turn in some forms, but all the man got was a terse letter, declining it after all.

Robert remembered nothing of the sort.

Was the man crazy? Robert looked into it and found out he was telling the truth. Who would impersonate him? Only Sophia knew about any of it.

It was here that the idea that she could be a revisionist got hold of him. It had made him sick to doubt her, even the tiniest shade of doubt. He became determined cleanse himself of all doubt by ruling it out. He set up a test—fake news about a scholarship, and he would tape the interaction on a hidden tape recorder. He did it to prove her innocence. But just in case his wildest doubts were true, he'd left a note to himself about the tape recorder with instructions to *push play*.

He remembered his surprise upon finding the note, knowing what it might mean. Then he played the tape and he heard the whole thing. His exciting news. Her fake happiness for him, followed by some mysterious moments of silence, and then her voice. *Idiots. I can't believe this. They would reject you? Are they insane? You should be the one rejecting them! Uh! I'm so sorry, Robert. The hell with them, anyway. You don't need them.*

The discovery had sent him reeling. He'd loved her with all his heart. She'd said she loved him.

But it was all fake. Those mysterious moments of silence were her revising him. It made him sick just to imagine it, but there it was, the proof.

He went after her, looking for her all over, but couldn't find her. On his way around town he destroyed all of the projects they did together. It was the worst thing he could think of to do. The depth of her betrayal was nearly incomprehensible.

Years later, he'd heard Packard say that revisionists couldn't revise emotion, and he recalled thinking that Sophia would hate that—she hated doubt, hated a lack of control. It made him wonder if she'd been building her skills on him, as he'd been building his skills as part of the Sidway crew. Or was he just entertainment?

He never did find Sophia that day he learned the truth, or the next, and she wouldn't answer his messages. Then he learned she'd scurried off to college. Apparently Robert's value had ended with the dashed hopes.

He sometimes went back in his thoughts to that girl who was his collaborator, his friend, his fierce protector. And he would remember how her spirit would shine especially bright during those rare moments when she felt out of control. Like under the bridge. Was it fake all along? Was their love fake? A teen girl trying on personas?

It didn't matter, because it was over. Again he'd been discarded, again in the cruelest of ways.

But it was okay, because he now understood something important: that beautifying the ugly and hated corners of the city was a lie; it was a form of revision in itself. His art, up to then, had been a cover-up of ugliness and hatefulness, which was the true state of things in life. There was nothing to believe in, and no point to anything. Least of all love.

He was glad to know this.

He turned his full attention to the Sidway multi-turnpike project.

As usual, Sidway Construction had created fake blueprints; city commissioners would rubber stamp a child's drawing if that's what Sidway and their mob friends presented. Anyway, Sidway would be using Robert to shape the concrete and rebar, and Robert didn't read blueprints, he read pictures. Once he had the visual of what he wanted a structure to do, he would touch it and commune with its atoms, and slowly, it would shift to take his vision.

As the start date neared, Sidway and his foreman would show him photos of other turnpikes in other cities, as well as X-Rays of how the rebar was to run through, and Robert would nod. The Sidway Multi was to be a double-up of one of the more famous turnpikes from out east—it would merge five highways in different configurations.

Grentano had once written that sculpture should express the truth, and Robert was determined now to capture just that. Looking at the pictures for the multi-turnpike, Robert had a new vision for a new kind of sculptuary—a piece that would express the ultimate truth, and at the same time, destroy the reputation of Sidway Construction for years to come.

Alone in his shabby room at night, Robert created his own plans for a grotesque confusion of roads. He'd build it twice as high as they'd scoped, make it run to triple the budget. It would be a hateful and Mobius-like mockery of turnpikes, an ugly, bloated, Slinky of a triple cloverleaf that would seem on the verge of toppling, though it wouldn't thanks to his fields. He planned for extra curlicues that didn't need to exist, underpasses that shaved shockingly close to the overpasses. He'd build it backwards and from the inside so that Boss Sidway and the foremen wouldn't see the whole until it was too late. His work would be too slow for the eye to see, but it would be relentless. A relentless bloom of pointlessness and despair. Just like life.

As the project progressed, he talked the corner-cutting Sidway foreman into trucking in old discarded sections of highway from other locales and depositing them under the structure; he told them that as long as they connected the pieces physically to the structure, he could use his mutant power to mold and incorporate them, thereby saving on concrete.

Yeah. He *could* do that. But he wouldn't.

He also requested the metal skeleton of an old farm silo be deposited under there, and told them to pour a line of concrete to connect it, and he would re-mold parts of it to form the highway rail. This too, was well within his power. But he would leave it there, as a flagrantly senseless touch, a slap in the face of the taxpayers.

The Sidway interchange would be a monument to pointlessness. It would be sculptuary on a scale even Grentano had never imagined.

The thing would be unusable, unsalvageable. There would be an outcry, investigations. The national news might pick it up. Blueprints would be seized and Sidway's corrupt business practices would be exposed. How would Sidway explain it? It's not like they could claim to have been following the advice of an eighteen-year-old highcap. Highcaps didn't even exist. Heads would fucking roll.

As the interchange took its full outrageous shape, it occupied over two square miles of land. During the final stages of the project, he worked night and day, deep in the belly of it, feverishly interfacing with parts of the structure, raising, lowering, and twisting roads, undoing or crashing the corrective work the Sidway crews were attempting. He figured they'd be hunting him by then, trying to stop him, and they'd eventually catch him, and Boss Sidway would kill him. But that was part of the vision— Robert imagined himself going down in flames, a fiery comet off the top of the turnpike.

Some pathetic part of him also imagined that, after he was dead, Sophia would recognize the Tangle for what it was before it, too was destroyed.

He still loved her—that was the hell of it. The fact that he loved her showed the hell of everything.

Surprisingly, it was Boss Sidway who died. Robert was so hard at work deep under the massive structure, he didn't even realize when the anger and editorials started up. The investigations were instantaneous. By the time he emerged, Boss Sidway and his foreman had thrown themselves off the top of the structure—some said they were pushed— and Mrs. Sidway had fled to the Philippines with other Sidway heads. The company crumbled. Sophia stayed gone.

Much to Robert's surprise, his multi-turnpike wasn't torn down. Midcity crews attempted to stabilize it and started rerouting the highways to it. He went to the new commissioners and pointed out hidden flaws, begging them not to let cars on it—never in his wildest dreams had he imagined they would. They were grateful for the lifesaving warnings, but they had to use the turnpike—too much money had been invested to abandon it or knock it down. Robert got involved in the safety modifications.

Plus, there was always something more to add to it—a dizzying new tilt, a bent light pole, a grim twist of guardrail. He couldn't stop working on it.

Three days later, Robert was officially in charge of the stabilization efforts, given the title of Tanglemaster, and construction began on a tower for him to work from. He and the Tangle became deeply connected. The Tangle lived and breathed, or more, Robert lived it, Robert breathed it, morphed it to match his undulating despair.

And now he sat in his tower, waiting for Sophia. She wanted to see the Monk. He wouldn't have told her he was the Monk. Therefore, Sophia would reappear. Sophia couldn't stand to be told *No*.

SOPHIA SAT IN HER CAR AT THE FOOT OF THE TOWER, ENGINE running, heater on high, trying to focus on anything but the way Robert looked at her. The sense of a wall. He didn't want her, didn't want to see her. She could only imagine his expression if he learned what she was, what she'd done.

Back before it all went to hell, she'd wanted to confess how she used her powers to support her parents' criminal enterprises—that she'd revised enemies, witnesses. She was doing that work before she realized the harm of it. As she got older she felt guilty, but she kept on. It gave her power in the household—made her a kind of princess really, granting favors and getting treasure. Refusing to do it would render her powerless, or worse. It was always easier to say she'd stop tomorrow.

The closer she and Robert had grown, the more convinced she'd become that it would disgust him that she hadn't refused to do her father's bidding. God, she was a coward! Robert valued truth, and she was all about erasing it.

After she betrayed Robert, she really *had* thought of tracking him down and telling him what she'd done, thinking it might help him to know that Grentano and others had very badly *wanted* to work with him—even if it was too late to do anything about it, he'd know it.

But there had always been some excuse not to. She didn't know where he was. It would hurt him to remember. It would hurt him more to know the truth. Bla bla bla. In truth, she just couldn't bear for him to be even more disgusted with her.

She'd searched for Robert in other men. Not intentionally, but it was no accident she'd hooked up with Detective Otto Sanchez when she moved back to Midcity years later. She couldn't tell by looking at Otto that he had the power like Robert's—no highcap could recognize another—but early on she had noticed the way Otto pressed his hands to the wall at a crime scene. Communing with the structure, sinking into the atoms. She'd seen Robert do it a million times.

Like Robert, Otto was a visionary with big ideas—she found that exciting, and she'd encouraged him. They'd hatched grand plans for a safe, prosperous Midcity and she'd felt almost happy again. She and Otto would be partners, reigning over the transformation of the city. She was her old kitten-tiger self, managing perception and memory around him, using her power to further their schemes. How had it gone so wrong? The things she'd done …god, how she hated herself! She'd tried to stop revising, but she always had some reason to erase something. Or Otto did; Otto was a great believer in the end justifying the means. And there were times when the revision he wanted her to do was so outrageous, so impossible, she had to try it. Like climbing a mountain because it's there.

And sure, there had been times when she'd used her powers for the greater good, like when she and Packard and the gang were kidnapping and questioning people in connection with the serial killers—if she hadn't revised the people afterwards, the bad guys might have gotten warned about what they knew. She remembered how that righteous hypochondriac Justine had looked at her—the horror that Sophia would take a person's memory, even a few minutes of it. Sophia had just laughed in Justine's face, but inside she'd felt sick. She could act as if she didn't care, act as if she didn't hate herself, but that's what it was—an act—and seeing what she'd done to Robert was the icing on the evil cake.

She craved the Monk's brand of annihilation more than ever now.

She had to stop. Had to be stopped—she was just too weak to stop herself.

She would find the Monk, throw herself at his feet, beg him to do his whammy on her. She'd heard he usually got the targets after the other disillusionists had softened them up, but she felt sure she didn't need to be softened up—she was ready! Burning with regret over her many misdeeds. She had this fantasy that he'd disillusion her instantly, and she'd bounce back good, like that snake Corny Chambers, who now went around helping the homeless after years of butchering them and eluding prosecution.

She checked the time. Almost six. Robert would be leaving soon to go home. Or would he? He'd always been a night owl.

"Focus," she said aloud, putting the car in gear. She would go through Robert to get to the Monk. But she needed smarter tactics. You didn't threaten Robert. You didn't bribe him, either—saying *No* to her would be far more valuable to him than any amount of money. And trickery wouldn't work—she'd been stupid to try. She needed more information. Robert liked directness. And Scotch and curly fries, too.

S HE STEELED HERSELF, STANDING AT HIS DOOR, BAG IN HAND. SHE took a breath and knocked.

"Come in," he said.

And she swept in. "Robert." She said his name like a secret between them.

He spun around, regarded her warily. "What are you doing here?"

She set the fragrant hot bag on the desk; grease stains spread over the Moe and Curly's logo. He eyed it. He knew what was in there. She set down the bottle and pulled a matching pair of funny woodland animal shot glasses from her purse. Robert appreciated a certain level of humor. When you knew his sculptuary work, you could see that. His creations could sometimes be amusing in their extreme precision, their audacity. They made you feel happy, because they showed you his heart and his honesty.

"How are you?" she asked.

"What do you want?"

"Fine." She opened the bottle. "I need to see the Monk, and I know you know where he is. And how to get to him. I need a location. Packard told me you would know."

"What?" he said.

"Do I need to repeat myself or are you just saying *What* for the hell of it?" She sat up on the counter and poured an inch into each of the glasses.

"You want a different answer? How about *No*."

"That's not the answer I'm looking for either." She pushed a glass toward him with one finger.

"It's the one you're getting." He took the glass and drained it, and Sophia did too. As illegal teen drinkers, they'd always had a thing about drinking like adult men, or how they thought adults drank, with an open-throat shot.

She poured another and put the cap back on, glancing over her shoulder at the view. "What the fuck are you doing here, Robert? You holding this thing up?"

"You think I am?"

"You're doing something."

"Is that why you came? To discuss the Sidway multi-turnpike?"

"Don't call it that." Again she glanced at it. Why would he stay, even to keep it from falling apart? Was it possible he blamed himself? But why? He should hate that thing. A puff of steam came out when she opened her bag of fries. She set out the wax paper and put Robert's double order in front of him. "Got extra ketchups." She put out her curly fries.

"You think all this will make me tell you?"

She slid onto the desk, not quite in front of him.

"I've got work to do, Sophia, and we've got nothing to say." He rolled his chair over and typed on his computer, but she couldn't see what.

"What are you doing?"

"Part of what the Tanglemaster does is to manage the ramp lights. After six-thirty they need different timing."

"Ugh." She poured a couple more shots and threw hers back, then looked out the window. Robert had always wanted so badly to capture *essence*, whether he was creating a likeness of somebody or vivifying a junky old alley. What was the essence here? A dead end job, she thought, watching the circling cars.

*Misery.*

"How can you stand to look at that thing?"

He gazed up from his computer. "I like looking at it."

"Right." She snorted. "The only people who like the Tangle are murderous hobos, fugitives, suicides, and cannibalistic sleepwalkers who *file their teeth to better tear into living victims' bellies*."

"The Tangle resonates with them."

"Don't mess with me. We're not talking about art. We're talking about the Tangle." Was he punishing her even now? That was Grentano's thing: the public as artistic collaborator, even if only to destroy the art. "He lives down there, doesn't he?"

"Who?"

"The Monk."

Robert rolled back; his smile was smug. Imperious, even, but still, something in her belly tingled. God, she'd always loved when he smiled.

She crossed her legs. "Though, maybe he doesn't live down there anymore, huh? I know he's supposed to be dangerous, but, what's he going to do? Zing the cannibals? Destroy their faith and hope? Turn them into good cannibals? I mean…" She waited.

He drained his glass and slammed it down. Said nothing.

"Maybe the Monk's down there preaching to all the freaks," she tried. "Maybe he has some freaky church of freaks. The sleepwalking cannibals wouldn't attack a crowd."

He looked up at her. "As a matter of fact, he *does* lead a church down there, and it *is* called the freaky church of freaks."

She smiled. She used to love when he'd do that—take something silly she said and make a serious thing out of it. If this was old times, she'd laugh and make up more stuff about the freaky church of freaks.

"Shut up," she said, feeling like her heart was breaking all over. Looking at him there on his chair, she knew exactly how she'd fit on his lap, how they used to nestle in to fit themselves to each other. How it felt to kiss him, to rub her cheek over his, and run her hands over his shoulders, his chest. She used to love to feel the solid heft of his limbs beneath his soft clothes.

He ripped open a ketchup packet and squeezed it over the fries.

And she might feed him a fry, too, if this was then. He used do this thing where she'd try to feed him something, and he'd snatch it from her hand and toss it onto the floor and suck in her finger, maybe multiple fingers, and not let go. He'd suck and suck, and it would feel so fabulously lewd, and it would make her instantly wet.

"Why do you want to see him?"

She swallowed. "I have business with him."

"You're going to have to tell me what that business is." He dragged a fry through the ketchup and bit it in half, seeming to evaluate the taste, then he ate the rest of it. "Crispy," he said.

"But of course." They'd always ordered their fries well done. Nothing worse than soggy curly fries. "If I'm going to do a fat bomb, it better be delicious."

Sullen gaze. A look that meant, *Stop being full of shit.* A compliment.

She felt flustered. Couldn't think how to proceed. "Why are you up here doing this traffic management shit and not down there doing your real work, Robert? Your sculptuary?"

"Traffic management is useful. Usefulness is a form of truth, too."

"Unlike the bullshit you're feeding me right now."

He gave her a hard look, which she answered with a sly gaze. Their old connection was all there again, pure and true as a bell.

Shit! What was she doing? She had no right to re-engage like this. No right to *him* in any way, shape or form. She really was evil. *Get in and get out,* she told herself. She crossed her arms. "Come on, I need to see the Monk."

"Why?"

"There's somebody who needs to be disillusioned."

"Only Packard sees the Monk. Packard and the targets."

"I don't know if you follow the news, but Packard's not exactly available right now. Would Packard have told me to come here if he didn't want me contacting the Monk?"

"No go, Sophia."

"No go? What does that mean?"

She didn't like the hard gleam in his eye. "Means you're not seeing the Monk."

Frustration surged up in her.

"Packard doesn't roll this way," he added. "So why don't you tell me what's really going on here?"

"Did you ever think Packard might be rolling differently?"

"Nope." Robert ate another fry, seeming full of private thoughts.

"What? Does he send an engraved invitation for the Monk to meet him? Dearest Monk, would you do me the honor…"

"That would work."

"Sometimes a person doesn't have time for an engraved invitation, Robert."

"Packard would make it happen if he wanted to."

Casually she glanced out the window. So *that's* how Packard did it? He'd send written instructions that Robert would carry to the Monk? She could probably get a sample of Packard's writing at the restaurant. She could send instructions for the Monk to show up somewhere and she'd be the one to meet him. Maybe she'd need a note from Packard to give to the Monk, too. This was all getting a bit complicated, but at least she was making progress.

She tried to get a few more details from Robert, without success. She needed to come at him fresh again. Lord, how many times would she have to revise him? He'd finished his fries now, and wiped his hands on his napkin.

"Hey." She slid over on the desk, so that she sat right in front of his chair, and leaned in. "You have an eyelash about to go into your eye."

He looked at her strangely. "Do I, now?"

"Are you mocking me? Yes, you do. Hold still." She rested her hands on his shoulders, a stolen enjoyment. "It's in your left eye."

He looked at her. This was the part that was the sickest, where he gave her the clear stream of his trusting gaze, and she invaded it in order to rob him.

The gate to recent memory was through the eyes, of course—for sighted people, anyway. The first thing she'd do would be to sync up with his gaze—it would give her a kind of hold, and even calm him, and then she'd deepen her hold and invade.

"This'll just take a second," she whispered, as much for herself as for him. Robert seemed to be watching her with too much awareness—it was because it was him, that's all. She'd felt like that earlier today, and, just as she had then, she tried to convince herself this was some no-name reporter who'd seen something he shouldn't, just another job, just another pair of eyes. "Now hold still. It's right there." She placed a pinky on his cheekbone and worked on relaxing into the stream of his gaze.

She just needed to get to that point, get control. Once she fully synched up, she'd start getting the rough images, and that's when she had a person.

Even when she had a person, she couldn't read much of their memory—images were indistinct—but she could see enough to know where to erase to. Afterwards, if she wanted, she could imagine her own thing and plant it there, like playing a movie for both their minds to see. Or simply allow the person to lose time, which is what she'd do with Robert. He was such a daydreamer, he'd never know.

A daydreamer with dark velvety brown eyes, watching, waiting. Her chest felt fluttery; it was taking forever to sync in. She just needed to get fully in and seize control, and then she could relax. She was right on the edge of it when she felt his hand on her knee.

"Robert!" she scolded, her hold faltering. "Come on!"

She pushed at his hand, sliding backwards on the desk, trying to keep the hold she had on his gaze, but he smiled and pressed another hand to her other knee, and then he slid both hands up her thighs. "Does this help?"

"No!" She struggled to get back into sync, pushing back on his wrists, trying to stop his upwards progress. "Don't be crazy!" But he was too strong, he kept moving his hands up her thighs, sliding, gripping, until his thumbs grazed the insides of her thighs. "Jesus," she said. She was in sync with him, but not the way she intended.

He stood and pushed roughly between her legs. All at once, his hands were around her, gripping her ass, and he dragged her to him.

"Robert!" It was meant to come out like an admonishment, but it sounded husky, inviting even.

He kissed her hard. His hold on her was fierce, like he was on fire, and she was the fuel. "You want me to stop?" he grated into the kiss.

Him stopping was the last thing she wanted. She had no right, but she couldn't help herself. "No."

His hands were at the front of her, pulling down the zipper of her safari jacket. "No what?"

"No, don't stop." She closed her eyes as her jacket fell open.

"Hey." Gently he took hold of her hair, pulled her away. "Don't check out now." She opened her eyes to his piercing gaze; he seemed angry—at her? Himself? "Stay looking at me. Be here." He let her go and she watched his brown eyes, his stubby Robert lashes, as he undid the buttons of her shirt. And he watched her. What did he want to see in her eyes? What was he looking for?

The way he watched her, it was too much. She felt exposed, but she wouldn't look away—she didn't want to break this dark dream. Did he suspect? It didn't matter. Later on, she would steal this experience from him as she had stolen the others, but for now she wanted to give him something. And take something.

He pushed her shirt and jacket off her shoulders, and sighed. "Goddammit," he said. And then he kissed her.

God, she wanted him. And evil as it was, she liked that she had him. He continued to peel off her clothes, with those same furious movements, like he didn't care, but like he cared too much. She pushed her fingers up under his sweater, pressing her hands to his chest, felt him tremble. He roved his hands all over her body, palms on her breasts, over her hips, her thighs, thumbs around her slick folds. This was wrong on every level. And oh, she was so turned on.

She kicked off her boots. He wrestled her pants from her ankles and she grabbed her purse, remembering a condom in there. She held it out for him and he plucked it from her hand, not questioning where it came from, who it was for.

"You can have anything," she breathed.

"Anything?" He watched her impassively. The pause between them went on for maybe a second or two, but it seemed like forever.

*Anything.* It was a lie, of course. Or was it? What was stopping her from giving him anything he wanted—even the truth? "Anything," she confirmed.

They watched each other's eyes. He was still wary, still shuttered. He didn't trust her, and she saw it. And he knew she saw it; suddenly there was too much truth.

"Put it on me," he said, shoving the foil package back at her. "That's all I want."

She opened the little package; she would never let him know how it hurt, that that's all he wanted from her. Nothing more. But what did she expect? She was the ultimate taker; maybe on some level, Robert knew it. She unrolled the condom over his hard length, carefully, reverently—she would give him something even in this. She pressed it over him, smoothing it down to the base of his cock.

He stroked her hair. The tender gesture surprised her. "That is so good, Sophia."

Inwardly she smiled—he'd always said that whenever she touched his cock in any way. Lightly she ran her fingers up and down the marble-smooth latex while she kissed his chest, the wiry hairs. She kissed the freckle by his left nipple. That little freckle, like an old friend.

"That is so good," he said. She straightened up and looked into his eyes. The whole tenor of their interaction felt different now, like the anger and angst had burned out, and there was just the echo of what was past, and a strange sadness.

She put her hand to his face, slid her thumb along his forehead. "Come here," she whispered, wanting to comfort him. Comfort him and protect him—from herself. Lord, she was twisted. "Come here."

He moved in close to her and she held him, kissed his neck, enjoyed the feel of his arms tight around her. The tip of his cock probed at her core, then slipped upward. He took it with his hand, dragged it around in her wetness, panting, forehead tipped to hers.

"Yeah," she whispered.

Slowly he pressed into her, filled her. It was beyond delicious. She tilted, wrapped her legs around him so that she could take him all in.

"Oh, that is so good, Sophia." Like he'd discovered something unexpected. Always like he'd discovered something unexpected. He touched her legs, feeling them all the way around him. "So…"

"Yeah," she said.

He thrust into her. They fucked slow, and then they fucked hard, not looking at each other, as though by agreement, like the truth had become too painful. She pulled him to her, licking his neck, maybe sucking it—she didn't know, because his every thrust sent mindless sparkles into her nervous system.

Later he pressed his thumb to her clit while he thrust, rubbing her. She'd always needed a little something extra to get off—sometimes a lot of something extra, and of course he remembered. The kindness of it hit her. When he paused, all she could think of was that he needed to start again, and the instant he started again she was over the edge, thrumming and throbbing with wild pleasure, only vaguely aware when he came too, with a Robert groan. He stilled, vibrating inside her.

They stayed connected for a long time, him inside her, her face at his chest, him holding her. Their breathing sounded loud in the silence. She wanted only this, she didn't want to think anything, face anything. Only this. She had a feeling he felt the same way. Wildly she wondered how long they could stay like that.

A ringing sound startled her cold. The ring of an old-fashioned phone. Robert stiffened, and he pulled out of her, not meeting her eyes. He just turned and yanked to phone off its cradle. "Yeah." He turned away from her, grumbling into the phone, which he held between his ear and his shoulder, fumbling around. She saw him throw the condom in the little garbage can, and he pulled up his pants.

Quickly she pulled her clothes back on, feeling ashamed and abandoned. He was right there in the room, but gone. Maybe it's how he'd felt when she'd left. Of course he'd be mad. He should be mad.

Robert was typing now, fingers fast on the keyboard. Schematics appeared on one of his screens. Then he was barking questions into the phone. "Did he see a blue pillar? Any kind of machinery?" He gave what sounded like coordinates.

She was supposed to be in and out; she was just here to get the Monk's information. Not open old wounds.

Robert slammed down the phone, grabbed his coat, and pulled on a black winter hat. "I have to go. And I need to lock this place down."

"What's going on?"

"Some kid in the Tanglelands." He regarded her darkly. "I'm going to have to take you down in the bird." This like it was the last thing he ever wanted to do.

"Okay," she said, understanding the dark look all too well. There were men who'd feel pleased with themselves after a quick toss with the ex, but Robert would feel like a dupe.

He hit some buttons on a panel and led her out another door, up some narrow steps and out onto the roof where there was a small helicopter.

You could see everywhere from his windy tower top—the perfect blackness of Lake Michigan, ship lights in the distance, decrepit downtown Midcity, and sludging through it, Midcity River with its shimmery, oily surface.

Robert helped her into the passenger seat, and then he got in the other side and started it up. Like it was a car or something. It was weird he knew how to fly a helicopter.

The helicopter lifted off with a backward jerk, then jolted forward, and up up up into the night sky.

Robert wore his brown hat just a little crooked, and it matched his brown hair, his brows. He'd always looked hot in hats. He seemed to be concentrating with all his might on the task of flying, but she suspected he really just didn't want to deal with her.

So many homes and buildings in Midcity were sporting barbed wire, sirens, and floodlights these days, but that was no match for the feeling of guardedness the man next to her now exuded. And something else underneath. Hopelessness. Despair.

Briefly she wondered if she could ever revise him again. Could she get close to him like that again without it being strange? Reluctant subjects had to be restrained, their eyes held open. It made her sick to picture doing that to Robert.

They rose over the massive structure, all strange twists and lights, like an alien space station, terrific and awesome and a little bit terrifying.

"You must do this a lot," she tried, wanting to say anything, just to change the feeling in the small space. "People must get into trouble all the time down there."

"Not a lot call the authorities though. If they do try…well, it's hard to get reception down there. We find the bodies." He paused. "Assuming… you know."

She nodded. Assuming the sleepwalking cannibals didn't find them first.

"I've only got two guys tonight. You'll stay in here and wait."

"Why not let me go in and help?"

"Because it's a war zone."

"And if I go you'll have three instead of two." With a deliberately obvious movement, Sophia eyed the rifles on the rack behind them. "Plus I'm probably still a better shot than you are." They'd had a range on the Sidway compound.

"Nope."

"I know the Monk's in there, and I'm going in either way. Frankly, there's not a lot you can do about it."

Robert frowned.

Soon they were nearing the airspace directly above the Tangle; she could see a large span of darkness in the center. She looked down at the twists, wondering, as she so often did, about her dad's last moments. It was terrible, the things he'd done, the people he'd killed. Well, she didn't know for a fact that he'd killed, but he directed a mob machine that killed. Still, he'd loved her—both her parents had loved her, and she'd loved them. Of the many highcaps she knew, she was the only one who'd been loved by her human parents. She was lucky in that. Yes, her father taken full advantage of her memory erasing abilities, but she'd never said *No*, had she? She pictured the three of them—her mom and her dad and her—at the Peanut Barrel, the peanut-shells-on-the-floor restaurant where they'd dine every Friday night. It was one of her favorite memories, the three of them. Their little family.

Fucking Tangle.

Her parents had gotten greedy—that's how it had all started. There had been talk on the city council of redoing the highway interchanges, and her parents couldn't bear to see the contract go to anybody but Sidway Construction. She remembered some of the conversations—they'd fight for the job and figure it out later. They partnered with another mob outfit, and called in favors to get the city to write the specs in a way that would exclude other construction companies, and made all kinds of deals to get the massive turnpike passed by the council. Lots of people invested and got lined up for cuts. Soon after they were awarded the job, her father regretted the whole thing. Something about concrete prices changing, and the fact that Sidway Construction would have to farm out more of the work than expected, due to other projects running late.

He let his cohorts know, recommended that they reverse course. That didn't go well. Mob goons kidnapped her mother, held her for almost two days. Two frightening, harrowing days.

Her dad promised they'd do the work, that Sidway would make it work.

That afternoon they found her mother wandering the Midcity lakefront in a drugged stupor, precariously near the big boulders. Sophia never got to see the note that was with her mother, but she heard the conversations about it, knew it threatened both her parents' lives. There was panic at home. They were having trouble pulling in subcontractors—people were scared of getting involved with such a mob-infused project—the price of failure was way too high. Sidway Construction's one saving grace was Robert's growing powers. *There's been nothing so big as to be beyond him yet,* she heard the foreman say. And another comment—one of the other leads: *those fucking crews couldn't build a doghouse without Robert.*

She and Robert had been in the thick of making their plans to leave at the time—if he received a *Yes* from a college, a *Yes* from Grentano, anything, they were out of there. She would be eighteen, so her parents couldn't stop her, and she and Robert would make a happy home. Robert, in particular was itching to go. He had grown increasingly angry at her father, blaming him for robbing him of his chance to know his mother, to find his own father, and laughing about what would happen when he left; he knew they couldn't build without him. It bothered her when he'd laugh about Sidway Construction crumbling, but she understood his anger.

But now she couldn't let Robert leave. The turnpike had to go up as planned or the mob families would lose big, and her parents would be killed. Would Robert give up his dreams to save her father? Her mother? Would he do it for her? She wanted to believe, but if there was one thing she'd learned working for her dad, it was that hate and vengeance were usually stronger than loyalty—stronger, even than love.

So she did what she always did. She controlled the situation through memory revision, the only sure way to control life. Looking back, she realized she could've confided in Robert. Given him a chance—given *them* a chance—to struggle through the problem together. But she hadn't even considered it.

She thought of that decision often. She saw it as the point where her true nature had fully and completely asserted itself.

And so the process began. Robert would come to her, excited about an acceptance, a scholarship; usually he'd have a letter to show her. She would read it and tell him how wonderful it was. She would draw up close and look into his eyes, and he would look back, so trusting. There was always this moment just before she took hold of his mind when he knew something was off, when the trust turned to confusion, and one time, horror. But usually by then she would have enough hold on him that he couldn't look away. And she would reach in and erase.

She couldn't just erase, of course. She had to picture new things to plant in place of the old memory. Robert opening the rejection letter. The feel of the paper on his fingers, and exactly where he'd sit; choreography was key. She'd realized by then that she couldn't revise emotions, but people would add emotion in as the memory grew roots and connected to genuine memory. Sophia made most of the letters kind, except Grentano's, which she made complainy, nit-picky, small minded—qualities Robert disliked. She hoped it would make him see the rejection as a blessing in disguise. Sometimes, as if to make up for it all, she would create a nice moment of Baron resting his fuzzy nose on Robert's knee and looking up in the way Robert always found amusing. Finally, she'd picture Robert texting her, and her arrival, and he'd give her the letter and she'd put it in her pocket and insist on burning it, and from there she'd cut him over to real time.

"Fuck 'em," Robert would say. He'd hold her slender fingers in his big meaty hands and say something like, "There's only one person I need with me on this."

But she wasn't with him. She was so full of shame during that time, she could barely look at him, could barely stand the shining goodness of his love for her. She wished she could run away, far away.

Then, one day, she saw their installation on the old bridge had been destroyed—erased completely in a way only Robert could've managed. She rushed around town and found everything else they'd ever done trashed, or effaced. Work he'd cherished. It was here that she realized how deeply the rejections had damaged him. Only a damaged Robert would destroy his own art. It shook her that she'd done that to him.

She'd panicked, unable to imagine facing him, and found ways to avoid him over the following day. Her parents had been pressing her to apply to colleges like her peers, but she'd put it off and off. That day she did a complete turnaround; she announced she'd like to tour her father's alma mater, Kenwell University in Northern California—immediately. She went that night. She toured and she stayed, signed up to major in political science. Her parents were relieved to get her out of town. They thought the reason she wanted her choice of college kept quiet and secret was because of the tension over the turnpike. They had no idea about her and Robert.

She got updates on the turnpike through her parents, and soon, the news of it all going bad. She felt sure that if Robert had been in his usual state of mind, he could've made it work, but she'd destroyed him in some essential way. Things went worse and worse, and it was all her fault.

By the time her father went off the top she was consumed with guilt. They said it was a suicide, but she knew better. Her mother fled to live as a broken woman in a Manilla condo.

Some of the guys on the Sidway crew told her that Robert was living a hermit-like existence within Midcity. Other people thought he'd left town after the debacle. She preferred the leaving town rumor; it allowed her to imagine him repairing and rebuilding, living the life he deserved. She repaired and rebuilt, too, or more, she hardened. Hardening seemed to help her forget.

Six years later she returned to Midcity and became confidante and ally to the rising city star, Otto Sanchez, clicking around town in her perfect hair and crisp safari suits. If you were in the know, you wouldn't dare to look Sophia Sidway in the eyes. She was glad to have spikes, metaphorically; it kept people away. Her life seemed to consist of her lounging about in top offices, posh parlors, and restricted areas, directing the past as she saw fit. And she'd mock people who judged her . "Me so evil," she'd sometimes sneer in a baby voice.

It was amazing she'd ever been that long-ago girl, scrambling across the nighttime cityscape, hand in hand with Robert, dressed all in black with long flowing scarves—one for her and a little one for scruffy little Baron. Dreaming. Laughing. Vivifying their stupid little scenes.

Sophia couldn't erase her own memory. Even if she could, her powers only let her reach back through one day, but if by some miracle she became able to reach back through the years, she'd yank that girl out by the roots. Because sometimes when Sophia was alone in bed at night, those memories felt like battery acid, burning her heart from the inside out.

Robert lowered the helicopter. Two strange-looking ATVs waited below; they looked like little tanks with massive rover wheels, white exhaust trailing into the sky. They seemed like toys next to the eerie mega-bulk of the Tangle.

"What are those, militarized clown cars?" Sophia said.

"You'll be glad for those militarized clown cars when we get in."

She sat up. "You're letting me come?"

"More like resigned to. It actually might be safer. And it's almost curfew."

"And you know I'm a better shot than you."

He gave her a jaundiced look and they landed with a series of bumps.

"Out," Robert said.

She grabbed a gun and jumped onto the noisy, snowy, garbage-strewn expanse that surrounded the Tangle, ducking until she got clear of the still-rotating blades. The outermost highway rose up above them on fat, gray concrete pillars. Beyond were more pillars supporting more highways, a web of thick roads rising up out of a nest of shattered concrete, rusted wire fences, and garbage. It roared like a motorized ocean, strangely cyclical, punctuated by horns and tire screeches.

Five minutes later, Sophia was buckled in one of the ATVs, and being driven over the broken barriers and into the maw of darkness by an EMT named Green. Their ATV followed behind the one that Robert rode in.

"Kids," Green grumbled. "Tangleland's a barrel of laughs until somebody gets caught by a deranged killer." Green had the thickest black moustache she'd ever seen, and he told her that his crew 'went in' with Robert only when they thought they'd have success. They had a firm location for this boy, and he wasn't too far.

They entered a space that was inky black except for the headlights. Green told her how to run the searchlight and she played the beam across discarded twists of guardrail and giant chunks of concrete, some as big as train cars. She felt like they were traversing the belly of an underground cave system, only instead of rock, it was made of chunks of old highway and garbage.

Deeper they went, down through a dark gulley, over a pile of rubble, and then they emerged into a dim, cavernous space. Shafts of light came down into the gloom from the curvy crosshatch of roads above. This *wasn't too far?* It seemed like another world.

They got out at the foot of a three-story high mountain of jagged boulders, eerie in the half-darkness. Green handed Sophia a flashlight and she strapped the gun over her back. The Tangle sounded different on the inside, more humming than roar.

The four of them scaled the pile, which was slow, dangerous going. At one point a boulder loosened under Sophia's foot and started a mini avalanche behind her. They reached the top and yelled down to the boy, who lay on the other side at the bottom. He lifted an arm.

"Alive," Green observed.

Robert told Green and his partner that he and Sophia would keep lookout up top, and that they 'could work.' This turned out to mean that the men could use their telekinetic powers in front of Sophia. Robert led Sophia to the edge of the pile next to a big pillar, and they watched the EMTs scramble down the other side, dislodging debris, which magically veered away from the boy. A stretcher, fitted inside a kind of plastic sled, slid right along down with them and stopped neatly at the foot of the hill. Powerful telekinetics, those two.

Sophia found the view to be weirdly spectacular, like several underpasses all munched together—pillars and supports rising willy nilly, tilted surfaces. It was like being inside a massive, bombed-out Salvador Dali painting. Was the Monk really down here? There would be something appropriate about that, she thought. The man with so much darkness inside him in this dark, twisted place. And weirdly, it echoed her feelings of hopelessness. It had been selfish of her to have sex with Robert, and now she was further than ever from finding the Monk. She felt like they should talk about it, but really, what was there to say? She crossed her arms.

"God, his friends left him trapped. I mean, he probably didn't come in alone, right?"

Robert nodded.

"Lucky for him it's still early evening," Sophia observed. The sleepwalking cannibals usually didn't come out until after bedtime—they were normal people who were commanded by a dream invader to kill and eat in their sleep.

"They've been coming out at nightfall now," Robert said.

Sophia stiffened. "Well, shit, I thought guns didn't stop them that effectively."

"They slow them. Usually that's enough, but if I have to, I'll throw up a field or suck them into a wall." He touched the pillar.

She nodded. She'd thought he wanted them to stand near it for cover, but of course he wanted to stay directly connected to the physical structure of the Tangle. Robert's powers only worked if he was touching the walls or floor, something directly connected to the structure.

"I smell fire," she said. "They like sharpening their teeth together around the fire, I hear."

"Fire doesn't mean anything. Anyone down here could be making a fire. And sometimes the oil slicks catch." He squinted beyond where the boy lay, at a massive rectangle of road sitting on the floor. When you looked closer, you could see it was two lengths of road, folded, like a sandwich, waiting for a giant with truck-sized hands. Whatever Robert noticed there, he didn't appear to like it. Way up above, car headlights swirled around on the angular surfaces, strobing the insane, futuristic cathedral ceiling. It was otherworldly, she thought, yet oddly familiar.

Green and the other EMT had gotten the boy up to the top, a bit away from where Sophia and Robert stood; he and the EMTs called back and forth; Robert and Sophia would keep a lookout while they got the boy down the other side. He instructed them to take 'the bird' and he and Sophia would drive back to the tower.

The EMTs eased the sled, with the boy in it, down the side of the boulder mountain. They used ropes, but Sophia suspected the ropes were there for the boy's psychological comfort. Those two telekinetics could probably ease him down with their minds.

"Is it hard being down here?" Robert asked suddenly.

*To be here where her father had died,* he meant. *To see it.*

"Less than I would've thought," she said, not looking at him. "It seems like another country. Like it happened in another country."

The EMTs reached the bottom. They transferred the boy into one of the ATVs down below and started it up. Robert's attention was on the other side of the giant hill; she followed his gaze to the buckled sandwich of road. Out the corner of her eye, she watched him flatten his hand on the pillar, and the buckled road rotated minutely and tipped up a bit.

Sophia's mouth hung open. The way it tipped made it look…better. "Jesus, did you adjust that for visual balance?"

Robert stilled, said nothing for a beat. Maybe he hadn't realized she was watching. Then he chuckled. "Is that what it looked like to you?"

"Yeah," she said. "It enhanced the *gestalt*."

"You're imagining things, Sophia."

Over on the other side, the ATV was disappearing into the darkness.

He hadn't meant her to see it. She grabbed his arm. "Don't screw with me. I know you. I know your work. You just adjusted a multi-ton section of buried highway for the purposes of visual balance. You vivified. Are you vivifying this whole thing?"

"Don't," he said in a warning voice.

"Something's up with this place."

"It's called traffic," he said. "Copy the way I go down."

Robert started down the boulder mountain. Carefully, Sophia placed her feet just as he did. Something was up. She knew she was right. Things were too…of a mind.

A rock suddenly gave way under her feet. Sophia scrambled, nearly losing her balance, grabbing something rusty to stop her slide, watching in horror as a boulder below her began to roll. She screamed. "Robbie!"

With a kind of terrible clairvoyance, she saw its whole path, heading right at Robert, and she couldn't stop it. "Robbie!"

He twisted and dove, but not fast enough. The boulder crunched onto his leg

And stopped.

"Robbie!" She scrambled down. "Oh my god!"

Robert craned up his neck to stare at the boulder pinning his leg, or at least the part below the knee, and then he lay back and looked upwards. Calmly, he said, "I think my shin is fucked. And my foot."

Shock. Robert was in shock.

She knelt beside him, hand on his damp forehead. "You're okay. You'll be okay." She tried to look calm, but her heart beat like crazy.

He turned his trusting brown eyes to her. Said nothing.

She eyed the boulder, the size of a small car. "I'm going to move this. Okay?"

He watched her calmly.

"I am." Sophia put her hands to the thing. She would move it. There had to be a way. "One, two..." she heaved.

It stayed.

Fear surged through her.

"Let's call your guys back." She pulled her cell phone from her pocket. No reception. She knelt and patted Robert's pockets and found his phone. She bit her lip as she got no reception on his, either.

"What the fuck! How can your phone not work in here? That kid's phone worked!"

"No, it didn't. His friends called when they got out."

"It's okay, it's okay," she said. She needed to remain calm.

He said, "Try punching a code for me - 6759 and a star."

Sophia punched in the code. A red light came on. "What is it?"

"A beacon. Installed years ago. I don't have high hopes..."

"It's okay, you have me." Sophia set the phone next to him, tilted so that he could see the light. It probably wouldn't work any better than the phone, but hope was important. She put her shoulder to the boulder and tried to get a foothold, thrusting herself against it, but it was like a wall. She tried again and again, then paused, leaning against it.

Robert was sweating, alarmingly pale. "You can't move it," he observed.

"Screw that." Sophia tried again. She'd heard of mothers finding the strength to lift entire cars off their trapped infants. Could she not have that for the man she loved? She tried and tried again. He would be losing blood. He was saying something to her. She couldn't hear anything but her grunts. She pulled her gun off her back and threw it down, and tried to push it with her back, using the power of her legs.

Finally his voice broke through to her. "Sophia! Stop!"

She stopped. She felt so insubstantial, so powerless.

"You'll have to take *No* for answer for once."

"What if I found a way to, I don't know, get you connected to the structure. Could you make the wall bend to push it off?"

"I'm halfway up a rock pile, Sophia. I can't touch the floor. And you can't bring the floor to me. Maybe if you had a cement mixer."

"I need something to lever this fucker." She looked around for a board, a metal beam.

A sharp intake of breath. "Sophia."

"What?"

"Sophia, I need you to pick up the gun. Now."

She looked around to see three sleepwalkers climbing up—two men and a woman. You could always tell them by the plodding way they moved. And the fact that they wore only pajamas, and no coat, even though it was winter. She grabbed her gun. Sleepwalkers under the control of Stuart, the highcap dream invader, Midcity's number one criminal.

"You have to shoot one," he whispered. "They need to see one of their own shot."

She cocked the rifle and crouched, balancing it on one knee, trying not to shake. Cold rocks ground into the other knee. "Jesus, they're regular people." But they were coming.

To eat her and Robert.

A man in a red union suit was closest. "Hell." Sophia aimed at his leg and pulled the trigger. The shot sounded like a cannon blast in her ear. He tumbled back down and the other two backed up. More would come now. Longingly she eyed the ATV, just yards from the sleepwalkers. Had they noticed it? They tended to notice only living things, the sleepwalkers. "We have to get you out of here."

"Listen to me carefully," Robert said. "Lift me up and pull my gun off my back and put it in my hands."

She touched his cheek, ears ringing. "I'm covering you," she said.

"Just do it! Lift me and slide out my gun."

Was it hurting him? Gently she lifted his back and pulled the gun out from under him.

"Put it on my lap."

"I'm handling the shooting part."

"No, you are going to that ATV. The keys are in the ignition."

"No fucking way. I won't leave you."

*Again.*

"Sophia, I'm losing blood and I won't be conscious much longer. We have a small window."

"Shut up." She squatted and stroked his forehead, brushing his hair back in the pulsating dimness.

"It's right that I would die in here," he said.

"No! It isn't right at all! It's the most wrong thing possible. And you won't. I won't let you. I will not let you."

"Some things you can't control, Sophia." He closed his eyes.

"Robert! No." Softly she patted his cheek.

"Stop hitting me, dude."

She gulped away a sob and knelt down, put her cheek to his, held him best she could. Moans down below. More sleepwalkers were approaching.

"Goddammit!" She wiped away tears, lumbered back up, cocked the rifle, and shot. They backed off. She crouched back down, brushed his hair off his clammy forehead, kissed his cheek, his nose. "I'm staying. I should've never left." A sheen of sweat covered his face.

"It's okay, Soph," he whispered without opening his eyes.

"It's not okay. You have no idea."

He said nothing.

"You need to know what I did, Robert. I have to tell you this— Grentano wanted you. He loved your stuff. They all did."

She took a breath and waited for that to sink in. Robert watched her, with a strange calm in his eyes. God, was he going into some sort of blood loss stupor?

"I erased your memory of Grentano's acceptance, Robert. I'm a memory revisionist."

"I know," he whispered.

"What? You know? You knew?"

He squeezed her hand in response.

"You knew?"

"At the end."

She watched him, bewildered, tears streaming down her cheeks. "I'm so sorry. I really did love you, Robbie. I loved you so much, but I was so frightened for my parents. I was such a coward—"

Confusion now. "Your parents?"

"They were going to kill them if the turnpike didn't go through, and without you, it was a death sentence." She rubbed his cold hand between her two warm ones. "I should've told you, trusted you. And then when I saw our beautiful stuff smashed…I couldn't face you."

"You were trying to save your parents? That's why you did it?"

"I'm so ashamed." She tipped her forehead to his chest. She felt like a boulder was inside her; crushing her. How long had it been there? "They loved your art and they wanted you, and I made you think they didn't. I betrayed you and ran off."

"It's okay,"

"Like hell it is. But I'm ending it. You're getting the fuck out of here and starting your rightful life, and I'm turning over a new leaf. I'm disgusted with how I am. I'm done with this."

The highways above them droned and droned. "The Monk," he whispered. "That's why."

"That's right. He changes people's whole deal." She sat up and craned around for cannibals and saw none. "I need to be stopped."

Robert shook his head. "You don't need that."

"I can't stop revising. Falsifying."

"You loved true things when we were together."

She felt the hot tears flow. "I was happy and in love then."

He winced. Oh, god, he was in pain and here she was talking about her stupid self. "Sophia, you have to go while you can."

If she left him, he'd be eaten alive. She leaned over and kissed him. The kiss tasted like tears. "I'll take my chances. They have to leave eventually. They have to return to their beds—"

"I don't have that long—" he breathed. "More sleepwalkers are going to be here. If I die or lose consciousness, I won't be able to cover you on the way to the ATV. It's okay," he said. "It's the culmination I'd always intended for this."

"The *culmination*?" With a shiver, she lifted her gaze to the fantastical forest of twisted metal and concrete. Its strange flow swept the eye, along gnarled progressions up to majestic visual offenses everything with a strange internal balance, like a grand atonal symphony. "Oh my god." She gripped his hand. "It's all yours. This whole damn thing is sculptuary." She took it in, anew. "It's a living, breathing…totally outrageous…" A massive sculpture fueled entirely by his despair. He was sunk into it— personally intertwined. "It's the most beautiful thing I've ever seen."

His hand was so cold.

"Fuck." She wrestled her coat off and put it over him, tucked him in. "It's beautiful, baby."

"No, it's not."

"It's the most beautiful thing ever." She could barely see anything for the blur of tears. "You made even despair and hopelessness beautiful. I erase things. You reveal them." He'd vivified his despair.

He looked up at her. He had something to say.

She waited.

"You really loved me?" He asked.

"I still do. I never stopped." She lay down beside him.

He touched her hair. "I never wanted you to go. Even after I knew what you did." Silence. "But you have to go now."

"You're in pain. Let me revise away the pain. Let me use my power for one good thing."

Weakly he shook his head. "There are some things a man wants to remember, no matter how much time he has left."

Moans from the other direction, above them. The sleepwalkers had circled around and climbed the other side of the boulder mountain.

She clambered back up and shot, and they disappeared.

She got back down by Robert. "I'll die before I leave you."


H E LOOKED AT HER, SO STRONG AND BRIGHT. SHE WANTED TO STAY with him! His heart swelled at the thought, not quite blotting out the excruciating pain in his leg—it was like the hottest hot, and the coldest cold, both at once.

He had to find a way to make her leave, but the fact that she wanted to stay, that she *would* stay, it meant everything to him. Sophia, always so in control of everything, Sophia who hated the word *No*, now she wanted to jump into the abyss with him—to embrace the most finalistic *No* possible.

She was stretched out beside him, head propped on one hand, watching his eyes. She seemed different, as though she was coming apart, somehow. In good way; like she was coming free of a hard, dark exoskeleton. And he saw the old truth in her eyes, or more, a new truth.

She wasn't hiding; she was with him—totally, completely and utterly with him. He wasn't alone anymore.

She tipped her head and pressed her soft lips to his. He grabbed onto her coat sleeves, fisting the fabric, pulling her to him and kissing her back, like the kiss was life itself.

Something cracked inside him. A sensation he couldn't quite place...a type of lightness...

*Hope.*

"No!" he whispered into her lips.

Rumbles. A crash.

Sophia jerked up her head. "What was that?"

It was his despair fading. "No," he said. His despair and hopelessness was what cemented the very atoms of the Tangle.

"What?"

"I'm feeling hope again," he said.

"But that's good, baby."

"It's not. The Tangle is fused with my despair. It won't stay up."

As if in reply, a section of ceiling crashed down nearby.

"You have to go!" he said.

More moans sounded from above. Pebbles started coming loose and hurtling down as the big cannibal set his foot onto their side. Sophia moved to cover Robert with her body. He loosened his hold on her. He had to make her save herself. "Get out."

Three gun blasts echoed out. Sophia gasped and straightened.

Robert could see one sleepwalker draped over the ridge, the others had disappeared. And a new head rose up. Gray hair in a prim little ponytail.

Jordan the disillusionist therapist?

Was he hallucinating? Robert had met her once. Of course she didn't know he was the Monk.

"Jordan!" Sophia screamed. "Help me! Help us!" Another figure rose up—another disillusionist Robert recognized. Shelby. Grimness, if he recalled. They were responding to the beacon he'd had Sophia punch in—he hadn't imagined it would have any kind of reach beyond the Tangle. Then again, the direction from which they came...had they been in the interior of the Tangle?

With a dark look Sophia averted her eyes from Shelby. Had Shelby done something to Sophia? Or had Sophia done something to Shelby?

Jordan was already scrambling down. Shelby came after her.

Sophia stood. "Please! He's trapped. If we can just get this thing off him."

The three women shouldered the boulder, rocking it. The pain was unbelievable and he screamed as the enormous weight lifted off. More crashes around them. Parts of the Tangle.

"Just get me down there," he said. "I can still reinforce this place."

"He needs to touch the floor," Sophia said. "Or this whole place comes down." She wrapped one of his arms around her shoulder, and he put another around Shelby and they started down.

Robert tried to help with his good leg; he couldn't feel his other one, though he was dimly aware of it banging over the rocks.

"You are structural interface," Shelby said, not looking at Sophia. Thick accent. He'd forgotten she was Russian or something. They got him to the concrete gulley by the ATV, and he lay back, pressing his palms to the rough surface, sending force fields through the key planes and supports of the mammoth multi-turnpike. He needed to place the force fields before he lost consciousness. So many people in the Tanglelands. He couldn't let them die.

From the edge of his awareness he understood that Jordan was pulling things out of the ATV and that Shelby was yelling at Sophia about the phone. "Only disillusionists have phone with beacon. Not you." She accused Sophia of stealing the phone from Carter, demanded to know the whereabouts of Carter...who was Carter again? It was all so confusing. There was so much bitterness between the two women. He wanted it to stop.

"The phone's mine," Robert grated out.

Silence. They were looking down at him.

"You have no right either," Shelby said. "Is disillusionist's phone. You are not disillusionist."

"No?" Jordan set a stretcher next to him. "We haven't met all of them have we?" She scrutinized his face. "The Monk, I presume."

Robert nodded.

"The Monk," Shelby whispered.

He knew what they were thinking—that they'd finally met the dangerous Monk, the pointlessness and despair man. Except he was feeling hope again. His despair was useless as a weapon if he didn't have an overwhelming amount of it.

Sophia appeared at his side, eyes shining with tears. Was he losing consciousness? Jordan was berating them and barking orders. She wanted him on the stretcher. He felt fingers under his shoulders, his hips, fingers poking his flesh, lifting.

H E DIDN'T KNOW HOW MANY DAYS HE WAS IN AND OUT OF consciousness. He remembered doctors and beeps and tubes. Kind nurses. Being awake and so tired. Being awake and in pain. Staring at the ceiling, all alone in the night, thinking about her.

But he was awake now. Alert even. The room came into focus and there she was, sitting by his side, absorbed in her sketching.

*Sophia.*

Silently he watched her, enjoying the sound of a colored pencil scratching on a sketchpad. He hadn't heard it for such a long time, but he remembered it well, and he welcomed the familiarity and warmth it added to the hospital's buzz of machinery. She seemed so bright, somehow—not just her bright red hair, or her silky shirt, but she seemed to him to glow with a kind raw strength.

As if she felt his eyes on her, she lifted her head. "You're awake."

"Yes."

She gave him a playful look. "How long have you been awake?"

"I don't know…"

"Oh, Robbie." She put down her sketchbook and came over. "How do you feel? Can I get you anything?"

So many questions. He shook his head, unsure how to answer.

She touched the bed. "Can I?"

"Yes." That was all he really wanted. Her there.

She lowered herself down, carefully, so as not to disturb him and his suspended leg, which was caged in a complicated-looking set of rods and joints. Dimly, he recalled a nurse telling him about it.

She winced. "Jesus, look at that crazy thing. Are there hydraulics in there?"

"God, it's good to see you," he whispered.

"Seriously, how do you feel?"

"Better," he said. "I guess."

She smoothed her hand over his forehead, a little like a mother, and a little like a lover. "You scared me. And everyone." She swallowed something back.

He'd lost a lot of blood. He'd almost lost the leg. Somebody medical had told him that. "I know," he said.

"They didn't let me see you forever, but they won't keep me away now. Try to get rid of me and watch what happens." She straightened his sheets. "You're going to be okay."

He nodded. He knew he would. He felt such hope now. Like a welcome new guest.

"Here." She held a cup with a straw in front of him and he sipped, and then she put it aside. "Jesus Christ. The Monk. All this time it's you."

"*Was* me."

She knit her coiffed brows. "I'm so sorry, Robert. I'm just so, so sorry."

He shook his head. "Don't be. It was my journey. Mine."

"Nevertheless."

He felt such a sense of lightness, remembering how she'd used to say that—whatever the obstacle, the objection, she'd always just cross her arms. *Nevertheless.* She took his hand and they just sat there. Even the hospital sounds seemed to recede against her strong presence. He was feeling more awake, too. The water had helped.

"Does it hurt?"

She meant his leg, but he was thinking about how much he still loved her. "It feels good right now, but it doesn't always."

"Is there anything I can do? Anything you want?"

He didn't know how to answer that. He wanted it not to hurt.

She narrowed her eyes. "Are you thinking of curly fries?"

He laughed hoarsely. "Definitely not."

The way she looked at him now, he knew what she imagined he was thinking. He pressed a hand onto her thigh, not at all seriously, considering his condition.

"This is a hospital, Mister. Anybody could walk in and see."

"Is that such a big problem for a memory revisionist?"

Sophia bit her lip. He didn't know why he said it. He didn't mean to hurt her, but he wasn't one to gloss over something.

"I'm done with that."

"Done?" he asked. "Meaning, never again?"

"Yeah, I'm just off it." She smoothed her hand over the back of his. "Hey, if they walk in, they walk in. Let them see and remember. Let everyone remember everything. Let the chips fall where they may. That's my new thing, baby."

He stared, amazed. The fact that she was making light of it showed him what a big thing it was. Here was a highcap renouncing her power. "That's huge, Sophia."

"If four days is huge." She shrugged. "But this is the longest I've gone. It's hard and kind of a bummer, but it's honest. And when I get in bed, I feel good that the day was true." She touched the cage around his leg. "This is all traction stuff?"

"And then I think they're going to put in titanium and pins and lord knows what."

"Hopefully not the skeleton of an old farm silo."

He smiled.

"I can't believe I never recognized the Tangle for what it was. I looked at it every day—I can't believe I didn't see it. But I've been over there a lot. I've been looking at it a lot these past few days."

"I wish you wouldn't."

"I like to. Why wouldn't I?"

"It needs to be destroyed. Evacuated and destroyed."

"Hell no," she said. "I mean, yeah, it's messed up, Robert." She smiled. "It's messed up in a totally awesome way."

"No."

"It's awesome. It's a part of your story, and a little bit our story." She smoothed her hand along his arm. "I don't want it to be erased. I say, fight for it. Punch through to the other side of it and find its transformative possibilities. I know you can find a way to make the Tangle something new and true and more itself. This whole goddamn city has been in darkness and despair, and the Tangle has been a symbol of that for people.

You would erase that?"

He caught her gaze, held it. She hadn't changed, he realized. She'd discovered herself. He felt like he was discovering her now, too. "Do it with me," he said. "Let's work on it together. Let's work together again."

"What? You would want to? After..."

"The revising bit was never you, Sophia. To run from the truth. It's not you. I know you."

"You don't," she said. "I have so much to make up for. You would be shocked to know some of the unforgivable things I've done. What I've stolen from people. I have a lot of big things to make right. I'm meeting with Shelby later on today—I have something to make right with her. I mean, you would be appalled."

He wound his fingers in hers. "Let me be appalled then. Just don't shut me out. Be anything but don't shut me out."

"I want to earn back your love."

"You have it already, dude."

Her eyes shone with tears. She tried to speak, then stopped a few times. His Sophia, she hated to cry. "Robbie," she said. "Is this a ploy to get curly fries?"

"No."

She shook her head, laughing, trying to shake off the cry, and then she nestled down next to him. They stayed lying like that, just silent together. Being together. They were back.

She kissed his cheek, a dry little kiss that was heaven.

# Fire & Frost

# Speed Mating

JESSICA SIMS

# Speed Mating

ESTRELLA SAT IN THE WAITING ROOM OF HER ALPHA'S AUTO repair garage and tried not to throw up her lunch.

It was just nerves causing her stomach to churn, but that didn't help matters. She perched on the edge of the plastic chair, sipping water from a Styrofoam cup and trying to distract herself from the sense of helplessness she felt.

A shadow fell over her. A pair of jeans and workman's boots moved into her line of vision, and Estrella almost choked on her water. She looked up and saw Vic towering over her seat. Massive, hulking Vic, who never failed to intimidate despite the fact that they were both the same height—six foot two. She always felt small around Vic, though. Maybe it was the immense breadth of his muscles or his thick arms sleeved with tattoos. Or maybe it was the fact that his usual expression seemed to be a displeased frown when she was around.

That frown was on his face at the moment as he wiped his fingers with a greasy rag.

"Morning, Estrella," he said casually, his attention more on his hands than her face. "You wanted to see me?"

She got to her feet, ignoring the eyes that glanced in her direction when she unfolded her legs and stood to her full height. She was a tall woman, healthy and muscular thanks to her liger background, but she wasn't dainty like human women. She never would be. Most men were intimidated by her size, which made it difficult to get a date. Add in the liger thing and she seemed doomed to live a life of solitude.

*Well, until now,* she thought, her gut clenching again.

Of course, why she was obsessing over her appearance at a time like this made no sense. It just went to show how incredibly distracted she was by…her situation. Oh, god, she had a *situation.*

She felt like throwing up all over again.

"Yes. I did. I…need to talk." When he continued to look at her with that patient-only-because-I-have-to-be gaze, she added, "In private. Please."

He gestured to the back office and she headed there.

Estrella didn't come in to visit Vic often. The were-tigers were a more loosely-formed clan of shifters than most, but they still got together several times a month for meetings and just general bonding. Being the only liger in the vicinity—hell, in the entire state—she didn't exactly 'blend' with the rest of her temperamental, fierce clan. She was only half tiger, but she fit in more with them than with the lions, who didn't welcome her at all. But even at the gatherings, Estrella hung back, quiet and watchful. The tiger clan didn't mind her around as long as she didn't cause trouble.

And she went out of her way to not cause trouble.

Vic's office was a small, glass-walled room at the back of the shop. It boasted a desk covered in scattered, smudged paperwork, a fan, and the world's oldest computer monitor. He moved to the far side of the desk and sat. "Let's make this fast. I've got someone dropping off an engine rehaul, and I'm going to need the time."

"This won't take long," Estrella said nervously, sitting down in the chair across from him.

He picked up a pencil, grabbed a stack of paperwork, distracted. Vic waved a hand in her direction, indicating that she should begin.

She swallowed hard. The words stuck to the roof of Estrella's mouth, and she stared at him mutely as he checked over a purchase order. His dark hair was sweaty at the temples but attractive. He was tanned, and his jaw (and neck) were wide. He looked like a big, mean bruiser. He wasn't, but that didn't make her feel any better.

When she didn't speak, he glanced up and gave her an impatient look. "Well?"

Now or never. She forced the words out of her throat. "I'm going into heat."

The pencil snapped.

Estrella didn't wince. She didn't even flinch. She just sighed, heavily. "I know."

He rubbed his jaw for a few minutes, saying nothing and clearly trying to compose himself. "Well. This wasn't the conversation I was expecting to have this morning."

Now she was genuinely confused. "What were you expecting this to be about?"

"I was expecting," Vic began, then cleared his throat and continued, "to hear that you'd taken an interest in someone in the clan."

She snorted.

He scowled. "I'm serious."

"So am I. They haven't shown the slightest interest in me, and you know it."

"They're tigers. You're tiger."

"No, I'm *liger*. Big, overgrown crossbreed of lion and tiger, remember?" She'd never forgotten that she didn't feel as if she belonged with the tigers. They'd been welcoming enough, but wary, and she suspected that the only reason they'd been open to her joining them was because she was female and they only had one other in their clan. But then again, she was sterile. All ligers were more or less 'mules' because of the crossbreeding, and they couldn't have children. At least, that was what she had always been told.

So why bring a sterile woman into a clan? It didn't make sense, and she'd never been able to figure it out, hence her unease around the other tigers. If she wasn't mate material because she was barren, what was she? Just a pair of bouncy tits to have around to look at?

Not an endearing thought.

Not that it mattered. Most of the tiger clan? Just not her type. They were too cocky, a little too confident, and with the exception of Vic, she was pretty much the only one over six feet tall.

She never knew how to interpret Vic, either. He always seemed to be scowling and bad tempered about something, but he was still courteous to her. It was a mystery.

"Big, overgrown, *sterile* crossbreed, I could have sworn," Vic drawled. "You sure about this heat thing?"

"I know how to interpret my own body, thank you," she said, trying to keep the growl out of her throat. "I've been feeling...things. Different things. It doesn't take a genius to figure out what it's leading up to." Things like waking up with her nipples erect, her hands between her thighs, and a pulsing in her blood. Things like her libido revving at the sight of a man's tight ass. Things like a constant, all-over sensitivity to her skin.

And she was moody as hell. She bared her teeth at him in annoyance.

He regarded her with a stern expression. "Feeling things?"

"I'm flippin' horny all the time," she exploded at him. "Is that what you want me to admit? I could rub one off against just about anything or anyone that walked past, and nothing helps. It gets worse every day." When he continued to regard her, she added, "And I'm a bit moody."

"A bit?"

"A bit."

He rubbed his jaw again, looking for a moment as if he wanted to smile, then thought better of it. "I don't smell anything yet. How long do you think you'll have? We need to make plans."

Her face turned bright red. This was the conversation she'd come here to have, but at the words *"I don't smell anything yet"* her mind had frozen. Was he going to *smell* her when she went into heat? Ugh. What did it smell like? God, she didn't want to know. "I'm not sure. This is my first time in heat."

Vic set down the broken pencil and linked his hands behind his head, all enormous biceps and tattoos. Her mouth went dry at the sight. Vic had such big, strong arms that he clearly worked out. A lot. Most of the tiger clan tended towards bulk, but Vic carried it like an Olympian. She... liked all that muscle. Quite a bit.

*Down, girl,* she told her libido. *He's the alpha. No, no.*

Lord knew that if any man flexed in front of her, she'd drop her panties to the ground in a flash, unable to control herself until her heat passed. It sucked.

"Are you going to have it?"

"Huh?"

A momentary flash of annoyance crossed his face. "You're going to be in heat," he said, words crisp and succinct as he sat forward, hands moving to the desk (and no longer flexing so attractively). "Heat means one thing—you're fertile. Are you going to have the child?"

"I…don't know." She raised a hand to stop him. "Before you can give me the spiel about how having a child has the potential to impact the entire clan, I want to remind you that it's my uterus, and I'll do what I want with it—or not. If I decide to have a child, it's going to be my idea, not anyone else's."

He scowled. "I don't care what you do. I just need to know so we can plan accordingly."

"Oh." That had gone a little smoother than she'd thought. For some reason, she'd anticipated…a protest. Shifter children were rare enough that an unattached female going into heat was a big deal. A heat only happened a few times in a shifter's life, and each time was impossible to predict. A woman would have no way of knowing how many times she'd go into heat in her life. And if she used birth control and rode out the heat? It was impossible to predict if she'd ever go into heat again.

It was a gamble. Worst of all, Estrella was single. She didn't even have a romantic interest. All she had were some rather short tiger clan cousins and…Vic.

Her stomach went queasy with nerves again.

"If you decide to have this child, do you have a father in mind? Tiger, I hope?"

"It doesn't have to be tiger," she protested. "I just want someone that will love the child and care for it."

"Tiger is preferable—"

"*My* uterus," she warned.

He gave her a piercing look. "Anyone in the clan would be thrilled to become a father and to take you as a mate."

She rolled her eyes. "If I decide to get pregnant, I'm going to pick the man I like the most, since we'll be tied through the child. I don't want to leave things to chance and just assume that the right guy will be around when the heat hits me. If I do this, it's going to be planned in advance. Right guy, right place, right time. I want my baby to be bred off of the best possible father. Just because I'm going into heat doesn't mean I can't have control of this."

This time, his mouth quirked, as if he were amused by her declaration. "It sounds like you've already decided."

"Maybe," she said defensively. "But if I can't find the right guy, I'm not going to go through with it."

"You'll need someone," he pointed out. "Pregnancy or not, the heat's still going to happen."

Her face flushed. "Yes, I know. Someone'll do regardless." And if it wasn't someone she could desire and respect, well, a lot of alcohol in advance would probably do the trick. There was no way around the situation—it had to be dealt with.

"I'm here to help you, Estrella. Know that." The look in Vic's dark eyes was intense. "You're part of my clan and we take care of our own."

"Thank you. I appreciate that, Vic."

"How much time do you think we have? Honest answer. Think you can hold out until the next week?"

Like she was directing her ovaries. But she didn't feel desperately horny yet. Not yet. Way hornier than normal, yes…but it wasn't dire. "I think I have at least until then. Maybe a bit longer."

"Good. I'm going to put the others on alert and instruct them to be ready to leave the territory at a moment's notice. The last thing you want is five horny tigers showing up on your doorstep when the time comes."

Well. In actuality, that didn't sound so bad. But she knew that was just the heat talking. "Thank you, Vic. I appreciate it."

"Quit thanking me. We're clan. That's what we do." He picked up his phone, and then paused. "You don't have anyone in mind? You sure? You can tell me."

She spread her hands in a helpless gesture. "I'm clueless."

He grunted. "Fine. You'll tell me who you choose?"

She nodded.

"Keep me posted, then."

* * *

S O SHE WAS GOING TO DO THIS AFTER ALL.

Estrella exhaled as she left Vic's office, her hand straying to her stomach. She'd gone in there to argue with him about how it was her body and her right, and she'd ended up going on and on about the father of her child as if things were a given. Maybe they were.

In a week or so, her entire life was going to change. Damn. She'd best get started.

"M AN, YOU'RE SO FREAKING LUCKY."

Estrella picked up a fry and gave her friend an inquisitive look. "What makes you say that?"

"Look at you. You're all boobs and legs and you're eating a burger and fries." Jayde Sommers stabbed at her salad with a vicious move. "If I smell one of those fries, I'm going to gain a pound. But not you. And now on top of this, you're going into heat." She shook her head. "Some people have all the luck."

"I don't feel very lucky right about now," Estrella confessed, grabbing a salt-shaker and dousing her food with it. "I don't have a guy, remember?"

Jayde waved her fork dismissively. "You're gorgeous. Someone'll turn up."

"I'm six foot two. Do you know how hard it is to find someone that's going to date a woman that's taller—and occasionally broader—than he is? Do you know how long it's been since I've had a date? Four years."

"Maybe that's why you're going into heat," Jayde said, waggling her eyebrows suggestively at her friend. "It's a desperate cry for attention from your girl parts. They figure if they don't speak up soon, they'll be forever covered in cobwebs."

"Oh please," Estrella said with disgust. "Lots of people go a long time between dates."

"Four years?"

She bit down on a fry and ignored Jayde. Okay, so her track record wasn't great and four years was a long time. A really long time. But what was she supposed to do? Fling herself at any man over six foot three that passed her way? Jayde probably thought that was a good idea.

But then again, her friend had never had trouble getting dates. Her problem was keeping them once they got an earful of her acid tongue.

Estrella sighed. "I just don't have any likely prospects to be a father."

Jayde's hand crept over the table and stole a french fry from the corner of Estrella's plate. "What about that sexyhot alpha of yours?"

"Vic?"

"Tattoos, right? Dangerous looking? Mmmm." Jayde's approval was practically a purr. "I wouldn't mind going into heat with him around. He could put a mate mark on me any time."

For some reason, Estrella squirmed in her seat. Hearing Jayde consider Vic in a sexual way made her feel…weird. Possessive. Which was stupid. And the mate mark thing? She hadn't even considered that. Shifters marked their mates on the neck with a love bite that only other shifters could see. It would brand her as someone's property, someone's cherished mate, and chase off all others.

Holy shit, she wasn't in this for just a baby. She had to consider a *mate*, too. Estrella swallowed hard, then shook her head. "Not Vic. He's not interested in me like that. I don't think he finds the liger thing appealing."

"Who does?" At Estrella's glare, Jayde chuckled and stole another fry. "I'm kidding, I'm kidding. In all seriousness, would it be so bad to ask your alpha to sire a kid? You know he's responsible, right? He's got a business. You'd never have to hunt the guy down for child support or worry if your kid has a place in the clan."

It all sounded nice, but Vic hadn't shown a bit of interest in her. If anything, he'd looked alarmed when she'd given him her pronouncement. And while Vic was attractive in a scowly, aggressive sort of way, she didn't plan on dragging someone into this 'heat' thing with her. She felt trapped enough as it was.

"Not Vic," she said one more time, and firmly. "I'll have to find someone else. I don't suppose you know of anyone?"

Jayde shook her head, reaching into her purse. "Nope, but I know someone you can call." She pulled out her wallet and produced a small business card, holding it out to Estrella.

She took it from Jayde, examining the small half-moon logo. "Midnight Liaisons. A dating agency? Seriously?"

"A dating agency for, you know." She sniffed meaningfully as if pointing out her unique shifter scent, and gave Estrella a firm look. "You should call them."

"I don't know. Like they're going to have more luck finding me a guy who wants to be a dad as of next week?"

"Just do it," Jayde told her. "I've gone out on lots of dates through them. There's a lot out there if you don't mind a little....variety in the gene pool."

"Mind? Remember that you're talking to a liger?"

Jayde pretended to crane her neck to stare up at Estrella. "Oh, I didn't forget."

"ALL RIGHT, LADIES! GATHER AROUND AND WE'LL BEGIN." THE too-chipper blonde at the back of the room waved a hand tipped with hot-pink nails, indicating that they should all move closer to her.

Estrella took a deep sigh to settle her nerves. She got up from the empty table she was occupying and moved to the center of the room, in front of the blonde. She counted five other women clustered nearby, and sized up the competition. Badger, rat, lynx, fox, and harpy, if her nose told her anything. Okay, well, she was the largest predator of the group. She supposed that was good.

She was a foot taller than anyone except the harpy, whom she only towered over by six inches. Damn. She was going to stick out like a sore thumb.

"Hi everyone! My name is Ryder, and I'll be the coordinator for our event tonight." The event hostess flashed them all a dimpled, candy-pink smile, her big blue eyes bright with excitement. "For those of you that have never participated in the 'Speed Mating' event, I'll go over the rules of our game very quickly. Does everyone have their name badge?"

Estrella touched the "Hello, My Name Is #6" badge stuck to her sweater, trying not to feel like an idiot. An optimistic idiot, which made things worse, because this was a set-up that seemed bound for failure, and yet the dating coordinators had assured her that they had great success with these kinds of events.

So she was hopeful. The more she thought about it, the more she wanted this possible baby, which meant finding someone who could be the father she needed for her child…within the space of about a week. Someone whom she could see sharing such a big part of her life with. Someone who wouldn't gross her out when she thought about sharing her heat with them. God.

"Each one of you has been assigned a number," Ryder said in a chirpy voice that was almost shrill as she strove to speak over the group. "You're going to sit at your numbered tables and one man will join each of you. You will have the chance to talk for five minutes, and then I'm going to ring the bell. When I ring the bell, each man is going to get up and move to the next table, and we'll cycle through all of our bachelors in that manner." She held up a small scorecard. "You'll have a card at each of your tables. If you like the man, make a mark under his number. You'll be turning in your card to me. If you and your date both mark your card as interested in the other, we have a match and I'll be contacting you both to coordinate a date. If there's no match, you can always come back next week. Any questions, ladies?"

The group was silent. Estrella wondered if they were half as impatient as she was. She just wanted to get things moving.

"All right, then! Please take a seat at your table and once everyone is ready, we'll bring in the men."

Estrella found table number six in the corner. A bottle of wine had been left, uncorked, on the table. That was nice—get them all boozed up before the men came in so the odds of making a match were better. She poured herself a glass and tipped it back, drinking quickly. Thanks to her liger metabolism, she'd need a couple more glasses downed at the same speed to even give her a bit of a buzz. It seemed to help her frame of mind, though.

She poured another glass and sipped as she picked up the card, examining it. There were no names—not surprising, since she was wearing a sticker that said her name was 'Six,' but it seemed a bit silly and juvenile to her. What was the harm in sharing names? She'd be able to tell what kind of shifter each man was as soon as he sat down, thanks to her enhanced senses. It'd be a parade of men—and a variety of shifters if the female pool was any indication.

For some reason, that thought made her uneasy, and she reached for the wine again, pouring herself another glass. Maybe she needed to get good and sauced before this started. It'd probably be her last opportunity to get drunk before the baby thing, or at least it would be if she got a decent date out of this.

The bell rang. "Date number one is about to arrive, ladies," Ryder announced. "As soon as everyone is seated, the timer will begin. Remember, you'll have five minutes for each date."

Estrella finished draining her wine and began to pour another glass as men filed into the back room of the restaurant. Each table was sequestered away from the others, and no one wandered too close. She could have craned her neck and peered at everyone, but that would have seemed overly obvious—and eager—so she forced herself not to. She flared her nostrils instead, trying to pick out individual scents. She smelled cougar, and the harpy, and…garlic bread. Lots and lots of garlic bread. Damn it. Now she was hungry.

A familiar scent enveloped her nostrils a split second before a massive, hulking form pulled the chair out and sat down across from her. Estrella looked up in surprise to see Vic, his hair still wet from a shower, black t-shirt stretched tight over his chest.

She sputtered at the sight of him, nearly spraying wine across the white linen tablecloth. When she was able to choke down a gasp of breath, she wheezed, "What are you doing here?"

He scowled blackly. "I came to supervise and that horrible little blonde insisted that I sit down on these stupid dates because she had someone cancel."

"Supervise? Excuse me?"

"Supervise," he agreed. "You're in a special situation, so the agency reached out to your alpha just to be on the safe side."

"Oh, I didn't know that."

"You should have. It was in the paperwork."

That would assume that she had actually paid attention to the paperwork. She'd been a little too fidgety to sit and read the ten-page disclosure. Estrella fiddled with her wine glass. "Well, it's nice of you to take an interest, I suppose."

"I have to take an interest. Your child is going to be part of my clan. I'll be his—or her—alpha." His dark gaze settled on her face. "Even if you can't find a decent father for your child, your alpha will be at your side."

Tears welled up in her eyes. That was so sweet. Hell, now she was getting emotional. Her own father hadn't stuck around to take care of her mother, and her mother had never forgotten it. Estrella couldn't forget it either. "What if I find a different kind of shifter? A fox or a wolf or something? Then my child will only be one eighth tiger—"

"Still a tiger," he told her firmly. "Or I wouldn't be here."

For some reason, that made her feel warm with acceptance. She'd never seen this side of Vic. He'd never told her that he didn't care how much tiger blood someone had running through their veins. She'd always felt like such an outsider. But, looking at his determined face, she wondered how much of it was truly real and how much of her insecurities she had projected on the others.

She couldn't know. "Thank you," she said softly again.

"Don't thank me. Just keep me away from that matchmaker woman before she signs me up for another event."

Estrella smothered the laugh bubbling in her throat, because she knew Vic wouldn't appreciate it. "So Ryder talked you into speed dating?"

"Speed *mating*," he corrected. "And that woman doesn't seem to understand the meaning of the word 'no'."

"I'm sure it comes in handy for her job." Estrella could just imagine the small, perky blonde trying to deal with the assortment of customers the agency probably saw over a regular basis. "Cheer up, Vic. Maybe you'll find yourself a nice mate."

He gave her a look of disgust and put his hand on the empty spare wine glass at the table. "I'm not here for me."

"But you're not mated."

His face grew hard. "Like I said, I'm not here for me."

"You're sure taking this baby thing seriously."

The look he gave her was tense. "I take the welfare of everyone in the clan very seriously."

"Yeah, but do you supervise all of them? Hey, you want to come and supervise the actual consummation? You can pinch hit if the guy I pick can't perform. I—"

The words died in her throat as Vic's hand clenched on the wine glass and it shattered in a spray of glass. He released it and shook his hand off, then glared at her so fiercely that it made her pause, mid joke.

All right. That was a 'back the hell off' look if she'd ever seen one. Estrella raised her hands, admitting defeat. Silence fell between them, seconds ticking past as a waiter rushed over with an apology and gathered up their glass covered tablecloth.

"Sorry," she told him. "Bad joke."

"Very bad."

Silence again.

He gave the restaurant a derisive look, as if the white linen tablecloths seemed out of place instead of the other way around. After another uncomfortable moment, he flared his nostrils. "There is apparently a harpy here."

She smiled. Safe territory—back to mocking the speed mating. "Well then, that should make me look pretty good in comparison. I'm glad she's here."

He gave her an odd glance. "Estrella, you always look good. If these idiots can't see it, I—"

The bell clanged loudly.

"Time's up," Ryder called out in her high pitched voice. "Everyone please move to the next station!"

Estrella stared at Vic with wide, wondering eyes as he got up from the table and left. "Have fun," he muttered. "Pick someone good."

She gazed at his retreating back, still stunned into silence. What had he been about to say? Did he really think she looked good or was he just humoring the broody female about to go into heat? And why did that make her entire body tingle with awareness? She stood up, intending to follow him to his next station, find out exactly what he had been about to tell her.

A man moved to her table, and the scent of were-badger filled her nostrils. He was short, rotund, and had a thick shock of black curls that stood up from his head. He looked like more of a hedgehog than a badger. She towered over him by at least a foot.

He wore a name badge that read, "Hello, My Name is #5" and he was blinking up at her, slightly aghast.

"Hi," she said flatly, dropping back into her seat. "I'm number six."

"T-tall," he mumbled, putting his hand out to shake.

She bared her teeth and gave a feline snarl and was somewhat pleased to see him jerk backward. Good. She stopped snarling and forced a polite smile on her face. "Nice to meet you, too."

He stared at her in uncomfortable silence. Estrella scowled back, not wanting to put the effort into talking with the guy. After all, they both knew at a glance that this match-up would never happen. As she regarded him, he reached into his jacket pocket and patted the card, as if double-checking it, and she knew he couldn't wait to write down a 'hell no' next to her name.

She was too scary. Too predatory. And too tall. That was fine. Her baby deserved better than a were-badger for a daddy anyhow. She needed someone stronger and more her type. More protective and open-minded toward whatever her child would be. Like Vic.

Her eyes widened. Oh god. Why had she just thought about Vic again? It was simply nesting instinct, right? He'd told her that her child would be safe with him, so her brain was automatically filling in the blanks. That was all.

The waiter returned with a new tablecloth and more wine, which she was glad to see. Estrella wasted no time in refilling her wine glass and chugging the contents.

She emptied her glass and refilled it again. And then again. All the while the badger sat there and stared at her.

The bell rang again a short time later, and Estrella wasn't sad to see Number Five move on. She'd had just enough wine that she was feeling pleasantly tingly and just a little bit bold.

The next guy sat down. He was almost six foot—almost—and seemed decent looking, with sandy blond hair and tanned skin. Not bad. Not bad. She sniffed the air. Feline breed, though he was wearing enough cologne that it was hard for her to determine which one. This one had potential.

"Hi," he said with enthusiasm. "I'm #4 tonight. You must be #6. It's nice to meet you."

She took another sip of her wine and decided to skip all pretense. "I'm going into heat in less than a week," she told him baldly.

His face lit up like he'd just seen Christmas.

"And I've decided to have the baby," she added. "Want to be a daddy?"

His face fell. "Um…"

She snorted and poured herself another glass of wine. Why were these speed dates a whole five minutes long? She didn't need more than thirty seconds to take care of business.

B Y THE TIME THE BELL RANG THE FINAL TIME, ESTRELLA HAD polished off the entire bottle of wine (plus the refill bottle they'd brought her) and was feeling pretty good. Every single man who had sat at her table was a big fat dud, but at least there was the wine.

As Ryder came by, Estrella hiccuped and waved the card in front of Ryder's face. "Don't even bother with mine," she said, and was amused to find her words slurring just a bit. "It's blank."

"You didn't find anyone you wanted to mark down as a possible match?" Ryder asked, a bit dismayed as she snatched the card from Estrella's weaving hand. "The only way you can get a call-back on a date is if both you and the man select each other as potential matches."

"No match," Estrella said mournfully, tipping over the empty wine bottle in the hopes that there might be a hidden reserve. "They were all wrong for me." Except Vic, but god, everyone would think she was a weirdo if she put down her alpha as her only possible match. And if that ever got back to him, she'd never be able to look him in the eye again. "No match," she repeated. "Too bad."

Ryder tucked the card into the stack and shook her head. "Don't give up just yet. If you come in to the agency tomorrow, I'm sure we can find someone in the database that will be more appealing to you. We're just getting started on your dating journey," she finished with a perky, determined nod.

Estrella glared at her, sitting upright. "You don't understand." She got to her feet and raised her voice just a little when Ryder began to protest. "No, listen to me. I'm going into heat in less than a week. I have to find a baby daddy—"

"You're yelling," a husky voice murmured in her ear. Vic, behind her. "Use your inside voice, Estrella."

"I'm not," she began, then realized how quiet it was in the restaurant. Gone was the clink of forks and the low murmur of conversation. Okay, so maybe she'd been talking about being in heat a *leeeetle* bit too loud.

Just a hair. She shook her head, her shoulder-length hair slapping the face of her alpha. "Vic, you're so cruel."

"And you're drunk. Hitting the sauce while you still can?"

"Maybe. Or maybe I was just blown away by the amazing selection of dates tonight." When Ryder frowned, Estrella bared her teeth at her and was pleased to see the blonde stumble backward a step.

"And now you're just being mean," Vic said with amusement. "Come on, I'll drive you home."

Warm hands grabbed her around the waist. He felt so delicious against her that she sighed and closed her eyes, draping her arms around his neck. "Carry me?"

A low rumble of a chuckle, and then an arm went behind her knees and Estrella was lifted into the air, and Vic carried her out of the restaurant. He didn't even have to strain to carry her gargantuan form.

"See, that's what I need," she sighed.

"What's that?" he asked as they headed out the front door of the restaurant and into the parking lot. As soon as they left the building, cold, crisp air slammed into them. It carried the scent of winter underneath the usual city smells.

Winter would be good, since the heat made her feel so flushed all the time.

"What do you need, Estrella?" Vic repeated when she seemed lost in her own thoughts.

"Someone strong. A real guy. Not any of those losers in the speed dating." She inhaled and was surprised at how good Vic smelled. It had to be the heat that was causing her to want to bury her face against him and lick at the cords of his thick, brawny neck, right? Or the heat that made her want to rip off his shirt with her claws and trace the lines of those tattoos with her fingers? Run her hands over his flat stomach...

A hot pulse of need flashed through her, and the scent of her own desire rolled through her nostrils a moment before Vic stiffened.

"Estrella," he warned.

"It's the heat," she told him. "Just ignore it. I'm going to." She put her face against his shoulder. "See, this is me, ignoring the heat."

He grunted, though it sounded less amused this time.

One of the strands of his hair fascinated her. It kept touching his ear when he walked, and she wondered how soft it would be. Then she touched it, and of course it was gorgeously soft. She decided her baby should have soft hair, too. "You find anyone at the speed mating, Vic?"

"You were the only one there worth noticing," he commented in that same gruff voice.

Estrella sighed miserably. "There were two guys who were interested until they heard the baby part. Everyone wants the heat but nobody wants the ramifications."

"It's good that you're finding out now, 'Strella. Better now than after the baby is conceived."

Her eyes began to water with sudden, weepy, ridiculous, drunken tears. "I need someone who's going to be at my side the entire time. Someone responsible who wants me just as much as they want a baby."

"I know, sugar. I know."

She reached out and smacked him on the arm just as he put her down. "I'm not your sugar, Vic Barlow."

He chuckled and pulled out his car keys, ignoring her turn of mood. "You're also not crying anymore, which is all I wanted. Now get in. I'm driving."

Evil, evil man.


THE COLD FRONT THAT HAD ROLLED THROUGH NORTH TEXAS hadn't brought more than gusty winds and a light, gloomy drizzle, but Estrella appreciated it all the same. With the temperatures firmly in the upper thirties, she wouldn't be breaking into a heat-induced sweat every time she went outside. She thought she'd get hot flashes when she went through menopause; apparently she got them when her hormones were ramping up to eleven, too.

Since it was a nice day out—well, for her—Estrella walked to Vic's garage. It was only a few blocks away from the gym she worked at, and in Texas, that was practically neighbors. She took her jacket so her boss wouldn't ask questions, and then ditched it into her car as soon as she hit the parking lot.

As she walked, Estrella inhaled the scents of the city. She loved the sharp, crisp bite of the winter breeze. The only trees she could smell were junipers; everything else was bare and brown. The sky overhead was gray, which suited her mood quite well.

The hunt for the father of her child was not going so well.

Estrella shouldn't have been surprised. Hell, it was close to impossible to find a date under normal circumstances. Finding the perfect guy who also wanted to be a parent in the space of under a week? Impossible. Still, she wouldn't stop hoping. Something was going to have to come out of this heat, after all. Waiting wasn't an option. Already her ovaries felt like they'd climb out of her body at the sight of the next sexy guy who walked past.

Maybe a human? Vic would kill her. Totally and completely kill her. If she'd ever felt like an outcast because of her liger ancestry, it'd be nothing to how she'd be treated if she were a liger knocked up by a human. She sighed, feeling defeated, and kicked a nearby can instead of picking it up and tossing it in the garbage. As much as she'd felt like an outcast growing up because of her dual halves? There was no way she'd subject any child of hers to anything remotely close to that.

Like it or not, she had no ideas. That was why she was going to confront Vic and ask—no, beg—for his help. Her face flushed uncomfortably hot at the thought. *Vic, could you help me with my heat?*

Why did that make her flutter low in her stomach? Stupid heat made everything attractive, apparently, even her formidable, scowling, often-scary alpha.

Vic's Garage was busy, all the bay doors open and cars on the lifts as men moved under them. The scents of motor oil and rubber tires filled her nostrils, along with the scent of other tiger-shifters. Vic hired family first, and several of the Barlow clan worked here. The scents of so many tiger males made a low, rumbling purr start in her belly, and she had to pinch her arm to make her purring stop.

As she walked up to the garage, men stopped and stared at her. It was disconcerting, especially since the looks they were giving her weren't the typical looks that she expected a female in heat would get. She knew she was at her sexiest, so why were they all staring at her with a mixture of wariness and unease?

It was because she was a liger. It was stamped into every ounce of her being—different. Tiger women were normally tall and strong, but

Estrella was taller and stronger than everyone else. Hell, she was taller than most of the tiger men. What, did they think she'd hold them down and take advantage of them? Sully their innocence? An amused smile curved her mouth. Judging from the wariness on their faces, maybe they thought that after all. Ignoring the men, she headed into the waiting area of Vic's Garage, closing her eyes for the blast of heat that would keep the room a comfortable temperature for the human and not-going-into-heat customers.

She'd prepared for the heat wave of seventy-two degrees Fahrenheit inside, but she hadn't been prepared for the barrage of tiger scents as she opened the door. She was familiar with most of the clan; these smelled different.

Different tigers? In the Barlow territory? Her uterus gave an excited little quiver of anticipation. Estrella's fingers curled and she crossed her arms over her breasts, lest her nipples betray exactly how she was feeling. Three men sat at the far end of the waiting room, talking quietly amongst each other. Their backs were to her, but as the door closed behind her, they turned…and stood.

Three men. Black hair. Two were about her height; the third was taller than her by an inch or two. They were all her age.

Her mouth went dry.

The door to Vic's office opened. "'Strella. Good. You're here. You saved me a phone call. Come in so we can talk."

Her body protested leaving the men behind, but she forced herself to turn around and face Vic. Of course, as soon as he came into her sights, she was drawn to him like a magnet. God, he was strong and fierce. The liger side of her liked the thought of having a fierce mate. She needed a man who would stand up to her, take charge when she needed him to, defend their territory…

She clenched her fists, willing the thought to go away. Vic was not going to be her mate. *Not.* He'd be horrified if he knew she was fantasizing about him. Hadn't he said at the speed mating event that he wasn't looking for a mate? The last thing he needed was her coming on to him because she thought he'd make some good looking babies.

When she walked into the office, he shut the door behind her. She delicately flared her nostrils, taking in his scent. Oh hell, he smelled amazing. Like hand soap and a hint of sweat and axle grease under that. It shouldn't have been such a turn on, but her claws were threatening to come out. The heat was getting worse, and she was out of prospects at the moment. Surely that was why she was going wild for her alpha.

"Vic, I'm desperate," she blurted, and it came out breathier and far more erotic than she'd imagined.

He froze in place.

"Not like that," she amended quickly. At least, not *yet*. "I need your help. For the heat." Oh god, she was blushing. "Not like that, either," she said when he raised an eyebrow at her. "I mean, I need help finding someone—"

"I know. Sit."

His voice was commanding; she immediately moved to the nearest chair and plopped into it, curving her long legs underneath, waiting for him to speak.

"Last night after the speed mating, I made a few phone calls to the other tiger clans. Told them what we—what you—were looking for in a candidate. And while I can't guarantee that any of them are into a long-term relationship, I want you to at least have a few options for your child that don't involve hooking up with the nearest were-badger. Or worse, a human." He leveled a hard gaze at her.

She felt herself grow flushed, sweat breaking out on her forehead. "Am I that obvious?"

"Yes," he said bluntly. "But I'm glad you came to me."

So were her ovaries. Especially when he said the word 'came'. Estrella clenched a hand over her stomach.

"It's obvious you're going to go into heat very soon. I've sent the rest of the clan out of town for the week, just until we're sure that you've covered all your bases. I also talked to the lion alpha—since you're half of each—and he's sending his boys out hunting in East Texas just to be safe. Unless you had your eye on one of them?"

She shook her head. She knew the local lions and they hadn't exactly been friendly. Or accepting. They were not even a choice for her. Her child would be fully accepted by his or her clan.

"Okay then. I've flown three males from other tiger clans into town. I want you to take a few days and talk to each one of them. Let me know what your thoughts are. Find out which one is best for you and the baby."

Suddenly she was weepy. "You did this for me?"

"Of course. I'm your alpha. If you have a problem, you come to me, and we fix it. I'm here for you."

Tears flooded her eyes. God, she was emotional lately. But just hearing that from Vic, well…it was something she'd needed to hear. She'd never felt more alone than this last week, being treated like a leper amongst men. Knowing that Vic was going out of his way to make this as smooth for her as possible? It made her giddy with happiness.

It also made her incredibly emotional.

Vic noticed her blubbering, and came around his desk with a sigh. "Don't cry, 'Strella. I can't stand to see you upset."

"It's just…I'm always just…" *so alone*, she wanted to say, but the words lodged themselves in her throat. A tiger wouldn't know what it was like to be alone simply because you were born a half breed. As one of the Barlows, Vic wouldn't know what it was like to be abandoned by your father, lose your mother. She was always so *lonely*.

Until now.

He knelt in front of her chair and put his arms around her, awkwardly patting her back. She wrapped her arms around him and snuggled her head against his shoulder, tucking her nose against his neck. It was fast becoming her favorite position with him, because it allowed her to take the most furtive sort of sniff of his scent. Not just his scent, but his skin—

"Did you just sniff me?"

Estrella bolted backward, flushing. "It's the heat."

"Uh huh." He looked more amused than annoyed, though. "If you don't want to go through with this, just say so."

"I kind of don't have a choice. My vagina's already prepping for the Shifter Superbowl." And she sniffed, loudly.

He stiffened against her.

"Sorry."

"Just glad I wasn't holding any wine this time," he grumbled.

She gave a teary giggle at that.

"'Strella…You know I'm always here for you."

*Yeah, but my brain keeps going to weird, dirty places when you're trying to be supportive.* So she said nothing.

He gave her another little pat on the shoulder. "Why don't you go out and say hello to my cousins before you start crying again?"

She nodded, then impulsively reached out and hugged him again. Why had she ever thought Vic scary? Under that fearsome exterior was the heart of a big pussycat.

Literally.

It might have been her imagination, but the hug went on for longer than she'd expected. She pulled away and glanced up at his face. Same old Vic. Must have been her imagination.

"Thank you," she told him one more time.

He waved her toward the door, the look on his face grim.

As she stepped through the door, she could have sworn she heard something crash in the room. She turned around to look, but then tiger scents were in her nostrils, and she was surrounded by three young, virile tiger males, and Estrella forgot everything else.

I N WHAT COULD ONLY BE DESCRIBED AS THE WORLD'S MOST AWKWARD quadruple date, Estrella took the three men out to lunch at the local barbecue pit. Her stomach was growling for food, and barbecue was a favorite with shifters—you could put away a ton of meat and no one said a thing about it. Estrella drove, and when she offered to pay for lunch, no one put up a word of protest. For some reason, that stuck in her craw. This was feeling a bit like she was auditioning for stud service.

Well, hell. That was exactly what she was doing.

Estrella's heart sank. Vic had made it clear that the guys probably didn't want a relationship, but if she wanted a baby that would be fully tiger clan, fully accepted, these three were her best chance. So she smiled and listened politely as they talked.

Two of the men were brothers. Nelson Maher was an electrician, twenty-nine, and single. His brother Montgomery Maher was twenty six, an X-ray technician, and single.

She immediately crossed Montgomery off the list. Too many X-rays, she told herself. What if her baby came out with radiation poisoning? Worse, what if he'd fried his junk by standing too close to the camera? For some reason, the thought of having sex with a sterile man repulsed her. Hell, if she was going to have sex for fun's sake, she wanted someone more like Vic...

She shut down that train of thought immediately and turned to Nelson. "So, what do you like to do in your spare time?"

Estrella could have sworn he flexed, just a bit. "I do some rock climbing and work out at the gym," Nelson said between bites of barbecue. "I like to stay fit."

She brightened at that. "You do? That's terrific. Did Vic tell you? I teach yoga and fill in as the Zumba instructor at my gym."

Nelson gave his brother a sideways glance that seemed a bit too competitive, and turned his smile on her. "Well now, I like to do real exercising. You know, get a sweat going." That time, he definitely flexed. "Bench presses and the like."

She bristled at his tone. "I see." Well, she could cross Nelson off the list. Arrogant prick. Like the father of her child was going to be condescending about what she did for a living. She was probably in better shape than Nelson was, if his muscle—or lack thereof—was any indication. "You must have just started lifting recently," she said sweetly. "When will you start to see results?"

Nelson frowned.

Montgomery smothered a laugh behind a mouthful of barbecue, which made her appreciate him a bit more. Shame about the possible sterility.

She turned to the third man. Tall. A bit on the lean side but still fit. Quiet, but good looking enough. He had pleasant features and serious eyes. "You're not speaking," she told him, forcing the smile to stay on her face.

He gave her an almost shy nod. "Cory."

"That's a nice name," she said conversationally.

"Cory Janitor," Montgomery broke in with a smirk. "You want your kid to be named Janitor?"

"I...what? Really?" She gave Cory a startled look. His bright red flush told her everything.

Oh. Oh no. If she were picking men for selfish, silly reasons...a horrible last name was definitely up there on things to avoid, in case her child wanted to hyphenate their last names at a later date. "I'm sure there's nothing wrong with that," she said politely. "So what do you do for a living, Cory?"

He shrugged. "I'm a manager at Super Burger."

"When he's not smoking weed in his parents' basement," Montgomery said with a snort. Cory elbowed him and gave a nervous laugh.

These were her prospects? A misogynistic narcissist, a possibly sterile asshole, and a pothead with the last name of Janitor?

Three men and she didn't want any of them. Estrella didn't think the day could get any more depressing.


To BE FAIR—AND BECAUSE SHE DIDN'T HAVE ANY OTHER OPTIONS— she gave them the weekend. Against her better judgment, she went out on dates with all three and tried to make the best of things. After all, she didn't have to marry the guy, right? He just had to get her pregnant.

Even after her date, she couldn't stand Nelson. He was polite enough, and he held doors open for her and acted like a gentleman. He was also controlling and a bit too old fashioned for her taste. They'd gone to a restaurant—his pick, since her pick wasn't 'any good' according to him. Once there, he'd promptly ordered for her before she'd had a chance to look at the menu, and when she'd tried to order a cocktail, he'd told her that he didn't find it appropriate for ladies to drink in public.

Of course, when she'd snarled at him, he'd changed his tune.

Montgomery was not much better. They'd gone out to a restaurant; the exact same one that Nelson had taken her to. Once there, Montgomery had grilled her about his brother. Had she liked Nelson? Had he purchased her dinner or had they gone dutch? Did she think his brother was the better-looking one? Everything seemed to be a competition between the two of them, and that was a major turnoff for her. She just imagined trying to sleep with the man. He'd probably quiz her on his technique and ask her who her best had been. Nor did she want to subject her future child to a lifetime of his father's competitiveness.

Cory had taken her to a bowling alley, and they'd played a few games while chatting. To her surprise, she genuinely liked Cory. He was nice, low-key, and easygoing. He was also a pothead who lived in his parents' basement, but she supposed she couldn't have everything.

Too bad his last name was Janitor.

Cory was nice enough, but just because he was the lesser of three evils didn't mean that she wanted to have his baby. After the bowling date, she headed back to her apartment—alone—and stared at her phone, debating. After a moment, she sighed.

In desperation, she called the dating agency one more time.

In what seemed to be par for the course, she got Ryder's voicemail. "Hi there! You've reached the desk of Ryder St. James," a perky voice chirped. "I'm unavailable to take your call at the moment, but leave me a message and your account number and I'll call you back as soon as possible. Have a super day!"

"Hey, um, Ryder? I don't remember my account number, but this is Estrella Townsend. The liger that's about to go into heat. I'm guessing you don't have many of those at the agency so I'm hoping you'll remember who I am. Anyhow, I wanted to say that I didn't mark down anyone on my card at the speed mating the other night, but…" She sighed, hating herself for even bringing it up. "But I was wondering if anyone marked me down. If so, can you let me know? I'm willing to reconsider dating anyone who put me down. Anyhow, call me back." Estrella rattled her number off and then hung up, hating that she'd had to stoop to this.

Pickings were definitely slim and getting slimmer all the time. Maybe she needed to make a list of attributes she was looking for in a man, and then she could narrow down her (rather sparse) selection. After all, she could always go turkey baster and raid a sperm bank or something, she supposed, but that wouldn't help with her heat much. She needed to have sex, period.

Her apartment was too warm. Fanning herself with a notebook, Estrella opened all the windows, letting the icy winter air breeze in. Sweat beaded on her forehead. Maybe she could make her list while having a nice, relaxing, chilly soak in the tub to bring her internal temperature down a bit.

Estrella undressed and filled the tub, adding some bubble bath. She gave a soft sigh of pleasure when she soaked her limbs in the cool water. It immediately felt better. Picking up her paper again, she tapped her lip with the pen and considered.

If she was man-shopping for herself, she liked tall men. Dark hair.

Muscles. A little bit dangerous. Someone with a take-charge kind of personality who wouldn't be overbearing or condescending. She liked a man who knew what he wanted, but trusted her enough to make her own decisions and wouldn't try to override her. She wrote down a few notes, then considered. Tattoos? For some reason she'd found tattoos sexy lately...

She froze in the icy water, and stared at her list. *Dark hair. Muscles. Tall. Tattoos. Take charge.*

Vic. It was all Vic.

Damn it. She tossed the notebook and pen to the far end of the bathroom and sank into the tub, cheeks flushing with embarrassment. She supposed she could lie to others but not to herself. Did she really want Vic that badly? When had her appreciation for him turned to full-blown desire?

It was bad to want your alpha. Bad bad bad. It mucked up a relationship that she couldn't afford to muck up. Things were awkward enough for her as one of the few females in the tiger clan. Mix in her liger heritage and things were already weird. Crushing on her alpha? Just made things even worse.

Her hand slid to her belly under the water, and she stared down at her naked body through the bubbles. She'd always thought she was pretty sexy, if it weren't for the height thing. Would a guy like Vic find someone like her attractive? Estrella raised one long leg into the air, studying it. Her muscles were tight, her skin tanned. She had a good body. Average face, maybe, but a good body.

Now Vic, he had an *amazing* body. She pictured his big, muscular arms, rippling with tattoos, and a shiver of desire flashed through her. Her hand slid lower, to her sex.

It was just the heat that was making her so turned on, she told herself. Passing phase. Even so, she pictured Vic's strong, muscular arms and her fingers slid between the lips of her sex, finding her clit. She was already aching with need; the heat gave her a hair-trigger reaction to anything sexual. A quick stroke of her fingers and she sucked in a breath. This... was not helping her ridiculous crush on Vic.

And yet. She couldn't resist sliding her fingers over her clit again and then circling the sensitive bud with sudden, sure moves. The heat that was making her crazy unleashed like a hurricane, and within seconds, she was gasping through the waves of a powerful orgasm, her other hand clenching on the side of the tub, splashing water over the side with the force of her movements.

The force of it rocked her to her core. She'd had sex before. She'd definitely had orgasms. But never quite like that. All that for a few quick brushes of her fingers? Jeez. When she finally found the man to father her child, she was going to tear him apart.

That left out humans and smaller shifters for sure. Estrella sank deeper into the frigid waters. Her choices seemed to be narrowing by the minute.

B Y THE TIME SHE FINALLY GOT OUT OF THE TUB, HER APARTMENT was a comfortable 42 degrees, her orgasm was a distant memory, and her skin was beginning to itch with desire again. Instead of sating the urge inside her, the furtive masturbation in the tub had only made things worse. As she toweled off her skin, she groaned every time the terry-cloth of the fabric brushed against her.

This was not going to work. She needed to burn off some energy. Best cure for that as a shifter was to either have lots of sweaty sex, or to shift and go for a run in animal form.

And since she couldn't do anything about the former, the latter would have to do.

Estrella dressed as gingerly as possible and then grabbed her keys and phone, heading out of her apartment and to her car. There was a definite icy bite to the weather, the skies, overcast. The sun was just about to go down, dropping the temperature further, which would be welcome given her state of mind. She would love a cold snap.

Jumping into her car, she dialed Vic's number as she drove.

"Everything okay?" he asked as soon as he picked up.

"Fine," she said, then exhaled sharply. Had her nipples just hardened at the sound of his voice? Jesus. She was a mess. "I'm coming over for a run. Be there in five."

"I'll run with you," he said, and hung up before she could protest.

Damn it. Bad enough that she had to call and let him know that she needed to run. As shifters that stood out like sore thumbs amongst the local wildlife, they didn't have the freedoms that the badgers, the foxes, or even the were-cougars did. A normal person would probably panic if they saw a badger or a were-cougar. They'd certainly call the cops if they saw a tiger—and the media would go wild. One of the Barlows had the clever idea of a big cat rescue project as a cover for their clan. So, when they needed to run, they headed out to Little Paradise and Kenna Barlow's farm. Kenna was Vic's sister.

She parked in Kenna's yard and didn't bother to head in to introduce herself—Kenna was used to the tiger clan prowling around at all hours and wouldn't bother to check on her. Instead, she glanced around for Vic's car. No sign of it yet. Damn. She lifted the floor mat and tossed her keys and phone underneath it, then headed to the gate on the side of the farmhouse.

The need to shift into liger form was bristling through her skin. Vic wouldn't like it if she took off on her run without him, especially after he'd told her that he was on his way. You didn't piss off your alpha with stupid, passive-aggressive moves like that. Not if you valued your place in the clan. If there was one thing Estrella didn't mess with, it was her tenuous spot in the clan.

Of course, nothing said she couldn't go ahead and shift herself. It would probably be better, considering her nipples would stand at attention as soon as Vic came into view, and she'd probably start giving off the scent of a cat in heat. With those embarrassing thoughts flaring through her mind, she hastily stripped out of her clothing and tossed it into a pile near the barbed-wire fence. Then, she crouched low in the grass and waited for the transformation.

It came a few moments later, ripping through her with a force that was almost orgasmic. God, it felt good to switch to her liger form. Yawning, she lazily stretched her large paws out in front of her, arching her back. Her tail flicked back and forth. She smacked her chops a few times, the scents of the night more powerful now that she'd shifted, the lighting as clear as day despite the sun's disappearance. The scents of the trees in the distance filled her nostrils, and she looked at them with longing, then sighed and flopped her large body to the ground, waiting.

Vic pulled up a few minutes later, just when her patience was reaching its breaking point. Good. Casually, she lifted a paw and began to wash it, acting as if nothing was out of the ordinary as Vic entered the gate and then shut it behind him. He gave her an amused look. "Sorry I'm late."

She ignored him, licking the pads of one foot as if it were the most fascinating thing ever. Her tail twitched.

"There was a cop behind me, so I had to go the speed limit all the way here," he explained, then grabbed the hem of his shirt and yanked it over his head, exposing rock-hard abs and more tattoos.

Estrella froze, mid-paw-lick. Okay. Okay. She could do this. She knew Vic had all those yummy tattoos and washboard abs. She'd seen him naked dozens of times. She'd seen every shifter in her clan naked dozens of times. So why was Vic's delicious body driving her wild now? She dropped her paw, and her claws curled. She might have kneaded the grass with her claws a little while he stripped out of his jeans and tossed his clothing over hers.

Damn. She had to do something about this, she realized as he began to change.

Even when her heat was taken care of, this infatuation with Vic was going to continue to be a problem.


"IT'S EMBARRASSING," ESTRELLA TOLD JAYDE OVER COFFEE. "AS soon as I see him, my kitty goes wild. And this time, I'm not referring to my liger."

Jayde snorted and stirred her iced latte vigorously with her straw. Her bracelets jangled with her movements. "So did you tackle him in the woods and show him your wild side?"

Estrella sighed. "No. I ran like a chicken. Did my liger thing and avoided him as much as humanly possible."

"Pathetic."

"I know."

"You should tell him you like him," Jayde said. The tip of the straw disappeared between her bright pink lips, and she slurped loudly. Jayde was a good friend, but she didn't know the meaning of low-key. Even now. They were having a quiet morning coffee between friends. Estrella was dressed in a T-shirt and jeans. Jayde wore a neon green mini-dress with a ruffled hem and enough bracelets to make a jewelry store pause. Her long black hair was pulled up in a high ponytail. "You want him, right? Just tell him. I bet he'll be flattered."

"Or horrified," Estrella said quietly, sipping her own iced coffee. She normally preferred her drink scalding, but, with the heat, the thought of putting anything warm in her system was repulsive. "I just don't want anything to jeopardize my spot in the clan, Jayde. Bad enough that I'm an outsider. I don't want to be that weird outsider who's crushing on the alpha. I'll never be able to look him in the eye again if he turns me down."

"So who are you going to go with? The chauvinist asshole, the competitive asshole, or the pothead?"

Estrella buried her face in her hands. "I really hate that those are my only options."

"So don't have a baby. Get hot and bothered, get a date for the night, and then go on with your life." Jayde shrugged. "It's what I'd do. No time for a kid. I don't know that were-jaguars are the most maternal anyhow. Maybe tigers aren't either. Skip it this time."

Not have the baby? But she'd spent the last week hyper-focused on the possibility of an upcoming child. Estrella touched her abdomen. "It's weird, but I want this baby."

"It's not a baby yet."

"No, but it's a sure thing," Estrella told her. "And what if I don't go into heat again? I'll have missed my chance to be a parent. The timing isn't great, but the more I think about it, the more I want this."

"Suit yourself." Jayde sucked loudly on her straw, and then eyed her. "Which one of the three screams daddy material to you?"

"God. None of them."

"Time to climb that alpha like a scratching post, then. I bet he'd make some pretty babies."

Estrella grinned. "You are single minded, aren't you?"

"That's why we're friends. I have the *cojones* to say things that you won't admit to yourself." Jayde winked and shook her cup, dislodging the ice at the bottom. "And I'm telling you, bag that alpha."

Estrella bit her lip, pushing aside her iced coffee. It was leaving a sour taste in her mouth…either that, or it was nerves. "I wish it were that simple, Jayde. I—"

Her phone rang. Estrella frowned and glanced at the screen. Unlisted number. After a moment's hesitation, she answered. "Hello?"

"Hi, may I speak to Estrella?" The chirpy voice on the other end was instantly recognizable. "This is Ryder."

"Oh, hi Ryder. This is Estrella. Did you get my message?"

"I did," Ryder cooed. "And I'm so glad you called me back! We did have someone mark you down on your card as interested."

Jayde wiggled her eyebrows at Estrella encouragingly, her shifter senses able to pick up every word of the phone conversation. Estrella crossed her fingers. "Who was it?"

"Let me get out my notes." On the other end of the phone, Estrella heard paper shuffle. "Ah, here we go. It was number six."

"Which was…"

"Vic Barlow."

Estrella's mouth hung open. Across from her, Jayde did a fist pump in the air, making her bracelets crash like cymbals. "I…he did?"

"Yes. Should I contact him and let him know you're interested?"

"I…no, no thank you." Her voice came out a breathless squeak and she clicked the call off.

"What are you doing?" Jayde tried to grab the phone from Estrella. "This is perfect!"

"He only went to that dating—mating—thing because he was feeling protective of me. That's probably why he put my name down."

"Uh huh." Jayde didn't look convinced. "Couldn't be that he wants to tap that ass?"

"He knows I'm going into heat. Why wouldn't he say something?"

"An alpha skeeving on a chick in his clan? That probably wouldn't go over well if he didn't know you were interested. Talk about an abuse of power. My guess is that he's being super careful." She gave Estrella a knowing look and sipped from her iced latte again. "Has he ever given you any hints that he might want you for himself?"

"No, I don't think so." Bewildered, she thought back to their recent conversations. *You're the only one here worth having, 'Strella.*

She'd thought he was just being a nice alpha. Supportive. Like finding her other tiger males to consider.

And yet…he'd snapped a pencil when she'd told him she was going into heat. He'd looked so rattled.

Maybe…maybe this would work out after all. Estrella reached across the table and grabbed Jayde's hand. "Should I do this?"

"Girl, I've been saying that all morning. Of course you should!"

"Then I need a plan."

G OD, THIS WAS A BAD IDEA. JAYDE WAS A GOOD FRIEND, BUT A good planner she was not.

Estrella paced in the woods, dressed only in a thong and a lacy, sheer bra. The heat was burning through her, making her thighs—and other parts of her body—ache with need. Even though nightfall was approaching and the wind was picking up, with hints of snow and ice in the weather, she didn't feel it. The heat was keeping her warm, elevating her body temperature to an almost feverish degree.

And heavens, she was horny.

Her fingers itched to touch herself, to relieve some of the pressure she was feeling, but she kept her hands clasped. Touching herself wouldn't do any good—her biological urges would override any sense of relief and this torture would just keep going and going until she either passed through the heat in another day or so…

Or until she found a man to make her pregnant.

A visual of that whole 'getting pregnant' process flashed through her erotically-charged mind. Of Vic, looming over her, muscles straining and tight ass flexing as he pounded into her.

She whimpered, shaking her head to clear it.

Her cellphone rang. Jayde. Her purse and clothing were hanging on a low branch nearby, though they'd soon be snow-covered if something didn't happen. The droplets were frosting her hair and turning the woods into a powdery white.

The plan was a simple one. Tell Vic that she'd been out running in her liger form and she'd gotten caught in some barbed wire. He'd come running to protect her—or possibly yell at her since she'd have theoretically gone out in cat form without his permission.

And then when he ran across her, he'd see her, oozing mating pheromones and dressed in sexy lingerie…and hopefully nature would take over. Problem solved.

She tapped her screen to answer the call. Before she even had a chance to say hello, Jayde's voice rang through the air. "He's coming and he's seriously *pissed*, girl."

Estrella winced, just imagining her large, often surly alpha angry at her. "Well, I suppose that's not a surprise."

"Maybe we should come up with a Plan B," Jayde said thoughtfully.

"This was your plan, Jayde!"

"I know, but I forgot the part where your alpha has a volatile temper. It's not going to do you any good if he gets there and he's too pissed to make babies."

Estrella groaned. "There's no time for a plan B! Are you kidding me? You said this would work."

"Well, it should still work," Jayde said brightly. "Call me when you're pregnant. Good luck!"

"Jayde—"

Click.

Estrella growled. Sometimes her friend could be really, really annoying. She tossed her phone back in her purse and ran her fingers through her hair, trying to make it look tousled and sexy. Fuckable. She'd even worn a hint of eyeliner, though that was all she dared as far as makeup went. Male shifters didn't like the scent of makeup. No perfume, either. Her own turned-on musk would scent the clearing. It was definitely a good thing that Vic had sent the others out of town, or she'd be dragging every half-interested tiger or lion male toward her no matter what she did.

So she paced. And she waited.

Vic's scent reached her first. Still distant, the masculine smell of tiger sent waves of pleasure rolling through her body. Her nipples tightened in response and she crossed her arms over her chest, shivering at the sensation. Her toes wiggled in the inch-deep snow, but she forced herself to remain where she was.

He needed to come and find her.

Of course, just waiting made her nervous. She chewed on her lip, thinking as she studied the naked trees nearby. Maybe a sexy pose? She could lean up against a tree trunk, cock a leg, maybe thrust out her breasts...

Vic crashed into the clearing in full tiger form.

Estrella yelped in surprise, flying backward automatically, her claws coming out. She could feel her cat under her skin, an automatic defense mechanism, and forced herself to calm, shoving away her shifter form. The last thing she wanted was to transform right now.

Vic's gaze moved to her, studied her for a moment, and then he opened his mouth and roared so loud that her eardrums vibrated.

Boy, he was *furious*. Estrella backed up to the nearest tree, automatically feeling that awful mental heaviness that came with disobeying your alpha. She leaned against it, forcing herself not to cringe away from his anger, and thrust her breasts out in the skimpy bra. "I'm so glad you're here, Vic," she murmured huskily. "I'm in trouble."

The tiger paced around her, nostrils flaring and scenting the clearing. His tail lashed wildly.

She patiently waited for him to finish checking out their surroundings, knowing that he'd find no other scents but hers. Once that was done, he leveled her another pissed off gaze and then hunched in the snow-covered grass, shoulders flexing as he began to change back to human form.

A few rather long minutes later, and he was in human form. She eyed him appreciatively, noticing for the first time that his chest was sprinkled with dark hair and he had the tightest buttocks she'd ever seen. God, she wanted to wrap her legs around them right about now.

She forced herself to meet his gaze as he approached her, his dark, damp hair steaming in the bitter cold. "What is it?" Vic growled. "What trouble?"

*Here we go*, she told herself mentally. *Now or never.* "This kind of trouble," she said in a throaty voice, and reached behind her to unhook her bra.

He growled again, the low rumble managing to come through despite his human form. The wild, furious look returned to his eyes. "What the fuck is this, Estrella?"

She stopped, humiliated.

She wanted to clutch the now-slipping bra to her breasts and run into the woods. Shame made the hairs on the back of her neck prickle. "A mistake, apparently."

Vic was still breathing hard, still furious. "This is a set-up, isn't it?"

His shoulders heaved with each angry breath.

She remained silent.

"Fuck, Estrella!" Vic turned and stomped away, snarling. "Do you have any idea of how fucking worried I've been? Here I thought that you—one of our females and near a dangerous mating heat—was hurt and in trouble. I've been mentally figuring out what the fuck to do if you need medical help, and you're just trying to seduce me?"

Bitter disappointment mixed with the shame. She reached behind her back and tried to resnap her bra, blinking back humiliated tears. "I didn't think—"

"No, you didn't," he roared again. "What if you were in tiger form and you were injured? What am I supposed to do? The Alliance doc can only do so much. Do I fucking call an animal hospital and hope they don't try to put you down? A fucking ambulance? What?" He continued pacing furiously, his hands clenched into fists that were so tight she could see white at his knuckles. "Never, *ever* fucking do this to me again, do you understand?"

"I understand," she whispered. God, she felt like a bug. An ant.

A really, *really* horny ant.

She closed her eyes, determined not to stare lasciviously at his naked muscles any longer. It was clear that she and Jayde had been all wrong about this—Vic was just thinking of her like an alpha thought of everyone in his clan. There was nothing more to it, and she'd embarrassed herself and jeopardized her place in the clan.

This was officially going down as the worst heat ever. Maybe she'd get lucky and never go into heat ever again.

"I'm your alpha," he snarled, pushing toward her. "Your safety and well-being are always at the front of my mind. You can't fucking jerk my chain and expect me to come running. Do you understand?"

"Yes," she said meekly.

"Look at me, Estrella."

She squeezed a cautious eye open.

His jaw was clenched harder than she'd ever seen it, and his eyes were so dark with anger they were almost black. As if to take the edge off of that, snow was falling in big, fat flakes now and dotted his hair and eyebrows.

"Never do that to me again," he rasped.

Yeah. She got it. She'd alarmed him. She yanked on the back clasp of her bra, determined to re-snap it, but her fingers were trembling from a mixture of the heat, nerves, and shame, and she couldn't quite do it. She gave up, crossing her arms over her breasts instead. "I'm sorry, Vic. I wasn't trying to scare you. I just wanted…"

Her voice trailed off with embarrassment. Now was not the time to confess her crush on him.

"The heat's clearly affecting you," he said after a moment, dark eyes glittering as he studied her face. "I'll forgive this lapse of judgment. It's clear you're desperate right now."

"Desperate?" She echoed. Did he just call her…desperate? Ouch.

"Approaching me for your heat. I must be your only option left. I just don't understand why you didn't pick one of the men I brought for you."

Well, it was a good thing she had no pride left after this debacle. Estrella shook her head, tamping down her own irritation. "Which one? The asshole? Or the chauvinist?"

His lips twitched with amusement, some of his anger receding. His arms crossed over his chest, echoing her own protective stance. She tried not to notice that he was really, really naked…and that it was incredibly arousing.

And not just to her, if the wood he was sporting was any indication.

But he was still talking, still arguing. "So you didn't like Nelson or Montgomery? I admit they're not my favorites, but they're both good candidates for a female in heat. Young, relatively attractive, tiger clan." He shrugged. "What more do you need?"

"Yeah, well thanks for that stunning criteria list, but I am not having the baby of either of those douchebags, much less sleeping with one of them."

"What about Cory? He seemed like a nice guy."

"His last name is Janitor, Vic," she cried plaintively. "If I'm picking men for ridiculous reasons, I don't want my baby to have a toilet bowl last name."

His brows furrowed. "Ridiculous reasons? Your heat's not ridiculous."

"But me picking men based on their looks and the fact that they can grow the same kind of tail as you? That's not ridiculous?" She sighed heavily, staring off into the woods. "It doesn't matter. They're not the ones I want."

"So who do you want?" The question was low, husky.

The words froze in her mouth. Vic had made it quite obvious that she'd made a bad call in inviting him out here. Like hell she was going to blabber about how much she wanted him. Her mouth remained mutinously shut.

"It's me, isn't it?"

Estrella remained silent, but she could feel the blush rising on her face.

"Fucking hell, Estrella. You're kidding me."

"I'm sorry that grosses you out," she cried. "Freaking sue me for having a crush on my alpha!"

"Goddamn it, why didn't you ask?"

"Hello!" She shouted at him, gesturing at her unclasped bra, her lacy panties. She felt like an idiot. "What do you think I'm doing?"

He charged forward. Before she could back away, his mouth claimed hers in a hot, hard, wild kiss.

Stunned disbelief rocked her. Vic was kissing her? The surprise of it almost overwhelmed her out-of-control hormones...

Almost.

A bolt of lust shot through her body, so strong it nearly knocked her over. She clung to him, her mouth parting under his hard lips. The kiss he was giving her was not polite, or tender. It was savage and hungry and punishing.

And she freaking loved it.

Vic's hands curled around her waist, dragging her nearly naked body against him. He rumbled low in his throat as his tongue slid against hers, as if pleased by the taste of her. She felt the stab of his cock against the crux of her thighs.

Oh god, this was everything she'd wanted. *If this is a dream, don't let me wake up.*

Then, he pulled away from her, the kiss ending so abruptly that she staggered against him.

"What is it?" She asked, the heat pounding through her veins.

Vic's eyes glittered with lust as he stared down at her. "Just tell me one thing. Am I the last resort?"

Estrella stared up at him, at the eyes as feverish as her own. The strong, stubborn set of his jaw. The dark hair that waved over his forehead. The big shoulders and strong arms covered in tattoos. A low moan of pleasure escaped her, just from looking at him. "God. Not in the slightest." She leaned forward, pushing her breasts against his hard chest, desperate to scrape her aching nipples against him. "I've always liked you, but I thought you didn't like me."

"Not like you?" He looked incredulous for a moment. "I practically browbeat you to join the tiger clan instead of the lions because I wanted to be around you. As it is, I've had to force myself to leave you alone since you never showed any interest before."

It was her turn to be surprised. "You wanted me? Even though I'm a liger?"

"Estrella," he whispered huskily, and his hand moved to ensnare her hair in his fist, an action that made a new rush of wetness dampen her panties. He slowly pulled her forward, until her lips were barely brushing against his. Her breasts flattened against his chest. "You're smart and utterly gorgeous."

"I'm six foot two. Most men don't want a giant in their bed."

"Their loss," he growled, then brushed his lips lightly over hers. "Do you want me for me, then? I want you to say it."

"I want you, Vic. So, so badly." Her hands slid up his arms, caressing his biceps. A purr nearly erupted from her when she felt how firm they were. "Are you sure you want me?"

"I've wanted you for years," he murmured, the look in his eyes making her knees weak.

But she had to clear something up, first. "Do you want me even though us coming together is going to make a baby? This is more than just a one night stand."

"Who said I wanted a one night stand?" he told her. "If you want me, I want to be your mate. Right here, right now. No more fighting it."

Her breath caught in her throat. "And the baby?"

"I'd be proud to be the father." And he lightly kissed her again.

Estrella sighed in pleasure, melting against him. "Do me a favor and pinch me so I know I'm not dreaming."

His free hand slid to her buttock and he lightly pinched it. "Better?"

"Yes and no." *Yes*, because she knew she wasn't dreaming. The delicious man holding her against him and declaring that he wanted to be her mate was the real thing. *No*, because even the slight motion of that pinch made the heat inside her pulse with need. Her skin felt like it was on fire—too sensitive and overly tender. She could feel her pulse throbbing in her veins, pounding a staccato beat that seemed to center right at her core.

"Should I pinch you again? Or do you want to get out of this cold?"

She growled low in her throat at the thought, and her fingers curled into his biceps, digging in like claws. "Still so hot, Vic. I'm burning up inside. We stay out here."

"Even in the snow?"

Her mouth quirked in a grin. "It'll cushion the blow when I knock you to the ground and ravage you."

His eyes gleamed with anticipation. "Will it now?"

She shoved at him, flinging him backward into the snow. As a liger, she was strong, just as strong as him. It intimidated most men, but she saw the excitement and challenge in Vic's eyes, and her own excitement grew.

He wouldn't mind that she was strong, fierce, and independent. For a man as rough as him, it was a turn-on to have a fierce mate. And that aroused her even more.

As he landed on his ass in the snow, her claws popped and she shredded the remnants of the bra loosely hanging from her shoulders. Her panties ripped away in the space of a breath, and then she was straddling his hips, bearing him back down to the thin blanket of snow in the grass.

He lay on his back and watched her with ravenous eyes. His hands reached for her hips, dragging her downward.

As if she needed any encouragement. Estrella took him into her hand and guided his hard cock into her body, seating herself fully onto him.

The breath escaped from her lungs. A small sound came from her throat, and she closed her eyes in pure ecstasy. He was big, and thick, and she was so very wet that he'd slid home perfectly. The sensation of it was amazing, and she soaked in the feeling of his cock deep inside her. Through the haze of her own desire, she barely heard his pleased groan.

All too soon, the delicious feeling faded, returned by the intense craving of the heat. She had him inside her, but she needed more, and she needed it fast. It made her crazed—this wild desire. Bracing her hands on his chest, she began to rock her hips, lifting up and down on his cock. Her movements were jerky and harsh, and she ground her hips into his with every movement. "Need more," she breathed. The heat was an inferno inside her, raging out of control.

"I've got you," Vic murmured, and she felt his big hands dig into her hips. All of a sudden, she was out of control. When she lifted again, he slammed her back down onto him.

She cried out—oh yes, that was exactly what she needed.

He stilled under her. "Estrella?"

Her fingers dug into his chest, claws gripping at his skin. "No," she panted. "Keep going. So good."

He growled low in his throat, and then he was slamming her down on him again, their movements so forceful that she was positive she'd have bruises in the morning, but she didn't care. She needed this—needed him—so badly. The heat was being fed, once and for all. It built inside of her, and she began to growl low in her throat, feral and rough. Her hips lifted with his thrusts, making each slam of their bodies together faster and harder than the one before. If he'd been human, she would have destroyed him. But this was Vic, her Vic, and he was as strong and fierce as she was, and when her eyes met his, she saw the intense excitement there. It didn't matter that she was rough—he liked it.

A shiver ripped through her, and then she was coming, the sensation so intense that stars swam in front of her eyes. A low, guttural groan ripped from her throat and she couldn't stop her claws from digging deeper into him as her entire body shuddered, flexing and tightening against him. Through the haze of the intense orgasm, she heard him bite out her name, and then she felt him come too, bathing her insides with warmth.

Estrella gave a wordless sigh and collapsed on his chest, breathing hard.

They lay there for long moments, the woods quiet about them, the only sound the symphony of their harsh, ragged breaths. Vic's hands slid to her thighs, and she felt his fingers lightly trace her skin, over and over, a soothing motion. She didn't move, though. She just laid on his chest, eyes closed, and tried to catch her breath.

Eventually, she cracked an eye open and surveyed her surroundings. Snow was falling in a thick blanket now, the snowflakes large and fluffy as they descended to the ground. Around them, the blanket of snow was patchy, the brown grass underneath exposed. And on the snow itself were dots of blood.

She flared her nostrils, alarmed. The scent of the woods touched her, along with the smell of her body and Vic, sex, and…blood. Warily, she lifted a hand and winced at the sight of the blood lining the beds of her fingernails.

Vic chuckled. "You play rough, 'Strella."

She sat up, pushing back on his chest, alarmed. Sure enough, the chest she'd been resting on was covered in scratches and gouges from her claws. Traces of blood dotted his skin and the snow around him. And Vic was smiling like he was pleased. "Oh my god," she murmured. "I'm so sorry."

"I'm not." His hand continued to stroke her thigh as she straddled him. "How are you feeling? Better?"

She shifted slightly, testing her body. Vic was still seated inside her, and that felt good. Her muscles weren't sore, but the heat didn't seem to be gone quite yet. Sated for the moment, but still lurking in the background. She grimaced. "I think we're going to have to do this again."

He chuckled. "Don't sound quite so pleased."

"It's not that," she began hastily. "It's that I want to have sex with you and just enjoy you. I don't want to feel like I'm going to flay you alive with my claws simply because the heat's driving me wild. It doesn't feel normal."

"Normal's overrated," Vic told her. "Are you better right now, at least?"

She stretched, working out her muscles. "I am. I feel pretty good, actually." Amazing, really, but she'd feel weird telling him that. "Thank you."

"Why are you thanking me?" His voice sounded funny.

A flush crept up her cheeks. "For, you know. Volunteering in my time of need."

His eyes narrowed. Suddenly, he moved, and she went from sitting atop him to being flipped onto her back in the space of a moment.

Her eyes widened at the sudden movement—and the surge of desire it sent through her. Vic loomed over her, pinning her to the snow. "Estrella. Let's clear one thing up right now," he told her in a hard voice. "I'm not doing this out of the goodness of my heart or because I'm your alpha. I'm doing this because I've wanted you for years. Me. Vic. It has nothing to do with free sex and everything to do with you."

Tears blurred her vision. "Good. I just didn't want you to feel... obligated."

He snarled. "Fuck obligation. I'm doing this because you're mine. And now that I know you want me too, there's nothing that's going to stop me from putting my mate mark on your throat. Understand?"

A surge of liquid desire rolled through her at the thought of Vic's mouth on her neck, teeth biting into her skin, and her hips flexed in response. "So what's stopping you right now?"

"Absolutely nothing," he growled, and leaned in. His tongue lightly moved along her throat, and she moaned at the sensation. "Ah, 'Strella, I can smell your desire. Smells fucking amazing."

She felt his cock, already hard, against her inner thighs and rocked up against him again. The heat was returning, but this time, she welcomed it. Relief was only inches away. "Need you, Vic."

"My 'Strella," he said softly, and she felt his tongue trace along her collarbone, making her shiver with need, her nipples hard.

Then, he bit down on her skin, at the spot where her neck met her shoulder. She felt his teeth sink in, ever so slightly. Another orgasm ripped through her, and she cried out, clenching his body close against hers. "Oh, yes. Vic. Vic. Vic."

He growled low against her throat, not pulling away, his mouth anchored there. She felt him shove her thighs forward, until they pressed backward on her chest and she was bent in half, knees almost to her shoulders. And then he sank deep again, and she cried out. Her claws popped again and she sank them into his back, clutching him to her.

"My 'Strella," he repeated in a hoarse voice, pounding into her.

"Vic," she cried out, and oh God, his rough strokes were driving her wild. She couldn't hold his body close enough to her. He sank so deep inside her that every thrust made her quiver with the orgasm that seemingly wouldn't stop. It kept building and building, her body quaking and muscles tight with the sensation, but it kept going and going, the fires stoked hotter with every thrust of his cock deep into her.

Too soon, he bit out her name against her throat, biting down on her again. And that made the orgasm skyrocket, until she was nearly passed out from bliss. She felt him come again, and then he collapsed on top of her.

After a few moments of panting, he moved away from her neck and leaned in to kiss her. In contrast to their rough, wild lovemaking, his kiss was tender and sweet. "Love you," he said gruffly.

Tears pricked her eyes and she ran her fingers along his hard jaw. "Love you, too."

"Your heat?"

"Still there," she admitted. "We might have to do this a few more times."

He grunted. "I see you plan on wearing your mate out."

Estrella grinned. "Are you telling me that I mated with a man with no stamina? That's disappointing."

"No stamina?" He gave her a mock-offended look, and then rolled his hips against hers in a seductive manner. "You want me to show you 'no stamina'?"

She moaned. "Yes, please."

They rolled in the snow and made love for hours on end, oblivious to everything but their own desires. Afternoon faded into dark, the moon came up and went away again, and sometime toward morning, they fell into an exhausted sleep in each other's arms.

When Estrella woke, the skies were orange and purple with the coming dawn, a blanket of snow was thick around them, and she was shivering from the cold.

Finally. Her heat was quenched. She gave a loud sigh of relief. Marathon sex was fun, but she was ready for the heat to be gone. Thank goodness shifter women only went into heat a few times in their lives. The intense craving—and hormonal craziness—was not something she wanted to experience on a regular basis.

A hard arm tightened around her hips, and she felt Vic nuzzle her shoulder. "You feel cold."

She burrowed closer to his warm body. "I *am* cold," she admitted, and couldn't keep the happiness from her voice. "Heat's gone."

His hand slid lower, to her belly. "So that means…"

"Yes." When he was silent, she began to worry. "What are you thinking?"

He kissed her shoulder again. "I was thinking about names. What do you think about Vic Junior?"

A happy giggle escaped her throat. "Uh, I think that's the worst name ever."

He gave her a mock growl. "That's my name."

"I didn't say your name was a good name. It's simply tolerable because it's yours."

He pulled her closer to him. "I see my mate is full of sass in the mornings."

"And afternoons. And nights," she told him happily. "Get used to it. You mated a woman who's not going to let you walk all over her."

"Good." Vic nipped at her shoulder again, and despite the exhaustion in her body, she felt a stirring of desire. Not because of the heat, but because of Vic.

She smiled. "Besides, what if it's a girl?"

He paused for a minute, thinking. Then, "How about…Vickie?"

She groaned. "You're clearly terrible at picking out names."

Vic's hand slid to her breasts, caressing them, and she sighed with pleasure when he began to stroke her nipple. His lips moved from her shoulder to her jaw, and he began to kiss her lightly. She turned her face so he could brush his lips against her mouth. "I suppose it's a good thing we have nine months to decide on a name, then. I'll bring you around to my way of thinking."

"I'm going to need a lot of persuading," she breathed, leaning into him.

"I know." His eyes gleamed. "I'm looking forward to it."

# Conjuring Max

## CAROLYN CRANE

# Chapter One

*January 12th, 1985*
*Malcolmsberg, Minnesota*

M AX DRUMMOND SAT IN THE OLD STUFFED CHAIR, SKETCHING the snow boots piled up by the fireplace while half watching Miami Vice.

Veronica lounged on the couch, fully watching Miami Vice. She slid the lid of her rectangular tin of lip stuff back and forth. Click, click. The clicking sped as a car chase heated up. The synthesizer music swelled. A truck slammed into a wall.

But all the crashing and music didn't keep Max from hearing a twig snap just outside the window. The distinct two-part crunch of a human foot. He sprung up, pulled out his piece, and flicked off the TV. "Hey!"

Max put his finger to his lips.

"Nobody's out there. My wards are perfect," Veronica said. "Turn it back on."

"Someone's out there," he said, listening for more snaps.

"Oh, you just hate Miami Vice."

He did hate Miami Vice. Don Johnson wasn't any kind of detective. "Your protective wards failed, Veronica."

Veronica tilted her head, one dark brow raised over blue-shadowed eyes. She was gorgeous and brilliant and cool as hell. Bitch Queen of the Witch World, he sometimes called her, which just about summed it up. "FYI, my wards don't fail," she said simply. "I'm feeling them now."

"FYI." Max turned off the lights. "I heard what I heard."

The moonlight reflected off the snow outside, brightening the night and sharpening Veronica's fine features. She blinked at him once, a long blink of patient annoyance.

Veronica's magical wards usually made the air crackle a good twenty minutes before a hit man would arrive. There had been no crackling this time. Never mind, he'd take care of whoever it was all the same.

Rich people had maids to clean their houses, cities had sweepers to clean the streets, and Veronica had him there to kill the hit men being sent after her. She could handle it herself, but she preferred to expend her energy on her computer experiments and her ogling of Don Johnson, aka Detective Sonny Crockett.

He motioned with the gun. "Get over there. Hide next to the clock."

Her brows knit. "I don't hide."

"Humor me," he said. "You think I don't know my business?"

"Fine. I'll go work in the basement while you handle this."

"You think I'm letting you waltz through that fishbowl of a kitchen right now? Wake up, Veronica. There are people out there looking to shoot you. They broke your wards without you knowing it."

She crossed her arms. "I don't see how."

"Maybe they brought a witch of their own."

She sniffed her haughty little sniff. "I very much doubt that. No witch would come after me."

"How about two witches? How about a group of really strong ones? You telling me there's nobody who could bring you down?"

With an air of amusement she tightened the flowered scarf that separated her dark, floppy bangs from the rest of her hair. "Let me think…" Oh, his witch had a very high opinion of herself. It was hot as hell, but it wouldn't do her any favors in a real fight.

"You want to stay alive?" he growled. "Let me do my job. You think

Salvo didn't get curious about how eight of his hit men died trying to kill you? You think he hasn't got wind of the townie tales about you by now? Figured out witches exist, and that you might be one? You got the attention of somebody very dangerous. You think he's stupid? Then it means you're stupid."

A slight smile played on her lips and her green eyes glinted against her porcelain skin. She liked his tough talk. The woman was addicted to cop shows—*Columbo, Baretta, Hill Street Blues*. He sometimes wondered if he was there partly for her entertainment.

"How would a mobster know about witches?"

"How about you check for witches out there all the same," he said. "You can check that, right?"

Her bracelets jangled as she made the hand motions that told him she was doing magic. It was her power that he loved most. Not her magical power, but her inner power. She was a scrapper who'd keep her chin up through anything. She thought he didn't know her, but he did—he knew all about her. He was in love with her.

Alarm replaced her weary expression. He'd never seen alarm on her face. "It's the Council."

"What does that mean? Can you fight them?"

She wasn't listening. "Salvo sent the Council? A man like that shouldn't even know witches exist."

"What is the Council? What does that mean?"

"Four witches," she said. "The four most powerful."

"In the world?"

Her silence told him *yes*. He'd never heard of a Council before. He'd put it together that she was some sort of outcast in the witch world.

"Can you defeat them?"

"Could you defeat the four best cops in the world, Max?"

"It would be a mother of a fight."

She smiled. She liked that.

Max listened for more snaps. "So. You got Salvo's attention and he's gone with the biggest guns he could find. If I was him, hiring witches for the first time, I'd team them with my best hitter—something familiar, something new." He had wondered if this day would come.

"They could kill me, Max. And we can't let them get ahold of the computers."

"I'll keep you safe." He motioned at the grandfather clock. "You're going to stand in that shadow."

"Stand in a shadow? That's your answer?"

"We do this the old school way," he said.

She winced as she pushed up from the couch, puffy bangs brushing her pale forehead. She wore a baggy cardigan sweater over leggings and leg warmers. He'd figured out that she liked the way leg warmers covered her mangled leg. He always wanted to tell her she didn't need to cover the leg, not for him.

Never for him.

As if she'd care about his opinion. He was the help, the thug of a cop who knew the Salvos better than anyone. The man who killed because killing was beneath her.

"Hurry." He motioned at the clock. "Keep down."

"I am," she whispered, disguising her limp. She didn't like him knowing things about her, but in the past three months, he'd learned plenty. Like the fact that her haughtiness was camouflage for desperate loneliness. And that her vast power was supposed to protect her, but it made her weak in all the ways that counted. And he knew that the way she was living was no way to live.

He nudged the curtains aside with his Glock, wondering who the hitter would be this time. He caught movement in the woods, somebody heading around back, it seemed. Moving like military. More distinctive movement some yards away. "Two. Two hitters. At least. Gotta think there's more in back." He pulled his other piece from his ankle holster.

"We'll fight them together," she said.

"Can you or can you not take these four witches?"

"Well…if you killed two. But they'll punch through my protection. They'll leave me open to gunshots."

This was bad. Max took a deep breath. "Your computer lab—those witches would have trouble getting to you in there, right?"

She sniffed. "Alls they'd need is ten days, a case of candles, and a few buckets of blood."

His Veronica. Cool and snappy under fire. *Alls they'd need.* She'd picked that speech tic up from him. It made him idiotically happy.

"We'll use your devil computer advantage."

"Oh, suddenly somebody *likes* the devil computers," she said.

"I like that it's the big thing you have that other witches don't know about. Here's the plan—everything I do now is to cover you on the way through the kitchen and down to the basement, got it? Whatever fireworks are going, you get down to that lab. You go, go, go. You hole up and you conjure reinforcements."

"And what do you do while we wait the 24 hours for them to appear?"

"I can handle a group," he assured her.

"For 24 hours?"

"If they kill me, you'll just conjure me back from the photo again. I'll pop in with the reinforcements." His witch could do that sort of thing with those devil computers of hers—bring things and people to life off photos.

"Oh no," she said. "That won't do."

"You conjure me from that photo every week."

"It's different if they kill you. For one thing, I'd have to conjure you off a different photo. I could never use that press conference photo again."

"You have other photos."

"And you'd remember your death," she said.

"So I remember my death."

"Don't talk of death so casually, Max. You won't enjoy remembering it."

"I remember plenty of things I don't enjoy," he said.

"Standing outside my front door tomorrow remembering your own death as if it just happened? You don't think that would be a problem? I don't want you losing effectiveness."

"Your concern is touching." She was probably right. He wouldn't want to remember his death.

He didn't remember the first time he died.

That's because the version of him she brought to life every week hadn't yet died. That version of him had been speaking at a press conference a few days *before* he'd died.

Needless to say, it had been quite a shock. He'd been standing in front of cameras in downtown Chicago one second, and then found himself 500 miles north, with a witch explaining to him that she'd made him appear off some newspaper picture, that he'd actually died weeks ago, and that he was her bodyguard now.

"You'll hole up in the lab with me and fight from behind the wards with me," she said. "Your duty is to me."

"We have an arrangement, sister," he said. "And me cowering is not in it."

"Your suicide is not in our arrangement."

Did she really not believe he had at least a chance against a group? He felt a little stung. It depended on the group, of course, and what the witches did to him. But he wanted her to believe he could handle more than one guy in a fight. God, what had he become? A Don Johnson primping peacock, all concerned with what she thought?

"It's not suicide if I fight them to the death and you bring me back to have at them some more. I'd call that a pretty big boon. Anyway, if that's how it's going down, that's how it's going down. Can't you do some anti-magic on my gun? Alls I need is a fair fight."

He caught the movement of her hands, the jingle of her jewelry. "This will work for a bit."

"You'll bring me back." A statement, but really a question.

"You don't get away from me that easy. Catch." She threw him a coin. It felt cool in his palm. "Protection. Imperviousness to spells," she said. "The Council witches will try to contain you and your gun. It won't hold up for long, but the witches will be going for me first. I'll rip off everybody's protection, but they'll be doing the same to us."

"Then we'll cancel each other out." For a while, anyway. It didn't sound like she had good odds against these witches unless she got into her basement lab. He slipped the coin into his pocket, wishing she were down there now, safe. A lot of killing was about to happen here; he knew it in his bones. He'd done a lot of killing as a Chicago cop on the organized crime beat, and he'd done a lot of killing as Veronica's personal thug. He was killing killers, but it was still killing. He liked to get their bodies out of there before she saw. He wanted to protect her from everything.

"Don't forget, I'll probably know the hitters. Which means I'll have a big ol' element of surprise when they bust in here and see me back among the living," he said. "And then I'll cover you through the kitchen. It means I shoot like crazy and drive them to hide while you scoot to the door, got it?"

"I get the concept of cover, Max."

"This isn't like Miami Vice. It'll be loud and you'll want to hide, but you just focus on getting downstairs. That's how you help me."

"FYI, I *won't* want to hide."

He rolled his eyes. *FYI.* Her pet phrase ever since that show with the Barney Miller guy. "Okay. There are only two outcomes here—I kill them, or they kill me. There'll be no Max lying on the floor bleeding, needing you to rescue me, got it? So don't let anybody trick you."

Silence. What a stupid thing to say. Why would she come up to rescue him? She'd just wait for him to die and reconjure him. They had a business arrangement: he killed the hit men, and she re-upped him every week. It was probably all wrong in some divine way but he loved getting the chance to rid the world of killers. To make the world safer for cops, safer for his little girl. He loved being alive.

And he loved Veronica.

Aloof and imperious as she was, he loved the hell out of her. Or, he wished he could, anyway. She wouldn't even let him see the leg. She didn't understand how completely he would love her.

Twig snap. She gave him a dark look.

"You're okay," he said.

No reply.

He smoothed his thumb up and down on the grip of his Glock, wishing he could touch her, hold her. He tried to make out her expression in the shadows. Was she frightened?

She was a classic overachiever—good at everything, and at the height of her powers. He'd put her age around 40, same as him. She liked to boast how no witch could best her. But now there were four witches working with hit men. The god-like power her computers gave her didn't apply to battles. It gave her the power to create.

And it took time to manifest.

*Crackle crackle.* More twigs. He'd purposely put them around the place, not trusting her wards. There had to be a half dozen people out there. He told himself Veronica could do this.

*Crack-crash!*

The mudroom door crashed in.

Intruders in the kitchen now.

A voice. "Veronica Harding?" A slight drawl. It sounded to Max like one of the Kite brothers. He'd arrested the Kite brothers numerous times in his cop days.

Max stole nearer to the doorway and made a patting motion. Down. She complied.

Max's heart pounded in his ears like it always did before a firefight. The voice again. "We just want to talk. We want to talk about Benny."

Ah yes, the familiar drawl: *We jess wow-n-talk about Benny.* This was Kenny Kite, a Missouri hitter. Which meant there were likely five Kite brothers in play—three back, two front, no doubt. Max had been worried that Salvo would send the Kites one day.

The Kite crew he could handle, but the witches were the wild cards. The Kites would come in before the witches to clear the way. "We just *wow-n-talk*," Kite said.

A squeak. Kite was creeping across the kitchen floor.

"How's the peanut biz, Kite?" Max asked, casual as could be.

Silence.

"Don't you remember? The last time I arrested you, you said you were out of the game. Gonna raise peanuts."

"Who is that?"

Max smiled. As far as psychological advantages went, you couldn't do much better than people thinking you were a ghost. It was possible that Kenny Kite might've even seen Max go down. Hell, Kenny Kite could've been the triggerman for Max's original death back in Chicago.

Another creak. More Kites on the scene.

"You should've gone with it. Peanuts are a lot healthier than all the candy you had me get for you in interrogation that last time. Remember that? All those Snickers. And did you give me the intel I was asking for?"

"Din' need to."

Fear in Kenny's voice. If Max showed himself now, he'd be able to get off two or three shots while the Kites absorbed the shock of seeing him alive.

Veronica held up three fingers.

Max stepped out and shot. Kenny went down first, wide-eyed and open-mouthed. Then Kyle. Kev got a shot off before Max plugged him.

He put another bullet in each of them.

He shoved Kenny's body out of the way of the basement door and yanked it open, shooting into the darkness of the living room with his left and back through the open mudroom door with his right. "Go!" She'd never have better cover.

Veronica limped across the linoleum and onto the top of the basement steps. Once she'd started down, he shut the door and slammed up against it, firing until everything went quiet.

He slid to a crouch. Two Kites still out front. And the witches were out there, too. He snuck over to the drawer and reached up and into it to grab one of the spare clips he liked to keep stashed around the house.

That's when a canon-like blast ripped through his head.

The blast overwhelmed him with a surprise he couldn't jerk himself out of. The world spun and screamed in the language of color: reds, blacks, yellows. Cheek against the smooth floor. The back of his head hot.

The back of his head cold.

Breeze where it shouldn't be. Yelling. Pandemonium.

They'd got him in the head. They'd undone Veronica's magic and got him.

The men bent over their dead brothers with a kind of anger that was really grief. The women, all witches in red cloaks, scried for Veronica, but Veronica was safe in her warded lab.

He didn't know how he knew any of this—his eyes weren't working. Things became simple. Feeling and knowing merged.

It all seemed to unfold further and further away—these new witches, Veronica, the Kite brothers, his little girl.

# Chapter Two

VERONICA SAT IN HER COMPUTER LAB, HER VIEW OF THE SCREEN blurred. She should be typing, but instead she clutched her chest, pushed against her ribcage, as if she could contain the horrible feeling there, maybe push it back inside somehow. But it kept growing.

He was dead. She'd pushed out to him with her magic and felt him on the floor.

And she was trapped like a squirrel behind her own wards.

She'd wanted to go out and fight them straight on, but Max was right. You have to use your advantage.

She wiped her tears and started setting up the UNIX command files she'd need to conjure him again. It would take a day to get him back. She needed to hurry.

Four or five sets of footsteps above. Voices. Oh, those witches and hit men would pay for what they did to Max!

She'd originally conjured Max because he looked mean and tough and was an expert on fighting the Salvos. It's why the Salvos had killed him in the first place.

And he loved being back alive, once he'd gotten over the shock of it, and was eager to reduce the population of hit men on Salvo's payroll.

*Clean kills*, he called them. *Right kills.*

Max was like that. Concerned about doing right.

*I'm finishing the job I started in life, baby.*

She loved how he spoke, and that he called her *baby*, though she got the sense from stories he told that he called guys *baby*, too.

And he'd talk tough right to her face. Even with all her power, he'd talk tough to her face. That had surprised and offended her at first. Well, she'd *wanted* a tough one, she'd reminded herself.

Now she wouldn't have it any other way. Nobody else would do.

She ran her fingers over the keyboard. He didn't remember his original death, of course, but he'd remember today's death if she conjured him back into this timeline. The memory from this timeline would cling. But Max could handle anything.

A thump on the door upstairs. One of the hit men going at it with his shoulder, probably.

She could do this.

The witches of the world had mocked her modern ideas about the new computer technology, and she'd mocked right back. People had ridiculed and rejected her for as long as she could remember. As a child, Veronica was teased because she was weird—not good-weird, but weird in a way that apparently made people dislike her. And then came the accident, the result of her futile attempt to impress the kids who always mocked her, monkeying around in the railroad yards. The chemical fire she'd accidentally started and the crushing fall she'd taken had landed her in the hospital for ten months, all pins and skin grafts and casts. Her family went bankrupt from it. She had to repeat third grade. She grew into a lonely and maimed teen trying desperately to hide her horrific injury, trying desperately to be normal, trying to reverse the stiffness and standoffishness that seemed to make her a magnet for mockery. But the more she was mocked, the stiffer and more unlikeable she became, and the more she focused on her leg.

And then she'd found magic.

*Thump. Crack.*

She pulled out her folder of Max photos.

Witches thought the only wisdom worth having came out of dusty old books. Veronica knew different. She could conjure anything in the world with her bespelled code—any person, any object, anything that could be photographed or even drawn. Everything was electricity, even the human body. Even emotions and thoughts—that had been her key breakthrough in computerizing the spells.

Hers was an innovation so powerful she couldn't even boast about it, much as she would've liked to.

Another thump. Another crack.

The door, they would get through. The Council witches would snap those wards up there with the crook of a finger.

The computer lab wards wouldn't be so easy.

She spread out the photos. Tried to decide which Max to bring to life now. Oh, they would pay for killing him…pay, pay, pay!

It took 24 hours for a conjured thing to appear, and it lasted only seven days. These seemed to be the laws of it all. No surprise, really: 24 hours and seven days aligned to the math of nature. She hated the 24 hour gap, but seven days had been a saving grace at times. She'd brought some disastrous things and people to life, especially during her rock star phase. It was a comfort to know any mistake would vanish in seven days. And, if not, she had a titanium cage out back.

She had a system for conjuring Max where she entered the code to bring him to life a day before he was scheduled to blink out. Result: the new Max would blink in the second the old Max blinked out. Cascading, she called it. He'd hate to know she had a name for it.

She'd have to wait the full 24 hours this time. Because they'd gone and killed him. It would've been painful. Bewildering. Her Max, lying on the floor.

The screen started to blur.

She grabbed the newspaper photo she usually conjured him from and ripped it in half. That Max was dead. She had to grab him from a different picture now. He called them her devil computers.

*Nevertheless.*

When the code was set up, she powered up all five of her computers—mini-supercomputers she'd home-cooked with kits and off-the-shelf processors, all configured in a daisy-pentagram. She pulled out her Scotch tape, ripped off eight small pieces, and stuck them to the edge of the desk so that she could grab them easily. She positioned the first electrode on her forehead and taped the thing on.

Thump. Crack. Through the basement door. Thumps down the steps.

She affixed the second electrode. How did a mob boss know to send the Witch Council after her?

She positioned the third electrode as they tore apart the basement, looking for her. The lab door would appear as a wall. More crashes. One very close.

*Concentrate!*

She affixed the last two electrodes.

Max always said that if she were a good person, she'd destroy her devil computers. He had a point. Even *she* knew it was too much power for one person, but the power was all she really had.

Max sometimes threatened to destroy the computers himself. She doubted he would. His will to live, to make things right—it was far too strong.

"Not here." A man's voice. "Nuttin' here."

"The bitch is here. I feel her." One of the Council witches. Veronica ran a quick side equation—an algorithm to scatter her voice—and wove it through the invisible wards that protected her. Then she laughed, loudly.

"The bitch is definitely here," she said. "And here, and here."

The modulating voice would unnerve the witches out there. Witches really were fools not to embrace higher mathematics and supercomputing.

She selected a different Max photo—one taken the same week as the press conference photo. This one showed him leaving a crime scene, ducking under the yellow tape. She chose it because he would have his gun with him, and he'd certainly be wearing a bullet-proof vest—he was a major mob target toward the end of his life. He'd be glad to have his gun and vest when he appeared on her front porch the next day.

She set the clipping onto her desk, tore a sheet of print-out paper in two halves, and covered the sides of the photo so that only Max was visible. She didn't want the guys walking next to him showing up. She taped the sheets into place. She needed to look at Max and concentrate during this part. She was the interface.

A woman's sing-song voice: "Ver-onnnnn-ica. Where are you hiiiiding?"

"I'm up your nose with a rubber hose," Veronica said, and then she laughed. She wanted them unnerved. Frightened.

It was only a matter of time before the witches got busy painting up the walls with all the blood they had at their disposal. They'd send the hitters around the house for candles. They'd pull hair from her hairbrush. It would be a spellcasting hootenanny.

"You won't hide for long, Veronica."

"I'm not hiding. I'm bringing the rain of hell down on you," she said. "If you knew the gnarliness of my power, you would keen and scream and fall at my feet."

She stifled a smile. Max, if he were there, would give her such shit for saying *keen and scream and gnarliness.* She missed him already.

Chanting. They were starting it up now.

Veronica took a deep breath. She'd exaggerated to Max about the witches needing ten days to get in, but surely the wards would hold for the day. The wards ran three layers deep, each embedded with algorithms that would lead to time-consuming rabbit holes. But there was a lot of blood available out there. And four masterful witches.

She twirled the voltage box knob to high and then set to concentrating on Max's image, letting her mind fill with him.

It was important to avoid experiencing feelings while viewing the image you wanted to conjure, because a computer could be tricked or confused. Not feeling things while looking at photos of Max got harder every time, because she had a kaleidoscope of feelings about him, this man who pushed her and criticized her relentlessly. Him and his overbearing cop attitude and moral views on everything. Max was a bull of a man who didn't think of himself as smart, but he was smart—his was a strong, simple intelligence that she couldn't tie in knots, try as she might. He loved whiskey and steak and tropical shirts and sketching funny little things and shoveling the walk until it was bone clear.

She tried not to picture him dead up there.

Max was always telling her that the devil computers were making her weak. Dependent. *Rotting you from the inside-out,* he loved to say. *A drug you can't quit.*

Well, he couldn't quit, either. He liked coming back, even as he resented her power. Most every living being wanted to continue living.

Crashes. That would be the paint cans. Max had told her to get them out of the basement. When she'd made to banish them with magic, he'd been disgusted.

"I'll be as magic as I want to be," she said to Max in the photo. Max, her bull of a cop and the number-one enemy of organized crime, squinting into a photographers' flashbulb.

She touched a finger to his thick cheek, as if she could touch him. He had a squarish face—not what you'd call handsome, but overwhelmingly male, right down to his wide brow and the cleft on his thick chin. His eyes were brown. So was his hair, which he kept shorn close. He got his haircuts at an old-timey barbershop he'd gone to since boyhood, he'd told her once. He was squinting in the shot, lips pulled slightly to the side of his face. That's how he smiled—sheepishly, and more on one side than the other. From the smile, she guessed that somebody must have just praised him, likely for the arrests of all the Salvo high-ups. The string of Salvo arrests that had gotten him killed.

The crashing and pounding grew louder outside her door. Somebody had found her sledgehammer.

A sledgehammer would do nothing against her wards.

She straightened the photo with a twinge in her stomach. A better person wouldn't bring him back after she'd let him get killed. A better person would leave him there in the photo where he belonged.

*She'd promised him,* she told herself. *He wanted to come back.* All excuses.

She concentrated on his image, immersing herself in him.

It was like getting lost in beauty.

# Chapter Three

VERONICA HIT THE ENTER KEY AND SAT BACK, RELIEVED HE WAS on his way. She could hold out one day.

It was in the very next moment that she realized what a spectacularly awful decision it was to conjure Max first.

The plan had been to conjure reinforcements. What was Max to do against the Council? She'd so badly wanted him restored to her world she'd made an emotional decision instead of a tactical one. What was wrong with her? They could kill him yet again!

*Shit.*

He'd arrive in 23 hours and 59 minutes, and he'd need backup. She grabbed a dusty three-ring binder full of the old Council newsletters from when they still bothered to send them to her. She flipped through to get to the *Now Vanquished* section of each, always on the back page. *Now Vanquished* was the witches' version of humankind's police blotters. She needed an enemy of the Council to appear ASAP after Max appeared. But it couldn't be a being that might harm Max. Or her. She rifled through. Various baddies had been photographed. Some killed, some sent off to other worlds.

Then she came upon the perfect ally: Jophius, a mini-bull dragon the size of large dog. He'd been kept caged by the Council for years as they tried to extract the names he knew, killed during an escape attempt. Oh, how Jophius hated the Council! Jophius would rip apart these witches like a bloody little banshee if he so much as scented them. But he didn't have a problem with witches in general—just the Council. Perfect.

She repeated the process with the electrodes. This photo had been snapped during Jophius' imprisonment. She covered the bars with the paper. She needed Jophius to arrive *sans* cage.

ALMOST 22 HOURS LATER, VERONICA LAY ON THE COMPUTER LAB couch studying *Ytonions*, an ancient tome, a kind of Holy Grail of witchdom, conveniently depicted in a 1871 painting by Brugese and now manifested into the real world via her devil computers.

She wondered if it was snowing yet. Malcolmsberg, Minnesota was due for a storm, according to the weatherman who'd appeared during a break in Miami Vice.

She'd subsisted on Dr. Pepper and Bugles while the witches and their hit-man helpers worked beyond the door. How in the world had mobster Johnny Salvo gotten involved with the witch Council? It was smart of him. Maybe she shouldn't have used magic to mess with Johnny Salvo's cruel son, but it had felt so good.

The power of the Council pressed in on her. They'd be pushing a hell of a lot harder if they knew Max and Jophius would show up in less than two hours. Veronica was starting to feel home free. Even if they got to her, she could hold up to almost anything for two hours.

Or could she? Max would say she couldn't. *Devil computers are making you weak.*

She frowned. The conjuring power of a god was hardly a weakness.

She surveyed the mini supercomputers that crowded the space with their metal bodies full of wires and circuit boards. The modern advances in computing were amazing; not long ago you'd need a computer the size of a two-car garage plus a massive water supply for cooling to do what just one of her refrigerator-sized computers could do today.

Red coils pulsed inside the space heater on the floor, warming the little lab. Even the electricity here emanated from her now—the witches' spells out there had drained the conventional electricity. She wished Max could understand how many breakthroughs she'd made. There was nothing she couldn't do!

Except, apparently, stop caring what he thought.

She hated that he'd have to come back remembering his death on the kitchen floor. It would feel like it had just happened, but Max would go into an action mode. Max was a pro…unlike Don Johnson. She smiled to think of his disdain for that show. "Detective Don *Johnson*," he'd growl, managing to load up those few syllables with total scorn.

She went back to her studies. This old book was giving her new ideas about extending the duration of things she conjured beyond seven days. She wanted to get the stuff faster, too; it really was inconvenient to have to wait for the entire rotation of the earth. And she wanted the power to cancel things, and she wouldn't mind more control over the beings she conjured, so she wouldn't have to use the titanium cage out back ever again.

It had taken her many years and a whole lot of luck she'd never be able to repeat to establish the basic commands for conjuring. Now that she had it down, however, she should be able to alter the rules.

The chanting started up again. Latin. An oldie. That one could do some damage.

Veronica grabbed her Walkman cassette player, cranked Grand Master Flash, and set to creating a modulating counter-pulse of magic. It put off their rhythm for her to be in a different sonic reality, and she loved how the Grand Master Flash guys boasted about their prowess. She liked their winning attitude. A lot of people hated them, too, but did they care? Hell no.

FIVE MINUTES TO MAX TIME. THE WITCHES HAD PUNCHED THROUGH two layers of warding and the last ward was getting ragged.

She'd turned off the music; she was fighting them with pure energy now and it wasn't going well, even with her warding head start. It would be hell fighting them in the open if it came to that. She felt cold already.

Power dwindling.

And she wanted to kick herself for not having Jophius arrive first. To let her neediness guide her like that was an unforgivable error. Hopefully Max would take a few minutes to collect himself when he remembered his death. Then Jophius would appear, smell the Council witches, and tear down.

"Snooty Veronica," Witch-ascendant Tami called, in her sing-song voice. "You had promise, but now you're merely sad. You see how we're shredding your walls? Your computer tricks are mere smoke and mirrors."

She could feel their enjoyment. The Council was on a hunt, and she was the prey.

"My smoke and mirrors are about to blow your mind."

If only she could hold out. She was at the last of her energy. She closed her eyes, weary of fighting, longing to see Max's face.

# Chapter Four

IT WAS JUST LIKE THE FIRST TIME AND ALL THE TIMES AFTER THAT. One second the camera bulbs were flashing in his face, the next he was on her doorstep.

And then the memories of this timeline came crashing in. Except this time the memories were violent. Painful. He hadn't blinked out after seven days like he usually did; he'd been shot in the head. They'd killed him.

Max pulled out his Glock and flattened himself to the side of the door, heart pounding, breath puffing out in white clouds.

Jesus.

It would've gone down a day ago. More memories. The plan had been for her to hole up in her lab and wait for him. He'd left two of the Kite brothers and those witches alive.

Faint boot prints were visible along the front of the house, made maybe an hour ago, judging from the rate of snowfall. Good. It meant they were still around, and that meant she was still in there, waiting. She'd be frightened as hell and pretending she wasn't, even to herself.

Probably giving them an earful. She always talked big when she felt small.

He peeked in the window. Candles burned. Electricity out. The place looked empty. The Council witches would be downstairs going for the lab, but the Kite brothers could be elsewhere.

Max turned the handle and pushed the door open, quiet as a mouse. Clear. The wood floor was covered in dark footprints—dried blood. He crept across and stopped at the doorway to the kitchen, feeling ill when he realized that this was likely his blood. Some of it, anyhow. His dead body was around here somewhere.

*Not me,* he told himself. *I'm here.*

Or was he? He sometimes wondered if these re-ups of him had a soul. Max wasn't frightened by much, but he definitely didn't want to learn the answer to that one. He'd asked Veronica once, then stopped her when she was about to respond. He didn't want to know.

The faint strains of a song started up. Singing in the basement? No—witchy chanting. Trying to break through. He took a breath and snuck smoothly around the entry into the kitchen where more candles burned. No bodies. Just a lot of blood splotches, footprints, and drag tracks. Hell, you could barely see the yellow linoleum for all the blood around. In the darkness of the mudroom beyond, he could make out a large heap. That would be the bodies, he thought with a start—his and three of the Kites. Piled up and already starting to stink. Better than outside, he decided, where the crows and raccoons would go at them.

The door to the basement steps was cracked open. The stairs would be a bitch—they creaked something awful unless you walked on the sides of the treads, and even then it was chancy. Murmurs. A man's voice. So at least one of the Kites was down there with the witches.

He crept down in the darkness, gun in hand, putting as much weight on the wooden rail as possible. Two silent steps, three, four. So far so good.

The front of the basement came into view. Candle glow from beyond. More like a blaze. A lot of candles. They'd be around a corner, in the back part of the space near where the lab was. The candles would help him, lighting his enemies while he stayed shrouded in darkness.

Five steps. Six.

*Creak.*

The chanting ceased. He banged down the last steps and flattened up against the wall. Even in the darkness he could see that Veronica's normally orderly basement had been turned to chaos, like a tornado had hit it.

"A man." A woman's voice said with disdain. "Deal with him."

He heard the clicks of guns being cocked. Both remaining Kite brothers present, then. Good.

He sucked in a breath. Something clattered onto the floor. Lighting flickered, dimmed; they were blowing out the candles. Time to move. He grabbed a paint can and hurled it toward the opposite wall, toward the pile of shelving and glass that had once been the canning area, creating a ruckus. Then he jumped out, both barrels blazing.

The men scrambled. The women kept chanting, ignoring him. Karl Kite fired at him from behind a concrete pillar. Kurt Kite popped out from behind a water heater and got off a shot while Karl ran for Max. Max opened fire and got Karl in the belly. The man was down, but he kept shooting, crawling toward Max, who took cover behind a different pillar. Kurt burst out and ran at him. Max shot him in the head. Kurt was down, but Karl still went, shooting, looking freaked. Maybe from being shot. Maybe from seeing a dead man come back to life.

Max leaned out for a shot and got one in the chest instead.

*Oof.* The blast knocked him off his feet; a vest didn't protect you from the impact, just the penetration. He lay dazed for a split second, unable to catch his breath when Karl came at him, all bloody and swearing. The witches increased their volume. Max tried to lift his gun. He got off a shot that stopped the man. Then he heaved in a breath, rolled over, and filled Karl with the last of the bullets. The wall behind the witches began to waver.

Veronica was coming to help him.

"Stay in there!" Max shouted.

A furious pain kicked up in his head. What was wrong with his head? He hadn't been hit in the head.

"No, you don't!" Veronica was out now. She scuffed furiously at the floor—going after the symbols, he guessed. He tried to move, but the pain wobbled him.

The Kites were dead. He stood uncertainly, focusing on Veronica, who was trying to pull something from the tallest one's hand, saying something. Tami, she called her at one point.

Another witch fell onto Veronica, punching her. The witches looked much bigger and stronger than Veronica with her lame leg.

"Leave her," Max bellowed, but again he was hit with that pain, like somebody was squeezing his brain from the inside. He collapsed to the floor. Veronica was thrown up against a wall, as if by a mighty wind.

"Stop it!" Veronica screamed.

"You have been quite the inventor, Veronica," the witch called Tami said, lighting a candle. "Brava. You crossed the seventh gate and hid it from all of us."

"You're killing him!" Veronica screamed as the vice grip of pain tightened.

"Yes, I am," Tami said dismissively. "Oh, Veronica, what made you get involved in mob business? Look at the trouble you brought on yourself. You pull a cop out of the umbra, create life, break every law of the universe...not that I don't approve, but let's do face facts. And you would get hung up on petty mob stuff? Why not just kill the guy? Was it worth it?"

"Screw you," Veronica snapped.

Max felt a popping inside his ear.

Veronica let out a frustrated yell, high and animalistic, a tone he'd never heard out of her. She forced an arm outward, uttered nonsensical syllables.

"You can't take us," Tami said. "Not even you." She seemed to be the leader.

Another witch spoke now in some other language. She lifted the candle.

Veronica's yells sounded strained, like her throat was being squeezed. Smoke filled the air. Something electrical spit sparks across the dark space. The witches chanted and babbled. Veronica squirmed and struck back, crashing a shelf. Wind roared. Candles flickered and flared.

Max shut his eyes tight, trying to counterbalance the squeezing inside his head. He was dying again, he realized suddenly. He flashed on his little girl. Teresa. And here was Veronica, fighting like hell. He clawed the ground, pulling himself toward her, struggling through the pain to get to her.

He wanted to stay. Even if he didn't have a soul, he wanted to stay.

He fixated on Veronica's desperate syllables, a streak of sound.

"You cannot!" One of the witches bellowed. Something clanged to the concrete floor. "You will not!" More yelling. Roaring in his ears.

The squeezing intensified. The roaring blotted out all sound.

And then it stopped.

Max collapsed, spread eagle. The pain was gone, but he wasn't quite right, as through the squishing and releasing of his brain had jumbled things. He opened his eyes and saw dark, swirling shapes. It was as if he'd pressed his eyes shut so hard he could only see inside his head now.

The place stunk of molasses and sulfur. More shapes came into view. Max blinked and pulled himself up, shaking off the stupor. He could make out the Kite boys, sprawled in pools of blood. One of the witches lay in a corner, eyes wide, face a rictus of agony. The others were slumped on the floor, looking alive but dazed. Finally he spotted Veronica, curled in a corner.

He scrambled over to her. "Veronica!" He touched her hand. Cold. He felt for a pulse. Weak, but there.

"Run," she whispered, looking alarmed.

He heard the chanting start up again just as the pain pounded back into his brain. Tami and the other witches were at it again. A crash and a roar sounded from upstairs. More witches? He grabbed his gun as a frothing, seething little monster tore down the stairs and right past them. It went at the witches, snarling rabidly.

"Jophius!" Tami screamed. "What have you done, Veronica?"

The monster seemed to be tearing at the witches...was it eating them? He heard agonized cries, frantic chants. The pain was gone...but Jesus! The thing was eating them alive. He pulled Veronica into his lap.

"A friend," Veronica whispered. She trembled violently.

"Baby." He pressed his lips to her hair, cradling her. He'd never held her before. She never would've allowed it. "That's a *friend*?"

She mumbled unintelligibly, teeth chattering. He held her closer, trying to still her. She was sometimes cold after using too much power, but he'd never seen her like this. And what *was* that thing? It was brown and scaly, like an aardvark, but thick and muscular, with a pug nose that was now covered in blood. And very sharp teeth, clearly. Reinforcements, he supposed.

"Okay," he said. "What do you need?"

A long silence. Had she dozed off in his arms? "I'm cold," she said.

"Come on." He stood up with her in his arms.

"No," she panted, pushing at him, weak as a kitten, but he was already moving, stepping over Karl's body. She wouldn't like being carried; she preferred to be the badass. Well, she was the badass who needed help now.

"Let me…" she protested.

Was it that unpleasant to be held by him?

"No go," he said as he mounted the stairs, taking care not to bang her feet on the narrow passageway, putting distance between them and the gobbling, crunching sounds he didn't want to think about.

She'd conjured a monster.

He carried her through the bloody kitchen and into the living room. He liked holding her, liked carrying her. He didn't know why he should be surprised she was so light; she was a small woman. It's just that there was so much substance to her. He set her on the couch facing away from most of the blood, and tucked a blanket around her feet. "You think you can drink some hot tea if I make it?"

She shook her head no.

"I'll heat some water just in case." She often rejected small kindnesses, but later changed her mind. He started the water, then he built a fire in the fireplace. After that, he went up to her room, grabbed her thick wool socks and the thickest leg warmers he could find and brought them down, setting them on the radiator to warm as she often did.

She groaned. Another protest, as though he was fussing too much. She lay there on the couch, glaring up at him like a beautiful, wounded panther.

"Is the thing going to eat all the bodies?"

She shook her head. "Council only."

"A taste for the Council."

She nodded.

"Looks like you retained your title as Bitch Queen of the Witch World, baby. You brought a monster to eat them. You are the baddest."

A smile in her eyes. She liked to be called bad. It came from the music she always played, where bad meant good.

"And I don't think you even needed the thing's help. Looked to me like you were doing pretty well against them on your own."

She sniffed.

He tucked the blanket around her feet. He had to get the electricity back on. And he'd need to get rid of the bodies the thing didn't eat. The smell was getting bad. "How much of a friend is that thing? Can I leave you alone with it?"

"He'll…protect. Very loyal."

Max felt a wave of irrational jealousy. *He* was there to protect her.

"The bodies…wait for…" She wiggled her fingers. Lord, she was weak.

"I'm not waiting for you to glamour them. You think I can't sneak through town with five corpses? Or…make that six." Because his corpse was one of them. That Max wasn't set to blink out for a few days.

Another feeble protest.

"You gonna be okay while I send these bodies down the river?"

"Yes," she whispered.

This was the dance they did with Johnny Salvo. Kill the hit man and send the corpse down the Mississippi.

"Though six is a lot to send. One body, okay. Six is gory. Maybe a boxcar, huh? That goes to Chicago, too."

"Yeah, Max," she said casually, as though nothing at all was wrong. "I like that better."

"You sure you're okay?"

"Don't look at me like that. I'm fine."

Max nodded. Unlike Veronica, he preferred a bit of jawing when things got rough. Back in the precinct they had counselors for you to talk with when you took a life. He'd always appreciated that.

He threw another log on the fire and stood, wishing he didn't have to leave her so cold.

A photo of Veronica and her niece, Alix, sat on the mantle. The little girl looked to be about eleven years old, just a few years older than his Teresa. The photo showed Veronica and Alix knitting in front of that very fireplace. He'd asked her about it early on, because he'd thought she was estranged from her family.

"Oh, I am estranged from them," she'd said dismissively. "They hate me, of course. I grabbed Alix from a swim team photo in the Minneapolis paper. I wanted a visit from my little niece."

"You grabbed her from a photo? You mean you conjured her? The way you conjured me?"

"That's right."

"You made a duplicate of her to visit you?"

"More or less." Max could still see Veronica's frown, hear her defensiveness. "What? I wanted a relationship with her."

"It's not a relationship when you blink people in and out like toys. And wasn't she confused?"

"I made up a story. It's not like she'll remember in her real timeline," she'd added. She'd offered to conjure his Teresa, then.

The idea had both tempted him and repulsed him. To make his little girl smile. Play her favorite games. His throat felt thick. "I don't want you conjuring Teresa. *Ever.*"

"It's perfectly harmless."

"Don't you ever, *ever* conjure my girl," he'd warned.

Max shoved at the logs. Veronica looked happy in that photo with her niece. It made him sad, because she deserved better. She deserved something real. Not that he couldn't understand the impulse—his wife had died when Teresa was a baby. Back then, he would've conjured her if he could've. It would've been a mistake, but he would've conjured her over and over just like Veronica conjured him.

And it would've stopped him from living.

He set the fire screen in place and turned to Veronica. She lay there on the couch, too feeble and too all-powerful, both at once.

"Is that monster gonna let me grab the Kite brothers' bodies from down there?"

"Jophius has no beef with you."

It had a name. Great. Max pulled a pair of gardening gloves from the pantry and went down to the basement.

The thing was curled up in a corner, sleeping. Its triangular brown ears stood straight up and blood covered its stubby snout.

It opened one brown eye as he began to drag out Kurt's body.

"Don't mind me," Max mumbled.

Twenty minutes later he was pulling the truck around back. He carried the bodies out from the mudroom, slinging them onto a tarp in the back. Rigor mortis had set in on the ones from yesterday, making them difficult to carry, and they got caught on things when you dragged them. It was grisly for sure, and he struggled to stay objective to the sights and sounds and smells of the scene, one of the tricks from his cop days for when things got ugly. A smell was just a smell. Cold skin was just a sensation.

He finally came to his own body, brown eyes staring into nothingness. A day of death had sunken his cheeks and made his skin gray. Max was glad he couldn't see the blown-off back of the head. He wanted to shut the eyes, but he hesitated. He would be cold to the touch.

*Not* him, dammit!

He reached out and brought the lids down. The eyeballs felt sickeningly flaccid under the pressure of his fingers. He swallowed back the bile and nodded, as if to confirm to an invisible audience that this had been the right choice, in spite of the small horror of it.

Did he have a soul? Was he just an animated version of this corpse? But that would make him a zombie, and he wasn't a zombie. He was the man from the picture, Max Drummond, human as he'd ever been. He was a man who ached and loved and everything else. He was the man from the crime scene brought into the wrong timeline, that's all. He didn't need Veronica to tell him he had a soul.

Or worse, to tell him that he didn't.

He crouched by his own corpse with a pang of…what? Compassion? He'd expected to feel revulsion toward it. Not this.

He buttoned the top button on the shirt of his body, feeling what he could only interpret as tenderness for it. *Him.* This man who'd never caught a break. It was strange to contemplate his own light brown hair, his own ear. To look at himself in death.

He'd felt like such a failure in life, but this man had tried hard to be a good cop and a good father. He'd died trying his best. A sob caught in Max's chest.

"Cut it, Don Johnson," he muttered.

He'd had these extra chances to make things right; that was something most slain cops didn't get. He'd made major strikes against

Salvo's organization. He and Veronica had set up a fake police charity to funnel money to his sister's family to help them care for Teresa. He'd gotten to know this extraordinary woman. But Salvo was on the warpath now—he'd known to send witches. Max had never even known witches existed aside from storybooks, but Salvo had figured it out. The fight would escalate in a supernatural way now. He and Veronica needed to go on the offensive or she was as good as dead. It would help to know why the hell Salvo was after her in the first place. The Council witches had seemed to know. *Why get involved in petty mob business? Why not just kill the guy?* the one had asked.

Who were they talking about? What had Veronica done?

Max grabbed his body by the feet and pulled it down the small hall and out back. The arm caught in the door and he yanked, forcing it free. A piece of meat. It wasn't him, dammit! It bumped down the steps behind him and onto the gravel out back. He grabbed it by the shirt and belt and heaved it up there with the Kite brothers.

Six bodies. Getting them through downtown Malcolmsberg would be bitch enough, but the railroad yard was manned at this time of night. Unless the trains were backstacked, he was screwed.

He returned to the living room to find Veronica asleep. He spotted Jophius curled up by the fireplace. Well, if she thought she was safe with that thing, then she was safe with it. She knew her business well enough.

He grabbed the warm socks and legwarmers from the radiator and sat next to her on the couch, slowly drawing off her leg warmers. Then he took off her cold, damp socks to reveal her feet. One foot was pale and pretty. The other was shriveled and striated with angry flesh from past operations. He'd seen this foot once before, purely by accident. Veronica hid it assiduously, but he loved it because it was difficult and strange and fiery, like Veronica herself. Gently he rolled the warm, thick sock over it, and then slid the leg warmer over that, over her leggings and clear up to her knee. He repeated the process on her good leg and left for the railroad yard.

# Chapter Five

*H*E'D SEEN HER FOOT.

She'd realized this immediately upon waking and finding new warm socks on her feet and her woolly leg warmers over her leggings.

He would've had to see her foot in order to put on the new socks. He may have seen her ankle and maybe even her leg.

She hated him for it with a sudden ferocity.

She knew it was irrational, that he was trying to help, but she felt invaded, stripped of dignity. The idea of his wide, frank face drawn tight with pity at the sight of her misshapenness filled her with horror and made her want to yell at him and banish him.

But she could barely lift her head.

She should be thinking about her frozen core instead of her leg. She was dangerously chilled, deep down to the cells. She needed deep, deep warmth. She wished she was strong enough to take a bath, but her muscles were jelly. And she'd enlarged and deepened the tub with magic at the beginning of winter; in her condition she'd slip right down and drown like a baby.

Unless she had help. But she couldn't bare her leg to him again. was stupid, because it was just a leg, but it had been the secret, festering center of her being and everything she should be ashamed of for so long that it wasn't just a leg.

It could never be just a leg.

Her teeth chattered. She eyed Jophius, snoring softly by the fireplace. He looked so cozy and warm with his little monster snout nestled between his cloven hooves. She wanted to go over and curl around him and be warmed by him, but she felt too weak.

Max returned at around ten, and she pretended to be sleeping. He touched her hand, then put his deliciously warm fingers to her neck to check her pulse. She wished he'd put his whole hand on her neck, her cheek. She felt as if every molecule in her body oriented toward his warmth and his strength the way sunflowers oriented to the sun.

He left then, and returned with a mop and pail.

It smelled like he'd mixed together every lemon and pine scented cleanser he could find. He'd also stoked the fire high, letting it get smoky. Maybe the place smelled; she couldn't tell. Her sense of smell was gone. Her taste would be, too. She felt like she was pinned to the couch by a ton of concrete.

Max scrubbed the wood floor with a sponge mop. He'd changed into jeans and a threadbare plaid shirt and every few minutes his sleeves would unfurl and flop around and he'd roll them back up. After they flopped down a few times, he rolled them up rather violently, clear up to the middles of his upper arms in two tight bands. Then he started back in on his scrubbing in quick, sharp movements that had his biceps straining and flexing against the unforgiving circles of plaid.

She found herself fixating on his arms, his brutal beauty. Her mouth began to water—actually water, like she was a dog or something.

This wasn't work he was used to doing and he wasn't particularly good at it, but his motions mesmerized her. It wasn't just a lust thing; watching him nourished her in a way that went beyond the physical. He was just so, so very *Max*, the tough-guy cop who'd gotten pissed and rolled his sleeves too high and tight. He was smart and generous and secretly artistic. Yet practical, too—a straight-line-between-two-points that line was a bullet. Every inch the fierce protector, purely who he was, so purely Max, that he was his icence, with a type of beauty that seemed to deepen ement. He'd hate the word beauty used on him, but that's what it was.

His beauty touched her in a way that no beauty ever had. She wondered if it was because he was so completely out of her reach. He was strong and good and everything that was right in the world, and she was a twisted-up witch.

And he'd seen her foot. He'd even touched it.

Oh well, it wasn't as if he didn't already see her as warped person, she told herself. Just tonight, before he'd hauled off the bodies, she'd watched him inspect the photo of her and her little niece Alix and was reminded of how she horrified him. She shuddered to think of his opinion on her conjuring Jophius.

When he finished scrubbing the floor, he sat down on the edge of the couch.

"Hey," he said. "You awake?"

"Kind of."

"Teatime."

The next she knew, he was holding a mug to her lips like she was an invalid. Christ, even lifting the tea cup was too much. But she allowed it; she needed the warmth.

She watched his mouth while she sipped. His lips were rosy for a man's lips, and there was a crease at the center of his bottom lip, a cleft that echoed the cleft in his broad chin. How many women had he kissed with those lips? A hollow feeling formed in her chest.

"Another sip?" he asked.

"Yes."

He put the mug to her lips. The liquid heated her throat as it seeped down. His body was warm from the physical exertion—she could tell even without him touching her, as if he warmed the very space around him. She wished he would check her pulse again, or feel her forehead or touch her hands.

She supposed she could command it; he did live at her pleasure. She'd commanded others she'd conjured. But not Max. Never Max

He sat, mug in hand, expression carefully neutral. Was he thinking about her leg?

"I'll finish the cleaning," she said. "Let me."

"How long until you can bespell it clean? A day? Two?"

"Maybe." It would be longer than that. "Surely you can do find something else to do."

"I don't think so."

"You'll let me handle it," she commanded firmly.

"Says who?"

Her gaze flew to his. The lines around his eyes had gone crinkly. Laughing at her. How she hated this!

He winked and got back to work. During a break in his mopping he ducked back into the basement and got the electricity back on.

No, she couldn't stop him from much of anything now, and she didn't like it. Outwardly she fumed at him, but really she wanted him to sit by her and give her more tea. She was dangerously cold. She'd almost died. She still could.

Maybe if he stoked the fire more…

Jophius stood up, snorted once through his miniature bull's snout, and curled up anew, just like a dog. His leathery scales glowed in the flickering flames.

Max took one look at Jophius and then eyed her darkly. "A wee monster curled up by the fire after a hard night of devouring witches alive. Isn't there a Norman Rockwell painting of this?"

She smiled in spite of herself. "His name is Jophius."

"I know." Max grabbed new socks off the radiator. He had a sock-warming rotation going.

"You think you're putting those on me?" She whispered this with as much strength and dignity as she could muster.

"Yup."

"I'll keep these socks."

"Yeah, yeah, yeah." He went to her and sat next to her feet. Watching her eyes, he squeezed the toes of her good foot through the sock. "Like tiny blocks of ice." She stiffened. Would he pull the sock off? "You're too cold," he observed. "This is wrong. You should be getting warmer."

"Just put the blanket over. I don't want new socks."

He squeezed the toes again, then he reached over and took her hand. He squeezed it and nestled it back onto her stomach, brow furrowed.

Concern. Not what she wanted from Max.

"Your core temperature's going too low. You need a bath, Veronica."

She shook her head. Out of the question.

"Why not?"

"Because I don't want one." She was getting her voice back. A bit of her breath. She managed to jerk her foot to show she wanted his hand off. Without his hand, her toes were so cold, though.

He grabbed the toes of her good foot again, rubbed vigorously, shocking her with his forwardness. "You want a bath, but you can't handle it on your own." He studied her face, then he reached up to her ankle and began to roll down the sock.

She watched him wildly. He would dare do this? And then the sock was on the floor.

He pressed his big mitts around her now-bare foot. It was invasive. It was impudent. And oh, it was heaven. He molded his flesh to hers, hands flat on either side of her foot, a prayer of warmth. For one delicious, forbidden second she imagined his whole body against hers, warming her, wanting her, loving her.

It made her feel stupidly sobby, how badly she wanted that.

He removed his hands and rolled the heated sock onto her good foot. Then he grabbed her maimed foot and rubbed it through the sock.

"Max…" she shook her head. "Don't." Yes, she needed a bath. Yes, she needed his warmth. She needed not to need. "No more."

"I read about these fish in National Geographic once," he said, rubbing gently. "They live beneath the ocean in caves way down deep where there's no light, and over time, they lost their eyesight."

She didn't like where he was going with this. "Can you remind me why I keep bringing you back?"

"They didn't need their eyes anymore because they live in darkness," he continued. "They could see perfectly before the caves, but after they lived in the darkness a while, their eyesight faded away."

"If you don't use it you'll lose it? And what am I losing?"

"Your courage."

The air went out of her. She swallowed, mustered up her voice. "I fought four goddamn witches tonight."

"Brilliantly," he said. "But that's not what I'm talking about. I'm talking about what really scares you. You won't ever do what really scares you. You think you can't, but you can."

She frowned. Max was such a pit bull with emotions, always wanting to tear into whatever thing you didn't want to talk about and shake the stuffing out of it. She wished she could crash some glass against the wall or make thunder. Or stuff him under a lid like a jack-in-a-box. A pit-bull-in-a-box. "You don't know anything about me."

"I know it frightens you to be vulnerable. To let me care for you."

She rolled her eyes.

And then he did something shocking—he brought her foot up to his mouth, so that his lips just grazed the wool sock covering her damaged toes, and he breathed.

She stiffened as the heat from his breath bled through the sock. She tried to jerk her foot away but he her held her bad leg tight and he breathed again, watching her eyes.

"Come on," she said, pulling weakly.

A glint of humor appeared in his eyes and again he breathed delicious warmth onto her icy toes, rubbing them gently.

"Max," she warned.

"You don't like it?" he asked into her sock, warming her more.

But that wasn't the issue. She closed her eyes. Yes, she liked it. She loved it. She loved him, that was the problem.

He rubbed and breathed. He would strip her of everything, this man.

"Max," she whispered. In the silence that followed, she opened her eyes and found him regarding her with a serious expression.

"I'm going to run you a bath now," he announced.

"No." She wished she had the energy to pull from his grip. "I'm power-drained, Max. I could slide down and drown."

"Not if I go in with you. Not if I hold you."

*What?* Her stomach did a flip-flop. "No."

"You have to get warm."

"I forbid it."

"Forbid all you want. You're getting a bath."

Her mouth dropped open. "You won't like the consequences of

defying me."

He squeezed her toes. "I'm already dead anyway, right?" He nestled her foot back into the blanket and headed up the stairs. It was with stunned horror that she listened to the crash of water. He would strip her down and take a bath with her?

A minute later he was back down, striding across the clean floor. "I *am* your protector, after all."

"You live at my behest."

"Yeah, yeah, yeah."

She glared up at him, hating her helplessness. The water crashed away upstairs, filling the massive claw foot tub. She couldn't allow herself to be on display for him, naked and needy. All the *fuck you* power she'd built over the years, it would all drain away, and he'd see her as what she was: a twisted little witch behind a curtain.

"I'll hold you," he said. "We'll bathe in our underwear, okay? It'll be just like we're swimming. And I won't let you drown."

She felt sick inside. "I'm telling you no."

"I got that, baby. You go on and get yourself Don Johnson the next round."

"Maybe I will."

He hesitated for a split second—she wouldn't have seen it if she didn't know him so well. Then he simply bent over and gathered her into to his chest, blanket and all, and hoisted her up. Just like that, she was aloft, in his arms, their faces close enough to kiss. She could feel his breath on her nose.

"I guarantee you, Don Johnson doesn't have the balls to do this." The room swooshed away as he carried her up the stairs.

# Chapter Six

UP THEY WENT, STEP BY STEP, OUTRAGE AND FEAR POUNDING
through her veins. She'd kick and struggle if her limbs weren't
heavy as lead.

The rush of water grew louder and the dry wintry air came alive with
moisture as they neared the bathroom. She could almost taste the warmth.
She yearned for it, even as the prospect of his bathing her horrified her.

Surely he didn't mean to go through with this! She, Veronica, was
the baddest of the bad. Fear tightened her belly. "I'll make you sorry," she
said.

"There's my Bitch Queen of the Witch World," he said.

"Don't patronize me."

"The bath is already working wonders and you're not even in it."

The breath caught in her throat. Would he actually do it?

He flipped off the lights with his elbow, and pale moonlight streamed
through the window. She felt grateful that he wouldn't see her leg in the
full, bright light. But also, she felt ashamed because he'd guessed it. A
truly powerful witch wouldn't care if her underling saw her ugliness; a

truly powerful witch might even enjoy having a man bathe her in all her despicable glory.

She needed to get her control back.

He set her down on the cushy chair in the corner and lit a candle on the shelf behind her. The glow lit the upper half of him. He tucked the blanket around her and sat on the edge of the tub, swishing the water. "Mmmmm. So warm and nice."

"Carry me back downstairs," she commanded.

"Sorry. You're going in."

Her heart swum with emotions she couldn't name. He didn't know what he was asking, what it was to be exposed, how deep the ridicule had sunk in. How it had poisoned her.

"I'm not."

"Not for you to decide, is it?" Then, casual as could be, he unrolled his sleeves and simply pulled off his shirt, taking the T-shirt underneath along with it, baring his thick, pale torso. His broad shoulders glowed strong and wide like muscled marble, with a series of scars low on one side. She swallowed as he tossed the garments aside and unzipped his jeans, stripping down to blue boxer shorts.

She'd fucked a good number of the rock stars she'd conjured, some in surprisingly dirty and imaginative ways, but this was already more intimate. And she'd always glamoured her leg for the rock stars. She couldn't glamour her leg now.

It had been a long time since she'd felt powerless, but she remembered it well. Frantically tuning into her environment, hanging on every sound. The stress of being on alert. Only the powerful could be oblivious.

Her devil computers were useless now.

He came to her and started to draw off the blanket.

She gripped it with all the strength she had. "No, Max. This has gone far enough."

"You think I've never seen anything like that? You think your injury's so special?"

"No more."

He scowled at her. This was how he'd been with perps, she thought suddenly; he'd overwhelm them with the force of his will. "You think it's special, but it's not. It's not anything special."

"I think it's my business."

"And keeping you alive is *my* business." He yanked the blanket out of her grip and clear off her, then he threw it aside and knelt in front of her and started unbuttoning her sweater.

"Max." She pushed at his arm.

He kept on. "I don't know what you're so worried about."

She glared. It's all she had left in her to do.

He undid more buttons, working gently and efficiently, hands grazing her belly through the tank top under her cardigan. She wasn't wearing a bra, though that hardly concerned her.

He paused at the last button and glanced up, face serious and shadowed in the candlelight. "I won't be your Jophius," he said. "I won't be some monster to do your dirty work and then just curl up like a pet." He pushed the sweater off her shoulders. The cool, moist air touched her arms. "I'll fight for you, baby," he said. "I'll fight to the last. But I'll never curl up at your feet." He looked at her strangely, and for one crazy moment, she thought he might kiss her.

"Fine," she barked. Not like she had a choice.

"You're on board."

No, more like she knew when she was beat. "Just do it."

Her heart beat like crazy as he pulled the sweater free of her arms and hands. She would reveal herself without a care. Isn't that what an undamaged woman would do?

"Ready?" He pulled her up against him and held her with one arm; he pushed her leggings and legwarmers off with his other hand, careful to leave her panties in place.

"It'll be like we're swimming," he said again, as though they were having any old conversation. As though they hadn't gone from boss and underling to something new and uncharted.

"I doubt that." She tried to make her voice sound casual as he lowered her back down to the chair and pulled the layers of fabric off her legs and feet.

Just like that, her leg was bare.

Her blood raced as she sat on view for him. She hated herself for worrying what he thought, nervous as a school girl. What did she care?

He hoisted her in his arms yet again and stepped right into the tub. The skin-to-skin contact would be nice if he wasn't touching the leg, which would be fully illuminated by the candle from this angle. *Who cares,* she scolded herself.

"Ready?"

"Do I have a choice?"

"Nah." He squatted into the warmth, lowering her gently in front of him. He stretched out like a human air mattress, pulling her onto him.

The warmth softened and enlivened her. She groaned her pleasure— she couldn't help it. She tried to avoid letting him take too much of her weight, but it was so tiring. What the hell, she'd gone this far. She was weak. Vulnerable as a kitten. She let her head rest back on his chest, let herself collapse and float back onto the hard planes of his muscles, let him hold her fully.

It was like a revelation, this feeling of being held.

"How is it?" he asked.

"Not so bad," she whispered.

"Not so *bad?*"

"Wonderful."

"That's more like it."

"Beyond wonderful," she confessed. It was beyond even that. It was like nothing she'd ever experienced, this sensation of being held, of giving herself over without reservation.

She trusted him. And he was holding her, helping her. And the more she let go, the more it meant. She felt open like a flower, skin to skin with him so silent and solid below her.

It was glorious and terrifying. Is this what normal people did? Gave themselves over? Was this a thing?

She'd had to almost die to get here, but now that she was here, she didn't want it to stop. She loved being in his arms. Even helpless, she loved it. Maybe even more so because she was helpless. The realization was a bit unsettling.

He seemed to have arranged himself underneath her—sideways or cross-legged, supporting her with his warm arms and thighs, letting her rest on his broad, muscular chest, which rose and fell as he breathed. As the minutes wore on she became hyper-aware of his masculinity. Not just him as a man, but as a male animal, virile and dominant beneath her.

And couldn't help but think that his cock was very near her ass. The way he sat, she couldn't feel it, but it certainly loomed large her mind.

She imagined melting and unfurling around him and feeling his hardness pressed between her legs. She wanted to fuck, even in this compromised state. Warmth blossomed between her legs.

He mustn't know. He didn't want her like that.

Max held her more firmly and slid them both deeper. She'd bared her rottenness to him, thrown herself on his mercy, and he'd simply held her. It was hard to comprehend.

She had another shocking thought: this is what a powerless woman had that she didn't have—vulnerability. A willingness to be held.

"More hot water?" he asked.

"Yeah, Max," she said.

He lifted his leg from under hers and adjusted the silver spigots with his feet, testing the water with his toe. All this touch. She hadn't been touched this much since childhood. Before the accident.

It was then she felt his cock brush against her butt, a steely surprise in the heat. She wasn't so stupid, though, to think it was her. Any man would grow hard holding a half-naked, wet woman. She looked at her mangled leg resting on his strong, thick leg. How could he ever want her?

"How's this?" He tested the water one last time.

"You're a regular monkey."

"That's right, baby," he said, his voice gravelly in her ear.

Was that sexual? But then, everything about him roared with sexuality.

"I want to stay in here forever," she said.

He kissed her hair. "I think you're amazing."

"For what?"

"You know what," he said.

He meant for doing something that scared her. As if consenting to life-sustaining warmth was brave. No, bravery would be for her to reveal how happy his joy made her. How she pined for him in bed at night. How he'd become everything in the world to her. How he was more real to her than any man alive. How she loved him.

Her love for him scared her, because there was no controlling it, no controlling him.

"Salvo'll come even stronger next time," he said. "He'll come fast and strong. Tomorrow, the next day."

"We'll handle it."

"We almost didn't," he said. "He's gotten a taste of going after you supernaturally now. I'd imagine there's a lot more supernatural where that came from."

"Maybe I'll go after *him*," she said. "It wasn't him I had a beef with. It was the son. But I'll go after him if I have to."

"Even if you killed him now, the vendetta's there," Max said. "The Salvo organization's a hydra. You cut Johnny down and there's others to take his place. They'll keep the vendetta strong. That's how it works with them. It's time to tell me why he's after you. Did you have something to do with his kid Benny getting locked up? Is that why they're after you?"

More truth. She hadn't wanted Max to know the reason they were after her because it had felt like a key to her somehow. Silly—she couldn't even give him that? A brave woman let people know things about her and simply dealt with it.

A pause. He brushed a bit of hair from her eyes. "Is that why?"

"Yeah, that's why. I made sure Benny Salvo got locked up."

"I'm glad. We knew all about the kid down in Chicago," Max said. "We sure didn't cry to see him go."

"The kid's a psycho," Veronica said. "If his dad thought he'd stop being a psycho just because he banished him to a small town in the middle of nowhere, he was wrong."

"The geography fix never works."

Benny Salvo, heir to the Salvo empire, had raped a Malcolmsberg girl, beaten her to death, and then left her in a local park, posed horribly. It had touched something deep in Veronica.

"They couldn't get him for it, so I stepped in. I produced his home videos of the rapes and murders. Supposedly anonymously, but…"

"Right," Max said. "What I don't get is, from what I recall of the trial, he'd seemed to truly think the videos had been destroyed."

"They had been destroyed," she said. "But there were *photos* of the videos. I conjured the videos with my devil computers, made copies, planted them, and then phoned in a tip. Then I blackmailed a judge and a prosecutor. Anonymously, just asking for a fair trial. I knew the Salvos would try and fix it."

"Because you wanted Benny Salvo to be locked up," Max said.

She swished the water. He was right to wonder why she'd gotten involved. And hell, she could've popped his brain like bubble-wrap—that would've stopped Benny from drugging and raping and killing another girl more surely than the justice system. "I wanted his own tapes to bring him down. For him to be brought down by his own folly."

"Why?"

"I don't know. I just wanted him helpless and bewildered, and to hate himself. I wanted him to have that feeling."

The candle flickered and guttered in the silence that followed.

"Because that's the worst punishment you could think of?" he whispered.

Her voice, when it came out, sounded hoarse. "Yes."

She felt his lips near her ear.

"Why?" he asked. "Because it happened here in Malcolmsberg?"

"No. It's not the proximity."

The candle cast eerie shadows on the ceiling.

"It's the way he left her, isn't it?" Max guessed. "Uncovered like that for all to see. You have a thing about that."

Always the detective, her Max. Too much the detective. Truth and vulnerability was losing its charm.

"Put on the hot," she said.

He flicked the spigot with his toe, said nothing more. But he knew.

THE MORE SHE REGAINED HER STRENGTH OVER THE NEXT DAY, THE more that night in the tub seemed like a daring dream. But it had happened, and she'd liked the woman she was back there. What's more, the incident had made her feel closer to Max, easier with him, and she sometimes imagined he felt it back.

She had the crazy thought that this was what a relationship was made of—taking risks and letting yourself be undone, undignified. It was surprising and fascinating.

He certainly seemed to take more command of the place—she noticed it in the bigger-than-usual way he sat on the furniture, and his heavy stroll; it was as though he'd sunken more deeply into life.

He also seemed more on guard. He really thought the next attack could be any minute. It frightened her. She wasn't strong enough to fight like again.

The next day she took her own bath, and afterwards, she went down to her lab and ordered up steak dinners from one of the photos in her gourmet magazine as a surprise for Max.

She wasn't quite up for steak when the dinner arrived the next day, but she sat across from him with a bowl of Donkey Kong Crunch and watched him devour both meals. She'd never seen a man so in love with being alive. The way he relished every bite of his food, how badly he wanted to walk around outside on sunny days. The way he padded down the stairs in the morning, opened the refrigerator, and then peered in while stretching like a grizzly bear, it made her want to be better for him, to be the woman in the bath for him, doer of scary things.

She could never tell him how she felt. She couldn't stand the silence. The pity. But she could do the second scariest-ever thing: she could try to give him a natural term of life. Total freedom and autonomy. He wouldn't need her anymore, but that was the gift of it—he'd be his own man. He could laugh at her and leave her. He wouldn't go back to Chicago, but there was a whole world out there for him.

*You won't ever do what really scares you,* he'd said.

Well, he'd eat his words when he learned of this new plan. He might eat his words on the way to California or something, but still, he'd see she wasn't some sort of coward, hiding behind magic. *If he leaves, he leaves, whatever will be, will be,* she told herself, ignoring the knot forming her stomach. Only a weak person kept people around by force. And anyway, she knew how to be alone. She knew how to live without love.

Jophius jumped up on the chair next to her. Jophius had taken to following her around everywhere. She put a handful of cereal in front of Jophius, and he gobbled it up in snorty delight, teeth flashing.

"That's nice," Max said.

She grinned. "He likes to eat at the big table."

Max rolled his eyes and sopped up the gravy with a biscuit.

A tweak of the code—she felt sure that's all it would take. But what tweak? That was the million dollar question. She'd figure it out—she always triumphed when she put her mind to something. In the technical realm, anyway. And she did things that scared her all the time—he was wrong to say she didn't.

Jophius scrunched his nose and eyes in pleasure as she rubbed his ear. If the tweak worked, she could give Jophius a natural life, too. Jophius would stay.

# Chapter Seven

THE TRAIN TO CHICAGO *THA-LUNKED* ALONG THE MISSISSIPPI past snowy river towns and half-frozen wetlands. Veronica sat next to the window, snuggled down inside her thick, black overcoat. Her furry black hat was adorned with a big jeweled pin, giving her the mysterious elegance of a woman from another era. As if she felt him looking at her she turned to him with a smile that lit her delicate features. Max resisted the urge to pull her snug to him; instead he offered her favorite part of the paper, the Dear Abby section.

"Thanks." She took it and folded it neatly.

He missed the intimacy he'd felt with her in the bath, but he certainly didn't want to see her broken again to get it back. If regaining her strength meant she needed him less, so be it. Though lately he felt like she was determined not to need him. And she was back to spending endless hours in her lab again, too. And here they were, pit bull and witch, riding a train. Handling business, albeit with a new level of friendship between them.

The train had left St. Paul at dawn. All the way to the station, he'd had the feeling of them being followed, watched. He didn't feel easy on the train, either. Salvo would move fast and hard.

They'd be in Chicago after lunch. Chicago, the home he longed for and dreaded seeing. The home he could never have back. Mostly he couldn't get his little girl out of his mind. Did she carry his death in her eyes? Back when he was a cop he'd seen a lot of kids carry death and trouble in their eyes. He didn't want that for Teresa.

He'd resisted going down to peek in on her these past months. It felt like haunting her, because he was a type of ghost. And what if she caught sight of him? It would mess her up big-time.

He flipped the paper to another section. More blather on Ronald Reagan's invasion of Grenada.

She'd be three months older. Nine and a half.

There was a chance he'd catch sight of her while carrying out their plan. Who knows? It could happen. Maybe his sister and her family would take Teresa to the natural history museum today—the natural history museum was near the old stakeout point, their destination. And Teresa wouldn't recognize him because Veronica was planning on glamouring them, magically changing their appearance. Still, haunting Teresa felt wrong.

He was less than a ghost, really, because one of these days his bitch queen would get pissed off enough at him that she wouldn't want him around, and she wouldn't even have to kick him out. Her simple inaction would end him. He was conscious of that fact each and every time he opposed her.

It was no way for a man to live. And it sure the hell was no way for a man in love to live.

He knew that if he mentioned the idea of seeing Teresa, Veronica would be all for it. *If you want to, why not?* She'd say.

But it didn't sit right.

Going to Chicago, however, was unavoidable. They had to travel for the plan to work. Max had come up with it after Veronica had explained how she'd conjured up the video tapes from a photo. If she could do that, he knew where they could get all kinds of dirt on Salvo. Veronica had assured him over and over that yes, if he could snap a photo of a certain file cabinet, then she could produce that cabinet with its contents intact.

"I got your brain when I ordered you, didn't I?" she'd joked. "I got your mulish attitude, right?"

"So out of curiosity," he asked, "what would you get if you ordered Don Johnson?"

"It depends on what picture I ordered him from. If I ordered him from a tabloid picture of him dining out at a Hollywood restaurant or something, I'd get the actual man. But if I ordered him from, like, a TV Guide picture where he's being Detective Sonny Crockett? I'd probably get that character." She snorted. "Ordering a character off the TV. That would be *so* irresponsible."

"What's the difference?"

"A character isn't human. It would just be insane, that's all. A Pandora's box." Then she looked at him, getting the real meaning. "You're human. A real man in every way. *Every* way, Max. You have no idea—" she seemed about to say more, but stopped herself, realizing, maybe the flimsiness of her arguments. He was neither real nor human. A man, yes, which made it all the more excruciating. Being with her.

They'd stopped at a camera store in Paupesha yesterday and purchased a camera with a telephoto lens. They would take a photo of the file cabinet in Salvo's lawyer's office, get it developed at the one-hour place, and go home and conjure it. Then he'd raid the thing for information nobody was supposed to have. They'd be able to blackmail the entire Salvo family with it. The plan would protect Veronica forever. It was a good plan.

Except they might not have time to carry it out.

And what if he did catch sight of Teresa?

*Stay away from her*, he told himself. *Photograph the cabinet and leave.*

Frozen wetlands turned to snowy fields outside the window. Dead, brown corn stalks popped up from the unbroken white here and there.

With her rosy red cheeks and dark, pretty hair under that hat, Veronica looked like something off an old-fashioned Christmas card. Almost innocent.

He thought about her leg in the bath, under the water that danced with candlelight. Her leg was outrageous and wrong and wild and unconventional and it refused to behave, just like her. He'd wanted to warm her that night with everything he had. And to kiss every inch of that hated, misshapen leg, and the rest of her, too—exploring her, tasting her. He'd wanted to pull her to him and slide his hands under her wet tank top and touch her breasts, and take over her body and invade her senses from every angle and fuck her until she screamed his name.

He'd contented himself with keeping her from drowning. He was a gentleman, however ungentlemanly his thoughts had been.

She tucked her coat over her lap. Then she looked at him, caught him staring. "What?"

*You're beautiful and hard and a little bit bad,* he thought. Instead he folded up the front section of the paper. "Want this?"

"Nah." She turned back to stare out the window.

# Chapter Eight

THE FREYER-KOPPS TOWER HAD BEEN 80% VACANT WHEN Max's men had taken over the 26th floor in order to stake out the 26th floor of the Griggs Tower across the street.

Three months later, the Freyer-Kopps was still mostly vacant.

Max hit the elevator button.

Veronica had glamoured them both before they'd left the train station. It was hard for him to get it through his head that the woman standing with him—the suntanned blonde with her red polka-dot power suit and giant shoulder pads—was Veronica. It put him off balance.

"Dare I ask what you bespelled me to look like?" he said.

With an impish smile she pointed at a mirrored section of wall beyond a potted plant. He walked over and groaned at the image of a young buck in a fedora and an oversized jacket with rolled-up sleeves. His frosted hair dipped over one eye. He gave her a dark glance. "I'm that Hungry Like the Wolf guy."

"Not exactly. But…" She shrugged. "…inspired by."

"Thanks a lot." The elevator door opened and they got in. He stabbed the button for twenty-six and the door slid shut. She'd made him into the kind of guy she wanted to be with, fresh off MTV. "Make me more regular. This is conspicuous."

Veronica switched her briefcase to her other hand. "We look just right. FYI, there's an ad agency and magazine offices in this building."

"You call this just right?"

"I didn't want you looking like a cop," she said.

"The only alternative to cop is a ridiculous man-child who can't even fill out a sports coat?"

She screwed up her eyes and lips in mock anger. He couldn't help but smile. The face wasn't hers but the expression was. He resisted the urge to grab her and kiss her.

She said, "Any more lip out of you and you'll find yourself staring at Boy George in the mirror."

The 26th floor was full of abandoned cubicles and cabinets, just as he and his men had left it after surveillance ended that past summer. He rolled a couple of chairs to the window. She sat in hers and spun around. He cranked up the back of another chair and knelt behind it, using it to steady the camera's bulky telephoto lens. "There it is. Still in full view."

He snapped a few photos. "Gotcha," he said. He stood up and had her look through it. "The window to the right of the one with the blue blinds is Salvo's lawyer's office."

"You sure they can't see us?" she asked.

"This building has mirrored windows. Find the blue blinds?"

"Yes. Marble wallpaper?"

"Yup. It's the middle cabinet stack we need. That cabinet holds the name of every judge, cop, and congressperson on the Salvo payroll, plus planted guys. We did everything we could to get a warrant. There was even some move to break in that I wasn't supposed to know about. Couldn't even breach the ground floor. So we had to sit here and salivate."

"Push me up to the edge," she said.

He pushed her to the window bank and she snapped a few of her own pictures.

"That's all we need?" he asked.

She grinned. "It's alls we need."

If this worked out, she wouldn't need him for protection anymore.

He wondered if she was thinking about that. "Let's get back to the station." They had tickets for the seven o'clock. It wasn't even four.

"You could see her."

"It's not rightful," he said.

"It could ease your mind. She wouldn't know."

"*I'd* know," he said.

"She won't recognize you."

"It's not just that," he said. It's what he might see.

"Kids are resilient."

He closed his eyes. The idea of leaving and not at least catching a glimpse of Teresa made him feel jumbled up. "I can't."

"I think you have to."

"Don't."

She limped to him—even glamoured, she limped. It was one way their enemies might recognize them. He hadn't said that, though. He didn't want to frighten her.

She rested a hand on his shoulder and set her chin on her hand. "I'll be the devil for you if you want," she whispered. "It's okay for you to hate me."

"Veronica—"

"Shhh." She flicked around her free hand. Scrying for Teresa. "Not very far," she whispered. "Teresa plays the oboe?"

He hissed out a breath. "Friday after school band practice." She'd had Friday band practice before his death. It struck him as strange that she'd still have it.

Veronica straightened up. "She's at her school. In the gym. We could be there in ten minutes. I'll make us repairmen. There's a panel on the wall near the stage."

"It's not rightful." And he didn't want to see his death in her eyes. So many kids were walking around destroyed. He couldn't bear that Teresa should be one of them.

"You need to give yourself a break sometimes," she said. "You need to see that she's okay."

"Did *you* see? Is she okay?"

"I don't know her." She fixed him with a gaze that was all cold, hard fire. "You need to see for yourself."

He pulled away. "I'm a ghost. I don't belong around a little girl."

"You're a man, not a ghost." She took his hand. "Come on." He felt a strange pull, like a magnetic river, urging him out of the space and back to the elevator.

He went willingly…yet not.

She hit the button and the door opened. Down they went, down, down, and then they walked across the lobby and out into the icy wind that whipped between the gray buildings and over ice-crusted sidewalks.

He recalled Veronica once telling him that she could compel people—she'd explained that she did it by repelling them from every other available option. In this way, she created pull. She was doing it now, he realized. There was only the school now. Teresa.

"Wait," he said.

"We're going." She signaled for a cab. There was nowhere else to go.

A cab neared. He would give the address of the school, almost like it was pre-ordained.

"Wait," he said. "Turn off the spell."

"No."

He pulled his hand from hers. "Turn it off."

"I'm making you go."

"I'll live and die by my own sword, dammit."

She looked unsure. He felt when she cut it.

A cab pulled up. Max motioned Veronica in and got in after. "Park Elm Elementary on Fourth and Zieman." He sat back with an *oof*. He was really doing it.

"You'll be glad."

Max kept an eye on the side and rearview mirrors to make sure they weren't followed. After a few blocks he told the cabbie to make a loop, claiming he wanted to see a favorite steakhouse.

Veronica gave him a conspiratorial look. She knew what he was doing—she always keyed into the cop stuff.

Without thinking, he draped an arm around her shoulders and pulled her close. He felt grateful that she allowed it, but then again, he looked like one of her music idols.

She snuggled into him. It felt good. Right.

It didn't matter why she allowed it; he needed to hold her. It shook him to see how all the shops and restaurants and people had all kept going. He didn't know how it could be that a man could lose so much so quickly and violently as he had the night he got gunned down, but the streets and restaurants he loved would look perfectly humdrum afterwards. He couldn't decide whether it was a monstrous joke or a kindness.

He paid and they stepped out.

The school was a long, low brick building with a fenced-in yard at one end. Veronica did the magic that would alter their glamour. She was in a ComEd jumpsuit, jacket, and cap with a badge on her pocket. She had the face she'd had in the tower. The camera she carried looked like a clipboard now, and she'd turned her briefcase into a toolbox, which she handed to him.

He took it, realizing he was dressed the same way.

They walked in. She went over and spoke with the night guard at the desk off to the side, showed him something on the clipboard and he waved them through. The halls were empty aside from a janitor mopping the floor behind a yellow *Wet Floor* sign.

Voices echoed down the hall as they neared the gym. A loud female voice rose above all others—something about starting where the horns come in. Strains of music went up. A march of some kind.

He and Veronica walked into the massive gym, melting into the darkness around the edges.

Up at the end was a brightly lit stage full of children. He saw Teresa right away, sitting at the edge of a row.

"That's her," he whispered, frozen in his tracks. She wore her favorite pink sweater with a black T sewn onto it. A massive tube of her favorite bubblegum lip gloss hung from a cord around her neck. She held her oboe in her lap and sat still as the horns blared on, then she leaned over and whispered to the girl next to her. He recognized the girl as her best friend, Patty. Patty whispered back and Teresa pinched her own nose— something she did when she wanted to keep from laughing aloud. Her little body convulsed with silent giggles, though, and his heart burst with emotions he couldn't name.

She was beautiful and perfect and lovely. And she was laughing. She'd always been a resourceful, happy girl, good at bouncing back from things. Could he trust this? Was she really okay? He couldn't see her eyes.

He needed to be closer.

A tug at his hand. Veronica pulling him. He allowed it, forcing his gaze away from the stage. Yes, they were inspectors of some sort. They needed to inspect.

She limped at his side. Before he knew it, they were on the far end of the gym. Veronica opened a gray panel. Then she took the toolbox from him and set it on the floor and took out some tools.

He could see Teresa's face more clearly from there. His girl had grown bored. The teacher had the horns repeat a section. Patty kicked Teresa's foot, and Teresa gave her an arch look. Ah, that arch look. Something of significance had happened in the horns section. A missed note?

The teacher had seen them by now—a few of the kids had, too, and Max knew they had an audience. The teacher had the children take out the next piece. A flurry of activity and chatter rose up from the stage. Patty and Teresa shared a music stand; Patty turned the page and Teresa looked in their direction. It was then he saw her eyes.

*They didn't hold his death.*

She'd be okay—she really would. He felt like shouting in gratitude.

"I suppose we're watching the whole practice," Veronica said wearily.

"The whole damn thing," he said.

"I could take a picture," she offered.

Horror shot through him. "No photos."

"Not to conjure," she said.

"Still. I want it like this."

The songs were played roughly, but with heart. He tried to maintain the role of the inspector, fussing with things from the box now and then, but watching all the while. His girl was a symphony of nuances and memories; every movement and expression heartened him and devastated him all at once. She was going to be okay.

Suddenly it was over, and the stage was a bustle of backpacks and chatter and instructions from the teacher. Teresa and Patty were among the first off the stage and out the door. Running.

Just like that she was gone.

He watched in a daze.

Veronica motioned to the teacher. "We got the lights," she said.

Five minutes later, the gym stood empty.

They stayed for a long time. Locker slams rose and dwindled. Voices faded. Doors squeaked. A hush fell.

The school was vacant now, except for the janitor.

"She always runs places when she's excited," he said when he realized how long they'd been standing there. "Happy."

Veronica put a hand on his shoulder. "She's happy. And you're okay."

Max wasn't sure if it was a question or an observation, but he wasn't okay. He loved that little girl. He'd lost so much. He slid to the floor.

"No." She kicked him.

"Ow."

"You get up. You help me. You're going to help me put these things away, Max." She motioned at the tools she'd pulled out of the box. Veronica. Always ready with a fix. He started gathering them up and putting them back.

"Don't just throw them in. Put them back in order," she said.

It was him she wanted orderly. He was unruly with emotion, and it frightened her. Veronica, with her temporary playmates and her carefully controlled world, the woman with the power to turn people on and off like water from a spigot. She'd never know what it was to be devastated by love, he thought with sudden sadness. The magic that protected her cut her off from all that.

He set a wrench into a slot with other wrenches. She didn't even understand tools.

"What?"

He looked up to find her watching him. "You pulled out a wrench to pretend to fix an electrical box?" he asked.

"So?"

His laugh sounded overwrought even to his own ears.

"Max, are you okay?"

"I'm all torn up inside, Veronica."

She regarded him helplessly. She hated him suffering, in part because it touched off her suffering, he suspected. Her pit bull, her Jophius, messy with emotion.

He forced a smile. "I'm okay, baby. We need to catch our train."

A silence. Was she relieved? "Okay, Max."

They caught a cab to the station, joining the late commuters traveling back to Milwaukee. They'd ride on through the night to St. Paul.

Inside the ornate and cavernous lobby, Veronica bought a detective novel from a used book stall, and she found a Louis L'Amour western for Max. She held it out. "You read this one yet?"

"No," he lied, because he knew she wanted him to have something nice for the ride, something to console him.

"Excellent," she said.

They settled into their seats for the journey home, restored to their regular appearances. The train lurched slowly through the Chicago yards, picking up speed as they neared Wisconsin. Max re-read the first few chapters of his book while she read hers.

The Milwaukee commuters disembarked some time later, leaving the car half empty. The lights were dimmed as the train set off once again, heading northwest. The horn blew whenever they approached populated areas—every few minutes at first, but less and less as they went on. Still Max would look up every time he heard the sound, desperate to get a glimpse into the lit-up windows of the homes and taverns they passed, as if he could find some life out there to latch onto.

Eventually the terrain turned rural. He felt hemmed in by the endless darkness, trapped in a train car with all the passengers and their murmurings and everyday lives and places they belonged.

As if she somehow felt his distress, she reached over and took his hand in hers. Gently, softly. "You okay?"

"Yeah," he lied, trying not to crush her bones out of wanting to hang onto her. She was all he had left, and he was about to lose her, too. His usefulness would be over once the Salvo bit was settled.

"That was hard for you," she said.

"Yet good." He looked out the window. At least he could rest easy knowing his girl was okay. "All this emptiness, does it ever make you feel all alone?"

"Max," she whispered. "You're not."

He looked over at her and saw the struggle in her eyes. Not saying all she thought, as usual. Regretting whipping him up, maybe. Dreading a slow goodbye. He pulled his hand from hers and made a show of flipping through his book, then he shoved it into the seat pocket.

"Be right back."

He headed down the tiny staircase to the lower level of the train, wandering to the very end. She'd think he was using the bathroom, but really he just needed to collect himself.

The *tha-lunk tha-lunk* was louder on the lower level, the darkness outside more profound. He sat himself on the luggage shelf full of backpacks and suitcases, all the essentials of those lives up there.

He suddenly didn't know what anything was, and it terrified him. He was dead, but not. He had a waterfall of grief inside him.

He felt her before he saw her limping down the slim hallway.

When she reached him, she rested her petite hands on his thighs. "I'm sorry, Max."

The weight of her hands comforted him. She affected him like she'd never know.

"When I wanted you to see her, I didn't want for you to feel like this," she said.

"It's okay."

"It's not," she said.

"No, it is, Veronica. I *want* to feel this." His words sounded growly, even to his own ears. "I *need* to feel it."

She furrowed her brow.

He took hold of her shoulders and looked into her eyes, feeling such crazy love for her. She didn't want things to touch her. That was their difference.

"I want to plunge down and feel everything if that's what's there," he whispered. "Bring it on, that's what I say. Even if it rips me apart."

"No, Max."

He tightened his grip, raw with love and grief. "It's what I have, Veronica. It's alls I have left that's still real. It's alls I have left that shows I'm alive."

"You're wrong, Max—that's not all." And she went up on her tiptoes and pressed her soft lips to his. She kissed him slowly and sweetly, but it was electric, too, as if she were shoving life right into him, and suddenly, miraculously, he wasn't alone. At least in that moment, he wasn't alone.

Before he knew what he was doing, he was down off his perch, pushing her against the wall, kissing her with everything he had. He felt her fingers wend under his shirt, around his back, pressing into his flesh, clutching at him.

"Veronica." He kissed down her cheek, trailing kisses down her neck, nuzzling her soft skin, drinking her up like a drought-crazed madman.

"You're more alive than everyone on the planet combined," she whispered in the darkness. "What's between us is real."

He pulled away, unable to trust it all. "Are you doing a pity number?"

She widened her eyes, a look she reserved for only the biggest of outrages. "Pity? *Pity?*" She snorted. "FYI, Max—" Then she stopped short.

"FYI what?"

"It's not exactly an FYI," she said.

"What isn't?"

"Well, it kind of is, but not on the level of, hey, this is teal, not green."

"Uh huh," he said.

"It's a different level." She placed her hands on his chest and squeezed his shirt front, gazing into his eyes with a mixture of fear and resolve. He'd seen that look once before—it was back in the bathroom, before she'd consented to let him bathe her, back when she'd let herself be so vulnerable to him.

A shiver came over him.

"FYI," she began again, then she tilted her head, eyebrows raised. Her expression for when she felt she was delivering the killer point in an argument. "FYI, I love you, so…"

He couldn't believe it. This crazy happiness washed over him. "So… so *there?* Is that what you were going to say?" he teased.

Her face went red. "No."

"FYI, I love you, so there?" He tickled her belly. "FYI? *That's* an FYI?"

She laughed. "FYI I love you, so it's not pity." She grabbed his hands. "Stop being a freak. Don't make me take it back."

He pulled out of her grip and caged her with his arms, pressing her up against the wall with the length of his body. This was real—she was right about that. "You can't take it back." He nipped her ear and she gasped. "I won't let you take it back." He kissed her hard this time, pressing his tongue beyond the seam of her lips and into her mouth, invading her. He couldn't get enough of her. He never could.

The train *tha-lunked* rhythmically, an erotic lull. *Tha-lunk, tha-lunk.*

He kissed her cheek, then her ear. He whispered, "I have an FYI for you, baby."

"Is it dirty?" she asked.

He pulled away and cupped her cheeks in his hands. "You are so freaking beautiful. Every inch of you. And I love the stuffing out of you. That's my FYI for you."

"Love the stuffing out of me?"

"Yeah," he said.

Her eyes went serious. "Oh, please do." She reached down between them and pressed the ridge of his cock right through his pants. "Please."

He looked up and down the hall.

She whispered into his ear: "Alls they'll see is luggage, Max."

His witch, on the spot with the magic.

With shaking hands he pushed her furry coat off her shoulders, then fumbled with the clips holding up her overalls, kissing her all the while. She pushed him away in a huff and undid them herself.

"Not fast enough?"

She watched his eyes as she wriggled out of her overalls there in the dim luggage area, letting them drop off her legs, letting her leg be bare in front of him. Even in the dimness, it was a risk for her because he could see it by the running lights, so much thinner and weaker than the other, especially below the knee.

"You are so goddamn beautiful and you don't even know."

"Oh, I know," she said, but it was her sing-songy voice, making a lie of something thorny. She pulled him close so the leg was out of view.

He pushed off his pants, and then unbuttoned her shirt and pulled down her bra. Slowly he kissed down to her breast. Her skin felt like silk on his lips. She held his head in her fists, managing to grab hold of bits of his hair.

He pressed his hands into the flesh of her buttocks, drew her to him as he kissed and sucked her nipple, letting his shaft slide along her seam. She gasped softly, churning against him to the rhythm of the train, *tha-lunk, tha-lunk,* fists balled at his skull, the short hairs of his crew cut caught tightly between her fingers. It was pain and pleasure and he relished it like crazy.

He pulled away and knelt, and he kissed her bad knee.

"Hey!" She tried to pull him up, but he wouldn't go. "What are you doing?"

He traced a massive scar over her calf, slid his hands over the mottled skin, feeling its texture. Kissed the roughest area. It seemed to be burned, almost. "You are beautiful everywhere."

"You stop that." Again she tried to pull him up. He allowed it this time.

He stood, looked her in the eye. "Or what?"

"I'll think of something." She grabbed his cock, trying to distract him from his mission of kissing some more of her bad leg. It worked. He wanted her like crazy. He'd dreamed of this. He picked her up and turned her around, setting her on the luggage shelf.

She wrapped her legs around him, opening to him, guiding him in. "Come here," she said, even though he was nearly there.

"Wait," he kissed her, hating to stop. "This could be dangerous."

"I'm a witch," she whispered. "Protection…" she bit his ear, slipped her hand down between them. "It's handled."

He kissed her some more as she guided his cock into her. He pushed into her with a moan and everything stilled.

Her grip on his hair went even tighter. He might actually lose a chunk of hair, he thought. He hoped he would.

He pulled out and slid in again. Then he pulled out and slid in from a high angle, sliding relentlessly along her clit to the rhythm of the train. Veronica was tight and hot around him. Sweat shone on her face. She moved her hands to his chest, let her head loll back. And then he fucked her at a new angle.

"Just like that, Max."

So he kept on just like that, needing her, loving her, fucking them both into the land of the living until she cried out and came, convulsing around him, fists tearing at his hair, setting him off in an orgasm that shattered his being.

# Chapter Nine

THE TRAIN SPED THROUGH THE NIGHT. SHE'D TURNED OFF THE spotlight above her seat, put up her armrest, and lay her head on his shoulder, pretending to sleep, but she was really watching him sketch.

*He loved her.*

It was the best feeling in the world. Unless you counted loving him. Just like that, she'd told him. She'd jumped and he caught her. It was such a good feeling. She didn't always have to be the one on the outside looking in. She just had to risk everything, that's all. It might actually get addictive.

He was drawing his little girl, up on the stage.

She straightened up, fished around in her pocket, and pulled out her Village Lip Lickers, sliding the top of the tin open. They had papaya flavor in Chicago. Very rare. "You wouldn't let me take a photo of her, but you'll sketch her?" she asked.

He filled in the hair with short, sharp strokes. "It's hard to explain," he said. "A photo, it's a way of capturing her. This drawing, it's a way of loving her."

Shivers went through her. He was loving his kid. Drawing her. He didn't need to have her, to conjure her. He was just loving her. It was a selfless love. Veronica felt ashamed to think of her relationship with her niece, Alix, the one member of her sister's family who didn't know her, didn't know to loathe her. The way she'd conjured the little girl for craft days and outings. Like a toy she controlled. Alix would never know about the time they spent together. It was selfish.

She didn't want her love to be like that with Max. She had to find a way into the code to give him natural life.

Now and then he put down the drawing and walked the train, up and back. He was on edge. She was, too. Salvo's next attack would be big and brutal, and without knowing what sorts of baddies he'd bring in, there was no way to prepare.

The next morning they developed the photos at the one-hour booth in front of the Piggly Wiggly, and she went right to work down in her lab conjuring the cabinet as he looked on from his seat on the couch.

"It's done?" he asked when she pulled the electrodes from her head.

"Tomorrow at this time it'll be on the doorstep."

He smiled. He was going to use the information to create what he called doomsday letters—letters that would be triggered by her unnatural or even suspicious death. The letters would be instantly sent to a long list of people, and each letter would contain the names of every government official and double agent who'd ever done anything for the Salvos. "They'll never bother you again once they know you have this. And they certainly won't send any more supernatural beings after you." He came up behind her and kissed the top of her head, sliding his hands over her shoulders. "We just have to hold out a while longer."

She gazed up at him. "Maybe we should go celebrate. We could go to the Malcolmsberg Supper Club for frog legs."

She didn't want to tell him the other reason to celebrate—she'd spent the day scouring magic books for ideas on normalizing his term of life, and she'd hit on something—the realization that she'd been approaching it wrong all this time. She needed a new kind of temporal notation altogether, bespelled to fool the computers. She couldn't be sure it would work, but things were looking good.

His seven days were up in two days. Normally she'd order him 24 hours and 10 seconds before he was due to blink out, so that no matter where he blinked out from, ten seconds later he'd appear at the door.

This new method of expressing time let her reset the term of life he had now. To a year, to 30 years, whatever. Max would simply stay. He'd age like a normal person. A few more tests and she'd implement it.

"I don't want to go out," he said, kissing her neck. "I want to stick around here. I can't get enough of you, Veronica." He said it as though it baffled him.

She smiled up at him. "All bodies are electric. All emotions are electric."

"Stop with the science shit." He pulled her up.

"It's true," she breathed as he lifted her clear off her chair. He carried her upstairs to the living room where he'd made a fire.

She pressed a hand to his chest, enjoying his solid strength. He would be his own person.

Roughly he grabbed her hand and kissed her palm, then the inside of her wrist. He undressed her and made love to her by firelight, sweetly. Max had so many moods. He'd died twice, but he was more alive than anyone she'd known.

Afterwards they lay side by side, naked on the couch under a blanket.

"Do you want to order a pizza?" she asked. He always wanted to eat.

"Too dangerous," he said. "This is not the time to be loosening your wards for delivery boys. Anyway, I want to draw you."

Her heart leapt. "You want to draw me?"

"You."

"Okay," she whispered.

He stood and flipped on a light. "Stay there. I'll get my stuff."

She grabbed her shirt.

"No," he said, "just like that, just as you are."

"Naked?"

"Yes."

She stiffened. "Max, you can't." It was one thing to let him see her leg in dimness or firelight. It was another to be laid out for him to stare at and sketch.

"Why not?"

"It's too much for me…"

He touched her hair. "Let me," he whispered.

"Don't ask it. I can't."

"You can do anything, Veronica. You're the baddest of the bad, baby."

"The baddest of the bad doesn't want to be drawn in the nude. Let's just hang out."

"Okay." He slid a finger over her shoulder. "Okay."

She looked away. She felt so pathetic. Why not? She thought about the time in the bathtub, the train, the strange and delicious luxury of letting herself be vulnerable to this man whom she trusted beyond anything. It had always worked out. But drawing the leg, it was too much.

*Do something that scares you,* he'd said to her. Well, she was about to give him a natural life and release him from her control. She'd told him she loved him. Wasn't that enough?

They watched the fire together. Why couldn't she have said *yes*? It was special that he wanted to draw her. Hell, he'd seen the leg. Still, for him to stare openly at it and sketch it, catalogue it in all its ugliness…

"It's okay," he whispered, as though reading her mind.

But it wasn't. She sunk into him, let him hold her, trying to remember what it was like to give herself over. Was she not the Bitch Queen of the Witch World? Could she not do this? She sat up. "Get the stuff."

"You'll let me draw you?"

"Do it before I change my mind," she said.

He slid out from beside her and headed to the stairs, broad back gleaming in the flames, ass radiant. He disappeared to get his drawing stuff.

She flipped off the covers and looked at her leg with its mottled skin and frail, wrongly formed bones. Just a leg, she thought to herself. But it wasn't just a leg. Her shame over it and the ridicule she'd suffered from it had driven so many of her choices. It was why she'd studied to become a witch, seeking out the most extreme mentors, traveling to the most remote places for the rarest charms, accumulating more and more power, having to beat everybody. It wasn't why the other witches had rejected her—they'd laughed at her ideas, not her leg. But somehow, when they laughed, she was still that kid in gym shorts, limping around, vowing to crush them all.

She closed her eyes as he came back down. He flicked on the lamp.

"Every single light?" She opened her eyes.

He smiled his crooked smile. "Shut up and get comfortable." He took the ottoman in front of the couch.

She stretched out sideways, with her good leg in front of her bad.

"No, no, no." He came to her, grabbed her good ankle, and set it in back.

"So pushy," she joked, just to cover the gravity of this.

"That's me, baby," he said.

She closed her eyes, feeling painfully exposed. The leather crinkled as he sat back down.

Lying there, naked, she couldn't help but think of the girl the younger Salvo had left naked and dead on display.

She banished the thought and focused instead on Max's pencil, which made a rustling sound. Her leg tingled at times—she felt sure it tingled from his sketching it, as though his eyes were too much for it. She fought the urge to cover it. This was Max. He'd said he loved her.

Still, it seemed like the sketch was taking forever.

"You okay like that?"

"Yeah, Max," she said.

A few minutes later he tore the paper from the pad.

"Are you done?"

"No. Got it wrong."

She groaned. "You're starting over?"

"Yeah. It was the wrong color." He crumpled up the paper and knocked through the pencils in his box. "I'm doing you in blue."

She laughed, overcome with the ridiculousness of it all. She was letting him sketch her naked, complete with her maimed leg. Not only that, but he'd already done one sketch, discarded it, and was starting over.

"I'm not a bowl of fruit,"

"Oh, I *know*," he said.

She snorted. "That had better be a good drawing or you will be illin' my friend."

"Yeah, yeah, yeah."

He sketched away, pausing only when Jophius scratched at the door. She felt a blast of cold as he let the little beast in, then he went back to work. She didn't know how much time had passed. It felt like an hour, but it probably hadn't been more than 20 minutes.

"Done." He smiled. "Was that so bad?"

"Depends." She pulled the woolly blanket around herself and sat up.

He sat next to her, pad against his chest.

"Am I going to regret this?" she asked.

He tipped down the pad. She looked at in confusion. In real life, her bad leg was much smaller than her good one, but he'd made it way larger, and more—it looked…vibrant. Energetic. Forceful.

*Magical.*

It was where the image of her came to life. She touched it. "Oh my god," she said.

"What do you think?"

Her vision blurred. Her throat clogged with tears.

He'd loved her, leg and all. In drawing her, he'd loved her.

*He loved her.*


VERONICA SAT DOWN IN HER LAB THE NEXT DAY, CREAKY FROM SO many hours at the keyboard. She was on fire with this new discovery, which she called a 'dithered time governance signature.' She'd experimented on Jophius first. She'd adjusted him to blink out that afternoon, and then dithered him, and he'd persisted.

The extension worked.

She wished she could share her breakthrough with Max, but she wanted him to be surprised. He'd already sent the doomsday letters to the Salvos and set up everything with lawyers and safety deposit boxes, ensuring her protection. Now she'd have something for him: natural life. He'd expect to blink out tomorrow at 6:07 pm, and reappear on the doorstep ten seconds later. But he wouldn't blink out.

He'd stay. He'd be normal. His own man.

The dithered time governance signature was a way of fooling the computers, totally outrageous in its simplicity—every time it hit the wall of seven days, it would bounce back and not realize it because of the way she'd bespelled it. Meanwhile, Max would age like a regular man.

She had to put in some limiting date, of course, just to not leave it blank, so she picked 2012. Instead of reappearing in a week as the man from the photo, he'd reappear in 30 years as the man in the photo. What the hell, they could always change it.

Then she thought about what a problem it would be for Max to reappear as a 40-year-old man in 2012 and not know anyone. So she put on the electrodes and conjured a recent photo of herself, and set that to appear in 2012 when Max appeared.

She needed a better place for them to appear, too, rather than January in Minnesota. It could be anywhere, if she had the coordinates. Maybe not even on this planet! The thought tickled her—the two of them materializing on some space station, like Mr. and Mrs. Buck Rogers. She put in the coordinates for a beach in Florida.

2012. Max might leave her by then. Or if the Soviet Union attacked, there'd be a nuclear winter and they definitely wouldn't want to come back. But for now, they'd both age normally until 2012. Then Max would blink out and reappear in Florida as a younger man. What 70-year-old man wouldn't want to blink out and appear on a beach as his 40-year-old self with his woman's 40-year-old self? It was a pretty good gift.

She went back to find his command, which sat a few rows above the Jophius code. First, she cancelled the command to re-up him at 6:07 tomorrow. Having two Maxes would be bad. It was bad enough that he'd had to cross paths with his corpse.

Once Max's cancellation went through, she copied in the new code. She hesitated over the enter key. Max would be free. But she wasn't like one of those blind fish. Real things sometimes frightened and threatened, but they were still worth doing. You could jump into the unknown and just trust. Max had given her that.

She took a deep breath and hit enter, setting the commands across the umbra where the images lived.

It was at that very instant that the lights went off. She sat up as the fans quieted and slowed.

Veronica frowned. Had the command taken too much electricity? Or was this just a coincidence?

More importantly, had the command to give Max a natural life gone through before the electricity cut out? There was no way to tell.

Great. Now she'd have to get the power back on and re-enter

everything, just to be safe. She grabbed a candle and went to the power box in the main part of the basement, but everything looked normal. Why was the power cut?

"Max?" She called up.

No answer.

Shivers prickled over her. A quick cast through the house told her she had visitors. Seven witches. In the same room with Max. The magical surge of seven witches at work had drained the electrical.

*Shit.*

Jophius was nowhere—probably out roaming the woods, too far for her to locate.

She limped quickly upstairs, and steeled herself and walked into the living room. The witches had arranged themselves on the furniture as though they were guests in for tea. She recognized only one of them: Kerucha, leader of the East Coast witches. Kerucha's assistant had Max bound with a magical Skiveto string.

"What do you want?" Veronica asked calmly. "And make it fast. I'm busy. And you'd do well to let go of my bodyguard."

"Funny story," Kerucha said. "About your bodyguard here. Apparently, he's been dead for three months."

"Doesn't look dead to me," Veronica said.

"Me either," Kerucha said. "But he is. See, it all started when I got curious about how the Council disappeared. One wants to avoid the fate of her unlucky sisters. My investigation led me to the Salvos."

"Is this supposed to be fascinating in some way?" Veronica asked calmly, trying not to look at Max. She couldn't let them know how important he was to her.

"You've been killing the hitters they send after you," Kerucha continued. "But this last time, the very fresh corpse of a certain cop who'd died long ago was found among your victims. The corpse of one Detective Maxwell Drummond. Almost as if he'd been brought to life only to be killed. And—" she held up a finger and walked over to Max, set it upon his head. "...here he is again. Veronica, we would love your secret recipe."

"Don't give it to them," Max said.

She tweaked his cheek. "Oh, she will. Or you, my friend, are in a world of pain."

"I'm dead already," Max growled.

*Dead already.* Was he? Had the command for him to have a natural life gone through? Or would he blink out tomorrow?

"You can't let them have it," Max said.

"Shut up," Kerucha said. Her assistant tightened the line on Max. He kept his face impassive, but blood seeped through his shirt where the Skiveto cut into his shoulders.

With a fling of her hand, Veronica blasted the thing off. Oh, it was folly to use her energy for a blast like that, especially if she was heading into a fight, but hell if she'd see him hurt. She wound a protection spell around him just as the collective power of the witches blew into her, slamming her against a wall.

She hit back, calling to Jophius in her mind. She crashed a lamp against the weakest witch's head, thinking to pick them off one by one.

"We just want your secret," Kerucha said. "It's your computer, isn't it? You actually did what you said. And kept it a secret."

"You'll never get it." Veronica swept a hand, stoking up wind that roared through the house in red gusts.

Max went for one of the witches and he was blown back onto the floor. These witches were brimming with power. They had been preparing for this fight.

"Nobody has to die," Kerucha said. "Just hand it over. With instructions."

"You'll have to kill me first," Veronica said.

"We'll kill him first."

"I won't let you!"

"Be happy it's us, Veronica. Your secret's out. Whoever controls life and matter controls the planet. Don't you prefer it to be witches? Your next callers will suck the knowledge right out of your brain."

But Kerucha would raise armies, slaughter millions, usher in a witch dynasty. Veronica should've destroyed the thing. She knew that now. She'd been so arrogant.

She mustered all her strength, crashing a bookcase onto them.

"Run, Max! Get out!" Her protection spell would let him get out of range if he ran fast enough.

Max headed toward the kitchen instead of out the front door.

No!

One of the witches started after him.

"No!" Veronica flung electricity, knocking her back, using an algorithm that would be strange to them all. Kerucha tried to punch through it. Another of the other witches tried to go after Max, and Veronica bespelled the floor with sparks, but the drain left her open to a jolt of pain from another. A window broke. Another tried to pull Max back, but bricks began to pop out from around the fireplace.

"Where is the computer?" Kerucha asked calmly, as if a fight didn't rage around her. "In the basement?"

"You can't have it." Veronica hit back with hellhail the size of baseballs. She'd fought the Council, hadn't she? She'd used everything she had, but she'd nearly won. The pain worsened as she rained fiery projectiles. One witch's hair caught on fire and Kerucha had to draw water. Veronica went harder, but she was losing energy. Growing cold.

The battle raged on, and in the noise and confusion of it, Veronica became aware of smashing coming from somewhere else. Rhythmic smashing, like metal and glass. At first she thought it was something the witches were doing. It came to her, as her strength finally drained, as she slid to the floor, that it was Max. In the basement. Destroying the computers.

"Noooo!" she cried. "Noooo!"

Kerucha pulled herself up from the ground. "What?"

The smashing went on and on.

Kerucha's eyes widened in understanding. "He's wrecking your computer!"

"He's wrecking all of them," Veronica whispered.

"Stop him!" Kerucha flew into the kitchen, heading for the basement with the other witches on her tail. Veronica heaved herself up, shivering, and went after them.

They found Max sitting on the floor in the shadowy computer lab, sledgehammer in one hand, flashlight in the other. The machines were destroyed. Utterly destroyed.

"Max, no!"

"It's over," he said. "And I wrecked your backup disks, too. Everything's gone. It ends here."

"You didn't!" Kerucha powered on the lights. The room blazed to life. Max had been thorough. Everything was destroyed.

Tears welled up in Veronica's eyes. "I can't recreate this code, Max. It's too complex, too full of accidents. I can never get it back!"

"I know."

She fell to her knees on the cold concrete floor, weak again. Her teeth had begun to chatter. She'd canceled the re-up of him before she'd entered the command to give him a natural life. "I can never get you back."

*Unless the command went through.*

"It had to be done, Veronica." Max knelt in front of her, took her hands in his. "It's done, baby."

Kerucha pointed at Max. "Check if they're telling the truth. This might be a ruse."

Her assistant waved her hands. Veronica allowed it, knowing Max would've gotten everything. She'd shown him her backup disks. She could see fragments of them on the floor. Even if a backup survived, slid under one of the machines, it would take years to configure new computers.

"They both think it's lost," the assistant said. "They both believe this."

A tear slid down Veronica's cheek. "I can't lose you."

"We have a day, right?"

"I should kill you," Kerucha said to Max. "I should kill you both."

A gasp from the doorway. The witches backed up as Jophius trotted in, snarling.

"Jesus!" Kerucha retreated toward her sisters, clustered in the doorway. "*Jophius?*"

Max grabbed the loose skin around Jophius's neck and pulled him close. "And he's been hungry for witches since he finished off the Council. You harm a hair on Veronica's head and Jophius will hunt you down and eat you just as he ate the Council. Now get the hell out!"

Jophius growled and snorted.

"Nothing here we want anyway," one of the other witches said, looking at Kerucha, clearly eager to leave.

Kerucha frowned. "We'll have our eyes on you. All of them."

Sparks crackled as they fled.

Max rubbed Veronica's arms. "Are you okay?"

"No, Max." She looked at her life's work, in shambles. And was he there to stay or not? "I don't want you to go."

He wrapped his arms around her, trying to warm her. "I was never really here."

"Yes, you were. Max…"

"Shhhh." He picked her up and carried her up the stairs, just like before, but he bypassed the trashed living room. "Into the bath with you."

"I'm not as bad as I was after I fought the Council," she protested. "I can walk."

"Humor me." Upstairs he set her on the bathroom easy chair and started the water. It crashed into the deep, deep tub.

"Max—"

"We have a day, baby," he said. "Let's get you warm. It was all stolen time, anyway."

"We could've had more," she whispered. "It was supposed to be a surprise, but I figured out a way to give you natural life."

He furrowed his brow, eyes intense. Was he angry?

"It's just that you love living so much, and you wanted to be your own man, and I wanted you to have that. To be free and alive. And just as I was inputting the commands, the power went out."

"You tried to give me a natural life?"

"Yes. I wanted you to be your own boss with your own life. Not dependent on me in any way."

"You wanted to set me free."

She explained how she'd re-set the time so that he'd age naturally and wouldn't blink out until 2012. "And, er, I had to put something, so I re-upped you as what you are now. In Florida."

"In 2012?"

"Yes," she said.

"So if the command had gone through, I would've grown old until 2012, at which point I blink out and reappear as the age I am now, off on some beach? And the same with you?"

"Well, except I wouldn't blink out. There'd be two of me," she said, "an old me here and a young me with you on a beach."

He scowled. "Jesus."

"Well, I figured we'd be able to alter it if we wanted. I didn't think the computers would be destroyed. If the command did go through, that's all set in stone now. We'd just figure something out. But Max, I'm almost sure the power was cut before the command went through. And now the computers…even if I worked around the clock for the next decade…"

"It's okay, Veronica—"

"No, it's not. Listen to me, Max. You asked me once if you have a soul and then you wouldn't let me answer. The truth is, I don't know, but—"

Max kneeled in front of her and kissed her, stopping her words in their tracks. "But I know," he said. "I know I have a soul because of how much I love you." He pulled away and pressed his palm to his chest. "This much love, no way could it all fit in here."

She put her hand over his. How could she live without him now? Tears blurred her eyes. "Why didn't I work faster?" she whispered. "Why didn't I input it just a minute sooner? Why did I have to test it on Jophius?"

"Stop." He kissed her. "You tried to set me free."

"I doubt it went through."

"But I'm here now." He broke away and swished his hand in the water, then turned off both spigots. "We're here now." He pulled off his shirt as he had before. It seemed like months ago, when she'd first let him bathe her. She brought her hands to her shirt, fingers trembling.

"Oh, please." He stood in front of her, undid her shirt for her. She really was cold. And so tired and drained. "You're going to have to stop using all your power on these witches."

"They won't come for me after this. And neither will the Salvos, thanks to you."

When she was undressed, he picked her up and stepped into the tub, lowering them both, slowly, letting the water surround them. He kissed her ear, her neck, and then stretched out under her, holding her. The warmth rolled through her, thawing her.

"So let me get this straight," he said. "Jophius got a natural life? But not me? Should I be insulted?"

Tears rolled down her cheeks.

"Hey, it's a joke," he said.

"It's not funny."

"What are you gonna do, not re-up me?"

She splashed him. "You're not funny at all."

They stayed up the whole night talking. In the morning, Veronica made his favorite breakfast of steak and eggs. She was feeling almost normal.

They ate. They made love. They made snow angels out in the sunshiny day, then came back in and made love in front of the fire. They tried not to watch the clock. He'd be gone at 6:07 p.m.

Unless the command had gone through.

That evening, Veronica made steak and garlic mashed potatoes with gravy, another Max favorite, and brought it out to the living room. The grandfather clock had just struck five. Max was busy hanging something over the mantel. The drawing of her. Framed.

She just stood there, speechless.

"I want you to see always how I see you. How beautiful you really are."

She swallowed back the tears and set down the plates. Neither of them felt like eating, though. They snuggled together, with Max getting up now and then to stoke the fire.

For the hundredth time, she went over that moment of hitting the enter key the day before, trying to tell herself that the command had gone through before the power went out.

It seemed too much to hope.

She said, "I'll keep an eye on her from a distance. I'll make sure that family has enough money."

Max tightened his arms around her. "Let's not talk like that, Veronica. Maybe the command went through. Everything's electricity. You said so yourself, remember? Emotions and thoughts. It doesn't only come from the wires."

"I just want you to know it, though. That Teresa's taken care of."

"I want us to stop saying goodbye," he said. "No more watching the damn clock. I want this to be a normal hour. As if we have a normal life."

"You're willing to watch Miami Vice?"

"Yes, Veronica. You know why?"

"Stop it." God, she was feeling so maudlin and weepy.

"Because I love you. You should've known just from my willingness to watch Miami Vice with you so many times that I love you."

"I love you, too." She sunk into him, let herself be held.

The fire crackled.

The grandfather clock struck six.

"Hand me the whiskey," he said. "This fucking suspense is killing me."

"That's not funny." She sat up, grabbed the bottle, and gave it to him. He swigged out of it, then handed it to her. She put it down and kissed him. He tasted alcohol-sharp.

She unbuttoned his shirt and kissed his broad chest, then laid her cheek against him, listening to his heartbeat. "After we saw Teresa's band play, you said you were all torn up. I wanted to feel like that, too. I was jealous of all your wild feelings. But I know what it is to be torn up, Max. I know what it is, now, and I don't want it."

"Don't say that. Being alive sometimes gets you all torn up, but you still want it."

"Not without you."

"Yes, without me. You're brave, baby."

"Stop it."

The fire crackled on.

Soon he'd vanish, and she'd be lying on the couch alone. She tried not to think of that. She just tried to soak up what they had left.

After lying there a bit more, she got the thought that it had been longer than seven minutes since the clock chimed six. She looked out the window at the moon. The moon had moved a lot since then, it seemed.

But if she said something, it might jinx things.

She kissed his chest. His cheek.

"Veronica."

"Yes?"

"Does it seem like…?"

"More than seven minutes?" She sat up. "I've been afraid to ask."

"I think it's been more than seven minutes."

"Should we check?" she asked.

He watched her eyes. Neither of them wanted to check. She kissed him, pressing herself against him, tasting his lips, his mouth. She loved him.

And what if…

Every second that ticked away made it more possible that he was staying. That the command had gone through.

He pulled away. "Now it seems really like it was more than seven minutes. That was at least a minute-long kiss."

She kissed him again.

"A minute and a half. That's it, I'm checking," he said.

"Wait," she looked into his eyes. "I don't want you to disappear while you're apart from me."

"This is stupid. I'm checking, Veronica." He got up and went around the couch and over to the clock. Veronica watched, gripping the back of the couch.

He regarded the clock for a while, then turned his head, looked back with that lopsided smile.

Her heart soared. "It's after six-oh-seven?"

"It's six-thirty." He came to her and she tumbled into his arms. He kissed her. "Twenty goddamn minutes we've been agonizing."

"You're here for good."

"You and me and Jophius, baby. Apparently you are the baddest of the bad."

She kissed his nose. "Don't you forget it."

"I won't," he whispered. "You hungry?"

"Starving." She warmed up the steak.

He stoked up the fire.

There would be no Miami Vice tonight.

# Wrecked

A Tale of the Iron Seas

## MELJEAN BROOK

# Chapter One

HER FATHER'S HUNTERS HAD FOUND HER.

Elizabeth recognized them as soon as she rounded the corner toward home—a man and a woman flanking the front door of her boarding house. Heart thumping in her chest, she resisted the impulse to dart behind a passing steamcoach. A quick movement would draw the hunters' attention.

Dear God. They were so close. In another twenty steps, she would have crossed the busy street and fallen straight into their hands.

Without a change in pace, Elizabeth tucked her chin deeper into her woolen scarf, burying the bottom of her face. Acrid smoke billowed behind the steamcoach as it rattled past, the dingy cloud obscuring her view of the hunters—and preventing them from seeing her slip into a tinkerer's shop. Inside, she pretended to browse the clockwork novelties displayed in the window, stealing glances at the hunters as she wound up a jumping frog.

Matthias and Amelia. Almost five years had passed since Elizabeth had seen either of them, but both looked the same as they had when delivering wild beasts to her father's sanctuary. Wide-brimmed hats shadowed their eyes. Ankle-length brown coats buckled over their chests and concealed the weapons harnesses they always wore.

Nothing about the hunters looked overtly threatening, but passersby seemed to sense the danger. A pair of gentlemen cast their gazes to the ground, as if hoping to avoid notice. A young boy and girl who had been laughing up at the sparsely falling snow and trying to catch the tiny flakes on their tongues suddenly had their hands gripped by their governess and were hurried past the boarding house. In this part of Brighton, where moneyed travelers browsed the shops for expensive trinkets and enjoyed the cleanest air that England had to offer, Matthias and Amelia were wolves among hens. But Elizabeth had seen a hunter receive the same wary glances from residents of the lawless smuggling towns she'd hidden in after escaping her father's estate. No matter where she ran to, people seemed to recognize what the hunters were.

Predatory, unrelenting…merciless. After they sighted their prey, they'd stop at nothing to bring it in.

Elizabeth edged a little farther away from the window, the instinct to flee yanking at her every nerve. Matthias and Amelia had been standing long enough that a dusting of snow had accumulated on their hat brims and shoulders. Had they searched the boarding house yet, or were they waiting for someone who was already inside?

Was Caius Trachter with them?

A familiar ache started in her chest. *Caius.* After she'd fled from home, he'd pursued her halfway around the world and back again—and two years before, he'd finally caught her in the Ivory Market, on the western coast of Africa. Elizabeth had made the mistake of bolting the moment she'd seen him, trying to lose him in the chaotic marketplace, but it wouldn't have mattered if she'd run or calmly continued walking. Caius had already spotted her. He'd taken her down with an opium dart as if she were an animal, and she'd woken tied to a bed in an airship bound for the Americas.

Caius had attended to her every need during the voyage…also as if she were an animal. Her father's hunters didn't kill their prey; they cared for the captured beasts until delivering them into her father's keeping. So Caius had fed Elizabeth, guarded her door—from inside the cabin, with his back to her—while she'd bathed, and walked with her on the promenade deck for exercise. For a week, he'd rarely left her side, sharing her every meal and sleeping on the floor beside her bed. In those few moments when he'd left her alone, she'd been tied again.

But animals didn't talk to their captors, and Elizabeth had barely allowed hers a moment's peace. She'd begged for Caius to free her. She'd threatened him. She'd promised to give him *anything* if he released her.

When she'd realized that she couldn't give Caius what he wanted most—his own freedom—she'd appealed to his compassion instead. She'd told him of the fate awaiting her at home and the horror that had forced her to flee on the night of her twentieth birthday.

For a short time, she'd believed that her pleas had affected him. She'd believed that Caius no longer saw her as prey—or as the pampered girl he'd met when he'd been forced into her father's service to pay off his family's debts.

Two years older than Elizabeth, he'd been a sullen, dark-haired fifteen-year-old boy with a gleaming shackle of indenture around his left wrist and resentment burning in his eyes every time he'd looked at her. Apprenticed to a hunter, then a huntsman in his own right, Caius had spent most of his time away from her father's sanctuary, returning only when he'd brought new animals in. The years had passed, and she'd watched him grow from a sullen youth into a hardened young man. By the time Elizabeth was sixteen, his resentment had cooled into quiet hostility—and with every encounter, his obvious dislike only made her determined to change his opinion. She'd wanted him to smile at her, to talk with her.

And with every encounter, she'd been increasingly bewildered and hurt by his icy, insulting responses. She'd done nothing to deserve them. Yet his hostility only seemed to grow.

But he'd warmed to her on the airship. At least, she'd believed that he had.

Though Caius had been all but silent during the first part of the voyage, in the days before they'd reached Johannesland he'd told her stories of his hunts for lions and rhinoceros and zebra—animals that she'd seen when he'd brought them in, but she'd never heard how he'd caught them or of the dangers he'd encountered transporting them out of zombie-infested lands. He'd joked about how a machete could be a man's closest friend when facing one of the ravenous creatures. He'd mentioned fighting mercenaries and rival hunters who'd attempted to steal the valuable animals for collectors or naturalists in competition with her father. He'd spoken of the people he'd met while pursuing her around the world, the letters he'd received from his mother and sister since leaving home, and of the life he'd planned to have before his father had died and left his family destitute. He'd told her of how he'd once hoped to attend a university, obtain a comfortable position as a solicitor, and marry the girl he'd loved at fifteen—a pretty blonde named Katarina.

But after they'd reached the shores of Johannesland and boarded the locomotive that would carry them over the last leg of their journey, Caius told her that if he brought her back home, Elizabeth's father had promised to release him from his service. All debts paid in full, and the thirty-year period of indenture would end the moment Caius walked through the door with Elizabeth in hand.

Aboard that locomotive, Elizabeth had realized two things. One, Caius hadn't warmed to her. He'd been explaining why he would never release her. Given an option between his freedom and hers, Caius had chosen his own.

Two, she couldn't blame him for it. After all, she'd been asking him to choose her freedom over his—and she understood all too well how the need to take charge of one's own life could drive a person to make selfish and desperate choices. And so as the locomotive's steam engine had chugged its way around a steep mountainside, she'd made her own desperate choice.

In a maddened effort, she'd broken away from Caius and jumped from the railcar.

Only sheer luck and a tree had saved her. The last she'd seen of him, Elizabeth had been clinging to the top of a tall white pine that stood on the side of a deep ravine while Caius had searched the rocky banks of the river below, calling her name until he'd shouted himself hoarse. His voice had finally failed him, but still he looked for her along the stones and the rapids. A full day had passed before he'd searched far enough down the river for Elizabeth to alight from her tree—exhausted and bruised but free.

She'd hoped that Caius would believe she was dead. Without a body, however, her father must not have been satisfied and sent his hunters after her again. And this time, he apparently hadn't trusted Caius to complete the job alone.

Matthias and Amelia still waited outside the boarding house door. Caius was possibly in her room at that very moment, searching through her belongings.

There wasn't much to search through. She never purchased more than a few changes of clothing suitable for blending in with the local population. Too many times, she'd had to abandon everything but what she carried—and so Elizabeth carried everything that she needed with her in a satchel and in pockets sewn under her clothes. When she'd escaped the sanctuary five years before, she'd taken a small fortune in gold and jewels. Some she kept with her; she'd hidden the rest of her money away in various cities.

Elizabeth didn't worry about what Caius might find in her room. She never left anything that might reveal where she spent her days or where her next destination would be if she was forced to run again.

And she was *always* prepared to run again.

At this time of day, she could easily leave Brighton by one of four routes: a boat at the pier, traveling by post steamcoach or boarding a locomotive to another town, or purchasing a fare on a passenger airship. If those failed, there were several other, more difficult routes by foot or horseback or steamcart, or by hiring a personal balloon. It wouldn't matter *where* she went; for now, she just needed to put distance between herself and the hunters.

But first, she had to wait until the hunters left. Every muscle tense, she watched through the window, winding up another toy. After a few minutes, a man emerged from the boarding house, and her heart stopped. Not Caius. *Her father.*

Tiny gears ground beneath her clenching fingers. She released the windup's key. Her hands shook as she replaced the little bird in the window, its wire feet skittering over the shelf. The music box chirped a cheery tune and the copper wings flapped, and Elizabeth was struck by the sudden terror that the noise would give her away.

Trying to control her panic, she glanced across the street again. Her father didn't look in her direction; he was speaking to the hunters. More gray peppered his dark hair. From this distance, she couldn't see whether her absence or time had lined his face, but she knew his eyes would be as sharp and bright as the mind behind them. A brilliant man, her father. But never a cold one. When he loved, his heart burned unceasingly.

She should have known he'd never accept death as the end. Her father never had.

While she watched, he gestured north along the street. Relief slipped through Elizabeth, releasing some of the tension holding her in its grip. He must have spoken with the boardinghouse matron. Elizabeth never left anything for someone to find—except for lies. She'd told the matron she intended to spend the day on Modiste Row. In truth, Elizabeth had walked to visit the menagerie at the Retreat, as she did almost every day. Now she would run south as soon as her father went north.

The three started in that direction. Movement near Amelia's feet drew Elizabeth's gaze. A pair of lean gray dogs were rising from the walk at her heels.

The hairs along Elizabeth's spine prickled with cold sweat. Hounds. Her father wasn't tracking her by scent yet—he would want to discover her himself, and follow her as far as his information took him—but as soon as he discovered that she hadn't been to the dressmakers' shops, he'd use the dogs. No doubt he had a handkerchief or some scrap of fabric from her room to provide a scent. When he did, Amelia's hounds would lead them straight to her.

And now Elizabeth's only option was an airship. One that was leaving within the next half hour. Any later than that would be *too* late.

She waited until they were out of sight and fled.

S HE WASN'T DEAD.
   Although he'd followed Elizabeth—*a living, breathing Elizabeth*—for the past hour, Caius couldn't truly believe it. Not until he spoke to her, until he touched her, until he heard her voice. He needed to now. But he forced himself to wait, standing in the shadow of a parked lorry with his hat low and his gaze fixed on the tinkerer's shop. From his angle,

the window reflected an image of the street, of passing steamcoaches and pedal buggies, but now and again he saw her face peering through the glass like an apparition.

But she was no ghost.

*Elizabeth Jannsen was alive.*

And now she was bolting out of the tinkerer's shop, racing along the walk on the opposite side of the street. Heading toward the airship field, most likely. Flyers departed on a more regular schedule than boats, and she would know that her best chance of escaping the hound was by sea or by air. Elizabeth always made her trail difficult to follow—so wary and clever, it had taken Caius three years to catch up to her the first time.

He couldn't lose her again now.

The need to pursue her tore at him, but Caius remained where he was until she reached the end of the street and rounded the corner, tugging her hat over her brown curls as she ran. She'd grown her hair out again. Careful to keep distance between them, he started after her, desperately seeking out any other changes when he caught sight of her darting across the high street crossroad. He would have recognized her back and shoulders anywhere—and it was fortunate he'd recognized them an hour before, or she'd have turned and spotted him in the menagerie, and this chase would have begun then.

Caius didn't intend to capture her now, though. He only intended to make certain that Willem Jannsen never would.

Elizabeth was already a step ahead of her father. Caius was, too, but only because he'd pursued her for so long. He knew her better than Willem Jannsen did—not the woman her father wanted her to be, but the woman that she was. So when Caius had arrived in Brighton just ahead of her father's airship and discovered that Elizabeth wasn't at her boarding house, he'd gone to the place she'd most likely be: the Retreat.

Over the Horde Empire's two-hundred-year occupation of England, the governors and magistrates had used Brighton as a summer retreat. When the Horde had fled during the revolution over a decade before, the governor had abandoned a collection of exotic animals rescued from the European continent. Now they were tended by volunteer zoologists who hoped to breed the rare beasts and restore populations that had been eaten to near-extinction by zombies.

Caius had known that Elizabeth would visit the menagerie as often as possible, just as she'd visited the sanctuary's keep each day. Even at thirteen years of age, she'd spent most of her time in the company of animals. That hadn't changed as she'd gotten older—or when she'd been on the run.

Or when everyone had believed her dead.

Caius could still feel the painful jolt his heart had given when he'd seen her standing at an enclosure overlooking an Iberian lynx. He'd barely been able to stop himself from going to her then and there.

He only wanted to keep her safe. But Elizabeth wouldn't have felt safe if she'd seen him. She'd have fled—and in her panic, might have run straight into her father.

She'd once been desperate enough to jump from a railcar to escape that fate. Caius would do anything to see that Elizabeth was never so desperate again.

That meant he had to follow her at a distance and be content with the little he saw. The flash of bright red stockings and sturdy black boots as she ran. Her strong grip on the satchel slung crosswise over her shoulder, preventing the bag from bouncing against her hip. The tail of her blue scarf hanging down her back, and the line of her jaw when she stopped at a street corner and waited for a spider rickshaw to pass.

As she paused, Caius drank in the sight of her. He'd thought the jolt to his heart would ease as surprise faded and truth settled in. *She was alive.* He'd thought the need to touch her and to take her into his arms would diminish, but that desire was only growing.

But that desire had always grown. From the day he'd met her until grief had shattered his heart, that need had never diminished.

Of course it wouldn't now, either.

The rickshaw skittered by and Elizabeth broke into a run again—still headed toward the airship docks. Caius kept pace at a jog that he could maintain for hours.

Elizabeth moved just as easily, as if she'd never leaped from a railcar into a ravine. But he couldn't assume she hadn't been injured. The menagerie might be the reason she'd come to live in Brighton…but more than half the people born in England during the Horde occupation possessed mechanical prosthetics or tools grafted to their bodies. Even if she'd lost a leg, it could be replaced here, and she had enough money to purchase one that moved as smoothly as a limb made of flesh. Until he saw skin, Caius couldn't know that she'd escaped unscathed.

A heavy ache filled his chest. How the hell had she survived that jump? Christ. He could still see her, that last wild glance back at him before she'd leapt. He could still feel the terror and disbelief when he'd lunged for her, when his fingers had brushed the hem of her coat but he'd gripped nothing in his fist. The memory had haunted his nightmares for two years.

*But she was alive.*

The street widened leading to the airship field. Almost fifty balloons floated overhead in ordered rows, from luxury passenger liners to sturdy ferries to flyers for hire that Caius wouldn't trust to carry him across the Channel. He slowed to a walk beside a steamcoach, using its bulk for cover when Elizabeth stopped at the schedule written on two slate boards near the field entrance. Choosing the next departing airship.

It wouldn't matter which one she chose. This would have been the best route of escape when Caius had been chasing her, because he would've had to wait until he found another airship headed in the same direction. At one time, it would've been the best way to lose her father and the hound, too. No longer.

His gaze rose to the south end of the docking field, where the private airships were tethered. A cloud clipper with a gleaming hull and twin balloons hovered in the fourth station, smaller than many of the personal yachts in the same row, but sleek and swift—the *Mary Elizabeth*. Her father had purchased the airship shortly after Caius had removed his shackle of indenture. In the past two years, the sight of that clipper had meant one thing: it was time for Caius to run. Not to escape Jannsen but to lay a false trail, leading Elizabeth's father and his hunters away from what mattered most—but Caius had inadvertently created a path leading them to Elizabeth.

He wouldn't let that trail end in her capture.

A moment later Elizabeth sped past the slate boards, into the northern docks. Caius waited until she was out of sight before going to look at the schedule, his gaze sliding down the list and stopping on one. *Kingfisher.* The skyrunner was leaving in twenty minutes—a four-day journey to the

Ivory Market. A fast flyer and a destination where she couldn't be easily traced. She would have chosen that one.

A glance at the fare made him suck in a sharp breath. He'd spent most of his money hiring an airship to bring him to Brighton ahead of her father. This would take every last denier he had.

He'd pay it, gladly. But Caius would be stranded in the Ivory Market until he earned enough for a fare home, and he'd already been away longer than he'd intended.

Caius's mother would understand. His sister would, too.

His daughter wouldn't.

The cost of this trip wouldn't be the money. It was the additional weeks of his daughter's life that he would miss and never get back. It was the four days of being on the same airship with the woman he loved—all the while knowing he would never have another four days with her again.

Yet it was well worth the price if his daughter and Elizabeth were safe. Willem Jannsen *would* come after her. But he wouldn't expect to find Caius standing in his way.

So the chase was on. And this time, Caius meant to end it.

# Chapter Two

As she entered her private cabin, Elizabeth's heart was still pounding from the wobbling autogyro ride she'd taken from the airfield's entrance directly to *Kingfisher*'s main deck. She could have boarded the airship via the cargo platform, as passengers typically did, but walking to the docking station would have led the hounds directly there. Eventually her father would track down the autogyro pilot and learn which airship Elizabeth had taken, but after the pilot had flown her to the skyrunner, she'd paid him to take a message to her boardinghouse matron. So that would give Elizabeth an extra hour, at least. Probably more. No other passenger vessels were leaving for the Ivory Market for several days, and even if her father hired an airship, that crew would need time to secure the provisions and coal needed for the long journey.

By the time he reached the Market, she would have already left again. The hounds might track her to another docking station, but it wouldn't matter. Unlike Brighton, the flights in and out of the Ivory Market weren't registered. She would board another airship and there would be no trace left of her to follow. Not even an eyewitness.

Opening her satchel, Elizabeth made certain her trousers and coat were still folded inside. She wouldn't alter her appearance yet. That had to wait until she reached the Market, or this crew would be able to give her father a description of a young man to follow. Let her father continue asking about a young woman, instead.

*Kingfisher's* engine suddenly thrummed, starting a vibration through the boards under her feet. Through the hull, she heard the faint rattle of chains as the cargo platform was raised against the deck, followed by shouts from the crew to release the tether anchoring the skyrunner to the station.

Preparing to depart—and she was still free. By the skin of her teeth.

Even now, her father might be entering the airship field. Elizabeth wanted to go up on deck, to watch the hounds lose her trail at the autogyro stand, but giving in to the urge could be a mistake. If Elizabeth could see her father then *he* could see *her*, and all of her running would have been for nothing. Better to wait in her cabin until they had flown at least a mile south.

The tread of boots sounded from the passageway. Already anxious, Elizabeth tensed as the steps paused at her door—then moved on. A moment later, she heard another cabin door opening and closing.

One of the other passengers, then. When she'd asked, the captain had told her there were four men aboard, aside from the crew. Not many, but the fare was expensive and the route dangerous. Most airships followed the Atlantic coastline around Europe to avoid flying over Horde territory. The higher price reflected both the risk the aviators took and the speed with which they'd arrive at the Ivory Market.

It was a risk Elizabeth was willing to take, as well—and speed that she was willing to pay for.

After a few minutes, she glanced out the porthole. Only water below. They'd already left Brighton.

She went up on deck to watch England vanish into the distance.

WITHIN AN HOUR ALMOST EVERYTHING HAD VANISHED INTO A thick swirl of white. Standing near the front of the skyrunner and looking back along the airship's side, Elizabeth could barely make out the shape of the balloon at the stern, as if the envelope simply faded away into the heavy fall of snow. Nothing on the ground was visible, but she'd flown this route before and knew what lay below. Hundreds of years ago, the French occupied these lands. But that was before the Horde's armies and war machines had rolled in from the east. Before the zombie infection had swept across the continent. Before most of Europe had fled to Scandinavia and the New World.

Now there were only the ruins of cities and villages overgrown by the surrounding vegetation. There were only forests and fields harvested by the Horde.

And zombies.

The ravenous creatures roamed unchecked over most of Europe and Africa. Only a few walled cities and outposts stood on each continent. Elizabeth thought the risk of flying this route wasn't that it took them over Horde territory—she'd hidden in several villages at the edges of the empire when Caius had been chasing her, and had felt as safe there as she had anywhere in the New World or around the North Sea. The real danger came from the slim chance that the airship would be forced to ground, its defenses overwhelmed by the dead, and the passengers' flesh torn apart and consumed while they were still alive—or worse, suffering a bite that would turn them into one of the creatures.

Animals didn't become zombies, though. They were just eaten.

Her cheeks stinging from the cold and wind, Elizabeth looked east. There was nothing to see but falling snow. But her father's family had originally hailed from that direction. Nobles from the lowlands of Holland, they'd migrated to Johannesland in the northern American continent, near the great freshwater lakes. With the permission of the local native trade federation—an arrangement strengthened by several marriages over the years—her father's ancestors had developed large tracts of land as a sanctuary for many of the animals brought from Europe and Africa.

But not all of the species survived. Of those that had, their populations—small to begin with—had declined over the decades, so that few breeding animals had remained by the time her grandfather inherited the sanctuary.

When her father had been a young man, he'd traveled around the world searching for a solution. He'd sent hunters to find specimens to reinvigorate the breeding stock—and to save the animals from certain extinction if they remained in zombie-infested lands. And he'd appealed to Horde smugglers, who exported stolen technology out of the empire to fund their rebellions.

The machine they'd found had surpassed even her father's hopes. Created by order of a Great Khan after he'd failed to produce a son or daughter, the device had been designed to replicate his flesh, creating an embryo that could be implanted in the womb of his favorite wife. Elizabeth didn't know if the Khan had succeeded in his plan, but it didn't surprise her that the Horde had invented such an incredible machine. They'd created other marvels, both wondrous and terrifying. The zombies' infection was not a natural sickness, but caused by tiny mechanical bugs in the creatures' bodies. In the occupied territories, similar bugs had allowed the Horde to graft prosthetics and tools to the bodies of laborers. Her father's hunters were infected with the same bugs, which made them faster and stronger than uninfected men and women—and allowed them to heal more quickly.

But the bugs weren't all the Horde had created. There were the monstrous kraken and megalodons in the seas. The boilerworms and the floating jellyfish. Towers which could broadcast a radio signal and control an entire population.

Few people knew of her father's machine. In the New World, any Horde technology was automatically suspect. But his success had been noticed by scientific societies and other conservationists. Soon he was not just replicating specimens from the sanctuary in Johannesland, but from other sanctuaries throughout the Americas. His hunters brought in more animals and he delivered their replicated issue to other naturalists struggling to renew failing populations.

He'd met her mother in that way. A naturalist from Manhattan City, she'd brought a chimpanzee to his sanctuary. Within a week, her mother had married him.

Ten years later, she'd died giving birth to Elizabeth.

A lantern flared to life near Elizabeth's post, radiating faint heat across her cheek. Startled, she glanced up. The day had grown dim—though white flakes still filled the air, night was falling. Each breath streamed from her mouth in a frozen ribbon, slipping away into the wind.

Suddenly cold, she made her way down the ladder to the second deck. She removed her coat and hat, grateful for the copper pipes that circulated hot water from the boiler room and throughout the airship, warming the cabins to a comfortable temperature. In her quarters, she lit her lamp and tried to fluff some life into her flattened curls. She would be expected at the captain's table before too long, where her conversation would consist of lies about who she was and why she was headed to the Ivory Market. That would be easy enough; she'd done it many times before. She always had different names and stories at the ready.

Blast it all, though—she'd grown weary of telling them. Just once, Elizabeth wanted to be herself.

But she never had been...except for the one week she'd spent on an airship with Caius. He hadn't expected her to be anyone else and she hadn't pretended to be. For the first time, she'd just been Elizabeth.

She would have preferred an opportunity to be herself while she *wasn't* tied to a bed, however.

A knock sounded at the door. Most likely the porter coming to announce dinner.

"I'll be there shortly," she called. "Thank you!"

Another knock. More insistent this time.

For heaven's sake. Did they think she needed an escort to find the captain's cabin? She wasn't likely to become lost on the way; it was on the same deck as her own quarters.

Frowning with irritation, Elizabeth opened the door and encountered a wide chest. She glanced up.

It was as if she'd conjured him from her wish to be herself. A tall man with broad shoulders stood in the narrow passageway. Dark hair. A face that had been a beautiful, sullen boy's—now harder, leaner, with shadows carving sharp angles from his cheekbones and jaw.

*Caius.*

Her heart plummeted.

She slammed the door and hit his booted foot, wedged against the frame. He pushed into the cabin. She turned to run and his left arm snagged around her waist. Kicking the door shut, he clapped his gloved hand over her mouth before she could shout for help.

"Don't be afraid, Elizabeth." His big body crowded her back against the bulkhead and she tasted the warm leather of his glove on her tongue. "I'm not here to— *Bludging hell!*"

Yanking his thumb from between her clamped teeth, Caius shook his hand as if to fling away the pain. He stared down at her, his eyebrows drawn and his expression dark. All at once, his lips quirked into a smile and laughter glimmered in the blue of his eyes.

Elizabeth hauled in a breath to scream.

Caius's head swooped down. His mouth captured hers.

And suddenly, she had no breath at all.

CAIUS HADN'T INTENDED TO KISS HER.

But she was so warm. *Alive.* And her lips were stiff beneath his.

He drew back before she recovered from her surprise and bit him again. She stared up at him, brown eyes wide in an expression frozen by astonishment.

"Forgive me, Elizabeth," he said, though he wasn't at all sorry. Caius had wanted—needed—to do that for years. But now wasn't the time, and he sure as hell didn't have the right. "You don't need to run. I'm not here to take you to your father."

As he spoke, Caius watched her anger burn away the shock. Her features tightened.

She didn't believe him. He didn't blame her.

*And she was alive.*

He didn't have the right but couldn't help himself. Catching her face between his palms, he kissed her again. Her body went rigid. God, he had to stop this. Her hands clenched on his biceps and he braced himself for another bite. Incredibly, she rose onto her toes, softening against him. Caius couldn't halt his disbelieving groan when her lips parted beneath his.

Elizabeth. Here, alive. In his arms.

And she was returning his kiss.

Heart thundering, he angled his head and delved deeper. Her chest hitched as he penetrated her mouth and tasted her, sweet and hot. A shudder ran through her slender frame. Her fingers slid into the hair at the back of his head and fisted, as if to hold him closer.

Or to hold him in place.

Sharp pain sliced through his lip. Caius jerked his head back, tasting blood.

Christ, he deserved that. He had to get this need under control. This wasn't what he was here to do.

Not to kiss her, not to touch her. Just to make sure she was safe.

She glared up at him, her lips reddened and a flush darkening her cheeks. Her palms flattened against his chest and shoved.

Caius didn't move. "Elizabeth—"

"I'm *not* going back." Her voice shook with resentment and frustration. "Get out. Leave me be."

He would. But not yet. "Come up on deck with me."

Her mouth compressed into a tight line. She averted her face, eyes bright with sudden tears.

Caius knew she would hate that. When he'd been twenty years old, no longer an apprentice but a huntsman, she'd happened upon him unexpectedly in the sanctuary's keep, her arms full of the alfalfa she was carrying to the giraffe paddock. Her startled gaze had met his before she'd given him a wry smile—and, as if they conversed easily every day, she'd suddenly told him,

*"Do you know what I despise? That I cry when I'm upset. I especially hate it when I'm upset and having an argument, because as soon as the tears begin falling they undermine my every point, no matter how rational."*

He'd noted that her eyes were red, then. As if she'd been crying—and arguing.

And he'd hated his desperate need to go to her, to offer comfort. He couldn't remember now what he'd said in reply, but it had probably been similar to so many of his responses to her. *What had upset her? Was her feather mattress too soft or her clothing too fashionable? Did she have a bag of jewels that was too heavy to carry?*

Caius didn't remember. He only remembered how hurt had darkened her eyes. He remembered the ache in his chest and the heavy weight of the shackle on his wrist. He remembered how she'd softly said, *"My father doesn't believe that I don't like apples,"* and how he'd scoffed and walked away, telling himself with every step that she wasn't worth the hours he'd spent wanting her, thinking of her.

He'd been such a fool.

Gently, Caius cupped her cheek in his left hand, wishing he could feel the warmth of her skin through his glove. "I know I've upset you. But I'm here to help. Your father has an airship and he's not far behind."

She sucked in a sharp breath. Her gaze searched his face as if looking for the truth. "I don't believe you."

He knew she wouldn't. "That's why I want you to come up on deck with me. I'll show you."

As if his offer was evidence enough, her gaze tore from his and wildly swept the cabin. Already beginning to panic. Trying to think of where to run.

But there was nowhere to go.

"Elizabeth," he said softly and waited until her eyes met his again. "I won't let him take you."

She shook her head and slid away from him, reaching for the door. "I have to see."

He caught her hand. She tried to yank it away but he held fast. She glanced back, her gaze snapping with anger.

"You asked me to go up on deck with you."

"Yes." His fingers tightened around hers. "But I won't let you jump again. I'm here to protect you."

Frowning, she glanced down—not at their hands, he realized, but looking for the shackle. Wondering why he would risk helping her when the price of breaching his contract of indenture was so high.

His coat sleeve and glove covered his left wrist, but she wouldn't have seen a shackle beneath them, anyway.

"I don't wear it anymore," he said.

Surprise lifted her gaze to his. "Did he give you your freedom?"

"No." On his last visit to her father's sanctuary, Caius had *taken* his freedom—along with something far more valuable: his daughter. "A friend helped me remove the shackle."

"Unlawfully?" Understanding lit her face. "So he's not only chasing after me."

"No."

But he wasn't chasing after Caius, either, as she probably assumed. For now, however, Caius would let her think so. Elizabeth would more likely let him help her if she believed they were running for the same reasons: they both wanted to remain free of her father.

On a deep breath, she closed her eyes. Debating whether to trust him, he knew. After a long second, she shook her head. Not rejection—resignation. Acknowledging how few choices she had.

But Caius swore that by the time they reached the Ivory Market, she would have as many choices as she wanted.

She reached for her coat and satchel. "Let's go up, then."

HER MIND WHIRLING LIKE AN AUTOGYRO'S BLADES, ELIZABETH didn't know what to think or what to believe. Everything was different. Caius had found her...but he wanted to *help* her. And when he looked at her or when he spoke, she didn't see coldness in his eyes or hear ice in his voice, as she always had before. There was no frost now. Only fire.

She couldn't make sense of it. She couldn't make sense of *anything*.

Especially those kisses. The first one, maybe he'd meant to silence her scream. But the second...

*No.* She wouldn't think of it. Because she couldn't make sense of her response, either, and remembering the heat of his mouth and his taste made everything inside her clench into an unbearable ache.

And he'd called her Elizabeth.

She hadn't even had to remind him that was the name she preferred now. All her life, she'd been called Mary—after her mother, Mary Elizabeth. Growing up, she'd taken comfort knowing that her father had given her the name of the woman he'd loved beyond any other, even though Elizabeth's birth had killed her.

After she'd learned the truth, the name hadn't comforted her any longer. And when Caius had captured her in the Ivory Market, she'd demanded that he call her Elizabeth instead of Mary...though not a single person aside from herself ever had. While on the run, she'd always used false names. But Caius had done as she'd asked—though he'd obviously thought she was being ridiculous. And he hadn't believed her when she'd told him *why* she called herself by another name.

Yet he'd remembered. And he'd called her Elizabeth.

Maybe he believed her now.

Or maybe he just wanted her to believe that he did. This could all be a lie.

He'd said his shackle of indenture was gone and that a friend had helped him remove it, but taking off the clockwork device wasn't easy. If it had been, many more indentured servants would tamper with them. Few people knew how to remove a shackle and even fewer could do it without triggering the blades or the poison inside the device; it was difficult to believe that he'd found someone who could help him.

If Caius *had* removed the shackle, she was glad for him. Abandoning her father's service would make him a fugitive and jeopardize his mother's and sister's freedom, but of all people, Caius would know how to protect his family and hide them away.

But he might have lied. Her father might have removed the shackle so that Caius could pretend to help her and lull her into complacency— not hunting her down but setting a trap. Giving her reason to trust Caius and to keep him near after she arrived at the Ivory Market, until her father could catch up.

Yet that made no more sense than anything else did. Caius must have boarded the airship in Brighton. He could have taken Elizabeth to her father then.

And she didn't know what to believe anymore.

Caius preceded her up the ladder to the main deck and took her hand as she emerged into the stinging cold. The wind caught the long length of his coat and swept it behind his legs like a brown woolen flag. The snow was falling more heavily than before. The speed of their flight made the flakes whip by at a near horizontal angle. Near the bow, an aviator cleared a drift piled up by the storage crates, tossing shovelfuls of snow over the rail. Lanterns cast a warm glow over the deck and illuminated a thick halo of white around the ship. Elizabeth couldn't see anything in the darkness beyond.

Caius adjusted his grip on her hand, turning their palms together and lacing his gloved fingers through hers. Her heart thumped. He didn't hold her hand like a captor holding a captive's. He held her hand like a lover.

No matter what he thought, Elizabeth wouldn't have jumped. He had no reason to keep hold of her. But she didn't pull her hand away.

He led her along the deck toward the stern, and she didn't look at the aviators they passed. She knew what they must be thinking—that she and Caius had planned an airship tryst. She'd heard it was common for illicit lovers to book different cabins to give the appearance of propriety and then spend the trip together. No doubt the crew believed that was what she and Caius had done.

Briefly she considered appealing for help from the aviators before discarding the idea. Caius wouldn't be an easy man to subdue, and any attempt would just endanger the crew.

And if Caius was telling the truth about his intention to help her, she might lose a strong ally. If he wasn't telling the truth...she couldn't do anything about it now except play along. Eventually, he might lower his guard, just as he had in the railcar two years before.

They passed the quarterdeck. The wheel stood at the center of the deck, behind a thick plate of glass that shielded the pilot from the wind. Approaching the stern, the noise of the engine rose until it reached a deafening roar. The twin propellers spun in a blur of steel, spitting swirling sheets of snow into the billowing trail of steam and smoke.

Without relinquishing his hold on her, Caius pointed beyond the propellers.

Elizabeth struggled to see anything beyond the white. The lanterns' glow illuminating the nearby flakes made it all but impossible—but even if the lamps had been extinguished, the snow fell so heavily she doubted there would be more than a few dozen feet of visibility beyond the sides of the airship.

How had Caius seen *anything* in this snowstorm, let alone an airship in the distance?

He couldn't have, she realized. He couldn't know whether her father was following them.

So he'd lied.

The pain of that realization was an unexpected knife through her chest. Blindly, she stared into the distant dark, her throat thick and her eyes watering.

Except...*there*. A pinprick of yellow light. She blinked.

It was gone.

Heart pounding, she watched the same spot, wondering if the light had been her imagination or if she'd truly seen it.

There it was again. A faint light in the distance. A lantern from another airship.

Caius *hadn't* lied.

The ache in her fingers made her realize how tightly she'd been gripping his hand. Now he was looking at her with concern, and when she eased her hold on him, he gently squeezed her fingers—as if reassuring her.

Because he thought that seeing her father's ship had upset her. It *should* have. But she'd been far more upset by the belief that Caius had lied to her.

Now she was overwhelmed by relief that he'd told her the truth, but she had nothing to be relieved about. Her father's hunters were on that airship, and they wouldn't wait until they reached the Ivory Market before attempting to capture Elizabeth. As soon as they flew near enough to *Kingfisher*, they'd come aboard.

And Caius intended to stop them. Two hunters against one. Why would he take that risk?

She glanced up at him with a frown. "Why are you helping me?"

Shaking his head, he leaned closer. To kiss her again? Her stomach clenched in anticipation.

But he turned his face away at the last moment and waited with his ear near her mouth. Just coming closer so that he could hear her over the engine's roar, she realized.

Elizabeth didn't know which was sillier: the anticipation she'd felt in that moment when she'd thought he might kiss her, or the heavy weight of her disappointment when he didn't.

Pushing that disappointment away, she called over the noise, "Why are you helping me?"

He pulled back to look down at her, the golden light from the nearby lantern warming the left side of his face and casting dark shadows over the right. His gaze searched her features for a long second before he answered.

His mouth moved. She didn't hear him over the engine. Yet she recognized the shape of those words, and they made her heart careen wildly in her chest.

But she couldn't believe them. His reply had to be a lie.

She'd thought he'd been lying about her father's airship, though—and he hadn't been. There was no reason to believe he'd lie now.

So she'd just mistaken the words, had misread the shape.

*"Because I lost you"* made more sense than what she thought he'd said. And he *had* lost her in that railcar. She'd escaped him.

But that wouldn't be a reason to help her. He'd failed to bring her home. If anything, that would be more reason to hand her over to her father.

It had more likely been *"Because I loathe you"*—because he *had* for so many years. She'd seen his resentment and dislike every time he'd come into the sanctuary. But that wouldn't be a reason to help her, either.

What she thought he'd said made no more sense, though—and Elizabeth was too afraid to ask him again.

Too afraid to find out it wasn't what she'd thought.

But she shouldn't care what it was or wasn't—she needed to focus on what to do now. Either Caius was truly here to stop her father, or he was just keeping her occupied and complacent until her father arrived. If it was the first, she would let him help her. And if it was the second… Elizabeth wasn't sure what she would do.

One thing was certain, however: jumping wasn't an option this time. The fall would kill her. And even if she used one of the emergency gliders stored near the lifeboats, the zombies would kill her shortly after she landed.

If Caius meant to hand her over to her father, she would have to let him do it—then escape as soon as she could. Until then, she would ally herself with Caius, and prepare to run again at the first opportunity.

God. She was so tired of running. Just the thought suddenly exhausted her, and a heavy ache settled in her chest when she imagined Caius betraying her after promising to help.

Could she trust him? She shouldn't.

But she desperately wanted to. Probably because he was her only hope of escaping her father.

No other reason.

# Chapter Three

SHE HADN'T BELIEVED HIM. CAIUS HADN'T EXPECTED HER TO. But his throat was tight and his heart pounding as he watched her struggle with his declaration.

*Because I love you.*

Emotions chased wildly across her face. Her expressive features were an open plain, concealing nothing—and after years of trying not to see her, he didn't want to look away.

Finally she tore her gaze from his. Doubt settled into her furrowed brow and wariness haunted the shadows in her eyes. Still uncertain of his motives and afraid he would hurt her.

As he had so many times before.

After entering her father's service, every time he'd returned to the sanctuary he prayed she would be there—and he prayed she wouldn't be. Her face had been as transparent then, sweet and earnest, but he'd never trusted what he'd seen. He'd never let himself trust it.

In turn, Caius had hidden everything he'd felt for her. Elizabeth was the woman he'd wanted from the day he'd first understood what wanting was. Not just arousal or an erect prick. It was needing not just anyone, but *someone*.

But he couldn't have her.

The law would have allowed it. He'd been in service to her father, but an employer couldn't prevent his indentured servants from marrying or living as they chose, as long as they fulfilled their duties. Indentured servants weren't owned; they weren't slaves. But with a shackle around his wrist that would poison him if he didn't return to her father at regular intervals to have the clockwork counter rewound, Caius hadn't seen the difference. He hadn't been his own man—and until he was, Caius couldn't call a woman his.

And the woman he wanted had been right in front of him.

So her sweetness had angered him, because he wanted to hate her, wanted her to be shallow and cruel and use her status as a weapon. Every breath she took angered him, a breath he wanted to feel on his skin and never would. Her attempts to flirt angered him, because he wanted everything her smiles promised.

But Caius hadn't understood any of that then. At the time, he'd only been angry with her—and angry with himself for wanting her even though anything between them was impossible. She'd had to know it was impossible, too. She was beautiful and wealthy, and he was bound to serve her father for thirty years. So he'd told himself that she was playing with him.

When she'd run away, Caius had been glad of it, because he thought she'd finally demonstrated that she was everything he'd told himself she was. A flighty, capricious, stupid girl, running into danger when she had love and security at home. He'd thought she was a fool for tossing it all away. For so long, he'd tried to make himself believe she was spoiled and selfish, and she'd suddenly proved him right.

Five years ago, his anger—and his shame that he'd ever wanted her— fueled his chase. He'd been determined to take her back to the sanctuary and wipe his heart clean of her.

But it hadn't been so easy. Tracking her meant seeing the places she lived and speaking with the people who'd known her. None of them described her as thoughtless or capricious or haughty, but friendly and quiet and sad. Just as she'd often been in the sanctuary.

Just as he'd told himself she couldn't truly be.

By the end, it hadn't been anger fueling his chase, but a desperate need to see her again. Yet he'd still tried to hold on to reasons to think less of her. So when she confessed the story behind her conception and birth—and that she wasn't truly her mother's daughter, but her mother's duplicate—he'd told himself that she lied. He'd thought it was a clever story, based on just enough truth to be plausible. Caius had known of her father's machine. He'd seen tintype photographs and painted portraits of her mother. Aside from small differences in their hairstyles and weight, she and Elizabeth looked exactly alike. But he'd already made up his mind about her, and so he'd believed her tale was a ruse to persuade him to let her go.

And it had been too difficult to believe her father would make Elizabeth take her mother's place, to step into her mother's role as his wife. Willem Jannsen loved his daughter. Caius had seen evidence of that so many times—and he'd seen the man's heartbreak when Elizabeth had fled. So it had been easier for Caius to believe that she would discard that love and impugn her father's name during her silly flight around the world.

He'd *wanted* to believe it.

But after he'd caught up to her, her panic and desperation had been real. So Caius had spent the last half of the journey talking to her, using every word to remind himself why he had to take her back to her life of ease and luxury.

Never for one moment had he believed that she'd toss herself off the side of a mountain—and that leap had destroyed him.

He'd driven the woman he loved to her death.

The wall of anger he'd put up around his heart had shattered when she'd jumped. Nothing protected him after that. For days he'd searched for her body, a broken man. But losing her hadn't been the only devastating blow. When he'd returned to the sanctuary to report her death to her father, Caius had learned everything she'd told him was true.

No pain could compare to watching her jump. But realizing how determinedly he'd clung to his illusions about her had wrecked him again.

Even now, with Elizabeth standing beside him and his hand holding hers, he was still wrecked. Two years of agony had receded in the joy of seeing her alive, but her jump had torn a jagged wound through his heart that he didn't think would ever heal.

He'd been such a fool. From the day they'd met, he'd systematically destroyed every opportunity to win her trust, her friendship…her heart. Two years before, he'd had a chance to help her. Instead he'd tossed away everything he knew about her, and had chosen to chase after the woman he'd wanted to believe she was.

After she'd jumped, he'd tried to make amends. Not to Elizabeth. That would have been impossible. But he'd given a toddling young girl the help that he'd never given Elizabeth, and he'd fallen in love all over again.

Now he had a chance to make amends to Elizabeth. Not to earn her forgiveness, and with no expectation of love; Caius knew he was too late for that. But he could help her now—and make certain she remained free.

He watched her search through the storm behind them. By the clench of her fingers, he knew when she spotted the *Mary Elizabeth*'s lanterns again. She glanced up at Caius and tugged him closer.

His body stiffened as he bent his head toward her. She couldn't know the exquisite torture of her heated breath against his ear, the lavender scent of her hair.

She raised her voice over the noise from the engine and propellers. "How long until my father's airship has caught up to us?"

Caius could have answered her by raising a few fingers to indicate the hours left, but he turned his mouth toward her to speak. A knitted cap covered the shell of her ear. Dark curls nested in the hollow between the curve of her jaw and her blue scarf, dotted by tiny drops from melted snowflakes that sparkled in the lantern light. God, he wanted to kiss those glittering beads away, taste her coppery skin.

With need curling a tight fist in his gut, he told her, "Two or three hours."

She drew back to look up at him, as if seeking confirmation. When he nodded, she cast her worried gaze into the falling snow and the darkness beyond. Then determination flattened her lips, her brows drew together, and suddenly she was pulling him away from the airship's stern toward the ladder leading below. She let go of his hand in the companionway. Reluctantly, Caius released his hold on her. He didn't fear now that she would jump—her posture and expression told him that she was prepared to fight rather than run—but the longing ache in his chest was a continual reminder of how few of these small touches he would have. Whatever occurred with her father would probably happen tonight. Afterward he and Elizabeth would continue on to the Ivory Market, but on that journey Caius would have no more excuses to hold her hand, to lean close as he spoke.

He would be fortunate if she spoke to him at all.

So he glutted himself on the sight of her, trying to memorize every detail as he followed her down the dim passageway to her cabin. At the threshold, he hesitated. He'd pushed his way in earlier to stop her from running before he could tell her of his intention to help. He wouldn't usually enter a woman's bedchamber uninvited.

It was a rare occasion when he entered a woman's bedchamber at all. Aside from Elizabeth's, he hadn't been in one for seven or eight years. And before that, a few taverns and alleys, with the image of her face burning on the backs of his eyelids whenever he closed his eyes.

Frowning, she glanced back and gestured him inside. Intended for a single passenger, the layout of her narrow cabin mirrored his. Darkness filled the porthole opposite the door. A wardrobe cabinet had been built into the corner at the foot of the narrow bed. Warm yellow light shone from a gas lamp atop a small vanity.

Her cabin was as empty as Caius's was. Even to go up on deck, Elizabeth hadn't left any of her belongings behind. Though her everpresent satchel had been slung over the bed when he'd forced his way in earlier, now it hung across her chest again.

Caius passed her at the door and crossed to the porthole in three strides. Not a thing to be seen outside. He removed his hat before facing her. His long coat was stifling in the warm cabin but he didn't unbuckle it. He wasn't here to make himself at home.

Elizabeth swung the door closed. Tugging her scarf from her neck, she eyed him warily. "I can't trust you."

Though Caius already knew she didn't, hearing her say it was an unexpected punch to his stomach, leaving him sick and shaken. But he didn't react; he only nodded.

Because he knew she had little choice except to trust him now—at least for a little while. Elizabeth knew it, too. She dragged off her cap and tossed it onto the bed, her eyes haunted. "So what do we do now?"

"You don't have to do anything. You'll go to dinner and return here to sleep. If they come aboard, I'll stop them—and by morning you'll be free."

"That simple?"

"Yes."

Unease slipped across her expression, her teeth briefly catching her lower lip before she asked, "How will you stop them?"

By killing them—or getting near enough to it that they wouldn't pursue her or Caius's daughter again. But he said, "I'll have the advantage of surprise. They don't know I'm here and an injury that incapacitates their legs or arms will force them to retreat. After you've reached the Ivory Market, they won't find you again."

"And you think *that* will be simple?" Sudden, wry humor lifted her dark brows. "I should have lain in wait five years ago and maimed you."

That wouldn't have stopped him. And even if it had, she wouldn't have been safe. "Your father would have just sent someone else."

"But he wouldn't now?" Realization darkened her eyes. "You don't really mean to injure them."

Caius didn't answer. Uncertainty tore across her features. She looked away from him, shaking her head.

"I don't want anyone to die."

Neither did he. But he wasn't just doing this for her. As long as Willem Jannsen lived, neither Elizabeth nor his daughter would be free.

"That will be up to your father," Caius said.

Still shaking her head, she sank onto the edge of the bed and rubbed her arms through the sleeves of her coat as if cold.

Or as if afraid. Maybe of him. Many people were. They didn't meet his eyes in the street and went out of their way to avoid crossing his path. He couldn't remember when the change had come—whether it had been while he was an apprentice or after he'd become a huntsman. He couldn't recall any change in himself. One day he'd just realized that no one looked at him as they once had.

Except for Elizabeth. The way she'd looked at him had never changed. Always hopeful and earnest when she first saw him. And always hurt by the time he left her.

It had been the same when he'd caught her two years before. Earnest and hopeful the first week on the airship. Then devastated by the end.

Now she looked troubled and defeated, her voice dull. "How did he find me?"

"By chance." Her father hadn't been looking for her; everyone had believed her dead. "He was pursuing me through Norway when he met with an acquaintance of your mother's, who mentioned that she'd seen a woman who could have been your mother's twin coming out of a boarding house in Brighton."

And when Jannsen had abruptly abandoned his pursuit in Norway, Caius had backtracked the man's path to discover why. The same fear that led people to cross the street to avoid him had helped Caius quickly extract the information from the woman. Within the hour, he'd hired an airship to Brighton.

Elizabeth closed her eyes. After a long second she glanced up at him. "My father was pursuing you? He hadn't sent Amelia and Matthias?"

"No."

Confusion creased her brow. "Why? Even if you're a fugitive…why would he come after you himself?"

"Because you jumped, and I would sacrifice anything to make sure it never happened to anyone else," Caius said bluntly. "So I destroyed his machine."

Though that wasn't the only reason her father pursued him. But Caius didn't know how Elizabeth would react to the news that her father had created another duplicate—or that Caius had abducted a child that wasn't his.

That child *was* his daughter now—and not a substitute for Elizabeth. Caius had never asked or expected his daughter to be like her. But given Elizabeth's history, he feared she might believe it of him. She might think he was yet another man who couldn't let go of the woman he loved.

"His machine?" Dismay filled her voice. "You destroyed it?"

"Yes."

She stared at him, but Caius didn't think she was seeing his face. That dismay was on behalf of the sanctuary.

It *had* been an incredible machine, and Caius believed in the necessity of the work it had done. But it had become a terrible device when used as Willem Janssen had.

With a sigh, Elizabeth nodded. "Perhaps it is for the best, anyway. I told my father that machine had become a crutch—and eventually conservationists would have been breeding replicated animals to their own offspring. Better to have a few duplicates spread across different sanctuaries to strengthen a population's overall numbers and stop there."

And Caius would hunt for new specimens, if necessary. He believed in that work, too.

"So you destroyed his machine." Her gaze sharpened. "What did you do then?"

"I ran. To England, first. Then other places." Though few in the New World, where anyone infected by nanoagents was forbidden from crossing many borders without special sanction. When he'd served her father, Caius had possessed the necessary permissions to travel almost anywhere. As a fugitive, he hadn't. "Many locations were the same that you'd run to. Chasing you taught me more about hiding than hunting ever had."

Her quick laugh left a smile on her lips. God, he loved her mouth. Her eyes. The way she tilted her head to look up at him again, not the dismayed stare but her entire face lit by humor.

"Truly?"

"Yes. I learned well from you." He smiled now, too. "So I avoided the Ivory Market."

Where he'd caught up to her the last time. She laughed again, nodding as if in agreement—then stopped herself, biting her lip. Uncertain. Nervous.

Her gaze flicked to the mattress beside her leg.

In the next moment she surged away from the bed, standing on the opposite side of the cabin with her back pressed to the bulkhead. Shoulders stiff, her arms folded tightly beneath her breasts. She didn't meet his eyes.

Perhaps remembering the days that had followed, and how he'd tied her after he'd caught her.

Caius remembered those days, too. That had been the most torturous week of his life. Not just because her pleas to let her go had tormented him.

*She* had tormented him. Her sweetness and her ferocity and her beauty, and her determination to escape, no matter the cost.

And at one point, Elizabeth hadn't begged or threatened. She'd offered herself to him—her virginity and anything else he wanted. She'd lain in bed with her wrists bound and her face flushed, and she'd asked Caius if he would take her body in exchange for letting her go.

God help him, he'd considered it for a moment. He'd considered climbing into the bed and between her thighs, then pushing deep inside her sweet warmth. He'd considered letting her escape, then returning to her father and claiming that he hadn't found her. He'd considered giving up his freedom for a few hours in her arms.

Caius had considered it—then had coldly told her that he didn't want her.

By the flush on her cheeks now, he thought she was remembering that offer, too. Perhaps remembering the lie he'd given in response. Her gaze fell to his mouth. "Why did you kiss me earlier?"

Even as she spoke, dismay returned to her eyes. She hadn't meant to ask, Caius realized. But she hadn't been able to help herself.

He couldn't help himself, either. "Because I've always wanted to."

Doubt filled her expression again—along with the same hurt he'd seen in her eyes so many times. Hurt that he'd put there when he lied, when he'd pretended not to care.

Now it was there because she couldn't believe that he did. She must think he was playing with her.

"That's not possible. Never between us." She looked away and her voice roughened. "I despise you. And I can't trust you."

Despising someone wasn't a reason not to kiss them. It wasn't a reason not to spend hours in bed with them. Caius had despised her, too, because of how she'd made him feel. He thought now it was the same for Elizabeth. The desire was there between them—it had *always* been there. He'd known it from her first flirtatious looks in the sanctuary, from those smiles that killed him and made him dream of running off with her. He knew it from the hitch in her breath the second time he'd kissed her.

But she didn't trust him. That was far more important than desire.

And he'd already accepted that nothing between them was possible. It shouldn't scrape his heart raw to hear her say so.

Yet it did.

"I know," he said past the ache in his throat. "And I won't attempt to kiss you again. After we reach the Ivory Market, we'll go our separate ways."

Still not looking at him, she nodded, her eyes bright and her jaw locked.

Upset.

He'd thought hearing that would have pleased her. But maybe she didn't trust that he'd leave her alone.

Blast it all. He shouldn't have kissed her. "I only mean to protect you now, and to make certain no one comes after you again. I only mean to help."

"How can I believe that, Caius?" Her gaze snapped to his, hard and angry. "You hate me. All my life, you've hated me."

"I didn't hate you."

Her laugh in response ended as abruptly as it started, as if the sound was too sharp and painful, cutting her as it emerged. Eyes glittering, she looked away from him again.

God damn it. He couldn't bear to see her cry. He couldn't bear being the reason for it. And he needed her to look at him, to believe him. Desperation carried him across the cabin, stopping an arm's length from her. Close enough to touch—but he *wouldn't* touch her.

"I didn't hate you, Elizabeth," he repeated hoarsely. "I hated that you were everything I wanted and couldn't have."

Her gaze shot to his face again. Lips parting, she stared at him. "Why would you tell me something like that when I've just said nothing could come of it?"

What would be the point of trying to protect his heart now? He couldn't damage it any worse than he already had. So he had nothing to hide. And he had nothing to gain or to lose.

"Does it matter what I tell you? Will you trust me? Will you no longer despise me? Does it make *any* difference?"

Wordlessly, she shook her head.

"Then the least I can do is give you the truth. And I never hated you."

Her chest rose and fell on a short, shuddering breath. Then another. Her gaze searched his face. Still uncertain what to believe.

Her throat worked. When she spoke, her voice was tight and high. "Was it true what you told me on deck—your reason for helping me?"

"Yes." Unable to stop himself, he took another step toward her. Close enough to kiss—but he *wouldn't* kiss her. The confession came more easily this time, but was just as gruff to his ears. "I love you."

Hope flashed across her expression. Doubt chased it away. "You don't even know me."

"I do."

"We only spent a week together on an airship. You never talked with me before that. And when you did speak to me..." Flattening her lips, she averted her face.

When Caius had, he'd been cruel to her.

Now his love was hurting her, too—because she didn't believe him. But disbelief wasn't enough to wound someone. Disbelief only hurt when someone *wanted* to believe.

He knew that too well.

"I followed you for so long, Elizabeth. And I lied to myself about who you were, despite everything I saw and everything I knew about you. Not anymore."

She huffed out a short breath and pinned him with a challenging glare. "What could you possibly know?"

"I know why the animals are so important to you."

"Because I'm a naturalist's daughter."

"That might be part of the reason. I don't think it's all of it. When your father sent me to hunt you down, the first place I wanted to look for you was with your friends. But I discovered you didn't have any. I thought it proved everything I believed of you—that despite your wealth and beauty, you thought yourself better than everyone, so that when the time came to run, there was no one for you to run to. But everywhere you went, no one said that. They said you kept to yourself, but you weren't arrogant or proud. And everywhere you went, you were still visiting animals. It didn't matter what sort. A donkey or a kitten or a cur on the street—petting them if they'd allow it and feeding them if they didn't."

She was shaking her head. "That isn't a secret. My life has always revolved around caring for them."

In the sanctuary. "Why did you try so hard with me, then—despite every insult I said to you? Because I'm so handsome?"

A laugh startled from her. Her gaze swept over his face. "It must have been the only reason."

But it hadn't been. "And because you didn't have anyone else. I never realized how you were kept secluded. I thought that when you returned to your big house every day, you would have entertainments and friends. But there was only your father and his colleagues…until I came. A boy, only two years older than yourself. And for the first time in your life, you thought you might not be alone with only animals to keep you company. You thought I might be a friend—finally, a friend with two legs instead of four. That's why you tried so hard."

"No," she said, but it was barely a whisper over a broken breath.

"But I didn't try at all. I *should* have been that friend twelve years ago. I should have been that friend five years ago, when your father sent me after you. I should have been that friend two years ago, when I caught up to you. So I'm trying to be that friend now."

Tears swam in her eyes again, but this time she didn't look away. She stared up at him. Yearning held her features absolutely still; her arms wrapped around her middle as if hugging herself tight.

"I *know* you, Elizabeth. You. Not who someone wants you to be, but who you are."

She closed her eyes. The tears spilled over her cheeks and she shook her head. Still not trusting him.

"I know you have no reason to believe me. I hid everything I was from you, and I never let you know *me*. But by the time we arrive in the Ivory Market, you'll know who I am. We'll go our separate ways." The thickness in his throat roughened his voice. "But there will always be one friend you can go to, no matter your troubles. A friend who will always believe you. Who will always help you. That's who I am."

She seemed to crumple. Standing stiff against the bulkhead one moment, in the next she buried her face in her hands, muffling a wounded cry. Her shoulders slumped. As if her knees had given out, she began to slide down the wall.

And God help him, Caius broke every promise to himself. Lurching forward, he caught her before she hit the floor and gathered her against him, letting her sob into his chest. His eyes burning, he tried to soothe her, pressing kisses to the top of her head and murmuring a vow never to hurt her again.

Elizabeth slowly quieted, but she didn't leave his arms. Her cheek lay over his heart, her fingers softly curled beneath her chin, her gaze staring into nothing. Now and again another shudder wracked her body, and with each one, he held her tighter.

But he had to let her go.

The knock came too soon. Through the door, the porter called, "Five minutes to dinner, miss."

Raising his voice, Caius thanked the man. As the porter's footsteps moved on to the next cabin, Elizabeth stirred in his embrace and lifted her head. Cupping her cheeks in his gloved hands, he looked down into her tear-ravaged face. Her eyes searched his, and he watched her wariness and uncertainty return—and the hope.

"Go on, then," he told her quietly.

She answered with a slight nod, a tiny movement that was heaven against his palms. "What will you do?"

His gaze fell to her softly trembling lips. But he wouldn't kiss her. "I'll keep watch above."

And try to prove himself the friend he'd said he was.

E LIZABETH HAD NO APPETITE, BUT SHE KNEW FROM EXPERIENCE that it was best to eat when she could.

As the only female passenger, she'd been placed at Captain Harker's right hand. She must have been proving very dull company. Barely a word had passed her lips since she'd sat at the table, but the captain bore it well. He spoke with the men, and though she felt his gaze upon her from time to time, he didn't attempt to drag her into the conversation.

Elizabeth was grateful for it. A gruff man with a weathered face and long black beard, Harker had already shown himself to be a kind man, as well. When she'd arrived for dinner, he'd taken one glance at her, eyes still slightly red and swollen from crying, and carefully pulled her aside for a private word.

She suspected that the crew had told him she'd been holding hands with Caius on deck and that he'd been in her cabin when the porter had come by, but the evidence of her tears must have alarmed him.

Quietly, Harker had told her, "We are no strangers to shipboard romances on *Kingfisher*, Miss Dvorak. But I want to be sure this is of your choosing. One word from you, and I'll make certain that you won't see Mr. Trachter during the remainder of this voyage."

Her heart still overwhelmed by Caius's declaration, the captain's concern had almost started her crying again. So many years alone, and in one hour, two different men offered to protect her without asking for anything in return.

Something her father should have done.

But although she didn't know whether to trust Caius, Elizabeth would take her chances with him. "Thank you, but you need not worry. I've known Mr. Trachter since I was young," she'd explained. "And our reunion was…emotional. He had to impart unhappy news to me regarding a mutual acquaintance."

The captain had nodded. "If that is what upset you, then I hope the remainder of your voyage proves more pleasant. You can be certain of privacy aboard this vessel. And because sounds of love and sounds of distress can often be mistaken for each other, I'll let my aviators know that you are not in need of rescue—so that you won't be interrupted at a delicate time."

Her face had flamed at that, yet the good humor in his voice made Elizabeth laugh at herself, too. It was scandalous, but so different from the stories she usually created to hide her identity. She was having an illicit tryst aboard an airship. Or rather, Miss Dvorak was.

With Caius Trachter.

In her bed.

At the thought of it, her cheeks had heated again, but not with embarrassment. Everything within her tightened when she imagined him there. *In her bed.* Caius—big and strong and rugged. When he'd kissed her, his unshaven jaw had scraped her chin. Leather gloves had covered his large hands, but when he'd tied her before, she'd felt the calluses on his palms against her wrists. She'd seen him bathe by the dim light of a candle when he thought she was asleep, watching from the dark as he lathered the coarse hair that shadowed his broad chest, her gaze following the water sluicing over ridges and planes of hard muscle.

He might be gentle. But a man like Caius would always be a little rough.

And she'd imagined being with him before. She'd imagined so many foolish things about him—at the sanctuary and after she'd fled.

She *had* kept trying with him, despite every time he'd hurt her. Because Elizabeth had believed that he was just as wounded and alone as she had been. And as she'd grown older, she'd begun building so many fantasies around him. Some romantic, some not. But in all of them, he hadn't hated her. She'd told herself that he was like the lion that had once roamed the sanctuary grounds before being moved to a preserve farther south, where the climate was more agreeable. She'd worked and walked near the lion before, always wary of the danger he posed. Yet he never attacked, watching her instead with his tail flicking, sometimes loping away as if irritated. But when he'd been caged for transport, he'd lashed out when anyone had drawn near, clawing through the bars. Not enraged by the person—enraged by the cage.

She'd thought Caius was like that. And she'd imagined that one day he would come to her and say that he'd never despised her, that he'd lashed out because of his own cage, the indentured servitude.

But then Elizabeth had wondered if she just wanted to believe it so much because she'd felt her own cage closing around her.

She'd let herself continue to have those dreams, however, because aside from studying and the sanctuary, she'd had little else. When she'd finally run, she'd dreamed that if Caius caught up to her, he wouldn't take her back to her father. That he'd just want her for himself, and they would run together.

But although she'd imagined it, Elizabeth never let herself succumb to those dreams. And a good thing, too. Because he hadn't let her go— and she would have been a fool, running straight into the arms of her captor.

She couldn't be a fool now, either. Even if the rough warmth of his lips still burned on hers. Even though his words still echoed in her ears, claiming that he was everything she'd imagined.

*I hated that you were everything I wanted and couldn't have.*

If that was true…then Caius was wrong: she knew who he was, too. If it was true, she understood Caius better than he realized. If it was true, he could be someone that Elizabeth could run to instead of running from.

If it was all true.

She was so terrified that it wasn't.

That fear and doubt lodged in her throat, making every bite an effort to swallow. Then the apple tart arrived at the end of the meal, and she couldn't eat at all.

Elizabeth never forced herself to consume something she disliked anymore. Apples, duck, sweetbreads—all were foods her father had insisted were her favorites and had regularly made her eat them...but it was her mother who had enjoyed their flavors. It was her mother who'd told her father that she'd grown up preferring the company of animals to human friends, and so when Elizabeth had complained of loneliness her father had insisted she didn't need any companionship but what she found at the sanctuary.

And Elizabeth *had* loved the sanctuary and studying to become a naturalist, just as her mother had been. But she'd wanted more.

So without her father knowing, she'd taken the entrance exams to the scientific university in New Leiden—close enough to the sanctuary that she could visit regularly. She'd announced her intentions on her twentieth birthday, the day she reached her majority. Her father had demanded that she attend university in Manhattan City instead.

Just as her mother had.

Elizabeth might have gone to Manhattan City, if only to finally be away from his controlling influence. Except during their argument she'd begun to cry, and her distraught father had confessed how he and her mother hadn't been able to conceive, so they'd created a duplicate—a daughter for them to love. That when Mary died giving birth, he'd known she'd been returned to him and that he'd been given a second chance. That Elizabeth was the same woman, and he believed that when she was twenty-five years of age, she would journey from Manhattan City and fall in love with him as her mother had.

Elizabeth had known for many years that her mother's death had broken something in him. She hadn't realized how those broken pieces had warped in his mind and his heart, and how desperate he must have been to make himself believe it so deeply.

But his belief was unmistakable—and unshakeable. He would

attempt to make Elizabeth into her mother, in every way.

Sheer horror had sent her fleeing.

Five years later, it had brought her here. Elizabeth wished she could hate her father, but she pitied him. A brilliant man, driven to madness by grief. And despite everything, she loved him. She had far more happy memories of her father than bad—and although they'd had arguments and frustrations, never once had he given her reason to suspect he saw her as anything but a daughter.

But in his madness, he did—and she didn't know how to stop him now. He wouldn't give up his search for her, and she had no protection, no power. Her only option was to run. And she was so tired of running, but there had to be an answer besides death.

Perhaps by hiding so well he'd never find her. By concealing herself until there simply wasn't an Elizabeth Jannsen anymore. She'd stop visiting menageries, attending to animals, and acting in any way that might draw attention to herself. Whatever crumbs of her identity that had allowed Caius to follow her around the world needed to be destroyed. She'd toss away everything she'd worked toward and wanted, and erase every lingering connection to her conservationist roots.

A fugitive, maybe Caius would want to run with her. She wouldn't be alone, then. There was no one better to hide with than a hunter. And there was no one else who would still know who she was, who she'd been.

There was no one else who had *ever* known.

But those were just more foolish dreams. When her father caught up to *Kingfisher*, he and his hunters would come aboard. She'd have no chance to hide. And Caius would have few options, too, except to lash out at the man who would cage them.

She didn't want anyone to die—and she wanted to remain Elizabeth. The very thought of losing herself made her heart seem to wither, and despite what her father had become, the thought of losing him this way made her want to cry. But she just didn't see a solution that would allow her to have both.

Movement near her elbow pulled Elizabeth out of her desperate search for an answer. The chief mate had entered the cabin and was speaking quietly into the captain's ear. Harker sighed and nodded, the tip of his beard brushing the buckle that fastened his jacket over his stomach.

On his order, a cabin attendant began closing the shutters over the portholes. The conversation around the table lulled as everyone looked to the captain.

"It appears that we have caught the attention of pirates," he said, and when a murmur of alarm rose around the table, he held up his hand. "We are taking precautions, but I promise you there is little reason for concern. This happens with unfortunate regularity. The pirates know that the fare to the Market is a steep one, and they assume we are carrying someone worth taking for ransom. But in ten years, not a single pirate has been successful in boarding *Kingfisher*. They won't be tonight, either."

Not pirates, Elizabeth realized. They'd mistaken her father's airship for a marauder's.

She supposed there wasn't much difference—and the captain's confidence was reassuring.

"They are probably relying on the snow to cover their approach, but the storm offers us the advantage," he continued. "Without lights to follow us by, they won't be able to track our heading. At this moment, my men are shuttering all portholes on the ship. I ask that when you return to your cabins, you keep those shutters closed, particularly if you spark your lamps. By morning, we will be far beyond the pirates' sight and their reach."

Hope lifted through Elizabeth's heart. Perhaps it would be that simple.

But it rarely was. And even if they did escape her father's pursuit tonight, he would still come after her. When she reached the Ivory Market, Elizabeth would have to give up everything that she was and hide as best she could.

She felt the captain's gaze on her again through the remaining minutes of their meal. Finally the glasses of spirits were poured—traditionally a male indulgence, and one that gave her an excuse to leave. As she rose and said her goodnights, Harker stood with her, offering his arm.

"Allow me to escort you to your cabin, Miss Dvorak."

It was only a few doors along the same deck, but she couldn't refuse. Elizabeth nodded and took his elbow.

In the passageway, he said, "Your man didn't come to dinner. Instead he remained on deck and was the one who alerted my crew."

Caius had? She'd assumed that one of the aviators had spotted the lanterns. But she couldn't feign ignorance. "Yes, sir."

"If you'll forgive me, it's a bludging snowy mess out there," he said bluntly. "My chief mate tells me that if Mr. Trachter hadn't pointed out the airship, no one could have possibly spotted it...unless he already knew it was there."

"Yes, sir," she said softly.

"Are they pirates, Miss Dvorak?"

"No, sir." As they stopped at her cabin door, she turned to look up at him. "It's my father."

His gaze thoughtful, Harker nodded as if he'd already suspected that answer. "And is your life in danger? Or that young man's?"

"Are you asking because you might have to decide whether to hand me over?"

"In the unlikely event that we do not lose them in the storm...yes."

Because his men might have to fight her father's men if they didn't. Not just gruff and kind, but pragmatic. A runaway daughter wasn't worth the lives of his aviators.

Though her chest hurt, Elizabeth tried to be just as pragmatic. "He doesn't mean to kill us, Captain. Just to return us home."

"Would it make any difference if you were married first?"

Married? Elizabeth frowned, then realized—the captain thought *that* was the reason her father was following them. That he had forbidden her and Caius from being together.

Now the captain was offering to perform the ceremony. Another kindness, but it wouldn't have mattered.

"No, sir. Mr. Trachter broke his indentured contract." And an indentured servant could marry whomever he wished, but a fugitive's marriage could be quickly annulled. "So my father's hunters would come aboard and take me, regardless."

"Then I ask you again, Miss Dvorak." Harker's gaze was hard and direct. "Should I hand you over?"

Her stomach in knots, Elizabeth struggled to find a response. But it wasn't her decision; it wasn't her life at stake.

Perhaps the truth was the only possible response, then. His crew would be in danger if they fought her father. If the captain was trying to decide whether she was worth dying for, then Elizabeth could at least tell him why.

"My father is…not well. I look very much like my late mother. Exactly like her. So he imagines that I am her and wants me to take her place."

A dark frown furrowed his brow. "That's unnatural."

Elizabeth stopped her automatic denial. All her life, she'd heard that word used to denigrate anything someone didn't understand—particularly Horde technology. *Unnatural* was why her father had to keep a wondrous and helpful device secret. *Unnatural* was why Caius couldn't return to the city where he was born without special papers. Many people would say Elizabeth was unnatural if they knew the truth of her birth. But a couple creating a daughter that they couldn't conceive on their own wasn't unnatural. It was wonderful.

What her father had done *was* unnatural, though. Grief had twisted his thinking, and it had never untwisted.

"Yes," she said. "And I am sorry, Captain. I didn't know he would follow me so quickly and endanger your ship."

His frown smoothed away, leaving an amused gleam in his eyes. "We're not in danger yet. A man doesn't fly as long as I have without learning how to disappear in a snowstorm—and this wily old fox knows a few tricks."

THEY'D EXTINGUISHED THE LANTERNS ON DECK. BUNDLED TIGHTLY in her coat, Elizabeth climbed up the ladder and into the rushing dark. The wind snapped at her scarf and whipped tears from her eyes. She stopped at the edge of the companionway near the middle of the ship, waiting for her vision to adjust.

Engine huffing and rattling, *Kingfisher* hurtled through the night and the falling snow. Somewhere above, a full moon was shining. Only faint light penetrated the thick clouds, but after a few seconds she recognized the shape of the pilot's wheelhouse and the framework of pipes warming the balloon overhead. Looking for Caius, she searched the deck for upright figures. Supporting timbers stood at intervals from bow to stern. Equipment lashed to the posts gave them irregular outlines, making it difficult to distinguish between the timbers and the aviators.

A shadow emerged from a nearby post. Her heart caught, then resumed on a thick, heavy beat. *Caius.* She couldn't have mistaken the silhouette of his hat and broad shoulders or the long column of his coat for anyone else's.

Without a word, he took her gloved hand in his. Pulse pounding, she let him draw her back into the shadows—where a lifeboat tied to the timber blocked the worst of the wind, she realized. From his position, he could watch over both sides of the airship and behind it.

His head bent to hers. Though loud, the engine wasn't as deafening as at the stern, and he didn't have to raise his voice as much to speak.

His warm breath caressed her cheek as he said, "Your father will either lose our trail or he won't, but you don't have to wait in the cold with us. If you want to return to your cabin to rest, I'll wake you as soon as we know."

After it was all over. "If you believe I would ever go below and wait for someone else to resolve my future, Caius, then you don't know me as well as you think."

His smile was a faint gleam. "You do often surprise me."

Good. But she didn't know what to do with the strange, heated tension rising through her. Feeling slightly breathless, she turned away from Caius and searched the sky behind them.

No sign of any lanterns. "Do you think we've lost them?"

"I don't know," he said, and when she glanced up, his profile was a sharp series of shadows layered over shadows: impenetrable from the brim of his hat to his eyes, the lighter slash of his cheekbone, dark again over his jaw. "We've changed heading and there are no lights to track us by. The storm will conceal the exhaust trail."

"But?" Elizabeth knew, though. Captain Harker might be a wily fox. But her father had hunters—and hounds. "Can a hound track an airship?"

"I've seen Amelia do it before. Though not in a storm like this—and the wind is at our tail now."

So *Kingfisher* might still have the advantage. "Have you seen their lanterns since we changed course?"

"No."

That didn't mean her father wasn't following them. When *Kingfisher's* lanterns went out, they might have realized that they'd been spotted and extinguished their own. The only way to be certain was to listen for her father's engine...but that meant hovering motionless in the dark with *Kingfisher*'s engine at full stop. In that time, her father might close the distance between them, and it wouldn't matter if the crew of *Kingfisher* could hear his engine then. Her father would be on them before they could fly ahead of him again.

The heated tension that had gripped her before changed into something sharper, tighter. No longer pleasant but roiling like sickness inside her.

Steeling her resolve, she said, "I don't want anyone to die for me, Caius. If they come, just give me to him. I'll escape again."

"No," he said. Not even raising his voice, yet she couldn't mistake the implacable tone.

It wasn't his decision, though. "You can't—"

"No. And if you argue, I'll tie you to the bed again until this is over with."

*If she argued?* "So this is how you intend to be my friend? If I scream, you kiss me. If I say something you disagree with, you tie me to a bed. I can't imagine what you'll do if I walk to the quarterdeck without your permission."

Oh, but the words had barely left her mouth before she *did* imagine what he could do—and she would not be tied, but her hands roaming over hard muscle and tanned skin. She saw the flash of his grin and was suddenly grateful for the darkness that hid the heat in her cheeks.

But he only said, "I'm a friend who will let you do anything but give yourself up."

Blast him. Yet Elizabeth wouldn't have let a friend give herself up, either. With a sigh, she stared into the dark again.

He took her hand and gave her fingers a reassuring squeeze before releasing her. "We *do* have a fair chance of losing them in this storm. We'll reach the Ivory Market. I know you can hide well enough that he won't find you. And if you need help...I'll tell you how to find me."

Heart full, she nodded. That was exactly as she'd hoped. Exactly as she'd planned, if her father and his hunters didn't board *Kingfisher*. Her alternative to anyone dying.

When Caius had warned the crew of the airship's presence, he'd known the storm was their best chance of evading her father's pursuit. Caius must have been trying to create the same alternative—because even though he'd planned to kill anyone who tried to take Elizabeth, she'd told him in her cabin that she didn't want anyone to die.

So he was attempting to offer her the chance to hide. Now she wanted to tell him, *Come with me.* But Elizabeth didn't speak the words, still unsure whether she'd begun to trust him just because she wanted to so badly.

And if they did escape her father tonight, she would have days to make certain that she *could* trust him.

"Well, I hope that we lose them," she said. "Then the next three days will be like a holiday."

Though the shadows concealed his eyes, she felt Caius's gaze on her. "And how would you pass the time?"

"Study, perhaps. Read more of Guerra's monograph on megalodon predation of whales in the North Sea." Along with clothes and money, she always carried the naturalist society's most recent publication in her satchel. "All of the crew believes we're having a tryst."

He didn't reply for a long second. "Does that worry you?"

"No. If there is a real woman named Magdalena Dvorak, I would worry that her reputation is ruined, but *mine* is not. I might use their assumption as an excuse to be very lazy in bed and rise well past a productive hour." She gave him a wry glance. "The truth is, I already do that more often than I should."

Caius abruptly turned his face away from her.

*Of course.* Her heart constricted. Throat tight, she said, "What do you wish to say? Do you wonder if I'll complain about the softness of my mattress or the many hours I can sleep?"

His head whipped back around. "No," he denied sharply. "I was trying not to think of you in bed. Or how I want to be there with you."

The huffing engine seemed to quiet, muffled by the pounding of her heart. She touched his sleeve. "What else do you want?"

He shook his head.

"You said that the least you could give me was the truth, Caius. So tell me, what else do you want?"

The shadow over his jaw deepened slightly, as if he'd clenched his teeth. "I want to kiss you again."

She wanted him to kiss her, too. To feel him cup her face in his hands and hold her as everything burned away into the heat of his mouth.

But that wasn't all he wanted. Roughly, he continued, "I want to taste the skin on the side of your neck. I used to watch you feed the mink at the sanctuary, and when you leaned over the edge of their pond your braid would fall forward over your shoulder against that spot and I would think of it for days, of holding you still while I licked and licked. I want to tear away your dress and worship your breasts with my hands. I want to kiss your nipples and suck until they're hard against my tongue. You destroyed me two years ago, offering yourself to me. Afterward, I stood at the door of your cabin and listened to you bathe, trying to imagine how you looked and knowing that I only had to turn around to see how beautiful you were. But if I did, you would have seen what imagining you had done to me, and you'd know how I'd lied about not wanting you."

Breathless, she had to know— "What did I do to you?"

"Elizabeth—"

"Tell me."

"Bludging hell, Elizabeth!" Voice harsh with frustration, he said, "My prick was hard as stone. Just as it is now, being here with you."

Her gaze dropped, but in the dark, there was nothing to see except the solid shadow of his body. But it didn't matter. Elizabeth had yearned for evidence that she could trust him, and his words now were enough.

Caius *was* here to help her. He would never admit to such things if he was working for her father. And whether the protective parent she'd known or the madman who believed she was his wife, if he'd had any idea that Caius wanted her, her father wouldn't have let him anywhere near her.

Her heart buoyed by joy, she turned her face away.

He was here to help her, to be her friend. And she *knew* him. It was so incredible to discover that Caius was the man she'd always dreamed he was.

"God forgive me, Elizabeth. I shouldn't have said— I wouldn't have…" Trailing off, he angled his head lower as if trying to see her expression. "Are you smiling?"

Elizabeth lifted her chin. No hiding now. "Yes. I was thinking that if this does become a holiday, I would like to have a tryst. Not as Magdalena Dvorak," she said, "but as Elizabeth Jannsen."

It seemed that an eternity passed, but it lasted only a few beats of her racing pulse. When he answered, tension strained his voice. "Would you?"

She nodded.

"With *me?*"

She nodded again.

And gasped when hard fingers circled her waist and pushed her deeper into the shadows behind the lifeboat, the timber post against her back and the edge of a folded glider pressing into her shoulder. Already difficult to see, now they were completely hidden from the sight of the crew.

His gloved hands rose and caught her face. "Are you certain? Because I would take *any* opportunity to be with you, Elizabeth, but I don't want to make a mistake and hurt you again. So don't play with me about this."

If not for the hoarseness of his voice, his doubt might have hurt her. But he was terrified of being wrong, Elizabeth realized. Just as she'd been afraid when he'd said he loved her. Because if he didn't…

It tore her apart to even think of it. She had to trust that he did. But she knew that wasn't easy.

"I never would play with you, Caius." She might tease him, but never mislead him. "Not about this."

"I know." His thumbs stroked her cheeks. "But it's so impossible to believe that you want me."

God, she did. So much. And all so overwhelming, so new. "I've barely grasped that *you* want *me*." After years of believing that he hated her. "What you told me—is that all you want to do?"

"It was not even near to all the ways I want to touch you."

"Then tell me that, too."

His groan was a low rumble. "Are you trying to torture me?"

"A little," she admitted. But everything he'd said had tortured her, too.

"Then I would part your legs and taste you until you're wet and begging for me to make you come. I'd cover your body with mine and drive as deep as I could again and again, watching your face because you don't hide anything, and I'd know how you felt when I was inside you." His voice deepened, so low and rough she could barely hear him over the engine. "I wish I could see you now. If I could, it would be easier to believe you want me as much as I want you."

He didn't need to see her. She would prove it to him. Sliding her hands over his shoulders, she lifted onto her toes. "Caius."

"Elizabeth," he said gruffly. The shadow of his head lowered—then stopped, as if he was waiting.

For her explicit permission?

Need overpowered her ability to speak. Heart pounding, she pushed her fingers into his hair and hauled him down to her lips.

Heat surrounded her. His mouth opened over hers with a demanding stroke of his tongue. His hands dropped to her waist and his arms gathered her close, his groan of pleasure a thrum through her chest and his arousal hard against her stomach. Hunger seared her nerves. She tried to push closer, closer, but Caius was pulling away from her, lifting his head.

Cold air kissed her moist lips. Breath ragged, she looked up. "Caius?"

His body stiffened. Still holding her against his chest, he turned toward the stern of the airship. She looked over his shoulder as a warning sounded from the crew.

Her stomach twisted into a knot. Had her father caught up to them?

Captain Harker began shouting orders, then his voice was lost as the roar of the engine changed—deeper, louder. Not a steady rattling huff but fast and irregular.

Not the sound of *one* engine, she realized with sudden horror. They were hearing *two* engines.

And both were at full steam. Her father's airship had caught up to them but his crew must not have seen them yet, because no one would barrel through a storm like this so close to another airship.

*How close?* Were they higher or lower? Off to the side and on a parallel heading or coming directly toward them?

Desperately, she searched the snow-filled night. Her arms tightened around Caius's neck. "Where are they?"

Even as she asked, a shadow moved through the swirling white on the portside tail. Just off to the side. Maybe they would miss each other—

All at once, the shadow's shape resolved into the jutting prow of an airship, like a spear tossed out of the dark.

Directly at *Kingfisher*'s propellers.

"Oh, dear God," she whispered, just Caius's arm cinched around her and he dove for the deck.

A heartbeat later, her father's airship rammed into them.

# Chapter Four

ELIZABETH'S BACK SLAMMED INTO THE BOARDS, KNOCKING AWAY her breath. A rhythmic *thunk thunk thunk* thumped heavily through the dark. Beneath her, *Kingfisher* shuddered in time with each thump—then jolted sharply to port.

Metal shrieked, a piercing scream that drowned out every other sound and resonated in Elizabeth's teeth and skull, spiking agony through her ears. She couldn't hear her own scream, only feel Caius above her, shielding her body with his and shoving her along the smooth deck. Around behind the lifeboat, she realized. Using it for cover.

The shriek rose and snapped. The boards trembled and the grinding of gears reverberated through the deck. The rumble of *Kingfisher*'s engine died.

*Oh, thank God.* Someone below must have thrown the engine to full stop.

Splintered wood hailed around them, pelting the boat.

Then nothing.

For a breathless second, Elizabeth couldn't believe it. She lay still, waiting, with Caius's tense body like steel over hers.

Well. That hadn't been as bad as she'd feared.

In the sudden quiet, joyful shouts rose around them. Murmuring that he loved her, he loved her, Caius pressed kisses to her forehead and cheeks. Laughing and coughing, she sat up, clinging to him.

A metallic *thwipkt!* whipped through the air. The deck lurched.

Silence fell for a taut moment—then a high-pitched scream of pain and horror split the dark.

"Get down, Elizabeth!" Caius flattened her to the deck. "Down!"

*Thwipkt!*

The deck seemed to drop toward the stern. More screams—but the first abruptly cut off. Glass shattered nearby. The pilot's wheelhouse. All around them, wood splintered and groaned. Another *thwipkt!* And another. Each followed by a jolt of the deck, as if it were falling out from beneath them.

The cables tethering the balloon to the wooden cruiser were breaking, Elizabeth realized—the tension snapping them like whips.

Terror dug into her heart with feral claws. The crash must have fractured the primary tether anchors at the stern. Now the weight of the cruiser and its massive steam engine were tearing the secondary cables from their anchors in succession, from stern to bow. Like a clamshell being forced open, the ship was ripping away from the balloon.

"Hold on to me!" Caius shouted.

The deck dropped again, a sharp downward slant. Elizabeth cried out as they suddenly slid past the lifeboat—then jerked to a stop.

Caius had caught the timber. But even that wouldn't save them. She could hear wood cracking all around them. It wouldn't be long before their support broke free.

Another *thwipkt!* and she screamed as the deck suddenly seemed to disappear beneath them. But they weren't dropping to the ground. They dangled high above it, Caius's arm around her waist and hanging on to the timber with his opposite hand.

A scream rushed past them. Someone falling. Dear God.

Wood creaking, the airship seemed to swing, as if the cruiser was hanging vertically from the balloon by the few cables remaining near the bow. It couldn't be long before the metal fabric of the balloon ripped. The envelope was strong, designed to carry the weight of the cruiser and withstand the effects of extreme weather. It wasn't made to do this.

Caius couldn't hold them forever, either—though she knew he would try. Thank the heavens he didn't have to.

"The glider!" she cried. "Can you reach it?"

"I can't reach it without letting you go!"

She tightened her arms around his shoulders. "Then let go of me. I'll hold on!"

He hesitated.

"Do it, Caius! I'll hold on!"

The ship groaned, swinging as another cable broke. Elizabeth's heart stopped for a terrifying moment when Caius's hold vanished from around her waist and her arms bore her full weight. Frantically, she wrapped her legs around him. Grunting with effort, he hauled them both upward with one hand, blindly reaching for the glider's hooks with the other.

Another scream as someone else fell. She prayed that others had gotten to the gliders, too.

A ratcheting series of clicks sounded by her ear—he'd opened the glider. Sheer relief made her weight seem like a feather's. Clinging to him, she tucked her head against his neck.

"Don't let go." Urgency hardened his voice. "Whatever happens, Elizabeth, don't let go."

Heavy muscle bunched beneath her hands. He seemed to swing—so his feet could push them away from the deck, she realized, jumping out away from the ship instead of just dropping—and then there was nothing around them, and the sharp jolt of their leap and the glider catching the air knocked her legs from around him. Gritting her teeth, she locked her arms tighter.

"Elizabeth!" Desperation filled his shout. Flying the glider required both hands. He couldn't hold on to her.

"I'm all right!"

Terrified, but alive and hanging on. Her stomach dropped and swooped as they leveled out, her feet dangling and skirts whipping around her legs.

Her eyes had squeezed shut. She made herself open them, looking into the dark beyond his shoulder.

An explosion of orange light burned her eyes. A blast of heated air hit her legs, seemed to toss the glider upward.

"Hold on!"

Arms shaking with strain, she did. The glider leveled out again and banked to the left.

Elizabeth dared another look and her heart pulled in two, ripping a denial from her throat.

On the ground, her father's airship had caught fire, the falling snow forming a glowing halo around the wreckage and lighting the scene. A rolling white plain stretched around the airship, broken here and there by bodies or crates and pieces of the engine. *Kingfisher* floated above, balloon up-ended, the cruiser dangling beneath. A small two-seater balloon was in the air, flying toward *Kingfisher*. More emergency gliders circled around the airship. Eleven or twelve. Not enough for everyone who must have been on the two vessels.

She glanced down again. *Oh, thank God.* There were more people down there, racing across the snow—

Not people. Fear slicked the back of her neck in a cold sweat.

*Zombies.*

Drawn by the noise and the light, the ravenous creatures were converging on the wreck. She watched in horror as a glider landed on the snow and four of the zombies sped in that direction. A figure burst away from the glider. Not fast enough.

Eyes burning, she looked away, then bit back her scream when *Kingfisher's* balloon suddenly split along a seam. The cruiser dropped—a lone glider flying away from the ship as it fell, a long sickening silence that ended with a deafening crash. The stern collapsed on impact, smashing in on itself. The bow snapped backward and slammed upside-down onto the ground. The remains of the heavy balloon flopped down around it.

More zombies turned toward *Kingfisher's* wreckage, then Caius banked the glider away from the site and she couldn't see either of the airships, only the glow of the fire illuminating the falling flakes of snow.

Flying away from the light and the noise and the zombies...but they had to land sometime. *Kingfisher's* bow might provide a shelter.

But she couldn't ask where Caius was going. She needed to be quiet, to avoid attracting the zombies' notice. And every bit of her concentration and strength centered on her arms, the trembling pain that weakened her hold with every minute that she dangled above the ground. A few more zombies roamed below—all heading toward the wreck while she and Caius flew silently above the creatures' heads.

Slowly, the glider lost altitude. Numbness had just begun to creep into her hands when her heels suddenly scraped over snow, her feet bouncing along until Caius's boots hit and then they were tumbling, rolling, the glider's frame cracking and the canvas shredding.

In the next second, he hauled her onto her feet. His coat was open, the brass buckles of his weapons harness glinting in the faint light. A machete gleamed in his left hand.

A man's best friend when facing the creatures. She was suddenly glad that Caius had one—and that he'd declared himself her friend, too.

"All right, Elizabeth?"

It was a hoarse whisper. Making as little noise as possible.

Elizabeth nodded in response. Bruised and sore, with needles of pain stabbing from her shoulders to her fingers, but alive.

He cupped her cheek. Not looking down at her, though. His gaze searched the snow around them.

Heart racing, she scanned their surroundings. The snow still fell heavily, and although a bit of wind scattered the flakes it wasn't the blinding torrent on the airship, offering fifty yards or more of visibility.

No zombies—but the fire burned in the distance, an orange glow against the sky. Any of the creatures heading in that direction might come across her and Caius in their path.

His hand dropping away from her cheek, Caius bent to the ground. Pinning the glider with his foot, he wrenched an arm's length of the broken frame free. Canvas ripped. He paused for a long second, watching the snow around them before turning toward her. Holding the broken piece in his fist, he mimed jabbing the sharp aluminum point into his eye.

She nodded to show her understanding. If they came across any zombies, stab them through the head.

Caius gave her the weapon and took her free hand, tugging her away from the light. She hesitated. They might find *some* shelter in the wreckage; there wasn't any out here in the open. He glanced back and lowered his mouth to her ear.

"There's an outpost ahead," he breathed. "I saw it in the flare of the explosion."

A Horde outpost? With high stone walls—and possible rescue for those left at the airship.

She nodded. "How far?"

"A half mile. The storm will help cover us as we move."

Then best to go quickly. She gestured for him to lead on, her boots sinking four or five inches into the snow with each step. Thank God not any deeper. He broke into a jog and she kept pace beside him, her heart thundering. She tried to be silent but her chest sounded like a bellows, each breath bursting into a frozen cloud, the snow crunching under her boots.

A distant crack split the air behind them. Gunfire. Someone was shooting the zombies—but that would only bring more, not scare them away.

All around them, shadows moved through the night, heading toward the sound of the shots. Faint moans and growls prickled the hairs on the back of her neck. She darted terrified glances over her shoulder as they ran, expecting to see one behind them at any moment.

But it came from ahead, rushing out of the dark and snow. Caius released her hand, sprinting ahead to meet it. Elizabeth faltered, horror slowing her steps. Covered in filth, the creature was naked, as if any clothing it had worn long ago rotted off. Some of its flesh had, too, skin hanging loose over its chest. She couldn't tell whether it was male or female. Gaping wounds exposed shredded muscle and bone in its lower abdomen and face. Snarls ripped from a nightmarish mouth, the lips torn or bitten away.

Fingers like claws, it lunged for Caius. With a quick sidestep and a powerful swing, he hacked through its skull. The top half of its head dropped to the ground, an upended bowl. The body took a few more running steps before plowing into the snow, thick blood drooling from the severed jaw.

Her stomach lurching into her throat, Elizabeth raced past it, catching Caius's hand again. A solid shadow stood directly ahead—the outpost wall. A hulking machine appeared on the left and they sped past an enormous segmented wheeltrack, larger than any vehicle treads she'd ever seen.

A harvester. Or a war machine.

They reached the wall. Elizabeth collapsed against it, catching her breath. His back to the stone, Caius's gaze swept their trail before he nodded. "This way."

Because the entrance to Horde structures almost always faced south. Without a visible moon, she didn't know how he could tell which direction they were running in, but soon after rounding the corner of the wall they came across the massive wooden doors.

The massive *open* doors. No sound or lights within.

Caius's jaw clenched. She knew what he was thinking. Those open doors meant the outpost had been abandoned or overrun. They couldn't know what was inside—whether the site would be infested with zombies or empty—and the worst way to find out would be walking through those doors in the dark.

He looked away from the outpost and his eyes narrowed. Elizabeth followed his gaze. Another giant machine stood twenty yards away, a long armored body on dozens of segmented legs.

A second later they were running toward it, Caius's hand holding hers.

Beneath the machine, only a powdering of snow lay over stiff, dried grasses. It must have been sitting for a while. Rust darkened the iron legs and flaked off beneath Elizabeth's glove. The body squatted low to the ground, the legs folded like a locust's—but the belly was still well over their heads. They peered upward, searching the shadows for a hatch.

How could they possibly see it? Tension gripped her chest as a moan sounded from inside the outpost. They both froze, watching in that direction.

Nothing.

Caius glanced up again and whispered, "We can't risk a light."

Only a fool would. But they were *already* being fools, Elizabeth realized. Even mobile structures had deliberately placed entrances.

She tugged on his sleeve. "South."

And there it was, on the side of the machine; an oval door with a simple lever latch waited above the third leg. In plain sight, but it took another five minutes of searching to find the ladder built into the leg—a disappearing ladder, designed to prevent more than one person from going up. Pulling on small metal rings while climbing opened handholds and footholds above her and closed the panels below. Only two holds were available at any time: one to stand on, and the next one up.

Because it was a war machine, she realized. They wouldn't have wanted an enemy to attack their entrance in force.

"Go on up and open the door," Caius said softly. "Zombies can't climb."

So the creatures wouldn't be up there…unless they'd already been trapped inside. But Elizabeth wouldn't think of that.

Tucking her aluminum poker under her arm, she hauled herself up. A tiny platform the size of her foot projected from beside the door. She gingerly stepped onto it and looked down at the top of Caius's hat ten feet below.

On a steadying breath, she gripped the latch. Rusted tight, the lever wouldn't budge, even when she threw her full weight onto it.

She glanced down, met Caius's eyes, and shook her head.

He gestured her back down and waited for her beside the leg. Her heart thumped when he pushed the machete into her grip.

"Will you stand guard?" he whispered. "I'll try to open it. If I can't, we'll head around to the other machine."

She nodded. A grin widened his mouth and his firm lips swiftly pressed to hers. Before she could kiss him back, he was climbing.

Smiling, she pivoted in a slow circle. A movement farther south froze Elizabeth's blood, her fingers tight on the machete's handle—but the zombie continued on, heading east toward the airships. She glanced toward the outpost doors to make certain nothing had wandered out, then looked up. Caius had reached the little step beside the hatch. Gripping the lever in his left hand, he hauled up.

A metallic *screeeech* ripped the air like a scream.

Snarls sounded through the dark. Elizabeth whipped around, searching for the zombies.

"Bludging hell!" He tore open the hatch, hinges squealing in protest. "Climb, Elizabeth!"

But one was coming fast, tearing through the outpost doors. She wouldn't be able to climb high enough before it was on her. Gripping the machete, she faced the zombie.

A heavy thud beside her. Elizabeth stifled her scream. Just Caius. He'd jumped to the ground and now he spun toward her, his long coat flaring out around him.

"Up!" He grabbed the machete, pushed her to the ladder. "Up!"

Another moan behind them. Elizabeth frantically yanked on the first ring, shoved her foot into the first step. A wet *thunk* silenced the first zombie's snarls. More were coming across the snow. Faster she went, yanking and climbing. She glanced back as Caius razed the neck of one zombie while slamming a second away with a boot to its chest. It staggered back and he chopped through its head. Then another came and she climbed faster, faster. Sick with fear, she reached the top and scrambled onto the step in front of the hatch.

"I'm at the door! Come up, come up!"

Below, Caius grunted as he hacked through a zombie's head. Another rushed at him and Elizabeth cried a warning as a small zombie came from behind—a child. His machete embedded in a skull, Caius reached back and caught the little one's face. Its head thrashed like a rabid dog's with Caius's gloved hand between its teeth before a hard shove knocked the creature back. Something dropped wetly from its mouth and then the child rushed him again, stopped suddenly with a chop through its head.

Caius yanked a ring and began to climb.

Her heart frozen, Elizabeth stared at the piece of Caius's glove on the snow. The zombie's teeth had ripped through the leather and torn it away.

Caius was moving too quickly and it was too shadowed to be certain, but she spotted a faint gleam on the side of his hand. Like something dark and wet.

Like blood.

Her chest seemed to fold in, crushing her heart. Her lungs only emitted short, broken breaths, and she clung to him when he reached the door, clung with tears in her eyes but she couldn't speak at all, because her throat was too thick and her heart was wrecked, smashed beyond repair.

*Caius had been bitten.*

"Shh," he soothed against her ear. "It's all right. It's over. Let's go in."

Into the cold and dark. A low ceiling forced them to hunch over.

He shut the hatch and they listened. Silence. He called out, his deep voice echoing. Nothing. If any zombies had been inside the machine, they would have been snarling and groaning.

But it was already too late. It wouldn't be long until Caius was one of them. That bite would take him away from her, and Elizabeth wouldn't be able to chase after him.

Her mind dull, she barely registered the sudden glow—a small flame from Caius's spark lighter. Copper pipes ran along the sides of a low passageway leading into the belly. Rust roughened the iron plates under their feet. To their right, a short ladder extended up through a hatch in the ceiling. Caius climbed up a few steps before dropping back to the floor, his boots clanging against iron.

"That looked like an access to the leg pistons and gun ports," Caius said softly. Bent at the waist, he led her into the passageway. "We'll find the living quarters. They walked these machines across two continents. They didn't come all that way without sleeping."

Throat aching, she nodded. They entered a chamber lined by two rows of levers and foot paddles—propulsion controls for the legs in this segment of the machine, she realized. An open panel in the floor exposed the machinery beneath, flywheels and long crankshaft arms with offset bearings that looked like teeth. On the walls, the faint outlines of several painted figures remained. A lion or tiger, and what she thought might have been a horse and foal. The ceiling had been painted blue—as if the men or women who'd worked those foot pedals were running across a cloudless plain instead of laboring inside the belly of a machine.

They followed another low corridor to the right, passing more chambers filled with levers and controls. A tattered cloth covered the entrance to the next; Caius glanced inside and pulled her in.

An altar chamber or a hearth chamber. Maybe both. It was roughly circular, and constructing that shape out of the metal must have been difficult; the room must have been important enough to warrant the effort. Embroidered fabric hung on the walls, the colors faded. Cushions covered in brown felt ringed the chamber, the stuffing all but flat.

A small dais sat opposite the door, topped by three clay pots. Caius strode across the chamber.

"Oil lamps," he said, lifting one and tipping it back and forth slightly—in the hand that was killing him. He glanced back with a grin. "With oil. And just enough of a wick."

She tried to smile, but the choking pain in her throat and chest must have made it look as false as it felt. His brows drawing in, Caius touched his spark lighter to the lamp and crossed to her side again.

His gaze searched her face. "Elizabeth?"

"I'm sorry. I don't mean to..." *Cry.* But that was becoming more difficult—and impossible when he wrapped her in his arms. Her heart a solid ache, she whispered hoarsely, "I shouldn't have run. I should have just gone with him."

But she hadn't. And now so many people were dead.

Caius soon among them.

"No." His voice was rough. "Your father gave you no good choice. And this wasn't your fault."

*This* was. She drew a sobbing breath. "I shouldn't have let you help me. I should have stopped you."

"Do you think I would have let you?"

No. Not the Caius she knew. Not the man who'd promised to be her friend.

And that promise had killed him.

Desperately she tried to stop her shudders. He was the one dying and she was the one crying. That was wrong, wrong—yet the tears didn't stop. He gathered her up in his arms and carried her to the dais, where the lamp burned with a steady glow. Kicking a few cushions together, he sank onto them, holding her against his chest.

So strong and warm. She couldn't let him go.

Her face felt hot and swollen. She dragged off her hat and curled against him, slipping her fingers beneath the chest strap of his harness. "What do we do now?"

"Wait until morning," he said softly. "And maybe we'll find something inside the outpost that'll take us out of here."

She didn't want to, but had to ask, "How long can you go on?"

Someone without nanoagents would only last a few hours after a bite. But the mechanical bugs in his body would allow Caius to fight off the zombie infection longer. Eventually, though, he'd succumb. There was no cure.

"As long as I need to," he said. And when her tears spilled over again, groaned and buried his face in her hair. "Don't cry, Elizabeth. I can't bear it."

Because he loved her. And she'd said that she despised him.

Elizabeth couldn't bear that he might still believe she did.

Shifting off his lap, she kneeled beside him, face to face. Kissing him, her tears still falling and her throat raw, she said, "I lied to you, Caius."

"Did you?" His hands tangled in her hair and she felt his smile against her lips. "Tell me."

"I don't despise you. I hate that you hurt me." With every cold response and his refusal to believe her—yet none of that seemed to matter now. On a broken breath, she said, "But I don't hate you. I love you. I think that I have for so long."

Caius's body stiffened. His mouth taut, he jerked his head up to look down at her. His dark blue gaze searched her features, and whatever he saw in her face must have echoed her words, because in the next moment he kissed her as if he'd never kissed her before, as if he would never let her go.

He would have to, but when the torrent passed he held her and tenderly pressed his lips to her cheek, kissing away the trail of her tears. "Then why these?"

"Because I can't bear to lose you now."

"You won't."

It sounded like a promise. Was he trying to protect her? "I saw the zombie bite you, Caius. Its teeth ripped through the leather of your glove." Her chest gave an agonizing hitch. "I saw it."

He drew back. His mouth curved, his lower lip still slightly swollen where she'd bit him earlier. "You're the only one who's almost taken a chunk out of me lately."

"But I saw—"

Untangling his fingers from her hair, he snagged the wrist of his glove between his teeth and stripped it off his hand.

His steel hand.

Stunned out of her tears, Elizabeth stared at it. The skeletal prosthetic resembled bones, yet when he made a fist his fingers curled as smoothly as hers. She pushed up his coat sleeve. The prosthetic melded smoothly into his flesh halfway up the length of his strong forearm, and the flex of tendons and muscle was mirrored in the subtle movement of small pneumatic tubes in his wrist.

Astonished, she wordlessly shook her head—then realization and dread slipped beneath her shock.

Caius had said the first place he'd gone after removing the shackle was to England—one of the few places where such an apparatus could be grafted to his arm. He'd said a *friend* had removed the shackle for him.

Her gaze dropped to the handle of the machete sheathed in his harness.

"Oh, dear God." The joy that the zombie's bite hadn't infected him collided with the horror of what he'd done. "You cut off your *hand*?"

"To remove the shackle." His voice roughened. "After you jumped, I went back to the sanctuary and discovered that everything you'd told me was true. And I realized that I should have cut it off five years ago, the moment your father asked me to hunt you down."

Elizabeth understood that all too well. She'd jumped, desperate for freedom. He'd made his own desperate choice. Nodding, she glanced up—and froze.

"Caius?"

His face bleak, he watched her. "You thought I was dying?"

"Yes." And because his stark expression and empty gaze made her stomach tremble with worry, she gave a nervous laugh. "So much crying over nothing."

He didn't smile. "Is that why you said it?"

Why she'd told Caius she loved him?

It *had* been. She wouldn't have dared say it yet, if he hadn't been dying.

She didn't know what to do now. What to say now. When she'd thought she would lose him, nothing else had mattered. Not fear, not doubt, not remembered hurt.

Voice ragged, he asked, "Were you lying, Elizabeth?"

Violent rejection shot through her in response. She'd said it because he was dying, but she hadn't been lying. She'd told Caius she loved him because she *did*.

And nothing else mattered now, either.

"No," she said softly. "Every word was true."

She just hadn't been ready to say them. But she was ready for this—Caius's rough, sweet kiss, the strong hands that lifted her against him. Smiling and laughing, Elizabeth said it again the moment she could take a breath—*I love you, Caius*—because he wasn't dying, and he was here with her, and she never had to let him go.

Then his kiss slowed and softened; her heart beat fast and hard. Her fingers clenched in his hair, everything inside her winding up tight.

She couldn't get close enough.

"Caius," she begged, and he knew what to give, dragging her over his lap to straddle his hips, his grip firm as he gently rocked up between her thighs.

*Oh, dear God.* Sensation exploded below, pleasure bursting into desperate arousal. Crying out, she arched her back, grinding harder against him.

With a groan, Caius tore his mouth from hers. His lips burned fire down her throat. A delicious shiver raced through her as he pushed aside her scarf and licked the skin where her neck met her shoulder.

The spot he'd imagined tasting—and he'd imagined so much more.

So had she.

Aching with need, she whispered, "All of it, Caius. Everything you wanted."

"Christ, Elizabeth." It was tortured, gruff. "Not here."

"Why?"

"You deserve better." His heated mouth met hers again. "A soft bed—in a bedchamber that isn't freezing."

And she could have those later. She caught his face between her gloved hands. "You're alive. I'm alive. We're safe. That's all I need—and to be with you."

His eyes closed and his jaw clenched beneath her palms. Fighting an inner battle.

This was one she wanted him to lose.

She trailed her fingers down his throat, over his collar, down to the first buckle on his harness. "I think the best way to keep me warm is to cover my body with yours."

The left side of his mouth quirked up in a smile, and that was the spot *Elizabeth* wanted to lick. She leaned in, softly parting her lips against the corner of his, and tasted.

Caius. A little salty—but mostly just heat.

And even hotter when he turned his head, mouth catching hers as she drew back. The battle over, the fight won. Eagerly, she returned his kiss, but this was already different, so different. Not just the joy and pleasure, but anticipation twisting them together in an urgent coil of desire. She tugged at the laces of her bodice, remembering—*I want to kiss your nipples and suck until they're hard against my tongue*—oh, but they were already hard and tight beneath her chemise, the delicate skin around her nipples puckering when Caius dragged the linen away from her breasts, exposing her to the frigid air. He bent his head and captured her nipple between his lips.

She caught fire. Elizabeth tried to ride it out, rocking against him as pleasure seared her senses. But though she could feel the wetness between her thighs, the fire burned higher, hotter.

His fingers suddenly slid through her slick heat. Caius groaned when he touched her, and her hips jerked, pushing wildly against his hand.

Sweet God. Her body had never been so uncontrollable. She hadn't known what she'd asked for. Her own hands had never felt like this, gentle and rough all at once. His fingers slicked over her clitoris, then returned to circle the sensitive knot of flesh when she cried out, her back bowing.

She hadn't known a touch there could feel like this, either, though she'd sometimes rubbed the same spot until a pleasant little jolt shuddered through her. But that had been a spark. This was a raging conflagration.

"I can't believe we've never done this before," she gasped. "Oh, Caius. We should have started at the sanctuary. We'd have been *such* friends."

With a sound that was half laugh, half agonized groan, Caius lifted his head. His frozen breath puffed across her nipple, so hot and wet from the attentions of his mouth that the chill in the air was another pleasure.

He tugged her bodice up, covering her. "We'll make up for it."

And he did within the next minute, tipping her back against the cushion. His features stark with need, he sat up and dragged off his coat, unbuckled his harness and let it drop to the floor. His ravenous gaze raked down her body.

"Pull your skirts up."

His demand stole Elizabeth's breath, but not her sense. She yanked them up to the tops of her woolen stockings, tied just above her knees.

Caius gave a satisfied nod. "You're mostly covered, then. But throw this over us if your legs become cold."

He tossed his coat beside her and followed it down—not settling between her thighs, as she'd expected and hoped, but gently pushing her legs apart and pressing his lips to the strip of bare skin between her skirt hem and her stockings.

Then moving higher.

Elizabeth stiffened, trembling, wondering if she should close her legs again and run away. He'd *said* he wanted to do this—but she hadn't given it much thought and had never imagined it.

But she wouldn't run again—and she would *never* run from him.

She squeezed her eyes shut, unable to watch, and she'd just realized that she could hide what he was doing by covering her legs with his coat when his mouth reached the apex of her thighs. His tongue slicked through the heat and wet.

Oh, God. Why had they never done *this* before?

The strangled cry she heard couldn't have been a human noise, but it must have been because it was coming from her throat while she bucked against his mouth and her fingers twisted in his hair. His big hands pinned her hips in place and he licked while she sobbed his name, and licked and licked and licked and when she thought her body might snap he gave her clitoris a firm rough rub with his tongue.

And she *did* snap, a thousand times, every nerve and muscle breaking apart all at once—except for her heart, that was all in one piece, thundering as Caius rose between her legs and kissed her, long and deep. She melted into him, trembling from anticipation and her release.

He settled into the cradle of her thighs, his weight supported by his elbows. His fingers slid into her hair and she felt him against her entrance, thick and blunt.

Sudden pain made her bite back a cry. She tried to hide it, but Caius was watching her face.

"Elizabeth." He gritted out her name between clenched teeth. "Forgive me. This is the last time I hurt you."

But it wasn't a quick, vanishing hurt like pulling out a splinter. Caius pushed deeper and the terrible ache moved deeper, too. How far did he have to go? Her teeth digging into her bottom lip, she curled her fingers into fists against his back and bore the thick intrusion. After an eternity he stopped, his body taut with strain and his breathing ragged. Softly, he pressed kisses to her forehead and cheeks and mouth, the rest of him motionless—as if allowing her time to become accustomed to the feel of the heated shaft buried inside her.

And she was. A little.

Then he suddenly shoved against her, drawing a surprised cry from her lips, but when he lodged even deeper the ache wasn't so insistent. Above her, Caius froze and shuddered. His rigid sex pulsed inside her sheath.

A tortured groan ripped from his chest, rumbling against her breasts. "I'm sorry, Elizabeth. Forgive me. I've wanted you so long."

Was he apologizing because he'd spent? That made no sense. "That *is* what this act leads to, isn't it?"

"But you should, too. I should have waited for you to come."

Well, she already had—when he'd licked her. She linked her arms around his shoulders. "It's all right. I like this, too."

Holding him in her arms and holding him inside her. Just having him so close felt wonderful, even if it was a little painful.

Though it wasn't so painful now.

His head bent to hers. "It won't be long," he said between kisses.

"For what?"

"I'll be ready again."

*Oh.* She'd thought it was done. But there would have to be more to this, or so many women wouldn't bother with expensive airship fares and illicit trysts.

Now she was all-too aware of the wide spread of her legs, of her bent knees and her boot heels digging into the felt cushions. Of her skirts bunched over her hips and his weight resting between her bare thighs. Of the sticky wetness where they were joined. Though he'd softened slightly, she could still feel his penis inside her, thick and heavy.

Caius licked that spot on her neck again, making her shiver. He tasted his way up over her jaw until his mouth slanted over hers, parting her lips with a possessive thrust of his tongue and a long, slow kiss. A moan rose through her chest when he suckled on the tip of her tongue, giving way to sharp, panting breaths as his hand slid into her unlaced bodice and teased her nipple to aching hardness again.

Heated arousal raced across her nerves, tugging and pulling them taut. Her sheath was tightening around him—or his shaft was stiffening. No painful ache this time, though she felt him so deep. Elizabeth moved her hips a little, testing.

Pleasure rippled through her flesh, clenching around him.

"Caius." Gasping, she moved again. "Are you ready?"

God, *please* let him be ready.

He reared up and braced his hands beside her shoulders, determination hardening his jaw. "This time, I'll come after you."

"You always do," she said breathlessly.

A laugh shook through him, then he rocked against her and there was no more laughing, just her cry and his groan and Caius pistoning his thick shaft back and forth inside her. Faster, faster. He'd worried about the cold but the flames were all but bursting through her skin, so much heat, stoked hotter with every deep thrust. Relentless, he pushed her higher, his gaze locked on her face—and she remembered that he wanted to see how much she desired him, needed him, but even in the dark he couldn't have doubted. Not when she arched and shuddered beneath him, crying his name as the world burned around her. Not when she clung to him as he still moved inside her, pressing wild hot kisses to his neck and jaw. Not when she held him tight as he pulsed deep once more, whispering against his lips that she loved him.

And that she would *never* understand why they hadn't done this before.

# Chapter Five

FOR TWO YEARS, CAIUS HAD WOKEN WITH A HOLLOW ACHE IN HIS chest and his fists closing over nothing—though only after the nights he'd been able to sleep at all. It seemed impossible that Elizabeth was here now, alive. Even though he'd held her and kissed her, a part of him feared that he would open his eyes and she'd be gone.

But instead of emptiness, his heart was full and he held Elizabeth in his arms. He hadn't needed to cover her body with his to keep her warm; he'd only needed to tuck her back against his chest and pile his coat and the wall hangings over them. Now she slept, her lips soft and her hands folded beneath her cheek. A small bruise marred her neck, marked by his mouth. Driven by desperate need, he'd had her like this in the middle of the night, pushing her skirts up and plunging into her slick heat. He'd sucked on her skin while his fingers had stroked the slippery bud of her clitoris, and her sweet cries had echoed through the chamber until her clenching sheath triggered his own explosive release.

The memory made Caius ache to have her again, but he only softly kissed the spot on her neck before pulling her tighter against his chest.

She loved him. That seemed even more impossible, more unbelievable than waking up with Elizabeth in his arms. But he'd seen it on her face, heard it in her voice. And he'd recognized the pain in her when she'd thought he was dying—he'd felt the same pain every moment for two years.

But he was here with her. And would be, for as long as she would have him.

A glance at his pocket watch told him that the sun would be rising soon. He didn't attempt to wake her, but simply held on, breathing in the lavender scent of her hair.

Necessity finally forced him out of bed. While she stirred under their covers, he took one of the lamps and found a small chamber that served the purpose. He returned to find her up and shivering in her chemise, her dress discarded. Her frozen breath formed a cloud in front of her lips as she dug through her satchel.

Without glancing back, she said, "It's easier to run in trousers."

Caius had never run in a skirt, so he didn't know firsthand, but he imagined it was. And propriety demanded that he turn around while she dressed, but it had been years since he'd looked at a woman—starting before she'd fled. He wanted to see everything now, while he still had the chance.

Elizabeth had said that she'd lied about despising him. He didn't think she had. Caius knew exactly what it was to hate someone because it was impossible to stop loving them. He also understood that when she'd thought he was dying, her reasons for wishing she could stop loving him didn't matter anymore.

But he'd lied to her, too. Or rather, he hadn't told her everything that he should have. And she might despise him for that.

He had to take the risk, though. Elizabeth's love meant everything. But so did a little girl.

"Elizabeth."

She pulled on a man's shirt, her head popping through the neck opening as she turned, her cheeks flushed from sleep and cold. "Did you look outside?"

"Not yet. This is something I need to tell you—" He stopped himself.

*Just tell her.* "I have a daughter."

"Oh." Lips softly rounded, she stared at him. Suddenly she looked down at her hands and pulled her trouser buckle loose, adjusting a strap that didn't need to be adjusted—hiding her face, but she couldn't conceal the tremble in her voice. "Did you marry? But I know you wouldn't be here with me if you were a husband."

He wouldn't have been. He'd have helped her, yes. But he wouldn't have taken her to bed, no matter how desperately he wanted to.

And her faith made his chest tighten. He was glad she knew that about him. That he didn't have to defend his character. It might be easier for her to accept *why* he had a daughter if she trusted that he would be an honorable man.

"I didn't marry. I returned to the sanctuary after you jumped. I still didn't believe what you'd told me about your father, but I'd begun to doubt, because you'd been desperate enough to..." *A wild glance back at him. His fist closing over nothing.* The familiar agony erupted through his heart. His throat was raw when he continued, "I had to tell him you were dead."

But she was here. Alive.

Her gaze touched his hand. "This was before you removed the shackle?"

"Yes."

And that hadn't been as great a sacrifice as he'd imagined. At the time, he'd been too overwhelmed by grief to grasp the horror of what he was doing. But it hadn't been an enormous loss. He got along well without it—and the steel replacement was a part of him now.

If the price of his freedom had been one hand, then it had been well worth the cost.

"There was a girl at the sanctuary when I arrived. About two years of age. She looked just like you." Copper skin, curling dark hair, wide brown eyes. Beautiful. "And your father called her Mary."

Realization hit her swiftly. "Dear God. Another duplicate?"

Caius nodded. He didn't know whether Willem Jannsen had replicated Elizabeth or her mother—but most likely Elizabeth, using some bit of her that she'd left behind. "He must have created her shortly after you left, in the event you never came back."

"So you took her?"

"Yes." And he would never regret it. But if Elizabeth believed he had any other reason than to help a young girl, it would destroy him.

"Of course," she said, as if she would have made exactly the same decision. Her response eased the bands of tension around his chest. She reached for her coat and slipped it on. "Where is she now?"

"With my mother and sister."

Her eyes narrowed. "And where are *they*?"

He had to laugh. His evasion had been automatic, and the same sort she'd used so often while running: giving an answer without really answering at all. "Krakentown."

A smugglers' town in Australia—where he'd been close to capturing her once, without even realizing it.

Surprise arched her brows. "You knew I was there?"

"Not until after you left."

"I heard you were looking for me. So I ran again."

He'd offered a fortune of her father's money to the residents there, hoping that one of them would have information about her. Not one had told him anything. A month after leaving, he'd found an aviator from the airship Elizabeth had boarded when she'd abandoned the town, and Caius had bribed the man to tell him where she'd gone. But if she'd stayed in Krakentown, he'd never have caught her. He'd have lost the trail and spent years trying to pick it up again.

So when he'd run with his mother, sister, and daughter, he'd known exactly where to go—to the town where no one would reveal that his family was there, even if offered a bag of gold.

"And the girl, the other Mary—she is just above four years of age now?"

Caius nodded, unable to prevent his smile as he pictured his daughter—unable to prevent the ache of missing her. "She calls herself Rainbow."

"*Rainbow?*"

"You chose which name you wanted everyone to use," he said. "I wanted her to do the same. In hindsight, maybe I shouldn't have left that decision up to a two-year-old girl."

Elizabeth's laugh rang out. "Perhaps not. But at that age I would have called myself 'Colicky Scream,' so you should consider yourself fortunate."

"I do." More fortunate than he'd ever imagined. "And I don't know if there is something of you in her, or if this is something that many young girls do, but she is already trying to bring home every animal she encounters. I expect to find a small menagerie when I return—and she's probably giving them the run of the house."

Her smile turned wistful. "That was one thing my father did right. He always gave them room to be what they are."

At the sanctuary. But giving the animals room hadn't been the only thing he'd done right. "It was important work."

"Yes." Sighing, she glanced up at him with haunted eyes. "I don't want to run anymore."

"You won't have to. You'll be free as soon as we're away from here." Maybe she would want to be with him—and with Rainbow. Caius would ask her. But she'd hadn't even been ready to admit her love. He'd give her more time before he asked for forever. "We'll search the outpost, see if there's anything we can use to return to the coast."

Where they might hail a passing airship or boat.

She nodded. "What do you think happened to the people here?"

He didn't know. "Maybe overrun by zombies. But there have also been rumors that a Horde rebellion is moving across Europe toward the empire, and that the people are abandoning the outposts to join it."

And Caius didn't know which he should hope for. If the outpost had been abandoned, the rebels had probably taken with them any machine in good repair that could be used for travel. If the outpost had been overrun, the machines would still be there—but more zombies would probably be roaming within those walls.

Elizabeth's brow furrowed. "So it will be one bad situation or another."

"Yes."

"If we were still on *Kingfisher*, our situation would be worse," she said matter-of-factly, and stuffed her dress into her satchel. "So I will hope that the rebels abandoned this place, because it means that fewer people died. And if we must, we will create our own machine from whatever they've left behind."

Such determination. Heart full, Caius crossed the chamber and caught her up, then kissed her while she was still laughing in surprise.

He didn't care which situation they found themselves in. All that mattered was standing by Elizabeth's side through whatever danger they faced, and that she was alive.

And that she loved him.


OIL FROM THE LAMPS LUBRICATED THE LATCH AND HINGES ON THE entrance hatch, transforming the screech from the previous day into a thin squeak. Elizabeth looked out through the hatch, blinking. After the darkness inside the war machine, the light from outside was blinding. Clouds still filled the sky. Only a few scant flakes drifted down—which meant they were no better or worse off than they'd been during the storm. They could see more easily across the distance, but zombies could see them more easily, too.

For a long minute, she stood with Caius at the war machine's entrance, waiting. Opening the hatch apparently hadn't drawn any attention. No moans or growls. No zombies in sight, aside from a single rotting foot sticking out of the snow beneath them—one that Caius had killed while she'd been scrambling up the ladder.

Caius dropped to the ground first. Machete at the ready, he glanced beneath the war machine toward the outpost. A second later, he gestured her down.

They raced across the snow to the outpost doors. While she watched for zombies behind them, he studied the courtyard beyond the open doors. A frown darkened his face. Between sweeps of the area, she glanced at his profile. What was he seeing?

But the outpost must not have been overrun. He took her hand and they slipped through the doors, staying close to the wall.

Nothing moved. The large courtyard they'd entered was shadowed by rows of tall wooden granaries that spoke to the site's purpose. A wind turbine's sails turned lazily. To the right, heaps of snow topped round stone buildings. More granaries stood beyond them. Still and quiet, an air of abandonment hung over the entire area.

Yet the workers must not have left very long ago. Not more than a year. The rest of Europe was a ruin, but not here. None of the roofs had collapsed. Elizabeth detected faint creaking from the wind turbine, but it wasn't the rusted squeal of neglect.

She glanced away from the turbine and saw that Caius's focus had narrowed on the center of the courtyard, where several lumps disturbed the even blanket of snow. He tugged her forward, his gaze sweeping the ground.

Because there were footprints, she realized. Nothing distinct, just depressions. But they must have been made while the snow had still been falling.

Her fingers tightened on his, her heart pounding. Zombies, then. They'd known there might be some about.

He stopped in front of the first lump and prodded it with his boot. Elizabeth stifled a cry as snow fell away from a zombie's ruined face.

Were they lying in wait under the snow?

But...no. Another prod of his boot, and the zombie's head rolled to the side. Decapitated. Frozen blood formed black ice in the snow.

Killed during the storm.

Eyes wide, she glanced up at Caius. She'd seen him hunt before; she'd seen him hunt *her*. The same predatory focus hardened his eyes now as his gaze swept the footprints leading in and out of the courtyard.

"They came from that direction," he said softly, gesturing around behind the stone buildings. "Then they retreated inside them. Two men, at least one of them injured when they fought the zombies. Accompanied by a dog."

Her heart jumped. "A hound?"

"Maybe. The snow erased too much detail for me to be certain, but it's probable that they came from the wreck." His grim gaze met hers. "The stride length of one of the men matches Matthias's stride."

Caius would know; he'd tracked the other hunter hundreds of times while apprenticed to him.

But Matthias and the other man hadn't entered through the outpost doors, or Caius would have seen their tracks there, too. They'd flown here on a glider, maybe, though the distance between the wreck and the outpost made that difficult to believe. More likely they'd arrived in the two-seater balloon Elizabeth had seen while she and Caius had been gliding away from *Kingfisher*—though she couldn't see that small balloon now. Maybe behind the stone buildings.

"Elizabeth," he said softly, dragging her attention back to him. "I think the second man is your father."

Chest tight, she nodded. "Let us find out, then."

Her hand in his, he followed the tracks to the entrance of the second stone building, a red double door that opened on a center seam. The left door stood a few inches ajar. A slice of daylight fell across floorboards trampled with tracks of snow. Caius hesitated and glanced back at her, eyes dark with concern.

She knew what he would ask and headed him off. "I'll go in with you."

Standing to the side of the entrance, he pushed the door open wide. A soft growl—but that wasn't a zombie. A hound.

The single room was large and open, the roof supported by wooden posts. Light spilled in through the door, but after the brightness from outside, her eyes had to adjust to the dimness and shadows. More evidence of abandonment here. A basket lay on the floor near the entrance. Near the center of the room, a small table with curving legs had fallen on its side. A broken pot. A woven mat. As if the people who'd lived here had forgotten the items when they'd left—or had decided they weren't worth the effort of taking.

Pulling her close to his side, Caius stared into the shadows at the back of the room. Elizabeth followed his gaze.

Her heart constricted. Against the far wall, her father sat on a pallet of cloth, his arm around a lean gray hound and a machete across his lap. Though it was freezing, he'd taken off his coat.

The hound growled again and she heard her father's soothing murmur, saw him rub the dog's ears. Saw the glint of tears on his cheeks, his joyous smile.

The bloodied bite mark on his neck.

Her heart seemed to drop out of her chest in a rush. "Papa?"

"You can come close." A hitch broke his voice. "I'm not done yet."

But almost. Eyes glassy with fever, his skin tight and hot. She fell to her knees beside him, her throat burning with tears.

"Mary," he said and took her hand.

"Oh, Papa."

"Is this Matthias?" A few feet away, Caius stood over a prone figure covered by a cloth.

Her father gave a weary nod. "Bitten, too. He ended it not an hour ago. Then I had to finish him."

Killed himself, then her father had to make certain Matthias wouldn't return as one of the zombies. Her breath shuddering, Elizabeth made herself ask, "How long do you have?"

"Not very. I've been trying to make myself destroy *her* first." He stroked the hound's back. "She won't leave my side. I left the door open, but I fear she won't run after my end has come—and that's an irony I'd rather not die with. I spent my life trying to save animals from these creatures, and in my death I would become one and tear her apart. Will you take her with you, instead?"

"Of course." She lifted her hand to the hound, and at a word from her father, the growling stopped and she received a wet lick across her fingers. "What's her name?"

"Artemis. A finer hunter you'll never see." His breath came in shallow gasps. "Matthias and I came here, hoping to find help. But it was dark when we landed, and the two-seater's engine brought the creatures."

"What of Amelia?" Caius asked, and Elizabeth heard the roughness in his voice. He'd have fought—maybe killed—both hunters while protecting her. But they'd been his mentors, once. He'd hunted beside them.

"She was at the bow of the *Mary Elizabeth* with Apollo when we flew into the propellers." Her father met her gaze again; his words thickened and trembled. "We tried to take the two-seater to *Kingfisher* to find you, Mary. I was coming for you when the cruiser fell. I watched... I saw—" His voice broke. "I thought you fell, too."

She squeezed his hand. "No. We made it safely away."

"I thought I'd killed you." A harsh sob ripped from him. "I thought I'd killed my daughter."

*His daughter.* Elizabeth couldn't breathe. "Papa."

"I should have known you weren't dead when he came to tell me you were. You always fought everything. You wouldn't give up and jump to your death." He cupped her cheek in a burning hand. "Now you look at Trachter as she looked at me. And my heart is full and glad, knowing that you weren't alone."

He thought she and Caius had been together the past two years, Elizabeth realized. That they had falsified her death. But there was no reason to tell him differently.

"And you took the young one as your daughter—as it should be. I never meant for this. We wanted a daughter and I tried to make her something else, Mary. I betrayed you and I betrayed our daughter."

Looking at Elizabeth, but talking to her mother. Slipping out of lucidity.

"I'm here, Papa." Her throat aching, she kissed his hand. "I'm here."

The sharpness returned to his gaze, but the same pain was still there. "Forgive me, Mary. My daughter."

Eyes swimming with tears, she nodded. "Yes, Papa."

"Is the young one well?"

Rainbow. She glanced up at Caius.

"She is," he said.

Her father gave a weak nod, closed his eyes. "I left the sanctuary to my daughter. I had meant the younger Mary Elizabeth, but the solicitors will know you and they won't quibble over which one of you it goes to. It could be yours or hers, if either of you want the responsibility."

"I do." She'd always wanted it. "I'll take care of it."

He squeezed her fingers, and she saw the pride in his smile. "There's enough coal in the two-seater to take you to England. There are other survivors waiting at the wreck. They're depending on you now."

"We won't let you down."

"You never have." His voice rough, he kissed her, then looked up. "You've already loved her better than I did, Caius. Please take care of her."

"I will."

That wasn't enough, because he couldn't fulfill that promise if she returned to the sanctuary—and she wanted him to be with her. "You must give him his freedom, Father," she said. "He's a fugitive."

"It doesn't matter," Caius said. "I've already taken it. I won't let anyone take it away again."

"It *does* matter," her father said. "And you will have it. Upon my death, all debts will be considered paid, all contracts fulfilled."

She hadn't known that. "Truly?"

"I never made it common knowledge. That might speed my end." He gave a wry laugh that faded quickly into a short breath. He pushed weakly at her hand. "Go on, now. Be away from me. Take my coat with you. You'll need the extra warmth in the two-seater."

Tears spilling over, she nodded and pressed her forehead to the back of his hand. She couldn't let him go yet. Not like this. Not yet.

"Elizabeth." Caius gently touched her shoulder. "Go on and wait by the door."

*Wait for what?* But she knew. Dear God, she knew.

Her father couldn't use a gun to end it—the noise would just bring the zombies. And if he used the machete, it wouldn't be enough to stop him from coming back as one.

Caius had to finish him.

"Take Artemis," her father breathed.

Blindly, she nodded. Artemis trotted at her heels as she made her way to the small, tipped-over table. Righting it, she sat and buried her face in Artemis's warm ruff, clinging to the hound as the terrible noises came from behind her. She didn't look around.

Caius joined her a few minutes later, carrying her father's coat. His face was tight and his eyes flat as he draped it over her shoulders. And they had to go—but first, she wrapped her arms around his stiff form and held him tight.

He hadn't had an Artemis to cling to.

Slowly, his arms came around her. He didn't say a word. Nothing could make any of it better, she knew. But this helped.

With a deep breath, he finally stepped back and looked down at her. "When we return with help for the others, we'll see that he's properly taken care of."

Throat too raw to speak, she could only nod.

His gloved hands cupped her face. "Ready, then?"

As she could be.

They quickly located the two-seater—and a zombie wandering nearby. Caius destroyed it with brutal efficiency, and the controlled rage in his eyes told her part of him was still back in that stone building with Matthias and her father.

Or perhaps just remembering how she'd cried.

Digging her spark lighter out of her satchel, she lit the two-seater's furnace. Now they had to wait for the boiler to heat—a silent process, fortunately. As soon as they engaged the engine, every zombie remaining in the outpost would come running toward them. They'd have to quickly fly into the air soon afterward; the aluminum frame provided almost no protection.

When steam billowed from the vents, she climbed into the rear seat and urged Artemis in. With Caius's help, the hound crowded in, sitting on the floorboards between Elizabeth's feet with her forepaws on her lap.

He looked down at her. No rage burned in his eyes now. Just love and determination.

"We'll make it through this, Elizabeth."

"I know it."

She lifted her face for his hard, swift kiss. A moment later, he closed the vents and the engine rattled to life. Her fingers tightened on Artemis's ruff.

Caius jumped into the front seat and shoved the lever between his legs forward, lifting the flaps. The small propeller at their tail began to spin. Slowly, they began to skim a few feet over the snow.

Not high enough yet.

Her heart pounding, she looked back. Nothing to see through the smoke and steam, nothing to hear over the engine. But they had to be coming—and a zombie only had to grab on to the frame to pull them back down.

Higher, higher. They were approaching the outpost wall. Caius banked slowly to the right and the zombies were suddenly there, running just below, grasping over their heads. A zombie's fingers brushed the bottom of the frame and Elizabeth cried out in terror, leaning over the rail and slapping it away. The two-seater rocked wildly and then they were safe, safe, flying over the courtyard that was teeming now, the zombies following them across the snow until the two-seater passed over the high outpost wall.

Artemis whined softly and licked her cheek. Laughing, Elizabeth kissed her furry face.

In front of her, Caius turned his head and she saw his grin. He shouted over the noise of the engine. "You always were good at escaping!"

Yes, she was.

NIGHT WAS FALLING AGAIN WHEN THEY FLEW IN TO BRIGHTON'S airship field. Exhausted, cold, and hunger digging a hole in her stomach, Elizabeth didn't wait to land before she was pointing out a skyrunner and calling to Caius, "That one!"

His jaw tightened, but he nodded and turned the two-seater toward the mercenary's ship. She tried to stand as soon as they landed, but the second she stepped out of the frame her legs folded. Sitting too long. But Caius caught her and swept her up against his chest, carrying her toward the docking station with Artemis at his heels.

"Are you certain?" He looked up at the skyrunner. "This one?"

"I've hired her before. Her captain will go anywhere for the right price." And more importantly, would get them there in one piece. "I used her to escape you once—though she captained a different airship then."

"I know," he said. "I bribed her for information later. She took ten livre of your father's money and sent me five thousand miles in the wrong direction."

Elizabeth laughed, then looked up as the skyrunner's platform chains rattled and began a slow descent. A woman stood on it—not the captain but the quartermaster, as tall as an Amazon and rigid in her aviator's uniform, a pistol tucked into her belt.

She looked them over, her accent heavily French. "You have interest in hiring *Lady Nergüi*'s services?"

"A rescue," Caius said. "Our airship went down on the plain southeast of Old Chartres. We've people waiting for our return."

"Then we need passage to Krakentown, by way of the Ivory Market," Elizabeth added, and Caius's arms tightened around her.

"Krakentown?" The quartermaster's brows rose. "That's a dangerous route."

Not for this airship. And it was the reason why Elizabeth had chosen it. These mercenaries weren't just the best choice for the rescue. They were also as dangerous as any pirate or smuggler that flew round the bottom. "Only because women like your captain are flying it."

The woman's expression didn't change. "An *expensive* route."

Which was what she'd really meant. "I have the money," Elizabeth said. "And we need to leave as soon as possible."

"Then I'll ask the captain if she's interested. Do you have a name?"

"I hired her before as Katherine Wallace," she said. "But we are Elizabeth Jannsen and Caius Trachter—and Artemis."

The quartermaster nodded and clanged her weapon against the platform chains. As it began to rise, Elizabeth glanced up at Caius, who no longer appeared doubtful at her choice of airships, but slightly stunned.

Carefully, he set her down. "Krakentown? You'll come with me?"

"Yes." Elizabeth grinned and rose onto her toes, linking her arms around his neck. "We'll have that airship tryst, after all."

Pain suddenly swept across his features and made a bleak wasteland of his face. "For as long as you'll have me."

Her heart clenched. He'd thought that was *all* she wanted? Urgently, she pulled herself closer to him.

"No, Caius. I want to go to Krakentown with you. Then I want *you* to come with *me*—back to the sanctuary. With Rainbow, too. And your mother and sister. Anyone you want, as long as you're with me." She caught his face in her hands. "And I'll have you forever, if you'll let me. I'll even ask the captain to marry us—though she'll probably ask a fortune to perform the service."

Caius stared at her. The pain and bleakness gone, thank God. But disbelief remained.

Nervous, she said, "Is that all right?"

"I'm wondering if I'm awake," he said hoarsely. "You want forever?"

"I do." But now she worried. "We don't have to marry, though. Or return to the sanctuary. If you feel that marriage is another shackle…and at the *same place*—"

"No." Caius shook his head, voice suddenly rough. "It's *not* the same, Elizabeth. Freedom is having a choice to make, to be who we want to be. And I want to be yours."

And she wanted to be his. "Then I'm going arrive in Krakentown a married woman," she said. "But first, I'd like to have an *exceedingly* illicit tryst."

He laughed, and she felt his smile against her lips. "I swore that I'd always help you, Elizabeth. As your friend, you can be certain that I'll help you with this."

"I knew you would," she said, and lifted herself into his kiss.

# Epilogue

BY THE TIME THE AIRSHIP REACHED KRAKENTOWN, ELIZABETH had indulged in a tryst that would have set a society matron's hair afire and married the man she loved. She couldn't have said which was better.

With a man such as Caius, both the tryst and the marriage were the sweetest pleasure.

She stood near *Lady Nergüi*'s bow as they flew over the darkened town, Caius at her side. Nervousness bubbled in her stomach and perspiration dotted her brow. The cold of winter in the north had given way to summer in the south, and even though night had fallen, the heat of the day lingered on.

Below, the airship's lanterns glinted off the carapace that had once been the armored shell of a giant kraken. There were other carapaces throughout the town, large and small. Many of them were used as residences, surrounded by more buildings made of red clay brick. It was a smugglers' town unlike any other, orderly and quiet instead of a glorified rum dive—and all of it humble compared to the city-towers on the opposite side of the continent.

At the southern end of town, the airship slowed to a hover over a modest brick house. A woman with dark hair stepped out of the front door and looked up before darting back inside.

"My sister," Caius said, and Elizabeth's nervous stomach tripped over into roiling anxiety.

As they rode the cargo platform to the ground, Caius's sister returned outside accompanied by an older woman. Caius's mother, Elizabeth knew, but she only had eyes for the little girl in nightclothes holding her hand.

It was like looking at a tintype photograph of herself at the same age. The same hair, the same eyes. And when Caius jumped from the platform while they were still a full three meters above the ground and the little girl flung herself into his arms, there was no doubt: Rainbow was very much like Elizabeth.

And her heart filled tight as a balloon when she saw Caius's face, eyes closed as he hugged the girl close, spinning her around. A father, with *so* much love for his daughter. She wondered how he had any left over.

But he did. So very much. There was no doubt of that, either.

The platform jolted to a stop. Elizabeth stepped off and felt the curious looks from his sister and mother—then from the little girl, who spotted her over Caius's shoulder.

Rainbow asked the question that the other women probably wanted to. "Who are you?"

Who would she be to this girl? A mother, a sister? She didn't yet know.

"I'm Elizabeth," she said.

"That's one of my names, too," she said, but the girl's interest in Elizabeth vanished when her gaze dropped to the hound at her side. Her eyes widened. "I like your puppy."

So did Elizabeth. "I think she would like to have you as a friend. She loves to be petted."

Obviously taking that as an invitation, the girl squirmed in Caius's grip. He let her down, and introduced Elizabeth to his mother and sister.

Within moments of the word "wife" being spoken, she was surrounded with welcomes and tearful embraces. Elizabeth was barely aware of the airship overhead leaving—heading toward the docks for the night. She'd already paid the fare for passage back to the Americas. By the same time tomorrow, she would be returning to take over the sanctuary. With Caius, her hunter. She couldn't have asked for more. Yet already, she *had* more—two women, eager to be family and friends.

So much—and so overwhelming. His mother must have sensed it, because not much time passed before she was scooping Rainbow up. "All right, love. It's back to bed for you." She started back toward the house, stopping to kiss Caius's cheek. "We'll hear everything of where you've been and what you've done in the morning."

After a hug from his sister, they were left alone. Elizabeth looked up at Caius—who was watching her, his gaze intensely blue and shadows deepening the sharp angles of his face.

"And who are you?" she asked.

His answer came immediately. "The man who loves you."

No. He was so much more than that. Caius Trachter, her husband, her hunter, her friend.

"The man who tied me to a bed," she said, starting toward the house.

His voice lowered. "And will again, the next time I catch you."

That wouldn't do at all. She stopped, dismayed. "But I swore to myself that I would never run from you again. How will you catch me without a chase?"

His slow, predatory grin held a heated promise. "If you run, we could find out."

Her heart tripped over with anticipation. *Who was he?* The man she loved. *Who was she?* The woman who loved him—and who desperately wanted to know what Caius would do after he caught her.

Laughing, Elizabeth whirled and ran.

But not very fast.

# About the Authors

MELJEAN BROOK is the *New York Times* bestselling author of the Iron Seas steampunk romance series and the Guardians paranormal romance series. *The Iron Duke* was one of *Publishers Weekly's* Best Romances of 2010. *Heart of Steel* was named one of Amazon's Best Books of 2011. *Riveted* claimed *RT BookReviews'* Editors' Choice for Best Novel of the Year in 2012. Meljean lives in Oregon, consumes too much caffeine, and can't spell *occasionally*.

**www.meljeanbrook.com**

CAROLYN CRANE is the author of the Code of Shadows series, a paranormal romantic suspense spy series with a dash of science-fiction and fantasy. She is also the author of the popular urban fantasy series, The Disillusionists, and a new romantic suspense series, The Associates. She's a writer living in Minneapolis with her husband and two daring cats. She works a day job as a freelance advertising writer; she's also waited tables at a surprising number of Minneapolis restaurants and bars (though not as many as her writer husband has). She's been a shop clerk and a plastics factory worker, which she was dismal at (think I Love Lucy). Also, if you invite her to your party, your cheese plate will be in grave danger. During rare moments when she's not at her computer, Carolyn can be found reading in bed, running, helping animals, or eating Mexican food.

**www.authorcarolyncrane.com**

JESSICA SIMS lives in Texas. She has some cats, but what writer doesn't? She plays video games and confesses to reading comic books. And she likes writing, but that one was pretty obvious. Jessica also writes paranormal romance as Jill Myles and hot contemporary romance as *USA Today* bestselling author Jessica Clare.

**www.jessica-sims.com**

# Carolyn Crane's
# THE DISILLUSIONISTS

**Welcome to Midcity, paranormal crime capital of the world…a place full of mystery, sexy secrets, and the legendary Disillusionists.**

## MIND GAMES

Justine Jones is a hopeless hypochondriac whose life is crippled by fear… until one day when a handsome, tortured mastermind named Packard peers into her soul and informs her that he can help her turn her fear into a crime-fighting power.

## DOUBLE CROSS

Serial killers with unhead-of skills are terrorizing the most powerful beings in Midcity. As the body count grows, Justine faces a crisis of conscience… and an impossible choice between two flawed but brilliant men—one on a journey of redemption, the other descending into a pit of moral depravity.

## HEAD RUSH

Justine tries to stay upbeat as Midcity cowers under martial law, sleepwalking cannibals, and a mysterious rash of paranormal copycat violence, but her search for answers leads her into the most dangerous mind game yet. With the help of unlikely allies, Justine fights her ultimate foe…and unravels the most startling mystery of all.

**"A violent U-Turn in a fresh direction…this is urban fantasy's new shot-in-the-arm." —National Bestselling author Vicki Pettersson**

**AVAILABLE NOW IN PRINT AND E-BOOK FORMATS**
**www.authorcarolyncrane.com**

# Jessica Sims'
# MIDNIGHT LIAISONS

**Where the paranormal go to find a date...**

## BEAUTY DATES THE BEAST

WANTED: Single human female to join charming, wealthy single male were-cougar for a night of romantic fun – and maybe more.

Me: The tall, sensuous, open-minded leader of my clan. You: A deliciously curvy virgin who's intimately familiar with what goes bump in the night. Must not be afraid of a little tail. Prefer a woman who's open to exploring her animal nature. Interest in nighttime walks through the woods a plus.

My turn-ons include protecting you from the worst the supernatural world has to offer. Ready for an adventure? Give me a call.

## DESPERATELY SEEKING SHAPESHIFTER

WANTED: Supernatural single seeks sexy she-wolf to help him bear all.

Me: A strong, silent type who doesn't care much about the creature comforts. You: Sweet as honey. No such thing as too big or too small— you're just right.

Let's take things slow. I'll start as your bodyguard, but hopefully soon I'll shift into your mate. You need a man who's born to be wild, and I'm ready to protect you from all the wolf pack can throw in your direction. Don't be afraid of your animal side. Show me yours, and I'll show you mine.

**"Funny, sexy, and lively." —Publishers Weekly**

**AVAILABLE NOW IN PRINT AND E-BOOK FORMATS**
**www.jessica-sims.com**

# Meljean Brook's
# THE IRON SEAS

**Swashbuckling steampunk romance…with an emphasis on the steam.**

## THE IRON DUKE

After the Iron Duke freed England from Horde control, he instantly became a national hero. Now Rhys Trahaearn has built a merchant empire on the power — and fear — of his name. And when a dead body is dropped from an airship onto his doorstep, bringing Detective Inspector Mina Wentworth into his dangerous world, he intends to make her his next possession.

## HEART OF STEEL

As the mercenary captain of the Lady Corsair, Yasmeen has learned to keep her heart as cold as steel, her only loyalty bound to her ship and her crew. So when a man who once tried to seize her airship returns from the dead, Yasmeen will be damned if she gives him another opportunity to take control…

## RIVETED

Annika serves on an airship, searching for her sister and longing to return home. But that home is threatened when scientific expedition leader David Kentewess comes aboard, looking to expose Annika's secrets. When disaster strikes, leaving David and Annika stranded on a glacier and pursued by a madman, their very survival depends on keeping the heat rising between them—and generating lots of steam…

**"Meljean Brook has brilliantly defined the new genre of Steampunk Romance. I loved it!" —Jayne Ann Krentz**

**AVAILABLE NOW IN PRINT AND E-BOOK FORMATS**
**www.meljeanbrook.com**

24698943R00216

Made in the USA
Lexington, KY
03 August 2013